A PLUME BOOK

THE HUMANITY PROJECT

JEAN THOMPSON is the author of six novels, among them *The Year We Left Home* and *City Boy*, and six story collections, including *Who Do You Love* (a National Book Award finalist). She lives in Urbana, Illinois.

Praise for *The Humanity Project*

"A bracing narrative stance and a tart political viewpoint . . . [Thompson] is eerily good at inhabiting a wide range of perspectives and has a fine ear for the way young people speak to one another. . . . A novel that doesn't pretend to have any answers, comfortable or otherwise, but that vividly, insistently poses questions we should be asking."

—Suzanne Berne, *The New York Times*

"Thompson achieves exceptional clarity and force in this instantly addictive, tectonically shifting novel. As always, her affection and compassion for her characters draw you in close, as does her imaginative crafting of precarious situations and moments of sheer astonishment. . . . Thompson infuses her characters' bizarre, terrifying, and instructive misadventures with hilarity and profundity as she considers the wild versus the civilized, the 'survival of the richest,' how and why we help and fail each other, and what it might mean to 'build an authentic spiritual self.' Thompson is at her tender and scathing best in this tale of yearning, paradox, and hope." —*Booklist* (starred review)

"A penetrating vision of a lower-middle-class family sinking fast. . . . Thompson has a knack for rendering characters who are emotionally fluid but of a piece [and] caps the story with a smart twist ending that undoes many of the certainties the reader arrived at in the prece⋯ getting it both ways: A formal, tightly const⋯ dates the mess of everyday lives."

D0816199

"[Humanity is] something that Thompson infuses into every sentence, striking true, clear notes . . . and telling [characters'] stories in a way that doesn't offer resolutions so much as a messy, imperfect kind of grace. And what's more human than that?"   —Leah Greenblatt, *Entertainment Weekly*

"In prose that is gorgeously written but never showy . . . *The Humanity Project* rewards readers with the kind of immersive, thought-provoking experience that only expert storytelling can provide."

—Justin Glanville, *Cleveland Plain Dealer*

"It's Thompson's own humanity project that's really interesting, heartfelt, and farther-reaching . . . a tribute to Jean Thompson's art, which, beginning so slowly and seemingly simply, expands and deepens to contain multitudes without ever losing sight of each singular soul."

—Ellen Akins, *Minneapolis Star Tribune*

"With godlike power, Jean Thompson, author of *The Humanity Project*, throws her dented (and entirely recognizable) characters into the crucible of the American recession to reveal what it means to be human: flawed, and yet somehow worthy of redemption that comes in glimmers instead of bursts."

—Christi Clancy, *Milwaukee Journal Sentinel*

"Virtue is thin on the ground in Ms. Thompson's book, which follows the disparate lives of a handful of Northern Californians loosely tied together by coincidence and united more firmly by their ethical lapses. . . . Ms. Thompson neither wallows [in] hardships nor sentimentalizes the grubby, compromised realities. . . . Her lucid, no-frills prose gives her depictions of the other half the stamp of authenticity."   —Sam Sacks, *The Wall Street Journal*

"*The Humanity Project*, the prolific Jean Thompson's sixth novel, weaves a rich, moving story of parents and children, money and poverty, virtue and evil. . . . Thompson manages this complicated choreography masterfully."

—Kate Tuttle, *The Boston Globe*

"Evocative [and] often colored by a smart, dark humor . . . Conflicted, complex, and compassionate when you least expect it: That's us in a nutshell—and in Thompson's ultimately profound novel."

—Connie Ogle, *The Miami Herald*

"Thompson has crafted an incisive yet tender novel—a disturbing portrait of a thoroughly modern, fractured family stumbling toward grace in difficult times." —Meredith Maran, *People*

"A forthright piece of social criticism . . . Thompson is also an accomplished story writer . . . attuned to the callousness of twenty-first-century society, its comedic elements, its misguided efforts to right itself, its often tragic results. . . . There's real beauty in the way Thompson has [characters] serve one another, even if that loving service is often not enough. It is, however, deeply human." —Helen Schulman, *The New York Times Book Review*

ALSO BY JEAN THOMPSON

NOVELS

The Year We Left Home

City Boy

Wide Blue Yonder

My Wisdom

The Woman Driver

COLLECTIONS

Do Not Deny Me

Throw Like a Girl

Who Do You Love

Little Face and Other Stories

The Gasoline Wars

The
Humanity Project

JEAN THOMPSON

᷈᷈

ℙ

A PLUME BOOK

PLUME
Published by the Penguin Group
Penguin Group (USA) LLC
375 Hudson Street
New York, New York 10014

USA | Canada | UK | Ireland | Australia | New Zealand | India | South
Africa | China
penguin.com
A Penguin Random House Company

First published in the United States of America by Blue Rider Press, a
member of Penguin Group (USA) LLC, 2013
First Plume Printing 2014

P REGISTERED TRADEMARK—MARCA REGISTRADA

THE LIBRARY OF CONGRESS HAS CATALOGED THE BLUE RIDER PRESS
EDITION AS FOLLOWS:
   Thompson, Jean, date.
   The humanity project / Jean Thompson.
   p.   cm.
   ISBN 978-0-399-15871-1 (hc.)
   ISBN 978-0-14-218090-7 (pbk.)
   I. Title.
   PS3570.H625H86   2013   2012028041
   813'.54—dc23

Printed in the United States of America
10 9 8 7 6 5 4 3 2 1

Original hardcover design by Amanda Dewey

The
Humanity Project

We were afraid of so many things: Of our children, who lived in their own world of casually lurid pleasures, zombies and cartoon killers and thuggish music. Of our neighbors, who were buying gold and ammunition and great quantities of freeze-dried food, and who were organizing themselves into angry tribes recognizable to one another by bumper stickers. We feared that our lives had been spent in piling up not treasures but great heaps of discardable and wasteful things. Television voices exhorted us to buy even more, and often enough we did, even though money seemed to be draining away from us like water in a leaky sink, and most of all we feared a future of privation and loss.

Our politicians were no help at all.

We feared those people who we believed meant to do us harm, although such fears fluctuated along with the most recent headlines. There were people who hated us with ancient, inexplicable, and undying hatreds. They might look harmless enough, unexceptional, but without warning they might precipitate some majestic destruction that we could not imagine, or no, we could imagine it all too well, the fire, the choking ash, the impossibly small spaces that our bodies would be made to fit.

We feared the very earth itself and took bad weather personally. The glaciers were melting, the oceans would soon boil like soup. Earth was visiting its slow revenge on us, payback for a million insults and crimes committed in our names. We might stop using plastic grocery bags or lawn chemicals, but our private virtue did nothing to prevent the next huge industrial discharge of molten silt. We felt powerless and ineffective, but also entirely guilty.

One bad year followed another. More and more of us lost jobs, houses, marriages. We were losing the future that had been promised to us, although now that we thought about it, we couldn't remember getting anything in writing.

But we could start over. It was our last and best hope, one we couldn't be cheated out of. We could reinvent ourselves brand-new. New! We had always liked new things.

We would cast off our old, damaged selves, peel back our layers of failure and sadness. The past would no longer count, would no longer have a hold on us. We would be born again, like the church people said. And indeed, some of us found our way to religion, different flavors of religion, new and passionate creeds. Some of us invested in ideas that had made other people rich. Some shed themselves of old wives or husbands and acquired different ones. And still others of us did what those down on their luck had always done: swept out our empty rooms and headed for a new place. As if "place" was what had defeated us.

We would think of ourselves not as refugees but as pioneers. We would find somewhere in the world that wasn't yet ruined, somewhere with clear skies and fresh mornings and orderly streets and people going about their business in expected ways. We would offer ourselves up, be recognized and welcomed there for our true worth.

And in our new place, our new selves, we would be better, smarter, saner. We would not make the same mistakes. We would give up our bad habits, bad food, late nights, lethargy. We would shape up, trim down. Because hadn't the entirety of our old lives been fat, bloated, and overstuffed with false desires?

Although if we were honest, we had to admit there were a lot of our old unworthy purchases that we would miss.

We would be calmer, wiser, braver. We would face down our fears. We would do a better job of loving. We would be more worthy of love.

ONE

D ad?"
  Gray morning. He'd fallen asleep in front of the computer again. The screen was gray too. "Yeah," Sean said. His voice was more awake than he was. He swung around in his chair. His son was standing in the doorway, tall, shaggy-haired, peering in at him.

"Yeah," Sean said again. "OK, buddy."

"You're supposed to call that guy."

"OK." Sleep was racing away and for another second he let himself follow it, his mind unraveling back into a dream that still held him under some impossible weight. Then he pushed the dream away, shut off the computer, planted his feet, and rose to meet the god-awful day. "Conner? Do I smell coffee?"

"I got some started."

"Thanks, bud." Coffee, then he'd call that guy in Santa Rosa to see if he could get a few days' work lined up, and if he couldn't, well, that was the next heap of crap to deal with.

"Conner?"

"Yeah?"

"Quit worrying."

Sean got the first of the coffee into him, then dialed. He could hear Conner moving around upstairs, getting ready for school. The phone in his hand came to life. "Hello, Mr. Nocera? Sean McDonald here, I was wondering if you could use me today."

He listened for a minute, then said, "Sure. Well thanks for your time. Have yourself a good day."

Nocera had already hung up, but Sean heard Conner coming down the stairs, so he pretended he was still talking while Conner opened the refrigerator and the cupboards, found a carton of chocolate milk, peanut butter crackers, a banana, and a handful of Oreos, which was either a weird breakfast or a weird lunch. "Dad?"

Sean put his hand over the phone, shielding his imaginary conversation.

"I already fed Bojangles."

"Thanks. Knock em dead out there."

"You too."

He waited until Conner was out the front door before he put the phone down.

Bojangles wanted in from the yard. He did his happy begging dance. "Scram, you con man," Sean said, and the dog went to his corner and lay down without complaint.

Another day of nothing stretched ahead of him.

He showered, fixed himself some eggs, then sat back down at the computer. The whole world was in the computer, if you knew how to figure things out, and you had to believe that somewhere out there were answers, solutions. Work and money, mostly.

He checked Craigslist for help wanted. It was the same old stuff—scams, mostly. Winter rain was going to start in soon and work would be even slower. He could fight the Guatemalans for landscaping jobs he didn't want anyway. He could enroll at the community college to take computer courses and be qualified for a whole new category of jobs where no one was hiring. Last month he'd printed up five hundred flyers advertising himself as Handyman Services—No Job Too Small! Stuck them under windshield wipers in parking lots, came up with two jobs cleaning gutters and another hauling brush, and somebody who wanted a garage framed but didn't want to pay white man's wages.

He'd get by. He always had. Things would turn around and you wouldn't feel like you were beating your head against the brick wall of the world. It wasn't just him. Times were bad for everybody, everybody had it coming. He guessed he was just a little farther ahead in the line than most people.

Finished with the job listings, he let his fingers do the walking over to the personals. Women seeking Men. Like the help wanted, he'd seen most of them before. *Princess looking for her prince. Where did all the great guys go? Friends first. Looking for something real.* None of them attached pictures, which was smart, he guessed, but made you waste a lot of time. Here was a new one: *Pretty Lady, 38.*

Maybe not pretty. Maybe not thirty-eight. Who knew? Sean clicked, and read:

So how was your day? Mine too. I miss having somebody I can talk to.

If you ever want to get out of the house some night for a while, you can pretend I'm your best friend and tell me all about it. Me: normal in most respects. You: tired of reading these ads.

Well at least she had a sense of humor. Sean thought for a minute, typed in the address.

Hi Pretty Lady,

I hear you loud and clear. I'm a single dad. My son is seventeen.

He already puts up with enough of my griping. Not that you have to put up with it either. But yeah, it would be nice if

Here he paused for a long time. Nice if you could just lie down with a woman, have some naked good times, not worry about anything more. But you couldn't write that.

I could get together with you some time and compare notes. I'm 45,
work as a carpenter, self employed, meaning I'm broke most of the
time, but I can always spring for a couple of drinks. I'm 5'10" and as for
looks, well, dogs don't bark at me. I'm free most nights, hope that
doesn't make me sound like a social reject, ha ha.

He signed it Sean, then sent it off before he changed his mind. She
wanted to talk. He was hornier than an eight-peckered toad, but he
guessed talking had to come before anything else.

He took his second cup of coffee outside and sat on the deck. The day
was going to work its way into hazy heat. The hillside beyond his back fence
was a tangle of manzanita and scotch broom and blond grass. So dry the
least spark would send it up in flames and then he guessed it would be good-
bye, house—that is, if Bank of America didn't get to it first, but there he
was getting down again, letting the negative thoughts in, and so he put his
feet up on the railing and smoked a little pot just to take the edge off things.

It wasn't the life he'd planned for himself but it was the life he'd grown
used to, it had its comforts, and it would be a sad and low-down thing if
he got kicked out of it.

His phone rang. Sean dug it out of his pocket, stared at the screen.
Floyd. "Talk to me."

"What are you doing, pencil dick?"

"Your girlfriend."

"Want to help me with some drywall?"

"When, today?"

"Whenever you can get over here."

"Half an hour," Sean said. Sat for a moment longer to clear his head,
then stood and stretched, and even if his body was sending out its usual
SOS's (back, shoulders, elbow), he just had to get moving, work a few
kinks out, tell himself he was thirty-five, not forty-five—well almost
forty-six. Floyd would buy him lunch and throw a little folding money
his way, a bad day turning into a not-bad one, and you had to have faith
that things would work out eventually.

He called to Bojangles and the dog leapt up, excited without knowing why, followed him out to the driveway, and ran in circles. Sean opened the truck's passenger door for him and the dog jumped in, happy all over again for no reason. Dumb dog. Sean checked the toolbox, grabbed a couple of Red Bulls from the fridge, and headed out.

Now that he had the day back on track, he was able to look out on the world with something close to pleasure. His house, his street, his neighborhood might be a little shabby, the whole town mostly a place where old hippies came to plant backyard pot and gradually fall apart, but he'd been here fifteen years now, almost all of Conner's growing-up time, and it was home. He liked the who-gives-a-shit attitude of people who let their gutters drip rust, and strung Tibetan prayer flags across the front porch and kept too many cats. The younger ones he wasn't so sure of, thought they were probably cooking meth or some other nasty business and Conner had better not ever get mixed up in anything like that, he'd beat his ass.

But live and let live and anyway, there wasn't a sweeter place on the planet than Northern California, with its soft winters and golden grass and yeah he guessed he was still a little stoned.

Floyd was trying to get his house in shape so he could put it on the market. He was one of those optimistic people who thought you could still get money out of a house. Floyd's house sat well back from the street in its own cruddy yard of foxtails and thistles. A pile of PVC pipe lay to one side of the driveway, along with two sawhorses and a sheet of plywood set up as a workbench. To the left of the house was scaffolding, and a blue tarp spread over the flat roof, and ten-gallon buckets of sealant. Also odds and ends like an orange heavy-duty extension cord snaking out of the open front door, a nail gun, a roll of fiberglass insulation, knuckle-shaped pieces of gutter. If you didn't know any better, you might think the house was being dismantled, not built up.

Sean parked and let Bojangles out to run around. Floyd was inside, in the bedroom at the end of the hallway. He'd taken it down to the studs and he was standing there like he was confused about where his walls had gone. He was a big guy who was going to fat, with a baseball cap jammed down on his ears and a beard that grew up practically to his eyeballs, so there wasn't much actual face visible.

"I just love what you've done to this room."

"Funny."

Sean popped one of his Red Bulls. "So, what's the plan?"

"I can't believe you drink that shit. It's nothing but chemicals."

"You get the sheets already, or are we going to Home Depot?"

"I got everything. We need to do the cutouts." Floyd took his cap off, scratched and pulled at his ears, replaced the cap. "This house is gonna kick ass by the time I get it finished."

"It's going to be sweet, Floyd." He would never get it finished and even if he did, it would still be a junky little undersized house.

They'd moved the first sheet into the room and leaned it up against the studs when Floyd asked, "You ever think about taking vitamins, you know, taking some of those formula kinds?"

"What kinds, the manly ones?"

"I'm just saying, it'd be nice not to have to get up and piss four times a night."

"You really should get that checked out," Sean told him.

"You mean that test where they shove a fist up your ass?"

"That's the one."

"Would you let somebody do that to you?"

"Yeah, but I wouldn't tell you about it. Let's hit it."

There was a rhythm to any kind of work and it always took a while to find it. You had to be patient with yourself until then, try not to bust up your hands or trip over your feet or break equipment. Just dig in, think it through, gradually let your muscles take over from your brain. He'd done plenty of jobs with Floyd. It made it easier to get to that smooth place where you used the least amount of energy to get a task accomplished. They sanded, did the cutouts for the electrical boxes, sanded again, then drove the screws, and even the first piece went up without too much of a fight.

Sean peeled off his sweatshirt and filled a plastic bowl with water for the dog, who lapped up half of it and then went back to sleep on the cement floor of the back porch. Floyd said who told him he could use his fine china for the damned dog and Sean said he'd had to look around a long time before he found anything the dog would consent to drink from.

It wasn't a big room but it took them most of the day to get the drywall up, and that with only a couple of breaks for smokes and a quick lunch from the Taco Shack. Floyd brought out two Coronas and they sat in the patchy shade of the yard to drink them. Floyd dug out his wallet and handed Sean two twenties. "Here you go. Buy yourself something nice."

"You want me to come back and help you mud?"

"No, I think I got it under control," Floyd said, and by that Sean knew Floyd couldn't afford to pay him for another day's work, probably couldn't even afford the little speck of cash he'd come up with. Everybody he knew was broke. It was beyond depressing.

Sean said, "You know what we are? Modern-day peasants. The guys who used to live in mud huts and sleep in straw and live on potatoes."

"Yeah?" Floyd considered this. "Potatoes?"

"Nothing but potatoes, come on, you know what I mean. There's all this money in the world and it never seems to get to the people who do the actual work."

"What are you, some kind of communist?"

"Sure, why not." Communist. It had an old-fashioned sound. They hardly even had communists in Russia now. From where they sat, they could hear the noise of the freeway, a constant low-grade roaring, because the world never ran out of people going places, like nobody was ever happy enough where they were.

Floyd said, "What's the news with the Bank of Asshats?"

"They get the house back."

"Aw shit, man."

"Yeah. Simple math. Only a matter of time."

"Sucks," Floyd said. "I mean, seriously, I'm sorry."

"Yeah, thanks."

"Can you get some kind of, I don't know, negotiation? They give you more time to pay?"

"That's what all us broke morons want." It felt worse to say it. It made it more real. There were too many other things crowding in behind that he didn't want to have to ask or answer, like where they'd go and how he could afford even such a thing as rent. He felt like he was losing out, like they'd changed the rules when he wasn't looking and drained all the good luck out of the world.

"Another beer?"

"No, I got to get back to the muchacho."

"One for the road." Floyd repositioned himself in his chair, heaved himself upright, and headed for the refrigerator.

Sean took the extra Corona, which Floyd probably wouldn't have offered if he hadn't felt sorry for him about losing the house, well, what good was total economic ruination if it didn't get you a free drink here and there. He checked his phone; no messages. He stood up. He'd done something unholy to his back. "Later, man."

"Yeah, thanks for coming over. This place is really starting to shape up."

He tried to call Conner on the drive home, got his voice mail. "Hey, let me know if you want dinner or you're doing something else. I can stop and get us something." The kid was probably chained to a video game somewhere. Him and his friends lived their lives in front of computers. He stopped at the Safeway, wrote a check for dog food, milk, laundry detergent, orange juice, cereal, frozen pizza, frozen vegetables, lunch meat, bread, and a roast chicken, and wasn't he a smart shopper because now he had two hundred and ten dollars in the bank and Floyd's two twenties in his pocket and maybe another thirty of his own and that was the end of the line.

Conner wasn't home. Sean filled Bojangles's food bowl and watched the dog eat it up in nothing flat. Whatever happened, the dog was staying with them. He wasn't going to be one of those people who left an animal tied to a tree, or took it to a shelter.

But maybe he was going to be one of those people who slid down bit by bit until you did things you never imagined doing.

Conner called and said he was at Tyler's house and he was going to eat dinner there and hang out for a while. "What about homework?" Sean asked. Conner always got good grades no matter what he did. Sean only nagged him about homework once in a while because he figured that was part of his job. Conner said not to worry, him and Tyler were going to study for the Spanish test and the only other thing was speech com. He had it knocked.

So he fixed his own supper and ate it watching SportsCenter and then he did the dishes and got the kitchen wiped down and took two ibuprofen for his back. There were times he liked the feel of the house with nobody else in it but this wasn't one of those times. He walked the circuit of the rooms just to keep his back from locking up, wearing a path in the sad sad carpeting that needed shampooing, but why bother when it wasn't really his anymore. Ditto the window that didn't open and the plugged-up shower drain and the leaking water heater, all things he could fix or attend to but what did it matter.

He tried to start each day with something close to a good attitude and by sunset he was always back down in the black pit.

He turned on the computer to check his mail. Pretty Lady, 38, had sent him a message three minutes ago.

> Hi Sean, well here goes nothing. I'm heading out to Ted's in a little
> while, you know the place? I'll be sitting at the bar, the hair is short and
> blond, the name is Laurie.
>
> —
>
> Hi Laurie, sounds good to me. As soon as I can get it together. See you.
>
> Sean

Here goes nothing indeed. She might have sent the same message to the fifteen other guys who answered her ad. He knew Ted's. It was a hike down the freeway in Novato and maybe a little more prissy and upscale than he liked. That might mean she just wanted to be a lady about picking up strange men she met online.

Sean showered, running hot water over the funky part of his back and pounding on it to loosen it up. He dressed in a clean pair of jeans, a plain black T-shirt, and a windbreaker. He'd said carpenter, she shouldn't be expecting anybody in a suit. He texted Conner that he was stepping out for a while, and got the dog a rawhide so he'd have something to do while he held down his spot on the couch.

Driving, he tried to dial his expectations down to zero. If she was really ugly, he didn't even have to say hello. Walk in, walk out again. Part of him almost hoped that was how it would turn out because then you were spared the stupidity of getting excited about something working out for once like it never did, and you just had to pour more attention and time and energy not to mention money into the situation before it crashed and burned.

He guessed it was fair to say his luck had gone bad all around, and that included women.

Ted's had a bar in front and a restaurant in back, so there were a lot of couples in the entrance, dressed up and waiting for tables. Sean stood behind them, trying to check things out. The bar was a big half-horseshoe and not very crowded. From the doorway he couldn't see all the way to the far end. No short-haired blondes in view.

Maybe she wasn't here yet. Nothing for it but to quit acting like a giant chickenshit, go in and sit down, and he'd just pulled out a stool when she came out of nowhere, that's what it seemed like, sticking her face in front of his and saying, "Hi, are you Sean?"

"Yeah, ah, Laurie? Hi." They shook hands. She was kind of pretty. He ducked his head so he wouldn't seem to be staring, and so he wouldn't see her checking him out. But then, she must have already done so, must have thought he looked all right or else she'd be hiding in the john or something. He said, "I hope you haven't been waiting long."

"No, just a couple of minutes." She took the seat next to him. She already had her first drink, some kind of margarita it looked like, and that was another point in her favor since he wouldn't have to buy it. She was wearing jeans and a short jacket that was made out of some shiny silver fabric, which was different and not in a good way, some fashion trend he guessed he'd been oblivious to. A little on the skinny side, but nothing he couldn't live with. He wondered if that was really her name, Laurie, then decided it didn't matter.

They smiled at each other. "So," Sean began. The perfume she had on fogged his head. It didn't matter what kind of foo-foo name they put on the bottle, it all smelled the same to him: perfume. "Did you get a lot of answers to your ad?"

The next second he wondered if that was an indelicate thing to ask, sort of like saying, 'How's business?' But she seemed OK with it. Rolled her eyes and made a wry face. "I sure did. You'd think if you say, 'Let's talk,' that wouldn't be taken to mean, 'Let's screw.' "

"Ha, no, you wouldn't." He was mildly shocked at her saying 'screw,' then interested, then disappointed that she seemed to be ruling it out. "I mean, that's not cool."

Laurie—he had to remember the name—got some more of her drink into her, then put the glass down. She had a cute face—blue eyes, pert little nose, smiley smile. She could have been a cheerleader back in high school, the kind of girl who everybody says ought to be a model or an actress or something, and maybe she tries that but it doesn't happen for her. Her eyes and mouth had a stretched-out look at the corners, and it was likely that she clocked in somewhere north of thirty-eight. She'd put some kind of goofy silver-colored makeup under her eyebrows to match the jacket, which he still thought was a mistake. The jacket made you think of spacemen in old movies. "So, where you from?" he began gamely. "You a local girl?"

"I am now." She laughed, like this was something funny. "I'm new in town, that's one reason for the ad. Meet a few people, feel a little more grounded."

The next thing was to ask her where she'd moved from, but just then the bartender came to take his order and Laurie said she was good for now and what he really would have liked to ask was what she meant by 'grounded,' since that was a different concept for the online community, a little bit of a stretch when it came to most people's purposes. He got his wallet out to pay and decided there was going to be a definite limit on expenditures tonight.

"A carpenter," she announced, before he had a chance to speak. "What made you decide to do that? Be that? I hope you don't mind me asking."

"No, that's OK." He was just as glad to have her steering the conversation. He was always afraid that something dumb was going to walk out of his mouth, and the woman would decide he was uncouth or just plain unfuckable. "I guess I kind of fell into it, you know, always liked the idea of building things, doing things with my hands. I took some community college courses in business, yeah, wheel and deal, be a big moneybags. So that didn't happen—" He was trying to remember exactly why. He thought he'd just stopped going to class. "—and one job leads to another—" Sean stopped himself, checked to see if she was still listening. He thought she was. "I'm just your basic working stiff."

"Well the important thing is to do what you love," Laurie said. It sounded like she was consoling him for something, like he hadn't quite made the cut in the cheerleader tryouts. "And you have children?"

She must have forgotten what he'd said in his message, or more than likely, forgotten which one he was. She finished the last of her drink and Sean looked around for the bartender. Two drinks. He was good for two, he decided, unless by then she was sitting in his lap or something.

"Yes, I have a boy, he's seventeen and he lives with me."

"There has to be a story there."

"We'll save it for another time," Sean said, not eager to start in on tales of marital failure. "How about you, any kids?"

"Ah," Laurie nodded. Her head bobbed in a way that made Sean wonder if the drink she'd finished was really her first. "That's complicated."

"It isn't usually."

Either she had not heard him or she was pretending not to. "Seventeen. I hope he doesn't raise too much hell."

"Naw, he's a good kid. Smart. Focused. He wants to work with computers. I'm all for that. I don't want him to get stuck in the same rut I'm in. Work your fingers to the bone, what do you get? Bony fingers." The bartender came then and Sean said to get them two more. He twisted incautiously on the bar stool and his back flared. "Case in point." He repositioned himself, trying to get the pieces of his spine into better alignment. "Messed up my back hanging drywall today."

"The thing about kids," Laurie said, her gaze following the bartender, "is you think you know them. Have them all figured out. I mean, who else knows them better than you? Then something happens and you have to ask yourself, who are they? Did somebody, you know, like birds do? Lay a different egg in your nest?"

"What are you talking about?" Sean said. "Birds?"

"Sorry." The silver stuff she'd put over her eyes was getting streaky. She smiled and he was distracted by the weirdness of her wriggling shiny eyebrows. "Sorry, I was just running off at the mouth."

"No problem."

"Tell me more about your work," she said brightly. "I think I'd like to hear more details. I find them interesting."

"Yeah, they are. Somebody's going to make a movie about it all someday."

Her new drink came and she latched on to it in a way that made him consider she might have run her ad just as a way to subsidize her bar time. When she put the glass back down she said, "What I meant was, with birds, everything is instinct. Birds always know how to be birds. They don't all of a sudden start acting like snakes."

He was beginning to think she was either drunk or flaky or both. "Yeah, flying snakes, that would be weird."

Laurie took a measuring look at the drink before her, as if it was part of the conversation. She said, "Do you come here often? I haven't, up until now, but I'm considering doing so."

"Are you feeling OK? Seriously."

"I am seriously, seriously fine."

"I think maybe you've had enough to drink already."

She appeared to give this some thought. "No, but there is a limit to what drinking can accomplish."

"You never told me where you were from," Sean said, mostly as conversational filler. He was getting bored with her. Normal in most respects. Whatever. He was only waiting to finish his beer and call it a night. His back was being tied into knots with ropes of fire.

"Ohio," Laurie said. "The Buckeye State."

Sean waited. "So, why did you leave?"

"It became very not grounded for me there. Like those old Road Runner cartoons where he runs off the edge of a cliff and just kind of stands there a second with a stupid look on his face and then gravity catches up with him and he falls and there's this whistling sound, and then he lands, ka-boom. I just had to get out of there."

"Sure," Sean agreed. As if any of that had made sense.

"Make a new start."

"Sure," he said again, and this part he did understand, though the closest he was going to come to that was bankruptcy.

"I'd like it if you talked to me," she announced. "About anything at all. You have a nice voice, Steve. All low and growly. Sometimes I think that's the thing I love best about men, their voices."

"I'm running a little dry on talk," Sean said. "Like I said a while ago when I was being interesting, I really messed up my back today and I should probably go home and tend to it."

"I have a son just a year older than yours," she informed him.

"Yeah?" Now that he'd announced his intention of leaving, she seemed to be making more of an effort. "Where is he, he come out here with you?"

"No. He's back in Ohio." She looked around the room, frowning, as if expecting someone who had not yet arrived.

"So it's really not a complicated question, whether or not you have kids."

"I don't know why I said that. It's more like, he got himself into some complicated trouble."

"That tends to come with the territory," Sean said. "Kids." They were all spoiled rotten these days, all of them except for his own boy, who was turning out to be the only part of his stupid life he wouldn't change or unmake and sorry, lady, everybody had problems and so far hers weren't doing the trick of distracting him from his own. Mostly the house and how long it was going to take to grind through the miserable jerk-off process of foreclosure and sheriff's sale and whether his ass would be on the street at that point or whether there was anything a lawyer could do, sure, throw himself on the mercy of the courts for being a hopeless fuckup.

"This is a little different territory," Laurie said. "Prison territory."

If she was expecting him to be all interested and sympathetic, she figured wrong. He said, "Yeah? That's a tough one."

"Excuse me," Laurie said, hoisting herself off the bar stool with a kind of careful clumsiness. "Be right back."

That seemed a little abrupt to him, like this particular incarceration trauma made her have to pee just this instant, but what the hell. Next time he had an itch to check out the personals ads, he'd remind himself just how depressing it was to spend time with some weirdo who mostly wanted to display her weirdness to the rest of the world.

He texted Conner: *U home?* And got back, *Yes wer r u?* Sean answered, *On my way.* He wanted to catch up with Conner, shoot the shit with him, impress on him all over again that if he ever did a bunch of stupid drug stuff he'd end up in jail with all the rest of the losers, and his poor old dad would spend his nights in the tavern, crying into his beer about it. *Home*, yes, as long as he still had four walls and a roof to his name, he might as well enjoy them.

When she did reappear, she'd visibly freshened up, put a layer of powder or something over the worst of the silver crayon. Before Sean could begin his how-nice-to-meet-you exit speech, she grabbed his arm.

"Oh my God." Laurie leaned in toward him to whisper, the kind of whisper you produced in a crowded bar. "Don't look now, but there's a guy over there who might be trying to find me."

"Yeah?" He took in the portion of the room in front of him, saw nobody who looked to be paying her any attention. "Where?"

"Don't look! Are you done with your drink? Can we go? Can you just pretend we're leaving together, you know, like a date?"

She still had a hand on his arm, pulling at it, and she looked excited or scared or both. Sean said, "Trying to find you, what, another one of your Craigslist pals?"

"Please." She reached up, kissed him. He was too surprised either to resist or kiss back. The sleeve of her silver jacket made stiff, crackling sounds, like the color had been sprayed on. "Just help me get outside."

"Jesus Christ, lady."

"I would be very, very grateful," she murmured, her hand still on the back of his neck, her face still close to his.

"All right, hold on. Jesus." It looked like he wasn't going to get out the door without her. He detached her hand, prepared for movement. His back wasn't going to quit hurting anytime soon. He stood, put on his windbreaker, and looked around the room again, nothing. He was irritated, he thought if there really was somebody who wanted her for some unknown reason, she should make the most of that. But the kiss had been an invitation, and even with a bad back, he couldn't help thinking what might come of it.

She was walking a little ahead of him. Maybe she wanted him to watch her tight little ass, which he didn't mind doing. She waited for Sean to open the door for her. "Where's your car?" he asked.

"Over there, I think."

He looked behind him at the restaurant. "I'm not seeing your stalker, if that's what he is."

"Will you walk me to my car?"

Sean sighed loud enough for her to hear it. Laurie led the way and again he trailed behind, thinking *stupid stupid stupid*, meaning himself, mostly. Head full of beer, fists jammed into his empty pockets, halos of blur around the parking lot lights, yup, one more wasted evening, and even though you wanted to believe you had an infinite supply of evenings available for wasting, you didn't.

"Hey, your car matches your jacket," he said, which he thought was kind of funny but the laughs weren't coming. She stood by the driver's side, again waiting for him to open doors. Which he did, leaning down, then standing back. "Well good night. Take care of yourself."

"That's him over there." She was whispering again, tugging at Sean's sleeve, and the next minute she'd fit herself next to him and was doing some serious grinding, and he couldn't have said at first whether he liked it or not. Not, he was thinking, but then he felt his dick come to attention.

"Where is he?" Sean asked, putting his hands on her shoulders to slow her down a little, but she tilted her face up toward his and pulled his mouth onto hers. He tasted something that might have been perfume, making him recoil, but he pushed past the feeling, pushed his tongue past the small fence of her teeth and into the hot space inside.

When they stopped and drew apart she said, "He's over there, don't look, he's just some guy who answered my ad and I was fooling around with him, online I mean, just going back and forth saying stuff, all this crazy stuff I didn't mean, yeah, dumb. But I didn't know if you were really going to show up so I told him I was coming and now he's expecting me to leave with him but he's probably not sure it's me and anyway I like you, I like everything about you. Can't we just go somewhere?"

"I don't . . ." Sean began, without knowing what came next, don't think so, don't want to, wanted to but wished she wasn't nuts. You'd have to be nuts to be humping in a parking lot with some guy you just met but maybe he was a little nuts too. "Where did you want to go?"

"Get in," she told him, shaking the car keys out of her purse. "Let's just get out of here."

His phone buzzed. Conner. Sean put it up to his ear to answer. "Hey. I got a little hung up. Yeah, go on to bed, I won't be real late." He shut the phone off, relieved, he guessed, that he wouldn't have to worry about Conner. He was covered, yes, free to follow his dick around all night, great idea. He walked behind the car to the passenger side, lowered himself with care—he was used to his truck, to climbing up—and shut the door behind him.

"Hey," she said, smiling at him. The inside of the car was small, some little undersized Nissan. She started the engine and it came to life with a rattle.

"Hi yourself." Sean draped an arm around her neck, tried to get some purchase on her left breast.

Laurie allowed this, waiting for him to be done with his probing and squeezing, then said, "It's kind of hard for me to see behind me . . ."

"Oh. Sure." He took his arm away. He needed to move the car seat so he'd have more legroom. It slid a grudging few inches. The pain in his back felt like a crack in glass, a radiating starburst. "Are you OK to drive? You want me to?"

"I'm fine. I just had to clear my head, you know, get some fresh air." Laurie steered them out of the parking lot, down an access road and past a strip mall, darkened, closed, then onto 101 North. She checked the rearview mirror. "Good. I don't think he's following. Anyway, he doesn't know where I live." She was in the left lane but not driving all that fast. Headlights kept coming up behind them, bearing down on them with glare, then pulling around to pass them on the right. "So, Steve . . ."

"Sean."

". . . can I ask you about something because I'm curious, nosy, whatever name you want to hang on it, also cause I don't see why we shouldn't know each other a little better. Did you used to be married? Or maybe you are now. I shouldn't assume."

They were coming up on Petaluma but she hadn't changed lanes and it looked like they were still heading north. Sean said, "You know what we should have done? Let me get my truck, so I can follow you, so you don't have to drive me back later." It had been stupid to leave the truck behind. You never wanted to be without an escape vehicle.

"Oh, I don't mind driving, don't worry about that. You know what they say about assume. It makes an ass out of you and me. Are you gonna tell me? Is this like, a sensitive subject, marriage?"

"No, I'm not married, we got divorced." The front seat was small enough that they sat almost shoulder to shoulder, which made it hard for him to see her face unless he was obvious about it and turned around to look. "What about you?"

"Ha. I've been divorced almost as many times as I've been married." She laughed at this, pleased with her own joke. "Don't worry. Every other way but legal, I'm divorced. Whose fault was it, yours or hers?"

"Depends on who you ask. So where is it you live? You up in Santa Rosa?"

"No, Cleveland." More of the laughing. Yeah, she was a scream. "I'm asking you."

"Hers." He was trying to keep his back braced, spare it some of the jolting. Crummy suspension. The car was so low to the ground, compared with his truck, that he had the sensation of the pavement skimming along just beneath his feet and one wrong move could make his door fly open, send him rolling under the wheels.

"Everybody blamed me when my son had his troubles. It's always the woman's fault, isn't it?"

Sean thought about this, about what would be best to say. "Well a lot of people are just way too quick to judge. I guess I'd have to include myself in that. There's definitely a case to be made for a lot of things between me and my wife, I mean my ex-wife, being my fault." He reached for his cigarettes, decided against it.

"Like what. What would you say you did wrong?"

It was a test question, he thought, so he made a show of thinking about it, and although the real answer was *Take up with her in the first place when she always thought she was too good for me,* he said, "I don't know, I guess I took her for granted." He still didn't know exactly what that meant, even after getting it tossed in his face on so many occasions.

"That's pretty tame, Steve. I can't believe that's the worst thing you ever did. The worst you're capable of."

He did turn his head to look at her then. She wasn't smiling or anything close to it. He wasn't crazy about the way she was driving either, lagging off the accelerator whenever somebody came up behind them. She said, "Did you ever hit your wife?"

"No, Jesus. What kind of question is that?"

"Push? Slap? Shove? Slam a door in her face?"

"Why would you think that? Come on."

"Well if you did, at least you aren't bragging about it. "

He let that one settle a moment, then he said, "You don't have a real high opinion of men, do you?"

"Just human beings in general."

"So I guess I shouldn't take it personally."

"Most people," she said, and now Sean was able to put words to the feeling he'd had all along, that she was not really speaking to him, only carrying on a conversation with herself and he was just a shape or an obstacle within her field of vision and he should not take anything she said personally because at no point tonight had he been an actual person. "Most people don't want to admit it, but they've at least thought about doing terrible things."

"No they don't. I don't. Give me a break."

"Things you hear about on the news," she said vaguely, peering into the trail of taillights ahead of them. "All the sick, twisted stuff."

"Yeah, well I'm not fascinated by anything sick."

"You sure about that?" Her face turned briefly in his direction. The dashboard lights gave the silver makeup an iridescent green cast.

"This is kind of a stupid argument, you know? I can't even remember how it started. You're not real good at small talk, anybody ever tell you that?" He moved as far as he could toward the door, away from the unpleasant stiff touch of her weird jacket. He couldn't remember what he'd thought was attractive about her. "You know what, I think maybe I should call it a night. I think you should take me back to the bar."

A moment later he said, "You need to get in the right lane."

They came up on top of the first Santa Rosa exit, then it was past them. Sean sighed. "Where we going, Oregon? I think you'll have to stop for gas somewhere."

She didn't answer and she didn't change lanes. He said, "This is really childish, Laurie. What is this, kidnapping? Should I call nine-one-one or something?" He was trying to keep it light, funny, even sound a little bored, but he was fighting a wave of sickness, as if the dread that had been following him all day or all of his unhappy days had finally caught up with him. *Conner.* His son's name the only charm he had against it, his son all that counted in a life where he had not done any one worst thing, only a long series of bad ones, for which payment had now come due. And one of his mistakes had been thinking that every new woman was a way to start over.

Laurie said, "I really didn't want to be alone tonight. I'm sorry if I got a little pushy."

"That's OK." He was relieved that she was talking again. "Sure, that can get to you, being alone." He waited. "I would really appreciate it if we turned around now."

"Let me tell you a story," she said, "about the worst thing somebody ever did."

TWO

Linnea's mom used to be married to Linnea's father and Jay used to be married to a woman named Angela. Now her mom and Jay were married and they talked about their "practice marriages," and this was terribly funny.

Jay and Angela had a daughter named Megan. Linnea's mom and her dad had Linnea. Linnea's mom and Jay had Max, who was still a little kid and unable to appreciate that he was the result of so much practice. Linnea guessed that she and Megan were the practice children. They were almost the same age (Megan fifteen, Linnea fourteen), and they hated each other and nobody at school better try calling them sisters because they weren't. Megan was one of those total bitches who ignored people, then once in a while for no reason gave them a big fake smile. Once, when Megan was visiting, she walked into Linnea's room and wrinkled up her nose and asked, "What smells so funny?"

Linnea's father used to live in Ohio with them and now he was in California somewhere. Sometimes Linnea thought she remembered him but really, she was probably making things up. Linnea's mom told people, even people who might not be expected to take an interest, that he hadn't ever paid a nickel in child support but it was worth it to get rid of the sorry bastard.

They'd gotten by all right on their own, Linnea and her mom, for most of Linnea's life, and then her mom decided she wanted a man around the house. Jay was OK. Except that he had big hairy eyebrows like Ugg the Caveman. And Max was OK, in fact he was one pretty cool little kid. But Megan was not OK. Angela was not OK, especially when she called the house for one excuse or another but it was all to try and remind Jay that she had the biggest tits in the world and didn't he miss them? Why did Linnea have to have these people in her life, taking up space and inflicting their stupid selves on her? Not to mention people even more remotely connected who came up from time to time, like Angela's loser boyfriend or the loser boyfriend's parents, who were going to get Megan a car for her sixteenth birthday except Jay would have to pay the insurance. One more stupid phone call, one more stupid fight, all these random people with the power to annoy and distress her. It was embarrassing to have such a messed-up family.

Linnea's mom said there wasn't any such thing as normal family these days. And that men, by which she mostly meant Linnea's father, had gotten it into their heads that life was to be lived without responsibilities, and expecting them to support themselves, let alone their women and children, was some kind of grave insult to their personhood.

Linnea's mom was cutting Linnea's hair in the bathroom and waving the scissors around to make her point. She used to be a beautician, so none of them was ever allowed to get their hair cut at a real salon. She added that Linnea might not like Angela or Megan, God knows she didn't like them much herself—the scissors dove in, took another bite—but at least Jay was doing right by them instead of pretending they didn't exist.

"Yeah, yeah," Linnea said. "All hail Jay." The view of herself in the bathroom mirror was discouraging. The mirror was never her friend. She was draped in one of the old towels and her hair was wet and combed down straight over her eyes. Her hair was an ordinary brown and her mom cut it the same way every time, shoulder length and with bangs. She was pretty sure Angela and Megan got their hair done at the kind of place that also offered massages and manicures.

But somewhere there was a mirror behind this mirror that showed her as she ought to be, was meant to be: wised-up, coolly amused, with her hair like a rock star's, all mussed and slutty.

"Uncross your legs," her mother directed. "Or I won't get both sides even." Her mother's fingers moved through Linnea's hair like a bird building a nest, making minute adjustments.

"Mom? Is Angela going to marry Bat Boy?" Bat Boy was the loser boyfriend. He was called that because of his peculiar, nearly lipless mouth.

"Now wouldn't that be nice. Then maybe she wouldn't always be pestering us. I don't expect we'll be that lucky."

A lot of what her mom didn't like about Angela was money. Angela took money out of their pockets and food off their table, Linnea's mom said. Angela thought she deserved to live better than Jay's new family and she wouldn't be happy until they were all in the poorhouse and that's why she called and said Megan needed all these extra expenses every month, like tennis lessons, and then physical therapy for her hand when she hurt it playing tennis. Linnea's mom was always talking about money and worrying about money because she was only working part-time at a dry cleaner's until Max was in school and meanwhile Linnea had better get good grades if she wanted to get a scholarship, because that was probably the only way she was going to get to college. College was supposed to be this thing she wanted really bad but she didn't. And was there even such a thing as a poorhouse?

"Well say she did get married," Linnea persisted. "Would she change her name to Angela Bat Boy, or whatever his last name is? Would Megan? Or would Megan still be Markey?" Jay's name was Markey, which was now her mother's name, as well as Max's. Linnea's name was Kooperman, after her dad. It was like there had been a whole forest of Koopermans and they'd cut down all the trees except her.

"I have no idea. Why are you even worrying about it?"

"Say you divorced Jay. Would you change your name back?"

"Flip your head upside down," her mother said, turning on the blow dryer.

"I want to marry a guy with an absolutely cool name. Like, Cullen." She had to holler over the scratchy noise of the dryer.

"Nobody's getting married. Nobody's getting divorced. Cullen? Where did that come from? Who do you know who's Cullen?"

"Nobody." Her mom was so dumb. Cullen was Edward Cullen from *Twilight.*

Her mother took a section of Linnea's hair, stretched it around a brush, and started blistering Linnea's scalp.

"Ow!"

"I'm not even touching you. Hold still."

Linnea hated this part. Her mom never quit until her hair was completely fried. Finally she got to sit up while her mom did some more tugging and blowing. Her mom shut the blow dryer off. "You're done."

Linnea contemplated her finished hair. It looked like it always did when her mom got through with it: a brown blob with the ends flipped up. "Don't put any hair spray on it."

"Just a little." Her mom held her hand over Linnea's eyes while she gassed her. "OK."

"Gee, thanks, Mom." She looked like Mary Tyler Moore. Or no, like she was dressed up as Mary Tyler Moore for Halloween. She was going to have to wait until morning to wash it and get it back to its normal dumb unremarkable self.

Linnea beat feet out of the bathroom. Max was playing in his room down the hall and Linnea stuck her head in the door. "Hey Spider-Man."

"I'm not Spider-Man," Max said. He was four and he knew all the songs to the television shows and movies.

"Spider-Man, Spider-Man," Linnea sang, trying to get him to join in, but he was busy playing with his army guys. Linnea got down on the floor next to him. Max had the army guys lined up on the edge of a Tonka truck and was pushing them off one by one, making explosion noises. "What are you doing to your guys?"

"They got shot."

"Oh, that's too bad. I hope they get better."

Max looked up from the army guys and scrutinized Linnea. "Your hair looks stupid."

"Shut up, Spider-Man."

"Not Spider-Man."

"Yeah, cause Spider-Man isn't ticklish!"

Linnea dove for his ribs. Max shrieked and squealed. Their mother looked in on them. "Don't get him all worked up, please."

"I'm a radioactive spider and I'm biting him!"

"Linnea," said their mother in a warning tone.

Linnea stopped tickling and Max took a few swings at her. "You're a big fat spider," he announced.

"I need you to set the table," their mother said, heading toward the kitchen. It was kind of funny that Max looked more like their mother than Linnea did, even though he was a boy. Their mother looked like a palomino horse. Max had the same goldy hair and light eyes. Linnea guessed she looked like her father. It wasn't the kind of thing anybody was going to tell her.

Jay came home and sat in the den watching the news. The news was all he ever watched. Linnea wasn't allowed to watch MTV or some of the movies. Her mom and Jay were so clueless. They didn't know all the things you could get on the computer or on a phone.

Jay worked at FedEx, scooting packages around on a forklift. He always came home tired, like it was so hard to drive around all day. Linnea set the table for dinner and tried to sneak back into her room. She was soft-footing it past the den when Jay called to her. "Hey sis. Come in here a minute."

Linnea edged around the doorway, half in and half out. "How was school?" Jay asked.

"It was all right." She figured Jay meant, did she get into a fight with Megan. But Megan was a sophomore and the two of them didn't have classes together. They only saw each other in the halls, and they could usually steer around each other.

"Your mom did your hair, huh?"

"Oh yeah."

"Don't let her catch you making that face."

"Can I do my hair a different color? Or even just highlights?"

"That's up to your mom."

"But you'd be OK with it, right?"

"You have to ask her."

Jay still had his FedEx polo shirt on. It made him look like he played golf for a living. His eyebrows practically met in the middle. He wouldn't let Linnea's mom wax them. Linnea said, "Why do I have to learn algebra? I bet I never have to use algebra in my whole life."

"Yeah, but what if you grow up and decide you want to be an algebra teacher?"

"You're killing me. I got a B on my French quiz."

"Why not an A?"

"Come on. Nobody gets A's."

"Linnea."

"How about you pretend I told you I got an A."

"Funny, kiddo." Jay called her things like kiddo and sis, because she wasn't his real daughter. And Linnea called him Jay, because he wasn't her real father, just some guy that she'd gotten used to having around.

On the television, a bunch of foreign people were marching along a street and hollering. Then the picture switched to somewhere else, a flood, and then the president giving a speech, then a man came on who looked like Mr. Field her algebra teacher but wasn't, and he said that the government was taking over everything now, taking over businesses and schools and banks and taxing everybody to death and coming to take their guns away.

"Do you have a gun?" Linnea asked, just to be saying something.

"That's nothing you need to worry about."

Linnea thought that might mean that he did, most likely in his closet somewhere, and that was kind of exciting, at least more exciting than most things about Jay. She was going to look around for it the next chance she had.

Her mom called everybody in for dinner. They were having cube steak and fried potatoes and green beans. Max got macaroni and cheese because that was all he ever ate. Linnea finished eating and took her plate to the sink and then went to the cupboard and fixed herself a bowl of Frosted Flakes. Her mom said if she was still hungry she should have had some more meat and vegetables and Linnea said no, what she really wanted was Frosted Flakes.

Sometimes she felt that these people she lived with, each one of which was related to her in some different way or not at all, were like a cartoon, like *The Simpsons*, and everything they did was probably really funny if you were just outside watching it.

The next day at school all the freshmen had an assembly about citizenship, and how they were all members of their community and they should all sign up for some activity, like helping old people rake their leaves or volunteering at the food pantry or reading to little kids at the library. They should get involved.

Linnea didn't think she was the community type. There weren't any windows in the auditorium and that sucked because outside it was a perfect October day, breezy and cool with the air full of colored leaves like fluttering birds. And today was only Tuesday.

She yawned and her friend Patti poked her. "Wake up. Get involved."

Linnea poked her right back, then one of the teachers gave them the stink-eye so they both put on their best paying-attention faces until he turned his back, and then they had to try not to laugh.

Finally it was over and they got to go back to third period, which was English. They were reading Maya Angelou so they would know something about black people.

Linnea had to go to the bathroom and she told Patti to tell Mrs. Beet that she'd be there in a minute.

The bathroom was at the end of the third-floor hallway, one of the small ones with only three stalls. When she'd finished peeing, she washed her hands and fussed with her hair. She thought her mom had cut it too short. It looked like it had gotten caught in a blender or something and they had to chop it off.

The bathroom door opened and Megan and one of her trashy friends came in.

They were both surprised to see each other and maybe if it was just the two of them alone they could have let it go. But Megan's friend was watching and so Megan said, "Oh lookee here. It's the little skank."

"Hi there, cupcake," Linnea came back with. It was a new one she hadn't used yet.

Megan's face turned blotchy red. She couldn't ever help it. She was growing big boobs, like Angela, and she always looked like a lot of her was squeezed upward, like her tops were too tight and about to strangle her. "Hilarious," Megan said. Then, to her friend: "Say hi to skank-head."

The friend smirked. She was one of those eyeliner girls. "Hi, skank-head."

Linnea clutched at her chest and pretended to crumple. "Dying here."

Megan and Eyeliner parked themselves in front of the mirrors. They made faces at themselves, sucking in their cheeks, and then they started in piling on more makeup.

"What happened to your hair?" Megan asked. "It looks extra queer today."

"Shut up, bitch."

Megan and Eyeliner looked at each other. "Oooh," they said.

Her hair was so stupid. Even if it grew out and even if she had somebody else do it from now on, it was always going to be ugly and stupid and wrong. You wanted to believe that getting older, growing up, would change everything, transform you into the amazing person you were meant to be. But what if it didn't? What if you had to stay you forever?

"So, you give any good blow jobs lately? Huh, Meggie?" Megan had once made the mistake of telling Linnea the things she had done with her last boyfriend.

"Fuck you!"

Now it was Linnea's turn to go "Oooh." She tried to get out the door then but the other two were in the way and Megan shoved her in the chest. Megan was big, but a total spaz, so it felt more like getting bumped by somebody on a bus.

Linnea ran into one of the stalls and shut the latch. She put her eye up to the crack in between the door and the metal frame. Megan was right outside, leaning in. "Oh wow," Linnea said. "The attack of the giant boobs."

"I am gonna beat your ass!"

"Not from out there you aren't."

Megan smacked on the stall door. "Get out here!"

"Make me."

Megan put her face up to the crack. Linnea wished she had her backpack so she could stick a pen right in her eye. Linnea saw their two pairs of feet. They smacked on the door some more and then pushed on it. Linnea pushed back.

They stopped trying to get in and the feet moved back to the sinks. "Maybe she should just stay in there," Eyeliner said.

"Yeah, because that's where she belongs. In a toilet."

Linnea said, "Hey, Meggie. Your mom is gross. I'm just saying."

"And your mom's a whore!"

"Yeah? Then I guess Jay likes whores better than big fat cows like your mom."

Megan rushed the door again and made it rattle. "He does not."

"Yeah, right." Linnea was running out of rotten things to say. She was going to get in trouble for cutting English when it wasn't even her fault.

Megan and Eyeliner were talking so she couldn't hear, all whispers. Then they left. The door swung open and they were gone. Linnea stayed put. She knew they were probably just outside so when she came out they could jump her. How long was she going to have to wait for somebody else to come in so she could leave? She unlatched the stall door and peered out to make sure they were gone. There was a window open just enough to let a little air in but she didn't know if it went anywhere and then she remembered the beautiful day outside and it wasn't fair.

Why did she have to even *know* Megan, but she did, she was somebody Linnea would have to drag around for her whole stupid life because Jay was stupid enough to marry Angela. And it was a purely horrible thing to realize that Max was what was called Linnea's half brother but he was Megan's too. Horrible horrible horrible.

Megan was going to grow up to be just like Angela, a big whiny top-heavy cow with a lot of boys always hanging around her. Did that mean Linnea would turn into her own mother and wake up every day in a bad mood and telling everybody else they were doing things wrong? Now that was depressing.

Some kind of noise started up, somebody shouting, but small and far away and Linnea couldn't tell if it was inside or outside, beyond the window. Then a ripping, popping sound. A door slammed. Then the echoing noise of feet running in the empty hallway. More shouting, she couldn't make out the words.

Was something happening? Was it some kind of crazy stuff?

She left the stall and went to stand next to the hallway door. She couldn't tell if anybody was on the other side or not. She put her mouth to the opening. "Megan?"

No answer. Her heart was jumping around and the commotion of it was making her head feel blurred. She had to decide something but whatever it was wouldn't stay still. It was about the door, which had always been an ordinary door but now it was like a door in a movie, something the camera stayed on for a long time so you knew it was important. She put her hand flat against it, as if letting the hand do its own deciding, and then came the sound of slow feet coming down the hallway and stopping just outside.

THREE

Foster's wife belonged to the Audubon Society, the Sierra Club, the Wilderness Foundation, Friends of the Earth, Greenpeace, and probably some others he'd forgotten about. Foster told her she seemed to join any organization that thought human beings had been a bad invention. His wife said he could make fun all he wanted, but they were all about worthwhile goals, like responsible stewardship and living in harmony with nature.

Harmony, Foster said, now that was a good one. Nature was a constant fight for food or territory, and every creature out there was either prey or predator or sometimes both, and that included forlorn polar bears on melting ice and lovable orangutans and anything else whose affecting, full-color photograph was used to manipulate people like her into writing more checks. Anyway, the next time the deer came down from Mt. Tam and munched on her roses, he wanted to hear her talk about harmony and stewardship. His wife told Foster that he just enjoyed arguing and being disagreeable.

He couldn't argue back without proving her point, so he silenced himself and waited for her to leave. She was preparing to go out, and this required phone consultations and marching back and forth between different rooms, and wondering out loud where were her shoes, her keys, and so on, and here was the lunch she had prepared for him, and this was how he was to go about reheating it, and he had to remember his medicine, which was all set out on the kitchen counter, did he want her to call and remind him?

"Feral cats," Foster said.

"What?" His wife's eyebrows rose and hovered like some old-time Applause-O-Meter, except here the dial went from exasperation to alarm.

"People *want* them to be endangered."

"Entirely disagreeable," his wife pronounced, taking herself off.

Foster waited while the car made its way down the long hill of the driveway, pulled into the street and receded, leaving a faint, stinging silence behind it. "Am not," he said aloud.

In fact, Foster was mildly in favor of preserving marine mammals and hummingbird habitat and scenic rivers, and mildly annoyed by most of his own species. What he didn't care for was anything he regarded as sentimental or falsely optimistic. Big fish ate little fish. Species evolved or failed to do so. Everything reproduced and died, everything wound up on the scrap heap of mortality. He'd had two bouts with prostate cancer and either that or something else was likely to finish him off sooner rather than later, and he didn't want to have to pretend it wasn't happening.

He had the house to himself for some blessed space of hours. She had gone into the city and there she would shop and lunch. She had an errand involving drapery fabric, or maybe it was upholstery fabric or maybe it wasn't fabric at all, but bathroom lighting fixtures or some other household trophy. It was often true, as she accused him, that he did not pay attention to the things she told him. They had been married more than forty years, and by now he figured he'd already heard everything she had to say.

So much of what came out of her mouth was just a kind of anxious noise, meant to reassure herself that she still existed, still retained her full complement of opinions, observations, preferences, imperatives. From time to time Foster dipped his oar into the stream, answered back, made listening noises, supplied information where required. But he simply couldn't keep up. What he called talking, she called "communication." On those occasions when she punished him by remaining silent, he usually had to have the punishment pointed out to him. It hurt her feelings, and her hurt feelings became one more of her infallible grievances, something used against him.

A good marriage? A bad one? A little of each, he thought, and anyway it hardly mattered by this late date, their children grown and gone, and only these last, exhausted years remaining. They'd knit themselves together and now, after the surgeries, the professionally sympathetic doctors, the explanation of what was meant by "recurrence," it was time to begin the process of unknitting.

There was a sense in which he had already removed himself from her. Dying was something you did alone; he needed to practice for it. He hated his wife's solicitude, her extravagant worrying, her inquiries after the state of his damaged, leaky body. He pushed her away, he said he was fine, leave him be. Of course her fears were in large part for herself. She was terrified of sleeping alone, waking alone, moving through her remaining days alone. Foster knew this. The future cast its shadow. But he could not allow himself to feel pity for her, lest he feel pity for himself, and so become entirely undone. He wanted to be left in peace, or the closest he could come to it.

Today he had his little space of solitude, and his excellent cup of coffee, and the thin winter sun angling through the windows of the breakfast room. He closed his eyes and let the sun warm his face. He didn't want to think about anything. He didn't want to be in pain, or dread being in pain. If only the light could go out and take him along with it.

A noise drew him back to himself. Something outside that scraped or scratched. Even before he opened his eyes he identified it as a rake moving over rough ground.

At the edge of the large and well-kept backyard, with its koi pond and footbridge and plantings of bamboo and Japanese maples, its bird-friendly shrubs and variety of feeders, a man—a young man? teenager? all he could see was a slight figure in a hooded sweatshirt—was raking the dead leaves out of the English ivy. They employed all manner of people to tend to the lawn and garden, and so this was not in itself startling, although Foster had not seen this person before, and his wife usually told him when to expect a crew—that is, the latest person who'd shown up at their door asking for work. Of course it was likely that she'd said something but he'd missed it. For once this bothered him, as if he should be making an effort not to let anything slip past him.

The boy had already filled a number of tall brown paper leaf bags—he must have started working along the driveway, out of Foster's view—and now he began hauling these around the corner of the house. When he came back to the rake, a black dog bounded alongside him, sniffing the borders and raising his leg on a teak garden bench.

Foster tapped on the window glass but they were too far away. A dog would not do, would not do at all. Who told him he could bring a dog anyway? His wife wouldn't have allowed it; dogs, in her view, were only slightly less destructive in a garden than deer.

Foster went to the back door and opened it, called out, but now the boy had a leaf blower going, running it along the edge of the beds. The racket was obnoxious. The boy had his back to Foster, the dog was pawing at the edge of the koi pond, onto some scent, maybe. "Hey!" Foster called. "You, scram!"

The dog raised his head, gave Foster a level glance, then went back to his absorbing task. The boy still hadn't seen him. Foster stepped outside—it wasn't really that cold—onto the bluestone path. His ankle wobbled—

—or maybe it was his head sending some scrambled electrical message to his ankle, because his vision went white and fizzy, like static, and he pitched sideways into a bush that wasn't dense enough to support his weight and he tried to catch himself but his hand went right through and then he was inside the bush itself. Twigs in his mouth and hair. He tasted them, a dry taste. He saw the patched sky through their crosshatching. He opened his mouth to speak, but the bush choked out any words.

It was the most extraordinary thing.

The black dog was nosing at him, almost delicately. Foster was aware of the snuffling, the small nudging. The racket of the leaf blower had ceased. Somewhere outside of the bush someone, a boy, he remembered, was saying something in tones of rising concern.

"Sir? Sir? Are you all right, sir?"

It was such a relief not to have to do anything. Be anything. Other than part of a bush.

"Sir? Can you hear me?"

Gradually, he came back to himself. Different portions of him—legs and feet—were on the ground, while the rest of him was suspended in the dense leafless branches, which both supported and imprisoned him. In another moment, he was pretty sure bad things would start to happen, and here they were. Damage reports from his neck and back. Places his skin had been scraped and scratched. His glasses knocked loose. Somewhere out there were all the unwelcome human components of alarm, fear, confusion, and embarrassment.

"Sir?"

"I'm . . ." He started to say "all right," since that was what you were meant to say, but there should be something else you could say instead. It was all the way back in his mouth where he kept the words. But now he had to contend with this boy, who was leaning over him and pushing through the branches, saying give me your hand, give me your hand, but Foster wasn't any good at that, so the boy had to stoop and try to get an arm beneath Foster's shoulders, all the while shooing the interested dog away. It was the kind of dog who wanted to be part of everything.

Getting himself upright took some effort. The bush had nearly swallowed him whole, and Foster wasn't much help, and the boy had to wade halfway into the tangled space. Back in the hospital Foster had been similarly helpless and other people had moved him this way or that. But then he had been drugged and punchy; now he was mostly curious about the whole procedure.

The boy hauled Foster back onto the path, still supporting his weight. "How about we get you inside," he suggested, and Foster said Yes, good idea, or tried to say it, but it was hard to do more than one thing at a time, and breathing seemed an even better idea. He hadn't gotten very far from the back door, so that when the boy draped Foster over his back like some big broken bird, it only took a few steps to get across the threshold. "Stay," the boy told the disappointed dog, closing the door behind them. Then, to Foster, "Is anybody else home?"

"Nnnn," Foster managed. He thought he could walk on his own now but nope, here he was falling over again, until the boy got a kitchen chair underneath him and he managed to land properly in it.

"I can call somebody for you. Like, nine-one-one . . ."

That joggled Foster's words loose. "No, don't. Call." His tongue unfurled, regained its strength. "Just need to catch my breath."

The boy had been bending over him and now he straightened and took a step back, seeming cautious, as if Foster might start flailing around again, or weeping, or any other unseemly thing. He went to the sink, ran water, found a glass on the drainboard and offered it to Foster. "Thank you," Foster said. He was aware that he was being monitored, and that he was going to have to behave reasonably if he didn't want ambulances and calls to his wife and every other fuss-making thing. He drank a little of the water. It seemed to stay in his throat a long time. "I guess I just lost my balance out there."

Cunning was needed. His head still felt gauzy, he scrabbled to hold on to the certainty that he had been, if only for a few moments, something other than himself, but he had to thrust it down and keep talking. "I have some problems with my blood pressure," not exactly a lie. "I probably stood up too fast."

He watched the boy weigh this as a reasonable explanation. He wasn't very old, a high school kid, Foster guessed. One of those god-awful rat's nests of hair. A baby face, but with something cautious and adult in his manner. His eyes never met Foster's. Foster said, "My wife will be home a little later. Really, you don't have to worry about me."

"You got a couple of pretty good scratches there."

He was going to have to explain those, he supposed, but first he had to establish himself as a competent person who did not need minding. "I guess my wife must have hired you," he said cheerily.

"How about I get you something for your face."

Foster closed his eyes again, giving up. He heard the boy in different parts of the house, looking for what he needed, something else his wife would not have liked. He felt weakened, defeated, a soiled old man. The boy was back. "I'm just gonna clean these up first."

Foster kept silent. The boy pressed a warm wet cloth to his face, then dabbed ointment. "This might smart a little," he warned.

Oh Jesus did it. Foster tried not to squirm. He flicked his eyes open, saw the boy's face close to his own, then the boy backed off, put a little more respectful distance between them.

"Thanks," Foster said. "I'm good as new."

"Sure." The boy's gaze lifted to the window, thinking of the undone job, or the job after that, Foster guessed. Or maybe trying to keep track of the dog. But he didn't seem ready to take himself off yet, since Foster might topple over again or worse. "This is a really nice house you have," he offered.

"Thank you." It was in fact a nice house, although Foster couldn't remember the last time he'd given much thought to it, and right now, in the aftermath of his peculiar episode, he had to look around him and consider it. Not just this particular house, his own, but the whole idea of houses. So much empty, complicated space, when all you needed was a few twigs. *And wasn't the body also a kind of house?* Foster shook his head loose from the strangeness of his thoughts, forced himself back into some familiar notion of himself: brisk and businesslike. "If you want to finish up back there, I'll just sit and rest. Then it's fine if you go."

"I need to put my dog in the truck," the boy said, which Foster guessed was a way of saying he was staying put.

The boy crossed the kitchen and the back door opened, shut. Foster would have liked to swear. He didn't think he had enough breath in him. Even if he could manage to get up and lock the door, shoo the boy away, that wouldn't be the end of it. Someone else would come tapping at the glass, breaking down the door, prodding at him with latex gloves. He guessed he'd be better off taking his chances with the boy.

There was a small, floating space of lost time—that is, of no time at all—before the door opened again. A draft of cold air walked along Foster's spine. The boy shut the door. "How are you feeling?"

"Ah. Lousy." Dumb answer maybe, but he didn't think "fine" was going to fool anyone.

"I could help you lie down."

"No, I think I want to stay more awake." He felt not sleepy, but vague, weak, diffuse. "What I really need is—"

"OK. Let me give you a hand."

The boy bent down and helped pull Foster out of his chair, then slow-walked him to the bathroom. Foster was aware of the boy's smell—something faint but unpleasant, unwashed clothes or unwashed body—he hadn't noticed before. Well, boys. What did you expect. They reached the bathroom and the boy said, "I can wait outside. Call if you need me."

For which Foster was grateful. He'd had enough of strangers helping him pee, watching him pee, enough of not being able to pee or not being able to stop, a whole universe of piss he hadn't been aware of until his troubles began. He closed the bathroom door, supported himself on the sink, and then the windowsill, and in this way managed to do the chore standing up, although there had certainly been days when this was not possible.

He flushed, got his clothes together, ran water in the sink, avoiding as much as possible the mirror above it. He couldn't escape it entirely. A gray-faced skull peered sideways at him.

When he came out, he didn't see the boy. Too tired to worry much about it, he hitched his way into the den and lowered himself onto a couch. The windows here faced the backyard. He saw the boy rolling up an extension cord into a coil, then scuffing around in the beds he'd raked.

The back door opened. Feet crossed the kitchen, halted.

"I'm in here," Foster called, his voice coming out thin and piping. Ridiculous.

The boy looked in at the door. "I was just clearing some things away."
Foster lifted a hand: Fine.

"The lady said you'd pay me."

Foster opened his eyes—he was not aware he'd closed them—sighed.
"How much?"

"Thirty-five. It's OK. I was going to hang out and wait for her anyway.
You know, in case you needed anything."

"Desk." Foster pointed. He couldn't get air all the way into his chest.

The boy scanned the desktop, held up Foster's wallet. "This?" He
crossed the room with it. "But, listen, I'm sorry if the dog got in your way.
He didn't mean to hurt you."

Foster shook his head. He wanted to say, the dog hadn't done anything
to him. Or only in the most roundabout way, since if the dog had not been
in the yard, Foster would not have stepped outside as he had. But maybe
whatever had gone wrong would have gone wrong anyway, in the bathroom or standing at the refrigerator or arguing with his wife. Whatever
it was didn't feel like the cancer, unless all the burning and poisoning
and cutting they'd done to smack the cancer down had made something
else in him fail. He hadn't wanted to think it, and now the thought took
root in him. So this was how it would happen. A bad thick taste was
climbing up the back of his throat. He would have the boy call the doctor,
because in spite of all his cheap, brave posing he was getting scared.
He said, "Dogger."

The boy held the wallet out to Foster, then, when Foster didn't take
it, he set it down next to him. "You could give me less, on account of the
dog. I completely apologize for that. I hope you aren't too mad about it.
Because I'd really like to do some more work for you guys. Also if you
know anybody else around here who needs yard cleanup, fencing, anything like that."

Foster let his head fall back against the couch. It was easier to breathe
that way. His hands had been fisted and now he let them uncurl. There
was something about a dog?

Dogdead dogdead dog.

"I've been trying to get a business going, you know, landscaping. People sure have nice yards in this place."

The boy waited to see if Foster meant to answer. When Foster didn't, he said, "Everybody has these great houses. This whole town is like, people here have it made. You drive around downtown and look in the windows of all those restaurants, everybody having a good time, eating and drinking, you'd think the whole world was one big party. You wonder where these people get all their money. Sorry. That was kind of rude of me. I didn't necessarily mean you."

Another space of waiting. The boy said, "Twenty-five bucks. Even twenty, that would be something. Maybe I should just shut up and let you rest."

Not just dog. All the poor dumb, baffled, nearly extinct creatures. They tried fighting back, making their noise. Roar, said Foster. Roaring here.

"Sir?"

Foster said, Afraid. The boy leaned over him, trying to make out the sound Foster was producing. There was that smell again, stale boy. Or maybe it was his own stink.

Afraid.

It did not take very long at all for Foster to die, not as the boy or anyone else watching would have measured it. Enough time for more of Foster's weakened blood vessels to give way and his secret bleeding to run its course. The boy had only just begun to realize there might be something serious happening here, something alarming, some mistake resulting from his inattention, and by then it was all over.

But for Foster, it went on and on. There was a sensation of something rolling, something heavy and extremely slow, along a chute or track, and once it reached the end, another rolling object took its place, and then another, and they were not thoughts, but the spaces between his thoughts. The frightened animal within him quieted. He had not wished to bother with thinking, and now the capacity to do so was leaving him. He recognized this new condition from his time within the bush. It was Not Be. It was a weight rolling away, a little heavier every time. The weight balanced on an edge and then dropped off. Not Be would allow you, if you wished, to look down on the leftover husk of yourself with gratitude, and in the last choice available to him, he so chose. His breathing had already ceased, and now black stars exploded behind his eyes. Then one by one, went out.

The boy had never seen a dead person before but there was no mistaking it, and soon enough he realized that nothing could be done. He took a few steps away from Foster, whose name he had not known, then back again. He spent some time looking at Foster, taking him in. With every moment, he seemed to become a little more dead.

Foster's wallet was on the edge of the couch where the boy had left it. Now he picked it up, opened it, and sorted through the bills. Then he stopped, replaced the money, and put the entire wallet in his back pocket. He went to the desk in the corner and rummaged through the drawers, finding those things worth taking. He left the room and from other parts of the house came more sounds of opening and shutting.

Finally, in the kitchen, he looked into the refrigerator and took some packaged lunch meat and a brick of cheese. From the cupboards he picked out a few canned things, boxed things, then loaded everything into a plastic garbage bag he found beneath the sink. He let himself out the back door, careful to flip the latch so that it locked behind him.

The truck started up, accelerated smoothly down the driveway, and was gone.

The house went about its business as before. The thermostat registered a drop in temperature and sent a warm wind through the vents. The water pressure in the pipes maintained itself. Electric current whispered in the wires behind the walls. The refrigerator's motor cycled.

The phone rang, and after the fourth ring the answering machine clicked on, unspooling its recorded message. Foster's voice said, "Sorry, we can't come to the phone right now, but leave us a message at the beep."

Foster's wife came on the line. "Lou? Are you there?" A listening silence. "I wanted to remind you about your medicine. Lou?" Her voice rose. "I know you can hear me. Or maybe you're in the bathroom? Anyway, you need to call me back."

The silence flattened. It could almost be heard, as if it were itself a sound.

"Lou?"

FOUR

Art Kooperman had been teaching himself Vietnamese: *Hoan ngênh,* welcome; *Chào anh,* hello! He often got takeout from the Saigon Palace, and he thought it would be nice to be able to speak to the people there in their own language. And anyway, learning Vietnamese was the kind of knowledge-for-its-own-sake project he enjoyed. He was practicing some of the basic phrases, *chào buổi sáng,* good morning; *khỏe không,* how are you? as he stood just beyond the security entrance at the San Francisco airport, waiting for his daughter's plane to arrive.

Not that his daughter was Vietnamese or anything. She was a normal, vanilla-flavored American. He should have been thinking about what to say to her, or getting his head wrapped around the imminent fact of her, but these were the last free moments he had, his last appearance as a nonparent, responsible to no one but himself, entirely unconcerned with his minor child's nutrition, hygiene, education, socialization, not to mention her seriously fucked-up behavior. *Làm ơn nói chậm hơn,* please speak more slowly. *Làm ơn viết xuống,* please write it down.

He didn't know what she looked like these days. In his memory she was still a chubby, staggering two-year-old. Too late, he realized he should have asked them to send a picture. Maybe some other, less problematic fifteen-year-old girl would show up to claim him as her father, and maybe his daughter would attach herself to some other, more competent dad, and everything would work out for the best, since the chain of events and bad decisions that had resulted in her arrival, indeed in her very existence, was turning out to be the greatest dismal circumstance of his whole shitcan life. *Cứu với!* Help!

But then, he had to keep in mind the absolute evil of what had happened to her.

His daughter was coming to stay with him as a kind of test drive, an exile, a visit of uncertain length. She had been having difficulties, and these difficulties had been explained to Art during an alarming phone call from his ex-wife, Louise. The fact of Louise calling was alarming in itself. It served him right for being incautious enough to keep the same phone number all this time, and for assuming that since Louise had not called him for more than ten years, she was finally off his case.

At one point in the phone call, Art had been imprudent enough to ask, "Well, is she seeing a counselor or anything?"

There was a silence, and he could hear Louise debating whether or not he was even worth the effort of sarcasm: My God, counseling! Why didn't we think of that? Instead she said, "All the kids got counseling."

Then she said, "Do you think I would call you if I wasn't desperate? We can't keep her here anymore, it's not fair to anybody, especially Jay, can you imagine how Jay feels? He lost his own daughter."

Art had begun to say something along the lines of commiseration when Louise added, "That's usually thought of as a tragic thing. Losing a child. You think I'm rubbing it in? Fine. I am."

They both listened to the silence for a time, then Art said, "What makes you think I'd know what to do with her? That I'd be any good at it. Huh?"

"She's going to end up in a juvenile facility, some horrible state-run program, if we don't get her out of here. Not to mention one more mar-

riage blowing up in my face. There's your answer. And I'd like to think
you'd want to help her. Maybe I'm wrong. Feel free to correct me."

"There's not a lot of space where I live," Art said, regretting the words
as soon as he spoke. No excuse was going to save him.

Louise said, "Honestly? Even if I tried to take you to court for, what, a
hundred thousand dollars of child support, you can't get blood out of a
turnip. Guilt? That's probably going to last you about twenty minutes
after you get off the phone. So how about, this is a chance for you to do
something different. Be somebody different. A good guy. A father. Oh, I
guess I shouldn't assume. Do you have any other children?"

"Just her," Art said, feeling as if he were making a damaging admis-
sion of some sort.

As if he should have had more children, or no, if he did, Louise would
find some way to use that against him, as in, she hoped he provided better
for them than he had their own daughter. Or say he was a model parent to
these other, nonexistent children, how did he justify his total neglect of
Linnea? Once Art reached this point, he was aware he was doing Louise's
dirty work for her, creating scenarios of fault and blame, and she was
wrong about the guilt, it did stay with him, but eventually it circled back
into anger.

He said, "Look, I'm either good enough for her, or I'm not. I guess you
think I am. I guess you need my help. So if you want me to even consider
it, how about you be a little nicer?"

"All right, OK then, sorry—" Louise started out snippy and nasty as
before, but here she seemed to swallow down a choking mass of tears, so
that words came out clotted and damp. "Such a horrible, horrible thing . . .
and she won't let anything get better. She tried to hurt . . . hurt . . ."

"Take it easy," Art said. "Hurt who, what did she do?"

"My little boy. She *loves* him, the two of them were always so great
together, and then she . . ."

"*What?*" said Art, as Louise started in bawling again. "Come on, calm
down." She wasn't calming down.

Didn't it always end up with tears, Louise crying over something that was traceable, either directly or indirectly, to a defect on his part, and the rest of it felt familiar too, the exhaustion of dealing with her, like one of those waves the ocean heaved up, the ones that clobbered you and knocked you flat and dragged you out to the murky, roiling sea. "What did she do?" he repeated, thinking of all the things a truly disturbed teenager might be capable of.

"We didn't see her do it, but his little arm was just black and blue. She hates us. We know she does because she tells us. She starts fights at school. She can't go back there this fall, they won't let her. She steals money from my purse and lies about it. She steals from stores. We think she uses drugs."

"What kind of drugs?"

"For God's sake, Art."

"No, really, there's a difference between a little pot and being a raging meth freak. There's some things you really ought to put people in jail for."

Louise said, "We can smell the marijuana on her. Don't start telling me it's a harmless, natural herb. Fifteen. Years. Old."

A chip off the old block, Art thought but did not say. Since it seemed like his turn to move the discussion along, he said, "This sounds like a real bad idea, Louise. Her coming here. Seriously, this is the kind of—"

"It was her idea."

Louise blew her nose, offstage, then came back to the phone. "She says she doesn't want to have anything more to do with us, and she's entitled to get to know her own father."

"She doesn't think I'm rich or anything, does she?"

"I don't think she's laboring under that misapprehension."

"What have you told her about me, huh?" Louise didn't answer. "Never mind that one."

"I've tried to talk her out of it, but she has her mind set on it, and honestly, we all need a break from her, it would be a relief, even though that makes me feel horrible, it's horrible not to want your own child. Oh, sorry. I forgot who I was talking to."

"If I say yes to this, Louise, and I'm not suggesting I will, you and I have to agree on some ground rules. Like, you can't call me up all the time just to heap shit on me."

They hung up. Art spent the next two days thinking gloomy thoughts. He didn't believe for a minute that Louise wouldn't sic the lawyers on him, or at least threaten to, or make some other kind of misery for him. There were other times when he tried on some jazzy, offbeat version of fatherhood, something from a quirky movie, but these moments proved difficult to sustain. In the end, it seemed easiest to agree to some kind of quickie visit, and he called Louise back and told her to put Linnea on a plane.

Her flight from Cleveland was on time, the arrival board said, and she had his cell phone number, in case there was any real problem finding each other. Art had come to the airport early and wandered the concourse, taking in its uninteresting restaurants and its gift stores selling Alcatraz T-shirts and sourdough bread, thinking too late that he should have bought Linnea something, flowers maybe, though he wasn't sure if she was a flowers type of girl.

They'd had one phone conversation before she'd left, and it hadn't really gotten off the ground. Louise had called him and said, without preamble, "She wants to talk to you. Here."

Some fumbling around on the other end, a conversation half muffled by someone's hand, a conversation Art intuited as hostile, the phone reluctantly handed over, then a girl's voice, light, cool, uninflected. "Hello?"

"Hi, Linnea. It's nice to be talking to you."

"Yeah," she said, unhelpfully.

"I'm glad you're coming out here." And at that moment he was; he had some dim sense of at least her ordinary misery, the things she contended with in that house. "Look, don't worry about anything that's going on with your mom, I mean anything you're fighting about. You're going to come out here and leave all that behind you. Like, a new start. Hey, for me too. Because I haven't been, you know, much of a dad. So you and me can take it from the top. Get to know each other. Oh, you need to tell me what kind of food you like so I can go shopping. Are you a vegetarian, anything like that? Because I can—"

"Art?" Louise was back on the line. "She eats most things. That will be the least of your worries."

And so he had undertaken the cleaning and overhaul of his apartment, a sobering project, considering his chronic lack of housekeeping. There were boxes of old papers, things that had never made it onto a computer: class syllabi, gradebooks, student evaluations, quizzes, xeroxed copies of articles. These were layered with a number of inactive wardrobe items, piles of possibly important mail, advertising flyers, receipts, a package of cocktail napkins bought for some forgotten purpose, a compilation of thriftily saved plastic bags, the cable attachment for a digital camera, and more more more: toppling piles of CDs, bands his daughter would sneer at, books she would find uninteresting, his collection of half-melted candles. He owned nothing that was not sad, dishonored, unworthy. In the kitchen the gas oven leaked gas. He threw out everything in the refrigerator and scrubbed it down with a powerfully lemon-scented cleanser. He couldn't bring himself to think about the bathroom yet.

Art's apartment was on the second floor, with an outside staircase, like a motel. He made a great many trips with trashbags dragging and bumping behind him on the stairs, and, as he was hoping, his downstairs neighbor Christie came out to see what he was doing. "You moving or something?" she asked.

"Just cleaning up. My daughter's coming to visit."

"I didn't know you had a daughter."

"No reason you would." Art paused mid-step. He had a hopeless thing for Christie. "She lives with her mom, in Ohio."

"Ah." Christie nodded, looking up at him with her amazing blue gaze. "How old is she?"

"Fifteen."

"A teenager, good luck." Christie was wearing one of her gauzy dresses with a little white sweater over it. She looked like she was wrapped in layers of cloud.

"So I'm trying to get the place cleared out a little. Want to see?"

"All right." Christie followed him up the stairs and in through the front door. Their apartments were identical in layout. Of course, hers was all girled-up. Art stood aside to let her take in the kitchen, or that portion of the main room that functioned as a kitchen.

"I can see you've been working."

"You don't sound real impressed."

"I'm not sure anybody else could see it. I mean if they hadn't been here before."

"I haven't gotten around to the bathroom yet," Art explained, as Christie continued her inspection tour.

"Could I suggest some new towels? And a new shower curtain. And put the toilet paper on the holder, don't just let it sit on the sink."

"I could do that. Sure."

"Where is she going to sleep?" Art indicated the small bedroom across from his own. "I think you should move the bed out to the sunporch and give her that."

"Why's that?"

"Because this room looks like an embalming chamber. How long is she staying anyway?"

"That kind of depends," Art said. He'd been hoping he could get Christie to help him clean up the place. Maybe he still could.

"On what, exactly?"

"How we get along, I guess."

"How do you usually get along?"

"I haven't seen her in a while," Art admitted, and before Christie could ask her next reasonable question, he said, "Hey, would you like some tea?"

"OK. But let's have it at my place."

Christie's apartment made his own look like some kind of evil twin. She'd painted her walls in sunset colors, gold and salmon, and she went in for things like houseplants and woven rugs and pottery that looked as if it had been fabricated by desert-dwelling Indian tribes. She made tea in an actual teapot and poured it through a strainer into matching blue mugs. There wasn't a thing she did that Art didn't observe with helpless fascination. "Now," Christie said. "Tell me about the mystery daughter."

"This is good tea, what kind is it? Green?"

"Art."

"I was married for a while. Not real long. It didn't work out. So we called it quits, and I came out here. From, you know, the Midwest."

Christie waited. Steam rose up from her teacup and twined through the baby curls on each side of her face. "That's it?"

"More or less." Art shrugged. It wasn't the kind of story that made you look good.

"How old was your daughter then? What's her name, anyway?"

"Linnea. Not very old. Two."

"That's a pretty name. Linnea."

"Yeah, it's, ah, Swedish. Her mom was Swedish. Is."

"So all this time . . ."

"It's not something you plan, you know? You don't say, 'I think I'll get married to the wrong woman and impregnate her and then bug out.' She wasn't ever happy with me. With who I turned out to be. She had all these expectations. She was glad to see me go. I was glad to be gone. Enough time goes by, you almost forget any of it happened." He thought he understood the parents in Hansel and Gretel, how they'd gone on with their lives after the abandonment in the forest. They had convinced themselves they'd never had children. After a moment Art said, "I'm just trying to be honest here."

"Yes, it doesn't seem like you're shining it up much."

"I don't think I would have been any good at having a little kid around anyway."

"You never know until you try," Christie said, meaning it as a reproach.

"I wasn't much of a family type."

Which was true. But what type was he? In another century, Art imagined, he might have had a nice life as a monk in some comfortable monastery, one with a good library. As it was, he'd been dragging out his education for the last twenty years. He had a master's degree in English literature, with a specialty in colonial literature, authors such as Kipling, Forster, Conrad. He'd always meant to go on and get a doctorate, and he still kept in touch with his committee, at least those who had not yet retired or died off. But over time his specialty had become somewhat dated. It was too easy to sneer at imperialism and cultural hegemony; anybody could do it, and many people had. It was harder and harder to come up with new and subtle variations, at least in English. In other languages, in other parts of the globe, you could be pretty sure that one population was still busy squeezing the juice out of another, and then sitting on top of the conquered tribes and writing about it.

He thought about starting over, tackling some newer, hotter field, where it was still possible to feel a righteous indignation: ecocriticism, or genocide studies. But as yet he had not taken up the sword. A doctorate of any sort, a dissertation, was such daunting work. Knowledge for its own sake had its limits. Nor was another degree going to land him some plummy professor job. He was forty years old, past his stale date, and anyway, jobs like that were long gone.

He tried to recall the excitement he'd felt when he'd first come out west, that sense of lightness and possibility, his life taking some new and unimaginable shape.

He taught composition courses at one or another junior college. He hired himself out to tutor the indifferent sons and daughters of the wealthy. He graded papers for a national testing service. He wrote online book reviews and attempted to get paid for them. These were the strategies of the overeducated and the underemployed.

In addition, he and a friend were developing a website, which did not yet earn money, although it had the potential to do so, where users could rate other websites. He'd written training manuals for an educational publisher to use in their New Delhi office.

He'd managed to get a trip to India out of it, and he'd parlayed that into three months of sightseeing and dysentery. He was working on a screenplay, a science-fiction epic of post-apocalyptic life on earth, where humans battled one another in huge arenas that were actually video games. From time to time, he made a little money selling pot. He thought about going to culinary school, learning about cooking. He was aware that there were ridiculous aspects to his life, ways in which he could not be taken seriously.

Louise had nagged him about quitting school and getting a real job, earning real money, and he guessed she had been entitled to do so. It was a wife thing. And it took them longer than it should have to figure out they never should have been married in the first place. What did they know? They kept waiting for marriage to take hold, do its thing, meld them into a single being. Each blamed the other for getting in the way of the process. Louise was beautiful, he was smart, or supposed to be smart. Sort of like Arthur Miller and Marilyn Monroe. Everybody knew how that had turned out.

Christie said, "So why is she coming here?"

"It was her idea."

Christie waited for him to keep explaining. Christie was beautiful too. Not in the voluptuous, strutting style of Louise, but in a way that made you take a second look, and then a third. And she was smarter than Louise because she was careful to keep a certain distance between them. She always behaved as if they were funny, sitcom neighbors, and was he going to spend his entire half-assed life alone and broke because he couldn't measure up to the things he wanted?

He said, "You know what your face reminds me of? A Victorian portrait. Of a fairy or something."

"Fairy?"

"They did a lot of these flower fairies. Little creatures wearing flower petals and flying with butterfly wings. They used, uh, all these very fine, delicate lines."

"That's kind of sweet, Art. A little icky, but sweet."

He was going to have to work up some more casual compliments. He said, "She's coming here because they don't know what else to do with her."

He told Christie the story. Maybe she'd seen it on the news, one of those school shootings. Did she remember? Last year? School shootings had kind of died down, but there had been this one. A boy with a grudge, it wasn't clear against whom. Most likely everybody. He'd come to school one morning with an automatic pistol in his backpack, and a hunting rifle with a scope, ingeniously concealed in its own canvas carrying case. For Christ's sake, weren't schools supposed to have security plans these days? What did they think was in there, lacrosse equipment?

Anyway, in he walked. It wasn't a huge high school, just medium-sized, in one of those depressed medium-sized Ohio towns that had grown up around a rail line a century ago. The place his daughter had moved with her mother at some unspecified point. Art knew the town, and thought he remembered the school, three stories of dark brick trimmed with granite cornices and a frieze of figures in togas, proclaiming the virtues of an educated citizenry.

The boy had chosen a place to sit and wait, a partially screened alcove at the end of the main hallway. From television, from certain muscular movies, from video games, he was familiar with the concept of the sniper's nest. The boy said later (because he had survived, to everyone's disappointment, had not turned a gun on himself or been shot by the tardy law enforcement officers) that he had meant to wait until class was dismissed and the halls full of students. But another boy had come out to open his locker and seen the boy with the rifle, and run off to raise the alarm. And so the shooting had begun early.

The shooter fired twice at the boy but missed. These were in the nature of practice shots. He'd needed to get some of the nervousness out of his hands.

And imagine for a moment that boy, spinning his locker combination, yawning his way through the morning, every part of him turned to the lowest possible setting in order to get through the boredom of his day, his week, and his foreseeable future. He hears something, most probably, and looks up at a place where he is accustomed to seeing nothing. Instead there is this thing that refuses to make sense, a rifle barrel pointed at him, jerking up and down as the shooter tries to adjust the scope. It will not resolve itself into anything real. It takes those first shots, the bullets hitting the wall a few feet from his head, kicking out some of the plaster, for the boy to start running.

The boy with the guns walked through the hallway, turned a corner, and entered a classroom where a sophomore civics class was in session. He knew no one there. He had never met or spoken to any of his victims. Now everything was real, he was the star of his own movie, which he watched from a little distance inside himself. He shot the teacher first, three times in the back with the handgun. He aimed haphazardly into the rows of students, who were all still in their assigned seats, because no one had yet fathomed any of it. The boy with the gun did not speak. Later it was estimated he was only in the classroom for fifteen to twenty seconds. For most of the students, it was the sight of blood, not even their own but someone else's, that set them to moving and screaming.

Those who had been shot did not realize it right away, or at all. The teacher, who had been bent over his desk, died without awareness or comprehension. Four students were wounded, one grievously. The boy returned to the hallways, where, unwisely, a couple of doors had been opened and people were looking out. The boy fired shots in their direction without hitting anyone.

And here was where the sequence of events became less certain, because the boy with the guns—only the handgun now, since for some reason he'd dropped the rifle in the main hallway—appeared to hide or evade for a time, and no one reported seeing him for a space of at least twenty minutes. By now police were assembling outside the school, and a team of officers was sent inside, wearing protective vests and helmets. They cornered the shooter in the cafeteria kitchen, surrounded him and wrestled him down in the middle of the stainless steel worktables and clanging pans, and only later were the two dead girls discovered in the upstairs restroom. One of them was Linnea's stepsister. Linnea had been there and watched the boy kill them. She herself had escaped only because his gun had misfired.

Art stopped talking. Christie said, "Go on, what happened?"

"That's what happened. She watched him shoot the others. He held a gun to her head. He couldn't get it to work right. Jammed or something. He kept trying for a while. Then he gave up and left."

"That's horrible, Art."

"I guess she's been having some behavior issues."

"I'd say whatever issues she's having, she's entitled to them."

"I don't know what I'm supposed to do with her, Chris."

"No school, I guess. Unless she needs to take summer classes. What's she going to do all day?"

"Shoplift. Sniff glue. I'm terrified."

"Well, try to imagine how she feels."

That was his problem, or part of it. He could not begin to imagine her. There was a thread of his own DNA in her, but that was braided into whatever she inherited from Louise, plus there was the confounding fact of her femaleness. What did he know about teenagers anyway? They were impossible, he'd been impossible himself, moody, hormonal, sullen. And that without anybody trying to shoot him.

He didn't guess it would have made any difference if he'd been a real father to her. The girls who had died presumably had real fathers.

Vietnamese was a tonal language, so the same words had different meanings, depending on inflections. That was alarming. What if you tried asking directions to the post office but you were really saying, "Do you know where I can find unusually large eels?" He could count with confidence only to six: *Một, hai, ba, bốn, năm, sáu.* What if one were to say to a daughter, "Good morning," but what she heard was, "I never meant to have children."

The airport's public service announcements about unattended luggage and smoking not permitted chimed overhead. Through the glass expanses of the corridor, planes trundled back and forth. Seven, eight, nine, ten, *Bảy, tám, chín, m something . . .*

A beat too late he heard his name spoken, then had to scramble because she was already walking away. "Hey, Linnea?"

She looked back at him. "I thought that was you."

"Sorry." In spite of all his apprehension, Art was grinning. He bent down and put both hands on her shoulders. "Wow. Let me look at you."

She muttered, embarrassed, but stood and allowed herself to be inspected.

She didn't look like Louise. She didn't look much like anybody except herself.

Small, with limp hair that had been dyed black, with purple fringes. There was more black involved in her wardrobe, which Art recognized as a kind of uniform: scuffed engineer boots, jeans, a leather jacket encrusted with zippers and other hardware. Earbud wires wreathed her neck. It was difficult to locate and focus on the face, which was probably her intention. The face was arranged into an expression of stony nothingness, which was another sort of uniform. Here, maybe, was a little of himself. Curve of eyebrow, eye color, pointed chin. He thought the hair was a mistake, and the clothes also were a little cartoonish—at least, they weren't quite what the hipster kids out here wore. She looked like a parody of a perfume ad, the kind where the models struck menacing, vapid poses. But he knew better than to say any of this.

"Welcome," he said, releasing her. "Welcome to California. So, you ever been here before?"

"No."

Her tone was heavily patient, but Art understood that he was meant to ask the kind of questions which allowed her to exhibit boredom. "How was your flight?"

"I threw up, but just the once."

"Oh. Are you all right? Do you need anything? 7Up? Crackers?"

"It was hours ago. It was from the plane. It's not like I'm pregnant or anything."

Art chose to pretend this was humorous. "Oh ha-ha. Come on, let's go get your luggage." He considered putting his hand on her shoulder again but decided against it.

They took the escalator down to the baggage claim. Linnea stood on the step below him, and he had a view of the top of her scalp, where an inch or so of normal brown hair had grown out around her part, bordered by the fried black color. There was something absurd and touching about her efforts to look hard and cool. It made him feel tender toward her, as if she were still two years old, and playing dress-up. He thought he should say something about the shooting at the school, how horrible, how glad he was that she was unhurt, but that moment had either already passed or had not yet arrived.

They stood together at the baggage carousel. Art hoped that her luggage, its amount and kind, might give him some clue as to how long she expected to stay. "There," she said, as the bags began to tumble out and circulate. "That one's mine." Art lifted it off the conveyor. It was large, plaid, and elderly, the kind of suitcase that gets hauled down from an attic or up from a basement, an extraneous, white elephant kind of suitcase, the kind used for the storage of old magazines. It was as if she was not expected back.

It weighed a ton, and Art kept shifting it from one hand to the other as they waited for the shuttle bus to take them out to the remote parking lot. It was late afternoon, and just about the best kind of summer day you could have in these parts: bright, warm, the cloud banks rolled up tight and staying put offshore. Art thought of the many useful and interesting features he could point out about the weather, climate, geography, and so on, and knew enough not to start in with the Clueless Dad narrative. And he should stop asking questions, those hopeful interrogatories designed to force the reluctant child to vocalize.

Welcome to parenthood, he guessed.

He'd cleaned his car too, but in such a way as to leave ghosts of the recently removed clutter and grime. The dashboard showed the tracks of the rag he'd dragged across it, and the zone of undisturbed dust he hadn't reached, a dividing line that reminded him of Linnea's dyed hair. The trunk, when Art opened it to heave Linnea's suitcase inside, still looked like a place you might stash a body. A Starbucks cup rolled around on the backseat floor. Linnea settled herself in the passenger seat. Music leaked out from her earbuds, a tiny, hectic noise. Art said, "It'll take most of an hour to get up to Marin. Did you want to stop for anything on the way? Food, drink, bathroom?"

She had extracted a pair of enormous white sunglasses from her whatever-it-was, purse, he supposed, a large satchel made of something meant to resemble suede, dangling with fringe and stray cords. "I'll probably just sleep," she said. "If that's OK."

"Sure." It was mostly a relief. "You had a really long flight."

"Thanks for letting me come out here."

"Sure," he said again. "Glad to have you."

"Because you could have said no. You could have just blown me off."

Art was trying to find the parking lot's exit. "Oh, well . . ." He wondered if that was how she thought of his absence during most of her life. Blown off.

"And don't get upset, because I assume it was at least partly your idea, or at least you went along with it, but I'm thinking about changing my name."

He glanced over at her. The sunglasses were disturbing. They made her look blind. "Yeah?"

"From Linnea."

"Oh." He wouldn't have blamed her if she'd wanted to ditch Kooperman. "To what?"

"I'm not sure yet. I'm trying out some ideas."

They'd reached the booth at the exit, and Art fumbled for his wallet and the parking stub. "What brought this on?"

"It just seems like a good time to be somebody different."

The clerk counted out Art's change, the gate lifted, and he merged into the highway entrance. "Well, sure. People do that. Decide to make a new start. Clean break, that sort of thing." Although he was agreeing, he wasn't really sure this was a healthy notion. It was either a harmless teenage thing, or else an announcement of mental illness. The highway signs loomed importantly overhead. He didn't come to the airport that often, and he always had to think through the different options: 101, no, 380 to 280. Traffic hurtled past him. You could never drive fast enough for some people. He took the 380 exit, then positioned himself in the right lane. "So, who do you think you might want to be? Penelope? Margarita? Claudette?" He was getting a kick out of this. "Prudence? Sharona?"

He glanced over at her. She was asleep.

She slept all the way through the freeway, and the stop-and-go traffic of the city, and didn't wake up until the Golden Gate Bridge. She swallowed and straightened and peered out from behind the ridiculous sunglasses. "That's the ocean out thataway," Art said, waving a hand at the open water, the sunset just beginning to color the waves. "And the other side's the bay. Over there is Alcatraz. I probably have a map at home you could use, get yourself oriented." He waited. "So what do you think?"

"It's different."

"From what?"

"Ohio."

Served him right for trying to elicit some admiring response from her. But he persisted. Below them, sailboats dotted the blue water. Above them, the huge, impossible ironwork. Everywhere around them, the storybook view of coastline, peninsula, headlands, rolling ocean. He said, "The bridge is more than a mile long. It took four years to build. It can withstand winds of more than a hundred miles an hour."

"Uh-huh. Don't people jump off it all the time?"

"Not exactly, I mean, not all the time. They usually stop them nowadays." *Crap.*

"Up thataway," he indicated the headlands on their left, "there are some, uh, nature things. Places they keep injured seals. Hawks. Are you interested in wildlife? They have some youth programs you could enroll in."

Honestly, it was the best idea he'd been able to come up with, and it was met with incredulous silence. "Hey, you know what we forgot, you should call your mom, let her know you got here all right."

"If she's worried, she'll call."

"How about I phone her from the house when we get there."

At this mild assertion of adult authority, the sunglasses turned to regard him, then once more away.

She said, "What's the name of this place? This place you live in?"

"Mill Valley." He was encouraged that she was asking an actual question.

"Because I bet it's a valley, and they have a mill, huh?"

"Bingo." Art decided not to tell her one of its nicknames: Ten Mil Valium. "We're almost there," he said, taking the East Blithedale exit. His apartment building was on one of the frontage roads just off the freeway, though there were trees planted in between to screen the view, if not the noise. It had always seemed to Art to be a reasonable place to live, though now, trying to view it as his daughter might, he saw how it might look as haphazard and accidental as a bird's nest built inside a shopping mall. By way of compensation, he said, "It's a great place, Mill Valley. You can hop on over to the beach, or to Muir Woods, or climb Mount Tam, right from here." He couldn't remember the last time he had done any of those things.

He pulled into his parking space. "Home sweet home," he said breezily. He was reasonably confident that Linnea would not offer any commentary, pro or con, no matter what she thought. And he was right. He lugged her giant suitcase up the stairs, ushered her inside, and stood back to let her take it in. "I've got you set up out here." Art pushed the suitcase across the tile floor, onto the sunporch.

Christie had picked out the sky blue bedspread and the bamboo shades. He thought it looked nice. "Why don't you get squared away, and I'll give your mom a jingle. Then I thought we could go out for dinner."

Linnea nodded. "Cool."

He guessed he was lucky that so far she was going along with things. He went into his own bedroom and dialed Louise. He didn't suppose his luck would hold to the point of getting her voice mail, and it did not.

"Hello?"

"Hi, I just wanted to tell you, her plane got in just fine, and we're at my place."

"You need to keep an eye on her," Louise said.

"That was kind of my intention." Art heard her crossing the hall and going into the bathroom.

"The term used in the legal system is 'person in need of supervision.'"

"Would you like to talk to her?"

"No."

"I'll tell her you said hi."

Art hung up and waited in the living room for Linnea to finish up in the bathroom. He wasn't used to having anyone else in the apartment besides his now-and-again girlfriends, and even these were infrequent lately. Certain realities about sharing his space were presenting themselves. And what did that mean, "supervision"? He couldn't spend his every moment with her.

Louise had probably made everything sound worse than it was. If she stole money, he didn't have anything much to steal. If she smoked pot, he hoped she'd do it somewhere he didn't have to know about it, and he'd try to do the same. Or maybe quit; it wouldn't be a tragedy if he cleaned up his act a little. He guessed he could look forward to a few tricky conversations.

There were the sounds of water flushing and running. When Linnea came out, Art was relieved to see that she'd gotten rid of the sunglasses. "So, you hungry? Anything you have a taste for?"

"Food."

"I mean, anything in particular? Thai? Seafood? Mexican? Burgers? Sushi? Ethiopian?" He thought he saw one corner of her mouth lift, a half-smile. It was like trying to win over a bored class. Clowning often worked. "Italian? Indian? Nicaraguan? Greek? Pizza?"

"Honestly, just grub."

"We'll head down to the café, then." He'd save any fancy waterfront dining or expeditions into the city for later.

They were back in the car when she said, "So, what am I supposed to call you?"

"What?"

"I mean, I don't think I can manage 'Dad.'"

"Well . . . Art, then. And when you figure out what name you want to go by, let me know."

He'd meant that to be a joke, sort of, but she wasn't going for it. He was beginning to see how having a teenager might be the equivalent of having a bad class in permanent session. There was much that seemed typically kidlike about her, the studied boredom and remoteness. Then there was the odd flash of wised-up humor, and the suggestion of something else unknown, down there deep in the water.

It was only a five-minute drive to the downtown district and the café, but he felt the need to break the silence. "It's kind of a neat little town. We have a big film festival. Art festival." That didn't sound nearly as interesting as he'd wanted it to. "This place, the café, sometimes they have live music." He was pretty sure it would be the wrong kind of music. "There's a bookstore too," he added. Bookstores, the last desperate throw of the dice.

The sun had gone down, the soft coastal fog was blurring the twilight, and lights were bright in the plaza and the shops surrounding it. The tops of the mountains overhead were black and mysterious. All in all it was just about the prettiest place he'd ever lived, and he hoped his daughter would see it with friendly eyes. She took in downtown's lineup of superheated boutiques—apparel, jewelry, antiques, gourmet pet food—without comment. Art said, "We have real stores too. Like, Safeway."

"Ha-ha," Linnea said politely.

In fact Mill Valley was one of those odd mixes of wealth and distress. The truly rich had houses up in the hills, while those like himself got by in their odd corners. People in tennis clothes drank white wine in the restaurants at one o'clock in the afternoon. But in the parking lot adjacent to Art's apartment building, a man had lived for some months in a huge stationary white Lincoln, attending to his private business in the line of bushes between the parking lot and the busy street. The scruffy man seated at the café's entrance, slurping coffee, might have been down on his luck, or just as easily a famous inventor of computer software.

Art and Linnea stood in line to order their dinner (he got pasta, she salad and a cup of soup), then found a table. Their food came, and they ate. Louise was right, she didn't seem to be finicky about her food, just bore down on it. He was trying to decide if she was pretty. If you had to think about it, he guessed the answer was no.

They were nearing the end of their meal, and Art felt a rising panic: they would have to speak. Linnea was poking at the wet remains of her salad, slouching in such a way that he was reminded posture was one of those things parents were meant to monitor. He decided he'd skip that one. "So," he began, a dumb, lurching start. "There's probably some things we should talk about."

"Mom told you to get after me about my hair, didn't she?"

"No, that didn't come up."

"Because she's been this huge, frigging bitch about it. Is it OK if I swear?"

"We can get to that later," Art said, already feeling helpless. Nothing was going to come easy here. "I think your hair's fine. I assume it will grow out eventually."

"Huh. So what did she tell you?"

"That you were unhappy."

For a moment her face was a child's face, something you could love and protect. Then the wised-up expression descended like a screen. "So? That's not some crime."

It was going to be trench warfare. Hand-to-hand combat. She wasn't going to give any ground easily. "Right," Art said. "No criminality. I'm thinking about getting dessert. You want anything?"

She shook her head, and Art got up to study the dessert specials written on the menu board. When he got back to the table with his slice of chocolate torte, she was gone.

Bathroom, he told himself, but he waited a long time, watching other girls and women come and go, before he was convinced she wasn't inside.

He got up to look in the adjoining bookstore. People often browsed there, bought newspapers to read in the café. He didn't find her, nor was she in the plaza outside, where people were doing placid, summer-evening things like eating ice cream and pushing baby strollers. Here was a kid around Linnea's age playing a guitar with noisy enthusiasm. A few other kids were gathered around him in an admiring circle, but none of them was a girl with purple-fringed hair.

Truly alarmed now, Art made a circuit of the building and the surrounding parking lots, calling for her: "Linnea?" Then he returned to the café to see if she'd come back. There was no sign of her. *A person in need of supervision.* He didn't even know the number of her cell phone. He talked to the restaurant workers, explaining that his daughter was new in town and might have gotten lost, and would they call him if they saw her?

Art walked back to their parking spot to see if she might have misunderstood him, if she'd said No, she didn't want any dessert, she'd wait for him at the car. She wasn't there. What if she entirely disappeared, Gretel lost in the deep forest? For two or three hours he'd had a daughter, but it had all been a mistake, a kind of optical illusion. He stopped on the dark sidewalk, trying to calm himself and talk himself in off the ledge of anger and panic. She'd done some aggravating teenage thing and wandered off. They'd have to have a talk about rules, once he decided what those would be.

He doubled back to the café. The guitar-playing kid in the plaza hadn't seen her, nor was she in the corner coffee shop, nor standing in line for ice cream. Did she even have any money? She might have been abducted, picked up by somebody. She might have gone with them willingly. She might have planned something like this all along.

After an hour of tracking up and down on foot, he got in the car and cruised the streets, expanding his circle each time, heading uphill, then down again toward the flats, keeping an eye out for kids or groups of kids, those congregating at the 7-Eleven, or in parking lots. He got on 101 and drove for a short distance south, thinking she might have hitchhiked into the city. But then, he had no idea what she might do, since he had no clear idea of Linnea herself.

By nine o'clock the café had closed and the crowds in the plaza had gone home. There would have to be calls made, to the police. To Louise. One more time he had failed and been found wanting. This would only be a different way of saying it.

Because he could not bear to make these calls just yet, and because he couldn't think of anybody else who might help him, he called Christie. He interrupted her chiming hello, he had a problem, a problem with his daughter, he couldn't find her. He hurried his story, interrupting himself, and stopped only when Christie said, "Do you want me to ask her friend if she knows anything?"

"Her friend?"

"There's a girl sitting on your steps smoking a cigarette."

Art's chest opened up and his heart flew out, cawing and flapping. "What does she look like?"

"Oh I don't know. Like the punks. You know, every day is Halloween. Black everything."

"Purple hair?"

"I'd say it's more of a fuchsia."

"That's her."

"I don't think so. Are you OK, Art? You sound like you're catching a cold or something. I thought maybe she was Linnea, I stuck my head out to say hello, but she says her name's Megan."

FIVE

Most nights, his dad fell asleep on the couch and woke at the ghost hour of two or three or four a.m. Conner would hear him in the kitchen or the bathroom, or flipping through the television channels. The pain pills knocked him out for a while, then the pain bled through. By the time Conner got up in the morning, his dad was asleep again, with his mouth frozen open in such a way that Conner always checked to make sure he was still breathing.

His mom wanted him to come live with her in Nevada. He put her off by telling her he had to take summer courses so he could graduate. By August he'd be eighteen, an adult, and nobody could make him do anything.

Even if some things had been his dad's fault, that didn't mean he deserved to get thrown out like some embarrassing kind of garbage.

This morning was like most others: Conner fed the dog, got himself showered and dressed, and made coffee. Coffee was something he was training himself to like. It went along with working. He ate some cereal standing at the kitchen counter, then put together a couple of sandwiches for lunch. The dog was getting excited at the prospect of going with him, but Conner told him No. Not today. The dog settled back into his corner. He was a dog who was used to disappointments.

Conner went into the living room and stood over the couch. "Dad?"

His dad didn't stir. He slept on his side with his bad hip in the air and his face pressed into the couch cushions. A white paste had accumulated at the corners of his mouth. The pills gave his sweat a particular smell, like fruit going bad. Conner left a note for him on the kitchen counter: Call me when you wake up.

Floyd had found Conner a couple of weeks' work in Corte Madera, helping a guy Floyd knew do some roofing. It was hard, hot work, and Floyd's pal was only too happy to let Conner know everything he was doing wrong. But he'd get paid cash, and maybe it would lead to other jobs, and a little more money, and a little more time they could keep treading water. People did whatever they had to do. He understood that now.

Sometimes he thought about all the really miserable parts of the world, Africa or India or wherever else you were supposed to send your charitable donations, places with water buffalo and mud huts and dying children. At least there it would be obvious you were stinking poor, and you wouldn't have to pretend otherwise. Here in America, you could walk around looking pretty much like everybody else.

He took the Corte Madera exit and drove west, then doubled back north, up the hill to the job site. They were still doing tear-off, and the dumpster was half full of the old shingles and sheathing. It was early and the roofing boss wasn't there yet, so Conner got out to stand in the driveway and admire the expensive view, the hillsides falling away below him, dense with treetops, the smell of eucalyptus and fog in the air. It had been a wet spring, and the grass in the narrow yard was still green and growing.

Say he lived in a house like this. Say this very one. He let the notion expand in him. This was his patio of tumbled brick laid out in a cunning circular pattern, and his grand expanse of triple-sealed glass across the front wall. His well-raked garden beds, and visible through the half-open garage door, his sweet, sweet Porsche.

He moved a little closer to the windows, trying not to be obvious about looking inside. Here were things everybody wanted and nobody needed, furniture made of leather and glass, a television like a big black sculpture. He guessed he'd have stuff like that, sure. But not all the gold-framed this-and-that. Or the antique clock, or the miniature sailboat. It was amazing, the things people went out and bought, instead of holding on to actual money.

Something moved toward him on the other side of the glass, and Conner took a stumbling step back, ready to pantomime some explanation or apology: he wanted to see what time it was? But it was only a parrot, a big red and green macaw, sidling at him along its perch, wings raised to scare him, and opening its beak so that Conner saw its small shriveled black tongue.

His dad called later in the morning. Conner was up on the roof with a pry bar and the boss was loafing in his truck. If he didn't keep making noise, the boss would poke his head out to see why not. "Hi Dad. I can't talk long."

"How's it going today?"

"Not bad." Conner one-handed some shingles onto the pile below. "How are you feeling?"

"Fine and dandy. Dandy and fine." His dad took different pills, and some of them made him kind of goofy. "If the sheathing looks good, you can leave it on."

"No, it's all coming off."

"I bet what's-his-ass priced it that way before he even looked at it."

"Uh-huh." The truck's door opened. "I gotta go, I'll call you later, OK?"

"This is the life, I tell you. Lie around while somebody else works."

For his lunch break, Conner drove downhill and ate his sandwiches at a bench in the waterfront park. It was only the third day of the job, and he guessed he should get used to feeling this sore.

Except for two kids walking their hyper little spitz dog, the park was empty. It was low tide, even in this small inlet of the bay there were tides, and the spit of land was surrounded by weedy mud. At a distance, the southbound 101 traffic passed over an elevated span, into the city and the million different lives people there led. There were so many things he tried not to think about.

Something tapped against the back of the bench, then skittered away. Somebody behind him had thrown a wood chip at him, and now another. Conner turned around. A girl stood on the far edge of the pathway. She had a handful of chips and was preparing to sidearm another in his direction.

"What are you doing?"

"Nothing." She dropped the chips and looked out over the mudflats, which suddenly interested her. "This is a really ugly park."

"It's just low tide."

She wrinkled her nose. "It smells gross."

"Sorry."

"Well it's not like it's your fault." Still not looking at him, she walked over and sat down next to him. She had black hair with the tips bleached a yellowy white. She was wearing cut-off shorts over a pair of black- and white-striped tights, and a red canvas shirt.

"Cool tights," Conner said, although he wasn't really sure if he liked them.

She raised one leg and turned her foot in its red tennis shoe this way and that, admiring. "Thanks. Sometimes you have to take fashion risks."

"Uh-huh." He still had half a sandwich left, but he didn't want to eat it with her watching. He put it away in the sack. He could finish it while he drove back to work. "So what are you, a zebra or a skunk?"

"Now is that nice?" She made a droll face and looked up at him, and he realized that while he'd taken her for a little kid, eleven or twelve, she was just small, and maybe only a couple of years younger than he was. "The legs are zebra. The hair's kind of skunk. You live around here?"

"Sebastopol."

"Where's that?"

Conner pointed to the highway and jerked his thumb north. "That-away."

"Yeah? Is there anything to do there?"

"Do?"

She sighed and kicked her legs so that the stripes blurred. "This place is so boring."

It was time for him to get back to work. He stood and stretched, trying to keep his muscles from locking up. "Maybe you don't have enough to worry about."

"You ever have somebody point a gun at you?"

Conner stared down at her. "I didn't think so," she said.

"I gotta go."

"Bye."

"Take it easy."

She made her thumb and finger into a gun and put it up to her head. "Ka-boom."

The next day she was waiting for him on the bench when he showed up. She'd pulled her hair back in a ponytail so that the whitish ends hung down like a tassel. She wore jeans and flat sandals and a plain white T-shirt. Conner followed the visible outline of her bra, then looked away. The clothes made her seem more normal, but she was still nobody he wanted to mess around with.

"Hey," she said. "You hungry? I got some burritos." She held up a paper bag.

"I brought my lunch."

"This is better." She waved the bag at him.

The food smell entered his head and landed hard in his stomach. All of a sudden he was starving for a taste of it. "Thanks," he said, sitting down. "You didn't have to get me any."

She shrugged. "Like I said, I'm bored." She began unwrapping the foil packages. "There's one bean, two chickens, and one beef. You can pick, I like them all. I got some Cokes too."

"Whoa, these are kind of big." He started in on the beef. Maybe he was just hungry, but it was the best burrito he could remember eating. "Thanks," he said again, once he was halfway through it. "Hey, what's your name?"

"Eowyn."

"You're kidding."

"Do I look like I'm kidding?"

She rolled her eyes at him. Of course she was the kind of girl who looked like she was kidding every minute. Conner said, "What, like, from *The Hobbit?* That's not your real name."

"Not *The Hobbit*, from *Lord of the Rings*. How would you know it's not?"

"Your parents didn't name you that."

"Maybe they were big fans. So what's your name?"

He hadn't finished with the food in his mouth. "Conner."

"Corner?"

"Con-ner."

"Well I think that's a dumb name. It's not even after somebody." She had a burrito unwrapped in her lap, but she hadn't started in on it yet.

"It's Irish."

She gave him a critical glance. "You don't look Irish."

"Well you don't look like a hobbit."

"Oh, good one," she drawled. She picked up her burrito and took a bite. Her lipstick left a crescent of pink on the tortilla.

The tide was higher today and they watched a few seagulls and plovers wade in the shallow water beyond the mud. Conner finished his food. It was a lot to eat and he felt sleepy. The day was already hot and would be still hotter. The afternoon was going to kill him.

"You get high?"

His eyes had closed and now he opened them. "No."

"That's too bad, because I found where my dad keeps his pot." She'd finished half the burrito and now she rolled the rest back in the foil.

"Good for you." Conner stood up. It wasn't a conversation he was anxious to have. "Thanks for lunch, ah, Eowyn. I gotta get back to work."

"Because, I was thinking, I could sell some of it."

She was squinting energetically out to the waterline. She said, "Because he wouldn't miss it, and even if he did he doesn't want me to know he has it, and it just seems like, an idea."

"Yeah, kind of a dumb idea."

"Because nobody ever does stuff like that, right."

"How about, because I have to go now," he said again, and this time he walked away from her along the path that bordered the water. He looked back once to make sure she wasn't following.

The next day, Friday, he stayed at the job site and ate lunch in his truck, and Saturday they worked only a half-day because of a party the homeowner was having, a party requiring the installation of a tent, and several white wooden boxes bearing miniature pink rose trees, and the lady of the house coming out to squabble with the roofing boss about why a portion of the roof visible from the backyard party area was still bare of shingles.

He spent Saturday night and Sunday hanging around the house with his dad, who got upset and fretful when he was stuck there alone. They grilled chicken wings and cooked up a big skillet of fried potatoes and onions. They watched a lot of ESPN, lame stuff like NASCAR races and golf. Sometimes his dad dozed off, but he woke up if Conner tried to change the channel. "Leave it on, they're just getting to the good part." The house was hot and they set two floor fans in the living room to blow crossways. The fans made enough noise that the television had to be turned up extra loud, with the commercials for motor oil and pizza blaring at top volume. By Sunday afternoon, Conner was so sick and sad and bored he announced he was going out on his bike for a while.

His dad said, Sure, have fun, and made jokes about being a pitiful old broke-down wreck. The jokes were meant as a way for his dad to pretend he didn't mind being exactly that, a pitiful old broke-down wreck.

Conner filled a water bottle and set off on the bike, fast enough to make his own breeze. He made a point of avoiding the houses of any of his friends. He didn't call them anymore and they had given up calling him. They tried too hard to be nice to him, which made everything worse. They'd all graduated, and most of them were headed off to some kind of school in the fall. Which wasn't their fault, nor was it their fault that they were spending their last free summer going to the beach, or sleeping late and helping themselves to their parents' refrigerators. They couldn't have fun with him in the room, couldn't talk about anything lighthearted with his big drag self sitting there. He'd broken up with his girlfriend because she wanted the two of them to live together in her parents' basement and he said he couldn't, he had to stay with his dad. She'd said, "I don't get it, why can't he go to a hospital or someplace, why do you have to turn yourself into some kind of giant loser?"

Then she said she didn't mean that, loser, but it had been the excuse he needed to walk away from her. No one understood what he was up against. He didn't want anyone to understand.

His dad still talked about Conner signing up for some community college classes. That was just his dad not ever wanting to look a thing in the face. His dad made jokes about them having to sleep in the parking lot at Costco. That meant he'd at least thought about it.

Conner biked a ten-mile loop that took him on a back road west of downtown and its halfhearted tourist attractions, the antiques stores and spas, out past the last scattered houses and the hippie goat farm, through a few acres of orchards and to where the vineyards took over. He climbed enough of a hill so that he could look back and see the town set out like a toy. It had been his home for all the life he could remember, and now there was no place in it for him. Maybe there was no place for him in all the wide world.

That night his dad said, "Buddy, we got to find a new base of operations."

It meant the bank was finally kicking them out. Conner had been waiting to hear it, but still it sent his heart right down to his shoes. "How soon?"

"Couple of weeks. We can do better than this here ghetto estate, don't you think?"

"Sure," Conner said, since that was what his dad wanted him to say.

"You'd think they'd show some charity to an old cripple."

"Quit calling yourself names."

"You ever think about the army? Joining up?"

His dad had one of his canny expressions, like he usually did when he came up with something out of left field. "You're kidding," Conner said.

"Free room and board. You wouldn't have to get shot at or anything, a bright guy like you. They'd probably put you into something like computers."

"No, Dad."

"Educational benefits," his dad said, but Conner could tell he was already giving up on the idea.

Conner went into the kitchen. Bojangles followed and thwacked his tail against the wall, food food food. Conner filled his bowl and put it down for him. Whatever else happened, it would be all right as long as he never had to betray his dog with an empty food bowl.

When he went back into the living room, his dad had fallen asleep again. The pills ran him now. It was one more kind of trouble.

For so long his life had been a kid's life, going along, going along without having to think much about it. There was school, and girls, and games, and anything else had been pretty easy to ignore, since after all he was just a kid. Then his mom had moved out and that had been a lot to deal with, but it was their problem, his mom and dad's, nothing anybody expected Conner to prevent or fix. The same with money, even when his dad's work got slow and they'd started losing altitude little by little. Sure Conner had worried, but he hadn't thought it was going to be that bad, and worse, forever and ever.

Then last October his dad went out one night and didn't come home.

Didn't answer his phone, and he always checked in, even when he was chasing women. No one had seen him. Three days later the police found him in a hospital in Ukiah. He'd been in a rollover accident on 101, seventy miles from home. His dad was trapped in the passenger seat. Whoever had been driving had disappeared, either unhurt or limping off. The car had been stolen the week before in Truckee. His dad had a broken pelvis, a ruptured spleen, some cracks in his neck. Those were the main things.

There had been a woman, a woman he'd met for drinks, but he'd either never known her name or couldn't remember it, nor could he remember the accident. He'd spent three weeks in the hospital, running up bills he'd never pay. Conner left the dog with his girlfriend and drove up north. His mom came in from Nevada and the two of them stayed in a motel near the hospital.

Conner's mom stood at his dad's hospital bedside and said, "Sean, you need to find yourself a steady girlfriend. This tomcatting around isn't working out."

His dad tried to laugh. It came out as a wheeze. "On the to-do list."

"Aim for one who's a better driver."

"Ah, I've hurt myself worse having a good time."

"McDonald, you're so full of shit your eyes are brown."

It was funny to see the two of them together again, carrying on the way they used to, all the old banter. The running joke was that his dad was a hopeless but lovable screwup, and his mom saw through him and disapproved, though she couldn't resist his rapscallion charms.

But when Conner and his mom went back to the motel, she said, "If stupid was a crime, he'd be in jail." His mom was pretty, with dark gold hair and wide-open eyes. Everybody said Conner looked like her.

"Come on. It was an accident."

"You take his side because you feel sorry for him."

"I'm not taking sides," Conner said.

"Honey, you always try so hard. You shouldn't have to be the only grown-up in the house."

Conner didn't answer. He was always surprised when people made pronouncements about him. He liked to believe that nobody really noticed him, while he observed and judged everyone else.

"I'm not going to come back and take care of him. I know it would solve everybody's problems but I can't. I've moved on from there."

"All right," Conner said.

"But I'll take care of you. I always will."

"I don't need taking care of."

"You don't know what you don't need," his mom said.

What did he know? He was supposed to be smart, everybody said so. If grades were the same thing as smart, then he guessed he was. Teachers kidded around with him, were fond of him, wished him well. Older people liked him, approved of him because of his seriousness and good manners. They looked at him and sighed and said what a great thing it was to be young, with your whole life ahead of you. As if your life was out there just waiting for you to step into it, like a new car all gassed up and ready to go.

Conner wasn't as sure as everybody else that he was such a safe bet, all-around great kid and yakkity-yak, whatever they saw in him that made them feel better about themselves. Maybe all along he'd had a low-down, untrustworthy nature that this run of bad luck had only now revealed. Maybe nobody knew who they really were until the world beat them up some.

His dad had one operation and then a second one, and more to come somewhere down the line, and then there was an infection, and the wrong medication, and the orthopedist nobody liked, and everything else it was possible to hate about a hospital. His dad claimed he was getting poor people's medicine, and that was a thought you didn't like to think, but you wondered. His dad told a story about an ironworker he knew, another big dumb Irishman, who fell face-first off a fifteen-foot ladder onto pavement, got up and said "Boy, I'm lucky, all I broke was my face!" His dad said he understood that a little better, now that he couldn't sit, stand, walk, or piss right.

Finally Conner brought him home, and he crutched around the house hating his own pain. He had to be taken to his doctors' appointments, and the physical therapy that was supposed to help more than it did, and of course the prescriptions to fetch, and all the while Conner was trying to earn a meager buck any way he could. The school had allowed him to make up his fall course work. He started his classes after Christmas but he kept missing days, and by the end of February he was sitting in the guidance counselor's office, having one of those conversations where the counselor kept saying "unfortunately."

"We need to find a way to make this work for you," the counselor said. "We need to look at all your options."

"Sure," Conner said. It was almost funny, to think he had these great things called options.

"Unfortunately"—there it was—"I don't think we can graduate you by June. Certainly not with the kind of grade-point average you're capable of earning."

"Sure," he said again.

The counselor fixed him with her expression of ineffectual sympathy. "I'm sorry. It's not like any of this is your fault."

Conner nodded and pretended to listen as she went on about her ideas of his future, involving loans and scholarships and applications and the different strategies he might use to nudge himself out of an economic dead end and into a more respectable middle-class anxiety. He was still working out the idea of fault, and wondering if the counselor meant it was his dad's fault for getting himself smashed up. For being in a badly driven stolen car.

His dad said he couldn't remember getting in the car, or else he had his reasons for not remembering. So it was their fault, this person who was driving or, at least, should not have stolen a car. But maybe fault was like the tail end of a snake, and you had to follow it all the way up to the head to reach the original pure badness that set everything in motion.

"So let's aim for summer," the counselor said, and Conner said yes, that would work, and thank you, and walked out of the school for what he figured was the last time. He signed up for online summer courses that were pretty much a joke; he could do the work in his sleep, which was lucky since he needed his waking hours for other things. By the end of summer they would send him his joke diploma.

He and his dad moved out on the hottest day of the year. Global warming, people said, and they were probably right. Him and his dad were moving into one half of a duplex in San Rafael. The other half was vacant, trashed by the previous tenants, and Conner and his dad were supposed to do some work on it in exchange for a few months' rent. Floyd and another guy came to help them load the beds and the rest of the furniture, and there was some talk of painting pentagrams on the floor for the benefit of the bank that now owned the place, or taking a sledgehammer to the walls, or some other eat shit and die gesture, but in the end they left everything as it was, and drove off, and it was one more place to leave for the last time.

The duplex was smaller than their old house, but at least they each had their own bedrooms, and a roof that didn't yet look like it was falling in. And it came with a couple of window-unit air conditioners. Once everything was hauled inside, they turned the air up as high as it would go and Conner lay flat on the floor with the sweat turning cold on him but that felt good. His dad got himself settled on the couch. It was a different house but the same old couch and his dad's same cussing as he tried to get himself into some comfortable position. It was their same clothes and shoes and lamps and kitchen gear and whatnot, all spilling out of cardboard boxes, and nothing had changed except there would now be less of everything.

By the second week of July they had unpacked as much as they felt like. They didn't talk about it, but there was a sense they might not be staying all that long. They ripped up the old vinyl floor and the subfloor in the empty half of the duplex, and started in replacing it. "Every job needs a boss," his dad remarked at least once each day, since he couldn't really get down on the ground, only drag things in and out or pass tools to Conner. The rest of the time his dad spent on the phone to the Department of Social Services, who were just about as helpful as you might imagine, and to Social Security, trying to file for disability. Conner's mom sent him some cash, with a note to not let his dad get his hands on it. The father of a kid Conner knew from school hired him to work some shifts at a grocery warehouse he owned, filling in for people on vacation. Once he put three cases of frozen steaks in the dumpster, retrieved them later, and sold them at the flea market. He cruised the nighttime streets in fancy neighborhoods and twice he found unlocked cars and stole a phone and a GPS system.

There was a rhythm to it, this getting-by life, and every so often Conner got scared at how used to it he was growing, like an animal gone wild.

After they had parted company, his old girlfriend called and texted him for some time, not willing to let things end. She was anxious to prove herself in this adult crisis and to stand by his side and offer him her sympathy and support, and in doing so, make it all about her. He knew that he was being unfair to her, and that if she had been the one to put distance between them when his troubles began, he would have accused her of being fickle and shallow. He had a confusion of feelings toward her. He wanted to be hurt, he wanted to be hurtful.

He hadn't heard from her at all for a couple of weeks. It gave him an ugly kind of satisfaction to think she'd given up on him. And if she had kept pursuing him, he would have felt scornful. In the same way, he both was and was not hoping to see her when he drove out of his way after work to go past her house.

It was nearly dark. There was a zone of heat and lavender-blue air in the west that seemed to fizz or strobe when his eyes tried to make anything out. He guessed if she was home she might see his truck and draw some wrong conclusion about his being there, like he was a stalker. What he really wanted was to revisit his old life so he could remind himself of what he'd lost.

Conner cruised her block, medium slow. Both her family's cars were in the drive, but that didn't mean she was home. Times when she'd had the house to herself they had made love in her narrow bed, and she had cried a little because it hurt her but told him not to stop, and he couldn't have stopped for the world. All that had been taken from him, as if it had never happened.

He turned and headed back toward the freeway. At the entrance ramp he pulled into an Exxon station to get gas, and then crossed the parking lot to the coffee shop to get a ham sandwich to go, dinner. He ordered at the cash register and waited there, looking out through the expanse of glass windows to the traffic queuing up on the highway.

Someone called his name. He turned and saw people waving at him, a table of five stoned-looking kids. He knew a couple of them from school, and as he walked toward them, his old girlfriend emerged from the restrooms and made her way to her seat at the table.

Conner made a point of not breaking his stride, but she stopped and seemed to look around for some other destination before she gave up and sat. She ducked her head in a nod, and Conner said Hi, without putting much into it either way. There were four boys and the two girls, and the other girl said, "You look hot, Con. I mean, all sweaty." She laughed at that.

"And you look totally wasted."

"You say that like it's a bad thing."

"Sit down, man," one of the boys said, and Conner was ready to tell them he couldn't, but instead he hiked an empty chair over to the table. His girlfriend was sitting between two boys, and he couldn't tell if either of them was anyone he should concern himself about. The other girl and one guy were a longtime couple, and the boy who had invited Conner to join them never had girlfriends. They had already eaten, and the plates were scattered with leftover food. It was all the things Conner wished he'd ordered for himself: french fries, bacon, pizza.

The girl who wasn't his girlfriend said, "We drove up to Forest Knolls looking for the place Jerry Garcia died."

"Yeah?" Conner said. A waitress came out of the kitchen with his sandwich. Conner stood to intercept her, then sat again. "You find it?"

"We couldn't tell. It looked like kind of a nice place to die. All woodsy, and there were these wild turkeys running around."

"Living on reds, vitamin C, and cocaine," one of the boys sang, and somebody else said that hadn't worked out so well for old Jerry, and Yeah, but that was rock and roll, baby.

Conner was just as glad they weren't paying any attention to him. He watched his girlfriend without looking at her, keeping his face impassive, wishing he hadn't ordered the stupid sandwich that he now had to keep track of. The paper bag kept slipping off his lap and he had to shift his knees around, juggling it. Finally he put it on the floor. His girlfriend didn't look pleased. He guessed that he had something to do with that. The guy to her right was staring at Conner, sending him little hate Valentines. So that's the way it was.

The boy who never had girlfriends was named Kenny. He was Korean and had black hair in a scrub-brush cut, and wore the button-down oxford shirts his parents bought him with the sleeves ripped off. He was talking about another weird thing he'd pulled off a website. Because there were websites out there designed for guys like Kenny, the deeply bored and the deeply lonely, and not just porn sites. Conner wasn't paying attention at first, preoccupied with the effort it took him to sit still in his chair. Then he said, "What?"

"The universe is going to end."

"Come on."

"It expanded for, what, a hundred billion billion years, that's from the Big Bang point. Then it's gonna start contracting, and fall in on itself and, whoosh. No more universe." Kenny looked happy, explaining the upcoming total death of everything.

"No way." This from the guy who'd been staring at Conner. The new, designated stud. "You mean there would just be this big blank sky?"

"There wouldn't be any sky. There wouldn't be any anything,"

A silence, while everybody tried to wrap their heads around that one. It was deeply unsettling, trying to imagine the nothingness of nothing.

"You are making this up just to annoy people, Ken-Bot."

"Uh-uh. Check it out yourself. It has to do with the density of the universe, how they measure that, and if the decreasing density of matter proves to be more of a force than decreasing temperatures as the stars cool."

"What is he talking about?"

"Ah, it's just a Kenny thing," said the guy currently fucking Conner's girlfriend. He was somebody Conner remembered seeing at parties, somebody's friend. He wasn't anyone special, one of those beach guys who worked on their tans to the point of skin cancer. He looked sort of like a baked potato. His girlfriend, meanwhile, was bent over her phone with her long, taffy-colored hair hiding her face. A moment later, Conner's phone buzzed. He pulled it out to read her text: YOU SHOULD PLEASE JUST GO.

Kenny said, "But the good news is there are probably alternate universes. Like string theory, where strings have length, but not width, and they vibrate in ten or eleven dimensions, not just the four we can perceive."

"That's awesome, Kenny."

"He's deep."

Kenny beamed, the way he always did when everybody gave him a hard time. He probably went out of his way to look up strange shit just so he could trot it out and be abused. Conner watched his girlfriend watch him not answer her text and not leave. It was stupid, he didn't want to start up with her again but he didn't want to be replaced either. Something mean and ugly and unfair was surfacing in him.

The beach stud was having an urgent private conversation with Conner's girlfriend, and she was tightening her face and looking away, and as he watched them Conner was made aware that everyone else was watching too, and they had been doing so all along, watching the three of them and hoping something interesting would happen.

A waitress came over, asking if they needed anything else, and there was some back-and-forth, they did and they didn't, no, finally. The waitress had the checks ready and ripped each one off a pad and set them down. Conner rose out of his chair and took his girlfriend's check. "I got this one."

It surprised everyone, including Conner himself, and it took the beach stud a couple of beats to say, "I don't think you do, bro."

"I'm not your bro, bro."

Now that there was the scene the others had all been waiting for, there was a drawing back—something fearful and recoiling—then an avidness as they settled in to watch. His girlfriend said nothing. Her face was remote and private, shut down until everything was over. It was all up to the beach stud. Conner waited, watching him and looking for reasons to hate him in and of himself: his idiotic tan, his short and somewhat piggy nose. He decided to wave it away, laugh it off. "Sure, knock yourself out. Want my check too?"

"No, Conner," his girlfriend said, because she must have seen it in his face, or in the cords in his neck tightening, that he was ready to kick his own chair away and take the four steps that would lead him to where the beach stud sat, and with any luck he wouldn't have time to stand up and Conner could break his oinky nose with his first punch. Why was she telling him no? Was she embarrassed? Did she care about her new piggy sweetheart, didn't want to see him bloody? Conner's muscles were one electrical charge away from motion

and in an alternate, parallel universe, some seventh or eighth dimension, Conner split the skin of his knuckles on the bone and cartilage of a thing that used to be a face.

—while in another universe, Conner invented the most terrible words ever spoken, spitting fire, dripping poison.

—in yet another, he and the girl never stopped never stopped making love.

—or he no longer cared.

—or he had never been born.

—or there was only the nothing of nothing.

But he had only what was here and now. Conner turned his back on the table and pushed his way through two sets of glass doors to reach the glare-lit parking lot with its baked-concrete and gasoline smells. He started the truck and made the tires squeal as he headed out, which was stupid, and also stupid was forgetting his idiotic sandwich, but he was glad for that because he wanted to feel hunger in the same way he wanted to feel hatred. Down deep, something he would guard in secret, because that was who he was, his true nature, and it was no one's fault but his own.

SIX

The name of God is Truth.

The mind persisted in making thoughts. You could not force yourself into not-thinking. You could only attempt to redirect the mind, through order, discipline, habit. Chanting helped. First out loud, then silently. Freeing yourself from the burden of comprehension. *The name of God is Truth. The name of God is Truth. The name of God is Truth.* After enough repetitions, the words shed meaning. The meaning became a part of your breathing, in and out, in and out, from the core of your being. The meaning was branded on the beating heart.

The name of God is

From upstairs, the sound of a long, rolling crash.

The name of God is

Followed by a door slamming.

The name of God

And feet in boots kicking something shut. A kitchen cabinet?

The name of

Then the music starting up, a troop of angry-cool black men, making rhymes out of cusswords. Christie opened her eyes, searching the corners of the ceiling. The bass vibrated above her. You almost expected to see plaster knocked loose. She couldn't understand all the words, but *mo-fucker* came through clearly, and often. Maybe you could consider the horrible music a kind of chanting.

Because everyone's reality was separate, different. Because—Christie was waiting for Mrs. Rubio's door to open, for Mrs. Rubio to go upstairs and complain so Christie wouldn't have to—different people gave themselves over to different energies. Automobiles, for instance. There was a surprising portion of the population for whom nothing was as important as automobiles. Or certain television shows. Or the long drama of enmities among families, or between lovers, or between oneself and anyone else.

On cue, like a cuckoo popping out of a clock, Mrs. Rubio's door opened and Christie heard her house slippers slapping and flapping up the stairs. She pounded on the apartment door, waited, pounded again, and when it opened, the staccato of her voice was added to the chorus of racket. A moment later the volume of the music was lowered just enough to comply, to a sullen, muttering noise. Mrs. Rubio descended the steps, slower now, pausing mid-stair to decide if she needed to go back up and make further demands. Not today. Her apartment door shut with a righteous slam.

Christie got up from her cushion and the small table with its careful arrangement of polished rocks and a single stem of plumeria in a vase: her shrine, although she would have been embarrassed to call it that to anyone else. Sunday morning. Where was Art? Probably at some coffee shop, reading newspapers and enjoying some adult alone time. Mrs. Rubio had already taken her complaints directly to him, and he had made his usual ineffective promises. Not that Christie herself would have known what to do if her own damaged and difficult child had boomeranged back into her life. Except she would not have had such a child to begin with. Or any child, as it happened.

She made herself a fresh cup of tea and took it outside to the picnic table that served the apartments as an outdoor leisure space. It was a fine summer morning, and up and down the cul-de-sac people were walking dogs and washing cars and opening their balcony doors to let the breeze in. She liked sitting out in the middle of so much ordinary human activity. She liked being part of it. Like it was all a kind of giant ant farm, and herself just another dutiful and obscure ant.

She was thirty-four years old. She was aware that she was different from those around her: less tethered to the things they considered urgent and important. More self-contained, detached. When she was younger she had tried to acquire those relationships other people thought worth acquiring. She had been married for a few years, in her twenties. It had not been an unhappy episode, not exactly, but she had been relieved when it came to an end by mutual and anticlimactic agreement. It was almost as if it happened to come up in conversation.

After the marriage ended she was miserable in ways she had not expected. She took the failure on herself, as evidence that she truly was deficient, damaged, freakish, incomplete. She embarked on a series of boyfriends who seemed to promise the kinds of passionate experience she lacked. Each one was worse than the one before, and when the last one held her head over a toilet and slammed the lid down on it again and again, she gave herself permission to stop trying.

She worked as a nurse, which suited her calm and undemonstrative manner. She was not overwhelmed by pain, either her own or other people's. She bore down on wounds, disease, infirmities, mortified bodies, and did what needed to be done, without fuss or becoming unnerved. When her patients were grateful, which was often enough, she felt as if she accepted their praise under false pretenses. They believed her to be not only skillful, but compassionate.

Yea, though I give my body to be burned and have not love, it profiteth me nothing.

She was thrifty with her money and saved what she could, although she was aware that this was one more cautious aspect of her personality: she did not wish to be dependent on anyone else. She allowed herself some small indulgences (of food, of household purchases), then worried that she was too attached to them. She took meditation classes at a Buddhist center in the city, although she avoided joining anything that resembled a practice or a congregation. She called her parents in Michigan every weekend, sent birthday cards to her nieces and nephews, kept up with her circle of hometown and school friends on Facebook. It was so much easier on everyone else when you did the things that were expected of you.

She had no reason to believe that much of anything in her life would ever change.

The teacup warmed her hands and she closed her eyes again, trying to reclaim the morning's peace. It did no good to be disappointed or resentful. If you lived around other people, you had to expect them to keep bumping up against your boundaries. You just wished they wouldn't leave so many footprints.

mofucker mofucker mofucker

Eyes still closed, she heard someone walking toward her along the sidewalk. They stopped short, regarding her, she felt certain. She wasn't really surprised when Art spoke.

"Hey Christie."

Her tea was growing cold. She opened her eyes. "Good morning."

"Mind if I join you?" He arranged himself on the other side of the bench, putting his untidy heap of newspapers on the table between them. She didn't really mind, but it would be nice if people stopped assuming she didn't.

"Linnea was playing music again."

"Shit. Loud?"

"Extremely."

"I talked with her about that. We had a whole conversation."

Christie let this remark settle. She said, "Mrs. Rubio went up there. She's going to get you in trouble with the property managers."

"Shit."

"I can't say that I blame her. I mean, Mrs. Rubio."

"I was only gone for an hour."

"Well, the first forty-five minutes were just fine."

Art groaned and let his forehead smack against the table, in the center of the pile of papers. "What am I gonna do?"

"Take her downstairs and make her apologize to Mrs. Rubio."

"I can't make her do that. I can't make her do anything." Art raised his head. Pieces of wispy hair floated up briefly, then drifted back to their place wreathing his scalp. He wore his hair in what Christie thought of as hippie comb-over style, although she reproached herself for being unkind.

"She's only been here, what, two weeks? It's like an alien life form taking over."

"Art."

"*Teenagers from Outer Space.* That's an actual movie. A cult classic from 1959."

"Very humorous," Christie pronounced. She didn't intend to encourage him.

"Maybe I'm trying too hard to be the nice dad. Making it up to her for, you know, not being around for so long."

"That's a good insight. Now, how are you going to integrate it into your behavior?"

"You are so tough on me," Art said, giving her one of his admiring looks.

"Well, someone needs to be." From time to time, it was necessary to deflect the admiration and everything that went along with it. She was fond of Art, in an exasperated way. She supposed they should have a Talk, though she kept putting it off. "She's still up there, go lay down the law. Man up. Dad up."

"Yeah, OK." He picked up his newspapers, then set them down again. "We actually did have a pretty good conversation the other night, her and me. I got us some dinner from Saigon Palace? And we were just hanging out in the kitchen eating? And I mentioned that I used to have a motorcycle. I ever tell you about that? A Honda V-twin cruiser. Just for tooling around. I showed her some pictures. Dad, the Forgotten Years. Me in leathers, if you can imagine that. She wanted to know why a Honda, she said, 'Better a sister in a whorehouse than a brother on a Honda.'"

He waited expectantly, but Christie's polite, interested expression didn't change.

"I guess I don't get it, Art."

"Because some people think the only real bikes are Harleys. Or maybe, the old Indians. They call the Japanese bikes rice burners."

"Oh." She nodded. "Sure."

"It just cracked me up, I don't know where she gets these things. Oh well. Had to be there." He was embarrassed now, telling a joke that didn't land right.

She hadn't meant to make him feel bad. "I don't really know anything about motorcycles. But that's very interesting, that you used to have one." She thought the point of the story was so that Art could tell her about having a motorcycle. A motorcycle sounded like a very Art thing to do. And of course he'd buy the clothes that went along with it. "Did you take any interesting drives? I mean, road trips?"

He must have sensed that she was humoring him. He muttered something and gathered up his newspapers, wadding them every which way. "So I guess I'll go talk to the problem child."

"Good luck. Try asking her why she plays it so loud."

"Pardon?"

"Have you ever done that? I mean, she's a kid, maybe she can't articulate it very well, but some kinds of music probably have to be loud. Because it's angry, it's supposed to be in your face. Maybe she wants to have people mad at her. So she can be mad back."

"Yeah?" Art, not very convinced by this strategy. "Yeah, I could do that. Sure."

She tried again. "How's your Vietnamese coming?"

"Oh, I kind of gave up on that. Don't have the time right now. You have a great day."

Christie watched him shamble off. Because she felt guilty about not being who he wanted her to be, not being personally available to him, she had attempted to make it up by being helpful. She'd only managed to aggravate him and put him off, so that he had to be rude to her in order to reclaim his pride.

You could not be all things to all people. You were allowed to have boundaries. But you could do more damage trying to keep your distance, trying to negotiate politely, than by being outright rude. If truth was the highest value, where did truth fit into human relationships? Should she just come out and say to Art, "You ought to not be enamored of me"?

Five minutes or so after Art had gone inside his apartment, Christie watched Linnea come out, slam the door behind her, and whip around a corner of the building, out of sight. So much for the Dad talk.

Art said she wouldn't talk about what had happened to her at school, the shooting. Just flat-out wouldn't. He'd tried a couple of times, tiptoeing around the edges. Nada. He didn't want to push it.

Christie thought that people shouldn't have to talk about such things on demand. But they ought to find a way to tell the story to themselves.

On Mondays and Tuesdays, Christie worked at a public health clinic in

spend on him. On the other side of the door was the waiting room,
linked orange plastic chairs and unfresh magazines and the play
the corner for the kids. On the walls, a number of public health
The posters showed multicultural citizens looking pleased be-
ey were following the recommendations for condom use, healthy
accinations. Beneath the posters, on the orange chairs, the crowd
nts waiting to be seen, the conveyor belt of bodily distress that
kept moving.

he was already headed for the exit. "Bye, Nursie. Think about me
e you hurt."

mind persisted in making thoughts, the thoughts had to be or-
amed, redirected. She sat before her little shrine, perfectly still,
as one of those times when the mind would not allow itself to fol-
Wednesdays and Thursdays she worked in a general practi-
office, and though you saw fewer patients than at the clinic, there
ps of boredom and irritation. *The greatest achievement is self-*
s. Mother Teresa regarded each of the afflicted poor she tended to
st in a distressing guise. But there was only one Mother Teresa,
e would not have been asked to provide diet pills to weight-
d Marin matrons. On Fridays and every other Saturday morning,
de visiting rounds to shut-ins and the frail elderly. So much in life
fering, but nobody ever wanted to die. *The name of God is Pain.*
er! No. Focus.

e *greatest precept is continual awareness.* And there were those
hen she could sustain whole moments of this, seeing the familiar
e were seeing it for the first time, with new eyes: the different
and lights of ordinary concrete, depending on air and sky. A piece
dy, fire-colored cellophane trash. *The greatest wisdom is seeing*
h *appearances.* Maybe she was too judgmental. Too quick to size
up by applying her own prejudices. She wanted to love them and
uldn't. She had tried to turn that into detachment, into a virtue, but
t only made her sad.

e gave up and got to her feet, disappointed with herself and her

San Rafael. The clinic was in the Canal neighborhood, where most of the
Mexicans and Guatemalans lived. Christie had learned enough Spanish to
get through the basics, and there was a translator for more complicated
situations. Twice a month, a dentist volunteered his time. They made re-
ferrals to mental health services, to employment services, to addiction
counselors. There were pamphlets, in English and in Spanish, on nutrition, domestic violence, birth control, prenatal care.

In addition to the immigrants, the clinic regulars included the homeless population, both regular and transient, and a certain number of people who fit into neither category. These might be young workingmen, or
mothers overwhelmed with small children, or those who had lost jobs.
Some of these looked like they ought to be shopping at Nordstrom, not
waiting their turn at a community clinic. But anyone could slide a long
ways down these days, and when they showed up there, furtive and di-
minished, it meant they had probably already maxed out the credit cards
and were afraid of answering their phones.

It was always a surprise that there were so many genuinely poor people in Marin County, where, as somebody once said, you could get tired
of seeing all the Lexuses and Jags. Where exquisitely dressed children
(they always seemed to be either blond or biracial) enjoyed ergonomically
designed playgrounds, and where real estate, even after prices swooned,
could still fetch obscene millions. At the clinic, you saw all this through
a layer of economic distortion, like a pair of glasses with the wrong
lenses, so that neither poverty nor wealth, viewed side by side, seemed
entirely real.

At the same time, you couldn't help noticing how many people (poor
or not, but most often the poor) were complicit in their own suffering. The
smokers, the addicts, the diabetics who would rather lose a leg than stop
eating sugar. The parents who let their children's asthma medicine run
out, the pregnant women who looked at her blankly when Christie asked
about birth control, the alcoholics with their scabies and untreated sores.
The ignorant, the obstinate, the quarrelsome.

Public health, she understood, was about providing services to those who were least likely to be good patients. She took their blood pressure, listened to their leaky hearts, tested for STDs, dispensed condoms, instructions, advice. Then the same people came back again and again, with the same complaints, bad habits, and neglect. The name of God might be Truth, but surely his middle name was Patience, to put up with so much repetitive and avoidable folly.

On this Monday, Christie saw a woman whose chest X-ray showed lesions, and a Guatemalan man with an ulcerated leg. The immigrants were always the ones in the worst shape, given to doctoring themselves with their own remedies until things turned truly bad. They couldn't afford to miss even one day on the job. There were children with pinkeye and earaches, sore throats and rashes. A man on crutches from an accident, and from what he claimed was botched surgery: "They had some beginner practice on me and it didn't heal right. Then they tried again so he could get more practice."

The clinic doctor made brief eye contact with Christie, a look that meant *drug-seeking behavior*. "And why is it that you think the surgeries were unsuccessful?"

"Because it feels like I got broken glass in my hip. Awake, asleep, sit, stand, lie down. Can't you give me something?"

There was a hungry, calculating look to the man, as if he was telling the truth but it was a story he'd repeated too many times. The doctor said he should go back to the surgeon and tell him he was having problems.

"Like I'd want to have anything more to do with that clown."

The doctor suggested physical therapy, a pain-management practice. "And tincture of time. We never heal as fast as we want to. You have to measure your recovery in terms of months and years."

"It's been almost a year."

"It may take a while longer."

"Funny how months can feel like years, depending on if the body in question is yours, not somebody else's." He wasn't going to get what he wanted, and he was unhappy about it.

On his way out of the examination area he lir[...] to Christie.

"Man, that doc is a hard-ass."

"So am I."

He made a pantomime of amazement and moo[...] ward on his crutches. You could still see the ladie[...] good-time guy in him, underneath all his layer[...] wasn't good, and the skin around his eyes and m[...] abraded, and his arms were ropy where the flesh h[...] he had the remnants of what Christie thought of [...] This registered on her purely as an observation.

She said, "You need to back off on whatever y[...] tin? Hydrocodone? After a while your body can't [...] tween pain and drug dependency."

"Yeah, because plain old pain is so much bette[...]

"I'm sorry," Christie said, taking a step to mov[...] attend to the next patient, whose medical history fe[...] and fastened to a clipboard, waiting for her at the [...] held out one of his crutches to block her, making a[...]

"Didn't used to be so hard to get a pretty woma[...]

Christie obliged him with a smile. He probab[...] guy. Just unlucky or dumb or both. She wondered [...] been in, if it had involved alcohol. "I think you sho[...] told you. Go back and see the surgeon who did the [...]

He shook his head. He was wearing a baseba[...] symbol of guy-dom, black, with a Raiders logo. "He[...] any more than I want to see him. Doctors don't like[...]

She thought this was probably true. She was [...] *me*, she had already said it in her mind, when his [...] folding-in on itself. "Ah," he said, coming out o[...] fashioned pain."

She hesitated, wanting to say something to this [...]

mood. Above her head, the indistinct sounds of Art and Linnea, talking to each other from different rooms. It must have been one of their good nights, Art finding something silly enough or harmless enough to get her to engage. Maybe getting to know a child wasn't entirely unlike meditation. You kept going at it from all different angles, and once in a while something clicked.

Mrs. Foster was neither a shut-in nor, at present, frail, having recovered from her anxiety-induced heart arrhythmia and breathing difficulties. But she had grown fond of Christie and was willing to pay out of pocket for the home visits. There was really nothing wrong with her, and she might have learned to read her own blood pressure and monitor her pulse. She only needed attention, and sympathy, and who was Christie to say that these were not forms of medicine.

Since Mrs. Foster lived here in town, it wasn't difficult for Christie to stop by, as Mrs. Foster called it, as if they were chatty neighbors given to sociable comings and goings. To get to Mrs. Foster's house, Christie left her economy-class apartment next to the freeway and drove downtown, then up into the hills. This was where the celebrities, both current and mythic, lived. There had once been a good many rock musicians and artists, not as many at present. The place cost too much now. Back in the old days, Janis Joplin had lived in Mill Valley. Now there was a television chef.

Mrs. Foster's house was a marvel of sleek redwood and expansive glass, arranged to take best advantage of the canyon views. There was some Asian-inspired landscaping Christie allowed herself to covet, with weeping cherry trees, peonies, ornamental maples, and bluestone paths. When she rang the front doorbell, it made a deep, bonging sound that was meant to be reminiscent of temple bells.

One of the furious captive cats appeared in the glass panel at one side of the door, hissed and spat and ran away again.

It took another couple of minutes for Mrs. Foster to open the door. She was wearing a sporty outfit with a nautical aspect, trimmed with red, white, and blue stars, brass buttons. There were certain looks that seemed to be associated with prosperous old ladies. "Come, come," Mrs. Foster urged, and Christie did the quick side-step necessary to prevent the cats from bolting to freedom. Mrs. Foster slammed the door shut behind her. "How are you, dear? You look very pretty today."

Christie said she was fine, and thank you, and followed Mrs. Foster back into the breakfast room, where Mrs. Foster had laid out teacups and teapot and a tray of thin wafer cookies and what looked like candied orange peel. In the center of the table was a bowl of peaches so perfectly formed and ripe and fragrant they might have been a magazine center-fold. "How does ginger tea sound?"

"That would be nice." She noted that Mrs. Foster's breathing was somewhat rushed and shallow, as if getting to the front door had winded her. "First why don't you sit down, and let me check you out."

Mrs. Foster's pulse was elevated and her blood pressure into the 160s. "You're a little speedy today," Christie told her. "Did you take your pills yet?"

"I can't believe those things are good for you. They make me feel like I'm a rag doll with the stuffing being pulled out of me."

Christie said yes, but they were necessary to regulate the system that was not regulating itself, and they had to be taken on schedule. "Do you want me to go get them for you? I can put the kettle on too."

Mrs. Foster agreed to this. Christie filled the kettle from the kitchen tap and set it on a burner. The medicine was upstairs in one of the bathrooms. As she advanced farther into the house, the smell of cat announced itself. Two adolescent kittens, one orange, one black, raced up the stairs ahead of her. A tiger-striped adult lurked on the windowseat, running off to hide as Christie approached. Cat noises, thumps and pattering feet, came from different rooms.

Christie retrieved the medicine, then took the opportunity to make a quick check of the upstairs. The guest bathroom had two litter boxes in it, neither of them entirely clean or entirely soiled. This meant that at least some of the cats were making use of them, rather than any handy section of carpeting. The bed was made, the laundry picked up. The cleaning service now came twice a week, which helped. The neglected medicine was a concern, as were the cats, which, although they were all supposedly spayed and neutered, seemed to have increased their population since her last visit.

Mrs. Foster was a widow and the cats were a project of her widowhood. First there had been Mr. Foster, all dead and tragic. Christie heard the story a number of times, because it was Mrs. Foster's heart's sorrow, the story she'd been left to tell. How she had screamed in disbelief when she'd come home and found him, had fallen insensible on the floor, awakening in the dark next to the dead man. How she had touched his knees and then his cold face, speaking to him in an ordinary way about the things she had done that day. It wasn't the kind of conversation he had ever taken much of an interest in, and so she was used to talking to herself. It was only a little normal space before she had to get up, make phone calls, and get on with the business of death.

The panic attacks and cardiac symptoms began once the funeral was over. They sent her to the emergency room on three occasions. They came on without warning, and sometimes she had what she called "grayouts," when her vision turned dim and her ears filled with roaring. Her daughter had come up from San Diego to stay with her, but she was either going to have to find some way to manage on her own, or else make the transition to some sort of sheltered, supervised housing. This was when Christie had first met her. She'd been sad and frightened, huddled in a quilted bathrobe and surrounded by Kleenex. Although her husband had been ill, she had insufficiently imagined his dying.

Christie organized Mrs. Foster's medicine, checked her vital signs, and listened to her talk about Mr. Foster. He sounded rather disagreeable, or else Mrs. Foster was still carrying on their long-standing marital quarrel, in which he stood accused of insensitivity, sarcasm, and condescension. But she missed him, if only because now there was no one to argue back.

By virtue of her not dying, Mrs. Foster's health gradually improved. Christie showed her some breathing exercises and brought her vitamins and calming teas. The daughter in San Diego sent a gift basket of spa products and the daughter in New York sent fancy cupcakes. One of them suggested that she might now acquire a small, companionable dog. Mrs. Foster was a great lover of animals, although Mr. Foster would never have put up with one in the house.

Instead the cats arrived. They were members of a feral colony in San Anselmo, and had been trapped by a group dedicated to feral cat welfare. "I thought," Christie said, when the cats began to take up space with their carriers and food bowls and catnip toys, not to mention their clawing, biting selves, "that you managed feral cats by trapping them, spaying and neutering and vaccinating them, and then releasing them again?"

"Somebody was poisoning them," Mrs. Foster said, her eyes and nose growing pink at the thought of it. "Putting out poisoned tuna fish. Can you imagine? There's simply no safe place for them right now. Besides, some of the young ones could get used to people and find homes. They just need a chance."

And so the lower level of the house, a place where Mr. Foster had retreated to practice his solitary hobbies (woodworking, the construction of remote-controlled rockets), had been turned into a cattery. There were a dozen feral cats in all, and supposedly only the tamest and most tractable were allowed upstairs and given names: Peanut, Handsome Devil, Lola, and Miss Priss. But more and more of them seemed to have migrated upstairs, where they shredded upholstery and hid under furniture, claws shooting out to inflict vicious ankle wounds. They seemed to make Mrs. Foster happy, in the same way that having a difficult husband had made her happy. The feral cat people came over on a regular basis to help with medications, or transport cats to the vet, so there was company in the house as well. "Some people go to the dogs. I've gone to the cats!" Mrs. Foster was fond of saying.

Christie came back downstairs with the blood pressure medicine and made sure Mrs. Foster took it. The kettle came to a boil and she filled the teapot, trying to ignore the thing in the corner of the kitchen floor that she was pretty sure was a cat turd.

Mrs. Foster poured out the tea and they drank, looking out to the backyard and its pleasing vista of formal plantings and fishpond and Mrs. Foster's elaborate collection of bird feeders. The cats, able only to watch from behind closed windows, must have thought they'd died and gone to hell.

"How have you been eating?" Christie asked. "Are you getting enough protein?" Mrs. Foster could be a picky and irregular eater, given to things like cheese and crackers for breakfast.

The nautical outfit made Mrs. Foster look like a captain in some small, loopy navy. "Cooking is so much fuss in this weather. I like a nice salad, watercress if I can get it, goat cheese, toasted walnuts, dried cranberries. You try it sometime."

"Add some cooked chicken."

"And a little high-fiber cereal. And some calcium pills." Mrs. Foster smiled in a way that was meant to be mischievous. She had once been a pretty woman, and there were still remnants of this in her coquettish manner. She had recently had her hair colored, so that it was no longer white but coppery gold. It poufed out thinly over her scalp like a tangled, vining plant.

"Seriously. You have to feed yourself at least as well as you feed the cats."

"I don't know how people get excited about cooking for themselves. Where's the comfort in it?"

"I do every night," Christie said, incautiously, because any such statement was likely to get Mrs. Foster started on one of her favorite topics, how Christie should find herself a nice man, marry, and have children before it was too late. But Mrs. Foster was listening to the sound of cat commotion in some distant precinct of the house: guttural war cries, attacks and retreats.

"I don't know why they have to fight like that," Mrs. Foster complained. "There's plenty of everything for everybody."

"Cats don't really like other cats. Most of them. They're solitary hunters."

Mrs. Foster waved this away. "Well they must get together once in a while. Or there wouldn't be any kittens. Oh, if there was such a thing as ghosts, my husband would be haunting me day and night. He didn't have any use for a cat. And he was so fussy about this house. It's a beautiful house, of course. But it's not a museum, it's meant for living."

Sooner or later, Mrs. Foster's conversations all led back to her husband, if only to complain about him. Christie didn't understand their marriage. But then, she hadn't understood her own. Trying to be discreet, she checked her watch. She had another appointment this morning. She didn't have much use for a cat herself.

Christie was about to make her final speech about better eating habits, when Mrs. Foster said, "He wasn't the easiest man to live with. He wasn't always sympathetic to different points of view."

Christie murmured that people were, oftentimes, and understandably enough, partial to their own way of seeing things. As she was herself. Her prickly, unbending self. She wondered if she should get a cat. A nice tame cat, not one of the feral hellions. She could pet its rumbly fur, watch its pink tongue paddle in water, attempt to bond with the creature.

"Of course I got mad at him. So mad I'd cry. Oh he could be an aggravating man. I came to understand, it was just his nature. Like the poor cats. There were things he couldn't help."

But what if you wanted to help it? Why were you so unhappy about it, if it was really yours, your true nature, the skin that fit you best? Wasn't she always trying to escape it, rise above it, step out of it like clothing? Be someone better? At times the bright edge of her finer self was almost visible, before it blurred and disappeared. *All truth is very ordinary.* Was that a teaching, or had she made it up herself?

Mrs. Foster was saying she wanted it to serve as a memorial to her husband. Memorial? Something Christie had missed, not listening; she put her teacup down on its saucer, centering it carefully, willing herself to focus. "Nothing to do with animals," Mrs. Foster said. "That would be a bad joke, considering the way he felt about them. Or claimed he felt. So much of that was just teasing, meant to upset me. Well, don't I have the last laugh. I could fund an entire endangered species. Too late for him to stop me."

"Ah," said Christie, nodding. The closest she could come to the humorous agreement that seemed required of her. What was Mrs. Foster talking about? She felt tired, scattered. Beneath the table, something furry brushed her leg and she jumped.

"No, this will be all about people."

"Ah," said Christie again. Sooner or later she was going to have to produce words.

"Because this is going to be my new start. My next chapter in life. I even have a name picked out: The Humanity Project. And who better to be in charge but you? If you would just consider it. If you would be able to help me."

"I'm sorry. I didn't understand, what did you need me to help you with? What kind of project, what did you mean?"

Mrs. Foster's smile turned girlish. The brass buttons on her jacket winked. "It means I would like to give you rather a lot of money."

The animals used to eat us but nowadays we mostly ate the animals. There were not many places remaining on earth, or many circumstances, where you could get yourself digested by a bear or a big jungle cat. Or alligator or hyena or great white shark. We could imagine such a thing, but only in a shivery, unreal fashion. We didn't actually think of ourselves as food.

Some of us were vegetarians, for reasons of conscience or health or both, but most of us were businesslike and untroubled about the creatures we ate. They came in so many unexpected and delicious varieties, things like snails and catfish and venison and the estimable hog. So much art and skill and effort had been devoted to pleasing our tastes. Cheeseburgers alone had been the subject of considerable experimentation and debate.

The Bible said: We had been made in God's image, and He granted us dominion over the fish of the sea, and over the fowl of the air, and over the cattle, and over all the earth, and over every creeping thing that creepeth over the earth.

"Dominion" was like a contract we could bring out to show any reluctant or recalcitrant fish of the sea or fowl of the air and so forth. Whereas: "Dominion" shall be understood to include, but shall not be limited to, the following. Confinement, slaughter, packaging, distribution, and consumption. Genetic modification, where deemed necessary and desirable by the party of the first part. The diversion and damming of rivers. The removal of forests and the leveling of mountaintops. Any other alterations of habitat for purposes of the extraction of resources or the expansion of agriculture, roads, or settlements.

For purposes of sport, for those creatures that provided sport, other practices were allowed.

But we were not easy in our hearts. It seemed that more should be required of us. We were aware that while some of us kept pets that we named and loved, others of us scissored the ears of fighting dogs. The huge feedlots and hog containment buildings polluted our air and water, the cramped and mistreated hens produced eggs that sickened us. The oceans filled with floating plastic trash, the bees died off, the migrating birds exhausted themselves and fell to earth in parking lots and freeways. We knew (when we thought about it or were forced to think about it) that the very process of dominion had made us, somehow, less than human.

If we were made in God's image, it remained to be seen if He would still recognize us.

We justified some of the things we did because they came naturally to us, and others because they were done out of necessity. But when we saw those pictures from the Gulf of Mexico, the oil pouring out like the earth's very blood, the great seabirds rendered foul and black and stinking and opening their doomed mouths to choke and die, their suffering shamed us because it served no purpose, and nothing could have been more unnatural.

SEVEN

The last thing she expected was that she'd end up bored.

Because here she was stuck with her father, the Prince of Boredom, a guy so squirrelly and anxious to please there must be some mistake about them being related. He was an *intellectual*, Linnea's mother used to say, meaning it as a putdown. Linnea had expected him to live in a house, not an apartment. That was one thing. She should have realized that what her mother meant was money.

By now Linnea had been in California long enough to believe nobody was going to send her back right away. She found the places Art hid his dope—in the closet in the pocket of a bathrobe, in the kitchen behind a rice cooker—and extracted enough to roll joints out of Tampax wrappers. When Art was at work, she smoked in the bathroom with the exhaust fan on, then sprayed Tropical Citrus air spray everywhere, a joke. The stuff just screamed dope, that you'd been smoking dope. She figured Art knew what she was up to but was too chickenshit to come out and say anything. Linnea imagined herself asking, all casual, "So, you get high?" Just to see him stammer and fall all over himself trying not to answer.

Her mother had built him up over the years as somebody cruel and powerful but really, he was just Art.

Mondays, Wednesdays, and Fridays, Art taught English to Dummies somewhere Linnea hadn't paid attention to, but it meant he was gone all day. Linnea waited until he left, then ran out to catch a commuter bus into the city. She transferred at the toll plaza and rode all over San Francisco, past neighborhoods of small yellow or pink or cream houses shouldered together, and Asian people with shopping carts, and hulking warehouses, and tough-looking streets, and parks, and traffic, and stores selling the whole world, and big humpy hills, and fog that made the bus windows drip and then a few blocks later unraveled into sunshine.

It was amazing that she could hand over her fare and sit on a bus and she was just a kid, ordinary, who cared where she was going? Nobody staring at her because she had been turned into some kind of pitiful freak when they didn't know one thing about her and never would.

Once she had to call Art to come get her from the toll plaza because there weren't any more Mill Valley buses, and he got all pissy and worried and wanted to know what she was doing out there and Linnea said, "Sightseeing." Then Art planned a big-deal night on the town for them where they had dinner at Fisherman's Wharf in a restaurant filled with Japanese tourists and Art asked her if she wanted to go on a cable car and Linnea said, "You're kidding, right?"

Once in a while they accidentally had a good time together, mostly when he forgot he was supposed to be a Dad in Charge.

Sometimes her mother called her, but Linnea never answered. Then her mother called Art, and Art made her get on the phone. "Yeah?" Linnea said into the receiver.

"Lose the attitude," her mother said. "No one's impressed. I hope your father isn't letting you get away with—" Murder, she might have been about to say, but she stopped herself.

Linnea had a sensation of dark feathers, wings, brushing past her head, just beyond her field of vision.

She shifted the phone at her ear and said, "He's right here, if you need to talk to him." Art was flipping through the TV channels, listening and pretending not to.

"No, I want to talk to you. I worry about you. I worry about you every minute."

"Well don't bother." Linnea stared at Art until he put the remote down and went into his bedroom.

"Have you met any kids your age? Made any friends?"

"Yeah, I'm part of a gang now. We do gang things."

"Very not funny. I'll take that as a no. You have to try harder, Linnea. You have to take responsibility for your own life."

Linnea didn't answer. Her mother had learned all these handy-dandy slogans.

"Aren't you going to ask about Max?"

"Sure." A silence. Linnea sighed. "How's Max?"

"He misses you. He keeps wanting to know when you're coming home. I tell him, we have to wait and see."

Linnea put the phone down and walked to the front windows. Beyond the roofline of the apartment building was a rim of orange sky left over from the sunset. Back in Ohio, it would already be dark. There would be fireflies, which they didn't seem to have in California. When she came back to the phone, it was making a tiny buzz, her mother talking and talking. Linnea picked it up. Her mother said, "There's nothing wrong with being a survivor. It's nothing you should feel guilty about. Linnea? Have you found a counselor out there? Because you need—"

Linnea shut the phone off. She yelled to Art that she was going out for a walk, and let the door bang shut behind her.

She sat at the picnic table, smoking a cigarette. She was supposed to be quitting, but she wasn't really. Her mother would probably call back, and then she and Art could have a grand old time going on about what was wrong with her.

She had learned to make everything she had left behind her feel less real, the same way you avoided touching a hot stove, or were careful to walk around a hole in the street. She learned to fill her head with *Don't don't don't*, a charm to take up space. The last thing she wanted was another counselor making her talk. Talking was always supposed to be this great idea, but only if you said the kinds of things that allowed people to feel better about you.

When she got back to the apartment, Art said, "Your mom wants me to tell you about some things."

"How about we don't but say we did."

Art smiled, in a sad, curdled kind of way. Linnea knew he thought her mom was a real piece of work. It was messed up to think of the two of them ever being married, which was maybe why she had turned out so messed up herself. "All right, great, go for it." She might as well get it over with.

"Your mom's been looking at schools for you."

Something sick-making crawled up her throat. *Don't don't don't.* She shoved it down. "Huh," she said. Bored here.

"Yeah, there are these private, yeah, private schools with pro-grams . . ." Art sketched an expansive shape in the air to illustrate programs.

Linnea didn't say anything. He went on. "This one's in Montana. They do a lot of outdoor stuff. Ranch stuff. Horses. Hiking."

The sick came back up her throat and she spat it out as words. "You mean a loser school."

"No, honey. Nobody thinks that about you."

"Who else goes to this swell school, huh? Druggies? Kids that weigh three hundred pounds and cut themselves up?"

Art looked miserable and hangdog but she wasn't about to feel sorry for him. "What did I do, huh, that I have to go away to some kind of jail?"

"I promise you, it's not a jail."

"Like everything that happened is my fault. That's what my mom thinks. That this is all some big excuse to act up."

"She just wants you to be happy. Me too."

"Why is everybody supposed to be HAPPY? That's asinine."

"No it's not. What do you—"

"It makes people HAPPY when I go away."

"You wouldn't be going anywhere anytime soon. Not until September."

"NOBODY. WANTS. ME."

And then she really was sick, barely made it to the toilet in time, kicking the bathroom door shut behind her, tasting the sour, foul mess, snot too because she was crying and she hadn't meant to, puking until she practically turned herself inside out. Like the cat—was it a cat?—so torn and horrible. She'd seen it yesterday on the edge of someone's yard, a coyote got it, the man said, lifting it up with a shovel, and once a thing was dead, it remained dead, was always and finally dead.

When she was done puking she got up and rinsed her mouth out and splashed cold water over her face. She wished she could just stay in there but it would have to be the only bathroom in the place. Art was waiting for her. "Seven Up," he said. "Come on, drink it."

Linnea did, and it helped some. Art said, "How about I talk with your mom. Nothing has to be decided yet."

"OK."

"You have to give her a break. Me a break. Yourself a break. Nobody knows what to do when there's a tragedy. Nobody practices for it."

"OK," she said again, because she was tired, wrung-out, shaky. She wanted to fall asleep and wake up somewhere else. She wanted everybody to forget about her, like she was dead. Plant another tree and move on. If you were dead, at least nobody thought it was all your fault, and no other girl's father would scream into your face, wanting to know *How is it you got out alive?* Even though Jay had apologized later. He'd still come out and said it.

Linnea had thought she could just keep her head down, cruise through one day and then the next and the next, until the end of summer, avoiding any mention of what might happen farther down the road. Then she'd enroll herself at Tam High, show up at the apartment with her textbooks and ask Art to help her with her homework, and that would be settled. Now her mother had wrecked everything.

Art could have said he wanted her to stay, but he didn't say it because he didn't want her to. Linnea didn't really blame him. She hadn't been very nice to him. He wanted her to like him, but mostly he wanted to be let off the hook, put in just enough time with her so that nobody would be mad at him. It was a stupid situation.

At least there weren't any more calls from her mother. Maybe she and Art were talking, hatching some new crummy thing to do to her. She needed to get her hands on some money. Art gave her a few dollars here and there when she asked. He wasn't cheap, exactly; he just wasn't a money kind of guy. Linnea had needed new clothes because everything she'd brought with her was wrong, and she'd gotten him to pay for them by telling him an affecting story about how every Christmas when she was a little kid, she pretended that her best present was from her daddy.

She could get a job. Or she couldn't. She didn't know how. But say she talked somebody into letting her do some moron teen job, scooping ice cream or flipping hamburgers. It still wouldn't be the kind of money she had in mind. She had to have enough to run away on and find someplace to stay, though she didn't have any clear idea of how she would do either of those things. And she had to have the money soon, in case her mother and Art ambushed her and announced that all of a sudden it was Montana time.

She was going to try and sell some of Art's dope, partly for meanness, partly for money purposes. She was handicapped by not knowing exactly what people charged or paid. Back in Ohio, guys had given her whatever they had some of, dope or different fun pharmaceuticals. She hadn't needed to buy anything. This was the one time Art could have given her actual fatherly advice, and she couldn't ask him.

The best way to proceed, she decided, was to take some small-enough quantity—no matter how much she took, the supply was always replenished—and try to peddle it in some casual way. Which she tried a couple of times around Mill Valley, but it didn't work because she was so lame. Really, she could not have been more of an idiot. She'd thought it would be easier to make friends, or at least talk to people. It was like she'd forgotten how to talk normal, like when she opened her mouth, animal noises came out.

This time she was going to go about it differently and be more businesslike, find some actual potheads. She took a bus into the city and headed for the hippie museum, otherwise known as the Haight. Art probably used to hang out here, being a groovy guy. About thirty years too late for the party.

She had been here before but only at night, those occasions when she'd managed to sneak away late at night, and if she tried that stunt again she guessed she'd be punching her ticket to Montana. So here she was, ten o'clock in the morning, disappointed to find Haight turned into an ordinary street. No music thundering out of the clubs whenever anyone opened a door, no costume parade on the sidewalks, where everything and everyone had a thrilling, illegal air. Once she'd hung out on the front steps of a house with a party going on inside, too shy to actually go inside, waiting for someone to talk to her, but no one did. And once two girls had pulled her back as she tried to cross a street. "Watch it," they said, nodding at the cop car at the curb. "Curfew."

"Thanks," Linnea had muttered, ducking her head, embarrassed. It was unfair and stupid that she still looked so much like a little kid.

A couple of times she saw kids she was pretty sure lived in Mill Valley. She kept her distance from them. She didn't want anybody thinking she was one of those rich Marin kids who came down here to get their kicks.

This morning she walked around for a while, pretending she had somewhere to go. She hadn't thought much about how she was going to sell the stuff, how she intended to connect with her fellow desperadoes. She read attentively the flyers taped in layers to the light poles, advertising concerts, a free clinic, work-from-home opportunities. The overcast daylight turned the streets with their painted murals into a used-up kind of place, tired and untidy.

She peered into store windows, as if she was contemplating the purchase of motorcycle jackets or vampire dresses or crystal jewelry. Tibetan art, steel boots, massage oil, Day-Glo wigs, incense, studded belts, skateboards, vinyl bras. She only had twenty dollars, and everything cost so much, as if money had taken over here too. Besides, she didn't want to go into anywhere they made you leave your backpack because she had two fat Baggies of dope in one of the zip pockets, and it wasn't the summer of love anymore, people outright ripped you off.

She went into a coffee shop and ordered a mango smoothie and sat at a table to drink it, killing time. The girl behind the counter wore one of those tasseled hats with the strings hanging down, the kind that looked like it was knit out of wool from really gnarly sheep. She had green and blue tattoos winding around both arms, a flower design. Linnea thought that would be something, to show up back at Art's with tattoos. A big FUCK MONTANA around her neck. And there wouldn't be anything anybody could do about it.

The counter girl washed dishes and chopped up different fruits for the drinks: strawberries, kiwis, honeydew, pineapple. Some kind of hectic dance music Linnea didn't recognize came from speakers in the corners. A boy and girl came in and ordered lattes and walked out again, draped and sagging around each other, as if they'd been having sex and were about to go back and have more sex and were just taking a coffee break.

She had to go to the bathroom; she hadn't gone since she'd left home, and now the smoothie was weighing on her bladder. NO PUBLIC WASH-ROOM, a sign said, so she bent over suddenly in her chair, cradling her eye with one hand. "Aaaouch! My contact is killing me!"

The counter girl said, "You must have the gas-permeable kind, huh?"

"Uh-huh." Not wanting to ham it up too much, she poked around her eye with one finger. "Could I go rinse this thing out?"

"Yeah, go ahead." She lifted a hinged gate to let Linnea pass behind the counter. There was a back room with a walk-in freezer and refrigera-tor, metal shelves lined with paper towels and jugs of disinfectant, and behind a door, a small, dank bathroom.

"Thanks." Linnea closed the bathroom door and ran water in the sink for a while, then, as if it were an afterthought, peed. She wished she was somebody who could just come straight out and ask for things.

Feeling she'd been hanging around the shop too long, like a jerk, she took the last of the smoothie with her and stepped outside. A little milky sunlight tried to burn through the clouds. There were more people out walking around now, but Linnea had the depressing sense that they were all of them just like her and came from other places. Everybody in search of some exotic good time that didn't exist anymore, or maybe they just wanted to buy souvenirs.

If you walked far enough along Haight, not that many blocks, really, past the taquerías and the African drum shops and vintage clothing places, you ran out of interesting street and it turned into an ordinary depressing neighborhood, more punk than hippie, with tax shops and industrial-looking clubs and the kind of hole-in-the-wall restaurants that made you think of food poisoning. But before then you came to a grassy space Linnea thought of as Bum Hill, because of the skanky men— and sometimes women—who slept there day and night, a coat over their heads, or maybe just sprawled in some passed-out, lewd heap.

There could be nasty things in the grass, wadded-up Kleenex glued together with suspect fluids, broken glass, needles. The first time she'd seen a needle she'd stared at it until she figured out it wasn't anything else. Today she was tired of walking and discouraged and didn't much care. Besides, the bums had arranged themselves in rows, each of them with a space around them like a substitute for privacy. She climbed half-way up the steep slope, inspected the ground carefully, then sat with her knees pulled up to her chin, her backpack beneath her. She wished she had a cigarette.

Her phone buzzed. It was Art, trying to do the Dad thing and check in with her. She'd ignore it like she always did, and then she'd get a few more calls and some texts, and after a while she'd text him back, some variation of, what's the big deal? It was so easy to get around him. She didn't think any real father would let her get away with it.

Two boys climbed up the hill and sat a little ways behind her. Linnea heard them goofing around talking, nothing she could make out. Then they got louder.

"Maybe she's deaf or something."

"Something."

"Doesn't want to play."

"Or she can smell you. She is downwind."

"Shut up."

"Maybe she's strung-out. So young too."

"Yeah, tragic."

Linnea turned around. "You guys are so, so funny."

"Hey! Not deaf!"

Linnea said, "No, but I kind of wish I was." Pretending to sound disgusted. One of them was sort of cute, but she didn't know yet if she wanted to talk to them.

"Look what you did. You got her mad."

"You haven't seen mad yet." She was glad to have a salty answer for him.

"What? Can't hear you."

"Now who's deaf?"

"Stay there, OK?"

The two of them scooted downhill until they were sitting one on each side of her.

"Much better."

The cute one said, "You got a name?"

They were sitting close enough to her that she had to turn her head from one side to the other to see them, like a tennis match. "Sadie," she said. She had decided on it right then and there.

"That's pretty."

Linnea shrugged. It wasn't one of her favorite names, she wasn't that attached to it.

"I'm Axe, like an axe," said the cute one. He made a chopping blade with his hand.

He had black hair with a blue piece in front that fell into his eyes. He wore a black T-shirt printed with white ribs to make him a skeleton.

The other boy said, "It's more like, Axe like a guitar." He was sort of fat.

"That's Jarhead," said Axe.

"Jared."

"Whatever. So what are you up to today, Sadie?"

"Just hanging." She decided she wasn't going to say that much. It was when she started talking a lot that she got into trouble.

"Yeah? Where you from?" Axe was bobbing around where he sat, like he was hearing a song in his head, so that sometimes his face was pushed close to hers and sometimes she had to swivel around to see him.

"Seattle."

"Yeah? You just get here? What did you do, hitch?"

"Uh-huh." Linnea said it like, no big deal. In her head she was already seeing herself hitching, standing by the side of a highway in the rain, probably. Somebody creepy had picked her up, but then somebody nice had.

"You going to stick around for a while? You got a place to stay?"

"With some friends," Linnea told him. *Friends.* It was a word that filled up space and explained things for you.

Axe jumped up and strutted, stiff-legged, as if he was on a stage. He threw his head back and sang an old Bruce Springsteen song in a grinding wail: "Glory days! They'll pass you by, glory days, inna wink of a young girl's eye, glory days, glory da-ays!" When he danced, the skeleton ribs did too.

Jared looked at Linnea. "He's deep." He was either mad at Axe, or just pretending to be.

Axe stooped, still in motion, put his mouth up to Linnea's ear, slurped at it with his tongue.

"Hey!" Linnea said, but he was already capering away from her. "Glory days, glory dayhhs!" Then he was done with the song and he sat back down, looking bored.

"What the hell," Linnea said.

"Real deep," Jared said. "Sometimes I just sit and marvel."

Axe said, "Because that's what he's good for. Sitting on his fat ass." He started singing under his breath, wah wah wah, some song Linnea couldn't make out. He had a skinny, paintbrush mustache and goatee and she thought he was probably a little older than her but not much. She couldn't decide if she liked him or not. Him douching out her ear was kind of gross. But she didn't want to give up on him yet.

She said, "Hey. Where would I go if I wanted to get some pot?"

Axe stopped singing. "You got a doctor's letter?"

"A what?"

"Forget it, you have to be twenty-one," Jared said. "Medical marijuana. If you have AIDS or something. You can go to a dispensary."

She'd forgotten about the medical pot. It was a disappointment, it probably meant hers, or rather Art's, wasn't worth as much. "Well I don't have AIDS."

Axe bent toward her, made his fingers into drumsticks, and did a quick drumroll on Linnea's knee. "That's good to know."

"What if," Linnea said, determined to get through it, "you have some to sell?"

They hadn't seemed to hear her. They were talking across her and they had started an argument, or maybe it was an old argument they were getting back to.

"Told you. Now we gotta pay up."

"Shut your fat face."

"Told you and now look."

"Shut up. I got it under control."

"Sure. Like you always do."

Linnea's phone buzzed and she pulled it out. Art again. Really, the guy had no life.

"Hey, can I see that?" Axe grabbed the phone from her. "Who was that, your boyfriend?"

"Give it back."

"This a pretty nice phone, Sadie." He flipped it over and spun it around. Linnea reached for it and he held it over her head.

"Give it back right now."

Axe let it drop and she snatched it up. He said, "Oh come on, what are you, mad? I was just messing with you."

Linnea didn't answer. She was beginning to think they were creeps.

"I'm sorry, Sadie. I'll make it up to you. I'll write a song about you."

"Don't bother." She got to her feet and swung the backpack around so she was holding it in front of her.

Jared said, "Hey Sadie, you got any money? If we had a little money, we could all go get some burritos."

She headed off down the hill. She had to get through two rows of bums to reach the sidewalk. There was a roll of toilet paper set on its end, unrolling in the wind. Some of this stuff was just gross.

She started walking back toward Stanyan. There were more people on the sidewalks now and it was slower going. She'd only gone a block when Axe and Jared caught up with her, once again walking on either side of her. She sped up. "You guys should just leave me alone."

"Come on. I said I was sorry." Axe danced along ahead of her, walking backward. "Is it OK if we just walk together? Since it's like, a public sidewalk?"

"Do whatever you want." She had a feeling it was a mistake to say anything to them, but for the moment at least they were quiet, walking. She still didn't have anywhere to go, and she was starting to feel stupid.

She slowed down and examined the window of a bookstore. They had arranged the books on pedestals, like it was jewelry they were selling. None of them were books she'd ever heard of. What she was really seeing was her own reflection. Her hair had grown out some and she'd just dyed it a bright, cellophane red. (Art had looked stricken at first, but he'd come around to a cautious compliment, telling her the hair was "nice all one color.") She had on her favorite dark green T-shirt and her best jeans. She looked all right. She really did. And here was Axe beside her, looking in the window to see what she was looking at, and for once he was quiet and not being an asshole so you could see what was cute about him, and they were together in the reflection and he might have been her boyfriend, she looked like a girl who might have a boyfriend just like anybody else.

"Hey Sadie. Want to go see a friend of mine? Hang out?" Axe asked.

She had to remember she was Sadie. She shook her head. She wondered what Axe's name really was. She didn't see Jared. She was glad he was gone so it was just the two of them and people would think they were together, a couple, for a little while longer. "Why not? Huh? What's so important you're doing instead?"

Linnea didn't answer. He was getting annoying again. They walked another block. She was going to have to go to the bathroom pretty soon, it was embarrassing she had to go so often. She didn't want to have to do it in the park, like the bums.

Axe saw somebody he knew, some guy and girl. He stopped to talk to them and they huddled together, ignoring her. Linnea walked on ahead, glad to be rid of him, mostly, but a little sorry too. Why couldn't she even have a pretend boyfriend?

She crossed the street and doubled back, and here was Axe walking toward her with his pals. "There you are," he said, like he'd been looking for her, though it was hard to see how he had been. "Let's go. Hop on the party train."

Her first thought was, bathroom. She could use whoever it was's bathroom. But she made a point of looking like she didn't want to go with him. She said, "I dunno," and shifted her weight from one foot to the other. The girl was pretty, with black hair and black-lined eyes and what could have been a little kid's party dress worn over leggings. The guy with her had plugs in his ears, which was always kind of gross, and a ring through his septum, ditto, but the rest of him was sort of normal-looking, a normal, goofy-smiling boy, like maybe somebody had done the piercings while he was asleep and he just woke up that way.

"I don't know," Linnea said again. "I should probably get going." Her phone buzzed again. It would either be Art or her mother. Nobody else called her. She was such a loser.

"Oh come on, Sadie. It's real close to here. This is Sadie. We call her Red. Ha!"

Nobody else thought it was funny either. "Let's go," the black-haired girl said. "This is boring."

"And you could be Black. Ha–ha."

"Hilarious," the black–haired girl said.

Crowds were trying to get past them on the sidewalk. Axe hooked his elbow through Linnea's and steered her around. Linnea just sort of started walking with them. She hadn't decided anything, but maybe you didn't have to. Maybe once in a while you could just *go along* with things and have them work out, come away with the kind of stories you could tell people, make them wish they were you. The next time Art called, she could text him back, say she was with friends.

They straggled along on Haight for another block, then turned onto one of the side streets. Axe had dropped her arm and was up ahead, talking with the boy with the plugged ears. The black–haired girl yawned. She didn't look especially friendly. "I like your dress," Linnea said, because that was something you could always say.

"Yeah?" The girl pulled the skirt out in front of her to see it better. It was yellow, with puffy sleeves and rows of fancy stitching across the bust. She was flat on top, even flatter than Linnea. She looked like a fancy doll come to life and walking around. "These leggings are crawling up my butt," she announced.

Linnea couldn't think how to keep a conversation going from that, so she just trudged along, hoping they weren't going much farther. The houses around her all looked old, in an interesting way, like anyone might live there, musicians or magicians, witch doctors, dancers, anyone who had already found a place in the world. Because weren't you allowed to have that, or at least want it? Somewhere that drew a line around you, a line you could put a name to.

After a minute she tried again. "So, who is this guy we're going to see?"

"Sinbad," the black–haired girl said, unhelpfully. "He'll tell you he's called that because he sins and he's bad. Make sure to laugh."

"Is he, uh . . ." She didn't have a real question in mind besides the one she'd already asked, and so she said, "Cool?"

"Oh yeah. He's kind of older."

"Older, what, twenty?"

"More like, fifty. He's not so bad. You get used to it."

Get used to what? Linnea wondered. She would have liked to ask the girl other questions, like, who was she, and where did she come from, and how did she know Axe, or Sinbad, or anyone else? Was the boy with the plugged ears her boyfriend? What did it feel like to touch all that metal with your hands, your mouth? How did she come by that expression of perfect, sullen boredom? How did you get to be you?

The black-haired girl looked Linnea over, as if it had just occurred to her to be curious about her. "Are you mad about something?"

"Me? No." Her first instinct was always to deny whatever people thought of her.

"Because you act like you are."

"Well I'm not," Linnea said, starting to get annoyed, which wouldn't do her any good because it would prove the other girl right. "I just don't get why everybody's so excited about going to see this guy. Sinbad, that sounds like a cartoon or something."

"It's just a place we can go when we need one." The black-haired girl stopped to pluck at her leggings, grappling with them. "He likes having a lot of kids around. For company."

Linnea kept quiet. She was trying to put together the things she had been told and the things she had not been told, and the things she could see but had chosen not to see until now, like the black-haired girl's seriously dirty feet, the kind of dirt that doesn't come off with just one washing. She guessed she could live that way herself if she had to.

They stopped in front of one of the houses. The front door was up a half-flight of stone steps and Axe rang a buzzer. Then they were inside, climbing up a long stair that led to a landing with more doors. One of these was open and music was playing inside, scratchy old-time low-down music, the kind that made Linnea think of nightclubs and dressed-up women singing into microphones. "Jeez," she said under her breath, because it wasn't exactly Ace Hood or Pitbull or even Chris Brown. But she followed the others, crowding into the space on the other side of the door.

The room was dim, all the window shades pulled down, and there was a smell that reached your nose in different layers, thick and sweet on top and then a hint of stink underneath, like spilled oil. Other people were there, a dozen or more, sitting on a pair of couches, on cushions on the floor. Linnea tried to look at them without staring. Some of them were kids and some of them she couldn't tell. There wasn't enough light and the music was loud enough that it too seemed to get in the way of seeing. Nobody acted like they noticed them. It didn't seem like the kind of place where anybody said hello. Axe and the others found a corner and squatted down. Linnea went looking for the bathroom. There wasn't anyone around she could ask for permission, and anyway by now she really really had to go.

The other rooms were lined up one after another behind the first, so you had to walk through them all. The windows were covered here too, but her eyes were adjusting and the music wasn't quite as loud as she went farther back, though it still made her ears itch. The furniture, beds, tables, chairs, was pushed together in dusty groups, like it was in storage. At the back was a bare-looking kitchen with a slopped-over pot of something on the stove, and next to it a closed door, the bathroom?

Linnea knocked. Nobody answered. She pushed it open, then yelped and shut it again. A man with Jesus-style hair and a beard was reclining in the bathtub, his knees drawn up and poking out of the water.

"Sorry," she said, once she was back in the hall. "I didn't think anybody . . . Sorry."

"That's OK, come on in."

"Is there another bathroom somewhere?"

"Sure, somewhere. Not in this house. Come in, I don't mind."

"No, I'll just wait." She heard him moving around, the water lapping and sloshing.

"You want the place all to yourself? You'll be out there awhile. I just got comfortable."

Linnea clamped her legs together. She had to go so bad, tears started up behind her eyes. Maybe she could wet her pants a little. Why wasn't she a boy? They could always pee in a sink, or anywhere else. She didn't think she could make it back down the stairs and out again to somewhere else. It was one of those stupid things that kept happening to her.

"Oh come on, what are you, pee-shy? I'll throw a towel over my head. I promise I won't look."

"I can't."

"How about, I put my head underwater and hold my breath."

"No."

"It's not that big a deal," he said patiently. "I've seen a lot of girls pee. I could get testimonials from them." She couldn't tell if he was joking, if he said things that were some kind of joke that nobody got but him.

"It's not . . . private."

"Whoa! Private!" There was the sound of the bathwater sloshing. "Private isn't a big priority around here. We aim for more of a communal experience."

He was talking like she'd come here to stay, and she hadn't. "If I could just please use the bathroom for like, please two minutes, I'll go."

"You already have my full and free permission to come in."

"Please," she said again. She could feel the pee starting to slide out of her, a hot trickle.

"You know who this is singing? Billie Holiday. You know Billie?"

The woman's voice wandered around the song, catching on a note, dragging it out into a moan. "No," Linnea said.

"One of the all-time great figures in American music. There's a hole in your education. See, if you knew Billie, I might be more inclined to get out of this tub."

"I'm sorry," Linnea said, her voice tiny. She tried squatting down. "I promise I'll find out about her."

"They used to call her Lady. Because, well, they just did. I'm thinking, that's what I should call you."

More water sounds, like a boat heaving around in a pond. Then the door opened, and the Jesus guy stepped out, a towel around his waist. Linnea guessed he was Sinbad, if names meant anything anymore. She didn't know how old fifty made you, but he looked like something that had been left outside in the rain and forgotten. His hair and beard were greasy gray. He made a little bow and pushed the door open wider. "Don't say I never did anything for you."

She barely got her pants down in time. Ordinarily she wouldn't have been able to pee with some guy standing right outside—she could see the shadow of his feet moving underneath the door—but Linnea didn't care, she was just grateful she hadn't wet herself like some giant baby. The bathroom was cruddy, with water stains in the sink. It was the kind of place her mother would have made her put toilet paper on the seat before she sat down.

She was just finishing up, just starting to pull her clothes back together, when the door opened. "Hey!"

"Relax, Miss Lady. It's OK if I call you that?" He stepped in and closed the door behind him. He was tall and skinny. There were hollowed-out spaces beneath his collarbone and at the bottom of his rib cage. He looked like Axe's skeleton shirt. "Why don't you say yes," he suggested.

"Yes." Her pants were up over her hips but she didn't have them zipped. Her belt buckle flopped to one side. She couldn't get the zipper to work.

He stirred the water in the bathtub with one hand, then pulled the plug at the bottom. "It got cold. See what you did? Now I have to run it again hot. What you got in there?" He meant her backpack.

"Nothing. Clothes and stuff." The music had stopped. Her ears tried to find something else to listen to besides the water draining away, but it was like all other sound was shut off with the record. She tried not to look at the towel he had wrapped around him, or the places the towel didn't cover. It was like the towel was some other kind of joke, one that was directed at her.

She felt the dark wings skimming over her, just beyond the reach of her eyes.

Now he replugged the tub and ran the hot water tap. He said, "Somewhere around here I got these Dead Sea mineral salts. Most excellent. Loosens you right up. Oh well. Maybe next time."

There wasn't room to get past him and out the door, and besides, she knew that he was waiting for her to try and make some kind of move. It was like she was an animal, or maybe they both were. Like the cat killed by the coyote. The cat frozen in place, all its nerves in its skin.

But no. She steadied herself and finished zipping her pants. Funny how much better that made her feel. Like, not a dead cat. She cleared her throat so her voice would come out right, because everything depended on making him listen. And so she would tell him, if not the truth, something closer to the truth than anyone else had heard. "You know," she began, just as he turned off the hot water and swept his arm across it in a gesture of invitation, get in, get in, "the last time I was stuck in a bathroom with some guy, I helped him shoot two people."

EIGHT

Do not speak, unless it improves a silence.

They were all looking at her. Christie wished she could risk a cleansing breath to steady herself, but they'd only think she was that much weirder. "I guess we should get started."

There was an industrious noise of paper sliding across the polished wood table. They were opening folders, straightening and shuffling, readying their yellow legal pads. Now what? Christie hesitated a moment too long and the attorney, Mr. Kirn, jumped in. No, not jumped; a smooth acceleration, born of his long experience with meetings, depositions, negotiations, pleadings. "You'll find the organizing documents in your folders. The name availability forms, the articles of incorporation, some of the tax requirements pertaining to 501(c)s. All of these will need to be filed with the secretary of state or the other state offices, or with the IRS."

Mr. Kirn was Mrs. Foster's attorney. He was in charge of the legalities necessary to setting up a nonprofit organization, or rather, a foundation, which was sort of the same thing but not entirely. The differences had been explained to her often enough that now Christie only nodded and went along dumbly with whatever it was being said. Today's assembled documents were meant to impress upon everyone the weighty responsibilities of such an undertaking, as well as make Christie feel completely unequal to the task at hand.

They were meeting in the conference room of Mr. Kirn's San Rafael office, which occupied a suite in a commercial park tucked in along the freeway frontage. The wall of windows looked out to the carefully edited greenbelt with its clipped grass and staked, half-grown trees, the unnatural nature that accompanied high-end California development. Also in attendance were: Mr. Alvarez, an investment officer from Mrs. Foster's bank. Mrs. Foster's aggrieved daughter, or one of them, Leslie Hart. Mr. Kirn's secretary, who had not been introduced. And the only person who Christie imagined was not entirely hostile to her, a youngish man from county social services. He had a furry chin and wore a T-shirt under his sport coat, and the lettering on the T-shirt spelled out, improbably, STAIN. She had forgotten his name but that was all right since he had told everyone to call him Scottie.

"Thank you," Christie said to Mr. Kirn, because if she didn't step up they would all ignore her and decide among themselves what ought to be done or not done. Which would be a relief, but also humiliating. "I expect once we've had a chance to look at these, we might have some questions for you."

Bluffing. She could read them for a week and not understand the first thing about them. Leslie Hart, the daughter, who was visibly unhappy about the disbursement of her and her sister's inheritance, launched her first complaint. "I don't understand, do we have an agenda here? An actual written agenda? I've yet to see one."

Mr. Kirn pointed out that there was no agenda because they did not constitute a board, or an executive committee, or any other body that operated under bylaws requiring agendas, and in fact, no bylaws had yet been set forth.

Then what exactly were they here for, Leslie Hart wanted to know, unwilling to be placated. Mr. Kirn said that this was simply an initial meeting of some of the interested parties. Covering some of the basics. Brainstorming.

"Ms. Schuyler," he said, indicating Christie, "has been in on the planning from the beginning, and is Mrs. Foster's choice for executive director." He said it with a straight face, and Christie imagined him using the same pleasant tone to announce that someone's entire estate had been left to their pet dog.

"Mr. Alvarez will have initial figures for us. He and I have come up with some suggested organizational steps. Mrs. Hart is here to represent the family's interests. And Mr.—"

"Scottie." A cheerful wave from his end of the table. Christie supposed that in his line of work, overcasual was the business norm.

"Yes. Has been kind enough to come and share some of his hands-on experience in working with disadvantaged populations."

Leslie Hart said, "Is that what this is all about? Disadvantaged populations? Because you can pour all the money you want into people like that, it never changes anything." She was the San Diego daughter. Christie knew, from Mrs. Foster, that she was somewhere in her fifties, with three expensive children of her own and a husband who worked in commercial real estate. She had gotten herself up in such sleek and polished fashion, she was so severely well groomed in her black-and-white suiting, that she looked nearly military.

Scottie spoke up then. "That's really not true. You do the right interventions, you make an impact. Give people better access to housing, health services, and job training, you get results you can measure. Reduced homelessness. Fewer sick kids. Less unemployment. You know, your basic benefits to society."

The others looked at him as if he was one of those talking babies in a commercial.

"I think," Christie said after a pause, "I'd like to hear what Mr. Alvarez has prepared."

Mr. Alvarez spent a long time clearing his throat. He was tall and stooped and dignified, with a waxy bald head and pink eyelids. He looked as if he'd been the Fosters' investment adviser since they were all in the sixth grade together. His voice rumbled and mumbled. He made reference to the necessity of a business plan, the formation of committees: executive, financial, fund-raising, and so forth. Provisions for audit and for annual reviews. The description of staff positions, the hiring and compensation of staff. He was so thorough and droning, that it would have been easy to miss the actual numbers: an initial endowment of five million dollars, with the possibility of further funding in the form of a bequest.

Meaning Mrs. Foster would put the Foundation in her will for further gobsmacking amounts. Christie couldn't bring herself to look at Leslie Hart. No wonder she was furious. Even though Mrs. Foster had said that both her daughters would be well provided for, would have no lack or cause for ill will. "That doesn't mean they won't kick up a fuss," Mrs. Foster had said cheerfully. "Just that they ought to be ashamed of themselves."

Well, they weren't. People seldom were, in Christie's experience. She forced her attention back to Mr. Alvarez, who was explaining that the actual operations budget for the Foundation would be the investment income from the endowment, minus expenses.

Christie stopped herself from saying, "Of course." She had been saying that too much lately, as a way of trying to sound knowledgeable.

Mr. Alvarez finished up with some projected investment income figures, based on this or that strategy, market condition, et cetera. Of course, of course. The whole enterprise still felt preposterous to her: that there should exist such enormous, free-floating sums of money in the world, and that they should in any way intersect with her own life. She studied Mr. Alvarez's graphs and charts, hoping to untangle the snarl of numbers.

It took her a moment to realize that Mr. Alvarez had stopped speaking, the same way you only gradually realized that a fan or a motor had shut off. "Thank you," Christie said belatedly. "This is all very helpful." She actually had come with a few notes of her own. She consulted her scribbled list, willing it to expand into something more eloquent. "I was hoping we might come up with a mission statement today."

Mr. Kirn's secretary was transcribing the meeting. From across the table, Christie could read, upside down, MISSION STATEMENT. It looked admirably straightforward and clear. It seemed a shame to scribble it over with everybody's opinions.

"Mission statement?" Leslie Hart echoed. Her pulled-back hair was so tight it drew her eyelids up at the corners. It was uncomfortable to look at, like plastic surgery gone wrong.

"For instance, the Robert Wood Johnson Foundation, dedicated to 'improve the health and health care of all Americans.'" Christie paused.

"Or," Scottie said, "the MacArthur Foundation, you know, 'building a more just, verdant, and peaceful world.' The kind of groups who support NPR. National Public Radio," he added, when Leslie Hart made another of her faces. "Maybe you've heard of it."

Christie wasn't so sure now that she wanted Scottie as her ally. He could shoot off his mouth as much as he liked, and she would be the one to suffer the consequences. She turned to Leslie Hart and said, in her most coaxing voice, "It's really just a statement of purpose. There's also the Bill and Melinda Gates Foundation, which is—" She consulted her notes. "'Dedicated to bringing innovations in health, development, and learning to the global community.'" Leslie didn't answer, only gave Christie a sideways look from her sideways eyes.

Once more Christie had let a silence linger, and the helpful Mr. Kirn filled it. "Perhaps you could give us a clearer idea of Mrs. Foster's intentions."

"She is calling her foundation 'The Humanity Project.'"

"If that name is available," said Mr. Kirn.

"Who else would want it?" Leslie Hart put in.

"And the aim of the Foundation, broadly defined, is to benefit humanity. I know, it needs considerable narrowing down. A lot more specifics. But it's a good, generous impulse." *The greatest effort is not concerned with results.*

"You just try talking to her," Leslie Hart said, appealing to Mr. Kirn and Mr. Alvarez, the grown-up powers. "All you get is this muddled, idealistic blather. And she's ruining her house with a bunch of feral cats."

"These days," Scottie said, "the preferred name is 'community cats.'"

Leslie Hart ignored this. "And now she wants to save the world. But from what I have no idea."

"From us," Scottie said. "We need to be saved from ourselves. I mean, most any problem in the world today, except, I don't know, sunspots or the decay of the earth's orbit, we caused it." Argument was making him animated. He raised his arms and his jacket opened enough to show that his shirt actually read SUSTAINA. Sustainable something? Growth? Farming?

"Incredible," Leslie said, as if providing commentary to an audience who agreed with her.

"I believe," Christie said, trying to put the unsettling notion of orbit decay out of her mind, "that Mrs. Foster would like to concentrate the efforts of the Foundation on local causes, at least at first." She managed another look at the secretary's notes. All she'd added was the word "Humanity," followed by a question mark.

Scottie said, "Five million. I can tell you exactly where to spend it around here. If you need ideas."

Mr. Alvarez swam to the surface of the discussion from the weedy depths where he had been dozing. "Five million is the endowment. The available funds will be, as I've said, dependent on investment results."

"Most people have no clue. They don't know how hard it can be for an immigrant family, or the disabled, or the unemployed, to put food on the table. Speaking of tables? With the money you could get for this one, I bet I could feed a dozen of my clients for a month."

Everyone took the opportunity to contemplate the conference table, its solidity, its fine-grained wood and shining depths. Christie raised her eyes and met Mr. Kirn's gaze. He looked unexpectedly sympathetic, as if the two of them, he and Christie, were in agreement about both the virtues and the drawbacks of young, passionate advocates. Whose idea had it been to include Scottie? She couldn't remember. It was possible that

Mr. Kirn had told his secretary to find them a social worker, and she had ordered one by phone.

"And when I think about the money some people spend on, you name it. Tennis shoes. Cell phones," Scottie began, but Leslie Hart cut him off.

"Funny how tennis shoes and cell phones are exactly what you see so-called poor people spending money for."

"So-called poor? How about if I said, sports cars and private schools?"

"How about, tattoos and crack cocaine?"

"You seem to be equating poverty and crime."

"I didn't say that, but draw your own conclusions."

The two of them were egging each other on into an entirely pointless fight. Christie tried to reach the calming center of herself and failed. They were both being jerks and you'd have to be the Dalai Lama himself to deal with them. She said, "I don't think there's any point in perpetuating stereotypes. I'd like to think that 'humanity' is the thing we all have in common. I'm sure that's why Mrs. Foster chose the word."

Leslie looked unhappy, in a complicated way, at the mention of her mother. Scottie said, "Sorry. Nothing personal." He subsided, but with an air of poorer-than-thou piety. Christie had a sudden intuition that he had been raised in a wealthy home, that he sat around his parents' own prosperous dinner table, berating them. And Leslie Hart? She was probably old enough to be his exasperated parent.

Moving on. "I've been doing some reading up on foundations." And she had, she had. "There are a couple of ways to proceed. You can function as an umbrella organization, making grants available to projects other people propose. You can run your own initiatives. Or you could do a combination of both."

Mr. Kirn dipped his head, a discreet nod. Somehow, she had won him over. Was it possible that she was making sense? Heartened, she looked at her list again. "That is a structural question, and it can be addressed somewhere down the line by the eventual board of directors."

"And who will they be?" Leslie Hart asked. "I mean, you can talk all you want about humanity, or giving people money for new, improved smart phones"—she wasn't one to let a good attack go to waste—"but it's money my father worked hard for. I don't want to see it handled carelessly."

Scottie asked, blandly, just how Mr. Foster had earned his millions, and Leslie Hart said that was none of his business. This time Mr. Kirn and Christie took care to avoid each other's eyes. There had been some inherited family money, then Mr. Foster had added to it, made his own fortune as an executive in one of the giant pharmaceutical firms and a substantial holder of its stock. It was a firm whose name was often in the news for its aggressive promotion of medications that were later found to have distressing side effects, like the patient dropping dead.

The meeting went on for almost another hour, and never got much better. Leslie, who was angry at her mother, had to settle for being angry at Scottie. Scottie kept on being smug. Mr. Alvarez slept. Christie asked herself what she'd expected. She knew well enough that nothing ever got decided by committee.

Finally Mr. Kirn thanked everyone for coming. It was a suitably anticlimactic finish. Christie waited until the others had left the conference room. She was depressed, and her nerve endings felt shredded, and the last thing she wanted was to have a lot of intense follow-up conversations in the elevator or the parking lot or, God forbid, in the ladies' room with Leslie Hart. But she hadn't reckoned on Mr. Kirn, who had stationed himself in the hallway. "If you have a moment," he said, holding open a door.

"Of course," Christie said, drooping but polite, and she followed him into what must have been Mr. Kirn's private office. There was a lot of dazzling window glass here also, and some sleek, angular modern furniture that Scottie would have sized up and sold off to fund the county's needy.

"Please," Mr. Kirn said, indicating a chair where she should sit. It was more comfortable than it looked. "That didn't go too badly in there."

"Really?" She was too tired to keep up mannerly pretense. "I thought it was a street brawl."

"It could have been worse. And you kept everybody in line."

"Barely. Thanks." She didn't necessarily believe him, but she was grateful for even insincere compliments by now. "We didn't really accomplish anything." She wondered what he wanted. Surely it wasn't worth any portion of his billable hours to give her a pep talk.

"You accomplished an initial organizational meeting." Mr. Kirn looked as fresh and pressed as he had an hour ago, and Christie had to remind herself that he was used to adversarial proceedings, probably even enjoyed them, the way some people enjoy boxing matches. He was younger than she'd first taken him for, certainly closer to her age than to Mr. Alvarez's. All his prosperous trappings had misled her, even as they put him in a much different world than hers. It depressed her to realize that money was such a large part of how she regarded people. It depressed her to think how much she had disliked nearly everyone in the room.

"Humanity," Mr. Kirn said, in a musing tone. "We didn't get around to a good working definition, did we?"

"No. Well, mankind. Human-ness. People. I expect Mrs. Foster means it in the sense of what's positive and aspirational about people. Altruistic." She wished he'd get to his point. She wanted to go home and take a long, soaking bath. She was often too critical. She was often too trusting. How did you manage this human thing anyway?

"Conscience-driven," Mr. Kirn suggested. "We're not supposed to act like animals, we know better."

There was some argument you might make to this, but Christie couldn't sort it out. She said, "Maybe money doesn't help anyone. Make any difference."

"Oh, I think you'll find it's going to make quite a lot of difference. To a lot of people." Mr. Kirn seemed to meditate pleasantly on the prospect. "I think you're going to have to put Leslie Hart on your board of directors," Mr. Kirn said, switching back to all-business mode. "Otherwise she might be inclined to try some sort of legal maneuver to keep her mother from endowing the Foundation."

"She could do that?"

"She could try. She could create enough obstacles to make sure the

Foundation never gets off the ground. And I suppose she still might, no matter what you do. Is it true what she was saying, about the cats?"

"There are several cats," said Christie faintly, thinking of them.

"She could raise questions about her mother's mental fitness. She could argue that you've manipulated her so as to benefit yourself financially."

Christie gaped. "None of this was my idea. I'm a *nurse*."

"I understand."

What, exactly, did he think he understood? "The whole thing just sort of *landed* on me. She had to talk me into it, I thought I'd be doing her a favor. And so far it's all been a real—"

She stopped herself from saying "pain in the ass," although that was what she meant, and shook her head.

"I believe you," Mr. Kirn told her, and she wanted to believe him, even though nothing that came out of his mouth seemed entirely believable, or at least entirely uncalculated. "But I really would advise you to try and head off trouble by giving Mrs. Hart some oversight."

Conquer the miser with generosity.

"Won't she just try to obstruct everything?"

"She'd only be one voice. One vote. And if she agrees to be on the board, she can't really object to the Foundation itself."

Christie was silent, thinking unhappy thoughts. It was true that the Foundation, and everything connected to it, had been nothing but a source of aggravation so far. But she had also tried on the idea of being a part of such an enterprise, which could, at least potentially, do good in the world. Fill in the hole of her own deficiencies when it came to the question of humanness. Put Mrs. Foster's money where her own mouth was. There was something wearying about going over your own moral inventory again and again, something her energetic midwestern parents would have called "navel-gazing." Didn't she want to actually accomplish something? She did. And by now she didn't quite want to give up on the prospect.

She raised her head. "I wouldn't have to have Scottie, would I?"

"Oh no. You'll want someone who's used to evaluating grants and familiar with community programs, but we'll find somebody with better table manners." There was a joke in there and he relished it. "You'll also want someone in charge of fund-raising, and a publicity director. An accountant with the kind of tax specialities a foundation requires. Depending on the size of your staff, maybe an office manager. Anyway, all those people would be paid employees. Not the board."

"So who else would be on the board?" She wasn't even sure what a board did. She was that ignorant.

"Anybody who's prominent in business or philanthropy. Or just prominent. Anybody who could raise your profile and give you instant respectability."

"Like, Bono."

She meant it as a joke, but Mr. Kirn seemed to consider it. He said, "Matt Damon has a foundation dedicated to improving global water resources. Did you know that?"

She didn't. She assumed that Matt Damon wasn't available any more than Bono was. She was really tired. She hoped that Mr. Kirn wouldn't keep making jokes. And in fact, when she asked him who else he had in mind for the board, and he smiled and said, "Me," at first she thought he was.

NINE

The dog wasn't eating. He'd stand at his food bowl, sniff, and walk away, back to his spot in front of the fan. It had come on gradually and now there was no way not to notice. Sometimes Sean or Conner coaxed him with lunch meat or hot dogs, and then he might get through a few mouthfuls of his ration before he lost interest.

His ribs were starting to show through his skin, moving up and down as he slept.

"It's the heat," Sean said, though neither of them believed it. They didn't want to think about what it was instead.

"I should take him in to the vet," Conner said. Both of them were watching the dog sleep, although there wasn't anything to see.

Sean said maybe they should wait a little, maybe he'd come around on his own. He was thinking that you never knew how much a thing like that was going to end up costing.

"I should at least call."

"Go ahead, see what they tell you. Sure."

How could he say anything else? But the vet would tell them to bring the dog in, and he'd want to do blood tests, X-rays, everything in the world. They didn't have that kind of money, and Conner knew they didn't have it, and that was one more thing there was no point in saying.

He'd always been Conner's dog from the time he was a pup, a little black fur ball tripping over his own ears. Not the smartest dog in the world. Just your basic dumb, lovable model. It killed Sean to watch his son steeling himself against one more shitty event. "Hey," Sean said to distract him. "Did you get me that stuff?"

"Yeah, I did." Conner got up and went into the kitchen, came back with a plastic bag. Sean opened it and fished out some bandage-shaped items in plastic wrappers.

"What am I supposed to do, slap one of these things on my ass?"

"If that's where it hurts."

"Funny," Sean said. He shifted positions on the couch, hauling himself up by the elbows so he could reach his hip and decorate it. "Like this?" It was just a square of sticky-sided gauze. "It smells like Vicks VapoRub."

"It's got camphor and menthol and soothing stuff. Just try it, OK?"

Sean let himself grumble a little more about it. Conner kept wanting him to use different kinds of herbal crap instead of his pills. Everybody thought the pills were a bad idea, but they didn't have any better ones. What did they know? Most days, he felt like this old Mickey Mouse cartoon, where Mickey was playing music on a xylophone made of bones. They were over in cartoon Africa, trying not to get eaten by cartoon cannibals. Mickey used two other bones to play the xylophone, banging out a tuneful melody. That was him now. A symphony of bone music.

The problem with pain was that nobody else could see it. Nobody had to believe you if you said it was bad, or worse, or enough to pop your eyeballs out of your skull.

And everybody got tired of your pissing and moaning, most of all you. He guessed he'd have to suck it up and at least pretend the patches helped, though he'd taken some Percocet earlier, before Conner got home and could give him a hard time about it. He sagged into the couch again to wait it out. The dog woke, raised his head, panting, then lay back down to sleep.

They were back to living in their old house again, though in peculiar, half-assed circumstances. The duplex hadn't worked out for long. The landlord didn't want to pay them for the work they'd done, and since none of what they'd agreed to was in writing, the guy was free to jerk them around as much as he wanted, and he had. Sean and Conner had stuck it out for two months, long enough not to pay any bills, and finally the landlord showed up with the sheriff and that was that.

He'd never had the sheriff call on him before. He'd done plenty of things that were illegal, sure, but up until now, he'd never felt like a criminal.

Then they'd moved their furniture and boxes into Floyd's garage and taken up residence in a converted motel in Santa Rosa. It was nothing either of them could stand for long, a single room with a couple of beds and a kitchenette. The rug had a pattern that looked like paint drips, and there were heavy plastic window curtains, and a smell of drains. The toilet sweated. It was exactly the kind of place that showed up on the news, where people got into stupid arguments and shot each other.

Then one night Conner came home and said, Funniest thing. Nobody was living in their house. It was just sitting there.

Sean drove past it. Not even a For Sale sign in the yard, nothing. The grass was a straggly untrimmed yellow. The blinds across the front windows were closed. Dead house. He guessed the banks had gobbled up so much property, they were having trouble digesting it all.

They went back later that evening. Not the middle of the night, when somebody might have called 911 on them, but dinnertime. Pulling up in the drive all casual, like they owned the place. Ha-ha. There was a heavy-duty padlock contraption on the front door, but they hadn't bothered to change the locks in back. There were some advantages to a house that wasn't worth that much to anyone.

"I wish we'd cleaned better," Sean said, as he kicked wadded paper trash and stray coat hangers out of the way. The place made him nervous. He felt like a ghost, coming back to haunt it.

"Dad? The water's turned off."

Sean flipped a light switch. No power either.

But a buddy of his had a homemade valve key you could use on the water shut-off. The next day Sean found the valve head out on the street and directed Conner to fit the key and work it back and forth until the valve gave and water shuddered through the pipes.

The power was trickier and Sean handled that himself, in case he got electrifried. You had to get the cover off the meter and mess with the plugs and receptors, strip the hot wires and reconnect them to the load. "Watch," he told Conner. "You'll either learn how to do this, or how not to do it."

He got a little anxious, hoping he wasn't going to get knocked on his ass with his hair on fire, but he guessed he was still good for something, because the meter clicked and started turning and now the juice was on, courtesy of Pacific Gas and Electric. If he was a criminal now, he might as well take full advantage.

They left the front door padlocked and went in and out the back. Moved some furniture in, just what they could get by with. Didn't unpack more than they needed. They were camping out, but at least it was free. They parked the truck on the street so it could have been anybody's. The neighbors were people who had their own problems and didn't ask questions. Sooner or later they'd run out of luck all over again, but by now they'd gotten used to making it up as they went along.

It was a good thing he'd had a son, not a daughter. You couldn't expect a girl to put up with rough living. A boy, it just taught him some of the hard things he'd need to get by.

"Conner?"

But Conner had gone to bed. Or maybe he'd left for work already. It was not quite dawn, and once more he'd woken up without being aware he'd fallen asleep. The television was on, turned down low, a gray program that might have been a documentary, some gray kind of history. His hip was on fire and his backbone was saying snap, crackle, and pop. He got himself to the bathroom and took two more Percocet from the bottle he kept behind the heating duct. He lay back down, slept some more, and when he woke up it was bright day with his mouth full of paste and the television turned off and a note on the kitchen counter saying that Conner had taken the dog to the vet.

Back when he'd only thought he had bad luck, he'd tried to stay positive. Ride it out, wait for things to turn around. Either he was stupid then or he was even stupider now, because all evidence and history to the contrary, a part of him still wanted to believe he wasn't entirely beat down and someday he could look the world in the eye again. But first there were some holes in his head that needed filling.

He remembered more about that night than he let on. He just hadn't known all that much to start with. *Pretty Lady, 38.* The whole stupid conversation was right there on his computer where he'd left it. By the time he was in any shape to sit at a desk again, she was long gone from Craigslist.

He invested in a few nights of drinking at Ted's, not that he expected her to show up there, and she hadn't. He found the bartender who thought he remembered her, or somebody like her. Heck, he saw a lot of girls. "Who's she, the one that got away?"

And Sean said it was something like that.

Then there was the wreck, and here his brain really didn't have much to contribute. It was possible that not remembering was a very good thing. He was sure he hadn't been driving, and lucky for him the police agreed, and after they asked him the same questions twenty different times, they satisfied themselves he hadn't been in Tahoe stealing cars. By then he was in sad enough shape that they quit pestering him.

They must have figured him for the kind of dumbshit that went joyriding with strange tail in the hopes of getting some, and they were right.

What about her? She'd either walked off unhurt, or she'd been able to limp away from the scene, or else she'd teleported to her spaceship and jetted back to her home planet.

He didn't think there was a *why* to any of it, beyond his own supreme idiocy. But maybe he could come up with a *what*, or a *who*.

The stolen car belonged to a guy in Nevada City. It took him a long time to get even that far, using the police reports to find out the license plate, telling them he needed it for insurance he didn't have. Then there was an actual insurance company to wrestle with, bluffing his way through one or another claims person, pretending he was going to sue, and maybe he should, why not. Sue somebody for having such an easily wrecked, easily stolen car. Almost by mistake, they sent him a name. A name wasn't as much as you wanted it to be, because then he had to come up with the rest of it. The only computer he could use was at the library, and it was a pile of work, but really, what else did he have to do these days?

Finally he found a work address, a place called Ecoland Systems, whatever that meant, and a phone number to go along with it. The guy who owned the cheap-ass car was called Wayne Horchow. Somehow that fit, though he couldn't have said why. For the last five days Sean had walked around with this information written on a card in his wallet, and the card was either a grenade or a dud, since people didn't necessarily know the person who stole their car, in fact more often than not they didn't. So Wayne might not have had anything to do with Miss Crazypants, and that was what had kept him from calling until now, in case it went nowhere and he was back to square zero and his own stupid life.

But today, stuck in the house without even the dog to talk to, and not wanting to think about why the dog wasn't there, he told himself to suck it up. He punched out the number, and asked the girl who answered for Mr. Horchow.

"Hi, Mr. Horchow? You don't know me, but—" I know your car? He hadn't thought this through very well. "I got your name from Allstate."

"Allstate? What do you want now?" Horchow sounded on the young side, and a little pissed-off. He drove a crap car, or used to, because he was just starting out. And now his rates were going up. Life was hard.

"I'm not Allstate. I'm not selling anything. I'm calling about your car, the one that was stolen."

"I only had the one car." Sounds of paper shuffling. A busy man, Wayne Horchow. "Who is this?"

"I was in your car when it crashed."

The paper noise stopped.

"But I didn't steal it or anything. I wasn't driving. I was with this girl, this woman, named Laurie." He waited a beat. "You know her?"

"No. Who is this?"

"She might have called herself something else."

"If you're the one who wrecked my car, I sure hope you're calling from jail."

"I didn't wreck it. She did."

"That's nice to know. I hope the two of you will be very happy together. I have to get back to work now."

"Hey Wayne? You ever go on Craigslist? Ever meet girls that way?"

For a moment he thought Wayne Horchow might have hung up. When he spoke, his voice was flatter, more cautious. "Why do you ask?"

"Because that's how I met her, Craigslist. Well, in a bar."

"Huh."

"Sort of pretty. Dogs wouldn't bark at her. She was drinking margaritas. Kind of a lot of them. That ring any bells?"

"I never said I knew any girl."

"But you know, if you did, Wayne, and if for some reason she helped herself to your car, one way to look at things is, I took it in the shorts for you. I mean, it was a pretty bad wreck, it left me real crippled up. It could of been you. You know what I'm saying?"

Another silence. Then Wayne said, "Are you in town here?"

"Nope. Sonoma."

"I told the police I didn't know who stole the car. I told my wife I was in Tahoe for a work thing, casino night."

That's my story and I'm sticking to it. "Uh-huh," Sean said, neutral, encouraging.

"Sometimes there's situations, circumstances, where you might not be in a position to keep track of your car keys. Your wallet. You understand what I'm saying?"

"Perfectly."

"She didn't call herself Laurie. She was Sandy."

"Pretty safe bet neither of those is her real name. Look, I'm just trying to figure out what happened to me, the accident and all. There's stuff I don't remember. She say much about herself? Where she was from, where she was going?"

Wayne's voice dropped. Nosy coworkers, maybe. "She wore this weird coat. It looked like aluminum foil."

"That's our girl. She say anything about Ohio, being from Ohio?"

"She might have. Look, friend." Wayne Horchow was trying to whisper, a hoarse sound. "There's things I don't remember either. It was that kind of a night. Let's just leave it at that. There was some goings-on I'm not about to tell anybody, especially not some strange dude on the other end of a phone. She kept saying she wanted to know what it felt like—"

"—to do the worst thing you could ever do." It was like a ladder of light opening up in his memory, and he climbed right to the top.

"Don't call here again," Horchow said, and hung up.

On Sean's good days he could just about do without his crutches and ride a bicycle, and today wasn't a good day but he got Conner's bike out of the back room and labored and cussed his way to the library. There was supposed to be a time limit on the computer, but the librarians felt sorry for him and let him sit as long as he wanted. For the rest of the afternoon, he went on Craigslist sites as far north as Vancouver and as far south as San Diego, then east to Austin, Las Vegas, Denver. And just for the hell of it, a few in Ohio.

Reading the personals was heavy going. They convinced you that the world was a failed, lonely, and loveless place, and only through dumb luck did men and women pair off for long enough to keep the species going. She might have been any of them.

She was all of them and none of them. In the end he logged on and left the same message on as many of the Missed Connections boards as he could find, an all-points bulletin, a warning beacon:

> Hey Pretty Lady 38,
>> What's the worst thing you ever did?
>> Well you almost did it to me.
>>> S. in Sonoma

The dog had a mass in his abdomen that the vet could feel, but without an X-ray, and probably surgery, he couldn't tell very much.

"What does that mean, a mass?" Sean asked.

"A growth."

"You mean, cancer?"

"He didn't say that."

But it felt too simpleminded and hopeful to think of it as anything else, and then let yourself be ambushed by bad news. The dog had been given what the vet called "supportive care," and that was a shot of B_{12} to stimulate his appetite, and antacids, and it had cost almost a hundred dollars. The dog had perked up a little and eaten his dinner. He'd shoved his head beneath their hands to get his ears scratched, and wagged his lumpy tail, and then went to lie down in front of the fan.

"So, if he has an operation, will that get rid of it?"

Conner said that the vet wouldn't know anything without more tests. "Dad? What if I called Mom?"

"No."

"He was her dog too."

"I don't think this is something we should bother your mother about."

"It's not like I'd be asking her for money for us. It's for Bojangles. And I'd pay her back."

"You know how much tests and operations and shit like that costs? You think your mother's rich? She's not."

Conner's face had a blurred, miserable expression, a kid's expression.

Working outside had tanned his face and neck and arms deep brown. He was roofing again this week, for the same bandit he'd worked for earlier in the summer, but this time all the way out in Yountville, where somebody still had money. He'd cut his hair short and that was something else to get used to. It made him look like a young convict. He said, "Bo's only nine years old."

Sean said, "Nine isn't the same for dogs as for people."

"I can talk to the vet some more, find out how much everything would cost."

"Con, we could spend all kinds of money we don't even have, and it still might not fix him. That's what the vet said, right?"

"So when you got hurt, we shouldn't have spent any money on you."

"That's different."

"Why, because you're not a dog?"

"Basically, yes."

"That's bullshit."

Conner so seldom swore, it took Sean a moment to register. "You need to calm down," he said, in the Dad voice he didn't use that often. "Look, let's think about this. He might start feeling better. He could go on for a long time, just the way he is."

"He's in pain."

"You don't know that."

"Why are you being like this? Don't say, 'Like what.' Like you don't care about him."

Because they couldn't afford to care about him, Sean wanted to say. Because the ailing dog was one more thing that made him feel low and worthless. Instead he tried again for Dad, the voice of serious, grown-up wisdom, as if he had some to pass around. "I don't want you to get your hopes up, he's a pretty old dog. He might be a pretty sick dog. It might be one of those things. Of course we'll try to keep him happy. Comfortable. Whatever he needs." He liked the sound of it coming out of his mouth. The sad reasonableness of it all.

Conner looked at him. "What," Sean said.

"Nothing."

"I'm sorry. Dogs never live long enough. It sucks."

Conner knelt down next to the dog and scratched him under the chin until he stretched his front and back legs out in pleasure.

They didn't talk anymore about the dog. Neither talking or not talking felt right. Conner left early and came back late. Sean spent most of his time calling to see if any of the disability claims he'd filed, with the state, with Social Security, were going to come through. Mail still showed up in the mailbox for them here, mostly from the hospital in Ukiah that was never going to get its money. The world was one big goddamn banana peel, waiting for you to slip on it.

Two more days went by and Conner was still giving him the silent treatment. What did he want him to do, rob a bank? The dog slept and slept. He got up to lap water or stand out in the yard, his nose in the wind. "Hey old dude, come here," Sean told him, rubbing his soft ears. "You want some hamburger, huh? You eat some hamburger if I cook it?" The dog rested his chin on the edge of the couch and sighed.

The next morning when he woke up, the dog was gone, and Conner too, and no note this time. Conner wasn't answering his phone. Sean stood in the center of Conner's room: a mattress on the floor, piles of clothes. He couldn't tell if Conner had taken anything with him. He had a sick, hollow feeling that Conner might have gone for good, just given up on him. Then he told himself that was stupid, stupid to even think about. He was the best kid in the world, he didn't pull stunts like that.

But what if he had? It wasn't like anybody would blame him.

He spent the rest of the day on the couch, too low to get up and do anything. This would be his life from now on, lying around waiting for the next kick in the head. He smoked the last bit of pot in the house and took one of his last Oxys and fell into a heavy sleep. He woke just before dark and heard the truck pull up on the street outside, and Conner walking around to the back door.

The first thing Sean could think to say was, "Where's Bo?"

"At the vet's. He'll be there overnight so they can watch him. They operated on him and took out this thing on his spleen. They don't know what it is yet."

"Jesus Christ, Con."

"He can probably come home tomorrow."

He'd just woken up and his head wasn't on right yet. "Tomorrow, huh?"

"I didn't tell you ahead of time because I knew you'd get all worked up."

"I'm not . . . what did you . . ."

"You don't have to worry about the money," Conner said, opening the refrigerator. The refrigerator wasn't the one they used to have. Nothing was the same as they used to have. This one cycled on and off every fifteen minutes with a lot of shuddering racket.

Sean said, "There's nothing in there. No food. Not a goddamn . . . Nothing."

Conner shut the refrigerator. "I can go to the Lucky. What do you want me to get?"

"Did you call your mother? Did you call and ask her for money?"

"Just leave it, Dad."

"I'm not the dog, buddy. Don't be giving me orders."

He was in between Conner and the door and he braced himself to stand his ground or take a punch, he was that kind of mad, a red film over his eyes, but he was too slow and clumsy and Conner was past him before he knew it. "Why don't you just take another pill," Conner said, from the other side of the door.

"Get back in here," Sean hollered after him. "I'm not through with you, pal, we're just getting started."

The truck started up and the noise of it rolled away down the street.

He wanted to haul off and break something, but everything here was already broken. His chest hurt from the hollering. The air in his lungs was heavy, and when he tried to breathe, a dragged-out noise, *huuuhhh*, came out of him. He had to sit down before he had a damn heart attack. He found his phone in between two couch cushions.

Number number number. It made him furious that he couldn't find it anywhere. Finally he thought to try the layers of folded papers in his wallet.

The phone rang for a long time, so that when his ex-wife answered, he was already in the middle of the conversation he'd been having. "Whad he tell you, huh? Whad he tell you?"

"Who is this?"

"I will beat his teen ass! You don't believe me, you hide in the house and watch!"

"Sean? What in the world?"

"He call you with some big boo-hoo story?"

"Who, Conner? What happened to Conner, is he all right?"

"He's fine." A small edge of possibility, how he might have really screwed up, inserted itself into his brain. "He's real fine."

"What are you talking about? Put Conner on."

"He's not here. It's nothing. Forget it."

"Sean."

He'd screwed up. It was nothing new. "You'd better tell me what's going on," his ex-wife said. "Are you drunk? You sound drunk."

"I am not. Drunk. Look, would you do something for me? Just this one thing? Call Con. Tell him I didn't mean it."

"Didn't mean what?"

"About the dog."

"About what? You're mumbling."

"The dog's real sick."

"Oh no, that's so sad. What's the matter with him, what happened?"

There was a rising wail to her questions that was beginning to hurt his ears. "He had an operation, he had a thing on his, this thing they took out. I don't know if he's gonna be OK or not."

"Oh, poor Bojangles. Oh, poor poor boy."

"Yeah." Sean felt himself giving way, giving out, as if a string holding his body together had been cut. The house was dark and walls he didn't expect turned solid, bruising him. He found the bedroom doorframe and fell onto the bed.

"Sean? Why were you yelling about Conner? What's going on?"

"I wish you wouldn't ask so many questions."

"What? I can't hear you. I'm going to hang up and call Conner."

"Wait, don't. Sheila? I'm sorry."

A little silence that might have been skeptical, but when she spoke, her voice had lost some of its anxious keening. "Sorry for what?"

"I dunno. Everything." His skeleton lit up with pain. He was an anatomy lesson in neon.

"What are you mad at Conner for?"

"Don't want to talk about it."

"He's almost grown up. You can't start hollering about beating on him. Oh yes you were. You called me just so I could hear you doing it. What a crummy stunt."

"Ah. Jesus. Crap."

"Sean?"

He kept cursing, softly now, so that she couldn't tell he was crying. Everything he'd had was ruined, shamed, lost, and he was a busted-up fool, and there was no end to the wrongness of the world. He put the phone down and let the pain roll through him. He hadn't cried since he was a kid, and he'd forgotten how.

He'd forgotten also that sooner or later, you stop crying. The phone kept making a small, piping noise, and after he'd calmed himself, he picked it up. "Sean, honey, are you still there?"

"Yeah. What."

"I'm sorry you're so unhappy."

Maybe she was. She used to have his back and he had hers, what people commonly thought of as love, and although that was gone, he felt the shape and the weight of it, the way people are said to feel an amputated arm or leg. "Yeah," he said. "I gotta go."

"Can you just wait a minute? Can I tell you some things?"

"Hold on." He put the phone down and reached for something to blow his nose on, came up with a scrap of paper towel. He didn't care anymore what she or anyone else thought of him. "Right."

"The Book of Job."

"Beg pardon?"

"You should read it again. If you ever read it in the first place. You're not exactly a church type, are you? If I say 'Job,' do you know what I'm talking about?"

"Yes." Annoyed now, since this was how things usually went with her. She never gave him credit for knowing anything he hadn't seen on television. "He's the guy who God kicks the shit out of. You been going to Bible study, Sheila? You got religion all of a sudden? Now that would be remarkable."

"I'm glad you're feeling better and can start in being nasty again. No, you're just reminding me of Job. When you have a body of knowledge, you can make connections that way. Cultural references."

He figured she was taking another evening course. "Thanks, Sheila. I'm real glad I can help you out. With the culture stuff."

"You didn't let me finish. See, Job is really a good, holy man. And God takes everything away from him. His, ah, flocks. Sheep, everything. His ten children die when the house collapses on them. He gets boils everywhere, from the top of his head to the soles of his feet."

"Everywhere?"

"Shut up. Then God appears in a whirlwind and tells Job, 'You know why I afflicted you? Because I can. Because I'm God. It doesn't have to be fair.'"

She finished up with a flourish. Sean waited, then he said, "Sorry, Sheila, I'm kind of tired. Anyway, I don't have any sheep. Just a real sick dog." If Conner hadn't asked her for money, who had he asked?

"I have to talk to Conner. He must be just miserable."

"Yeah." Why had he called Sheila anyway? All this time they'd spent learning to unlove each other and still he kept coming back around for the leftovers, the gnawed ends and snotty remarks. "Look, I gotta go. I forget, what finally happened with Job?"

"God felt sorry for him and restored his sheep and oxen and all, and gave him ten new children, and he lived to be a hundred and forty years old."

He wanted to ask her about the boils, but she had already hung up. He wasn't Job.

He hadn't had much that could be taken away in the first place. The pain in his back began its slow creeping dance again. Nothing was ever fair or had to be fair, and maybe that was the thing you had to get your mind around.

The dog came home with his side and stomach shaved, and a big pink incision, and one of those cones around his head to keep him from chewing the stitches. He licked their hands and walked unsteadily to the bed they'd made for him, lay down, and groaned.

Conner said, "The vet gave me this special food for him. I'll try some when he gets up."

Sean hadn't said much to Conner and he didn't say anything now. The dog looked bad, but maybe that was just from the operation. Conner was in the kitchen, washing his hands in the sink. Sean stood in the door, watching him. "What did the vet say?"

"He thought he got it all."

"Got what?"

"The cancer." Conner looked around for something to dry his hands with, found nothing, and wiped them on his jeans.

"We need some, what are they, dish towels."

"Uh-huh." Conner seemed to want to go in the next room and tend to the dog, but that would have meant walking past his father, and so he took his phone out of his pocket and flipped through the screens.

"Are you going to tell me how much of a vet bill we're looking at?"

"You don't have to worry about it."

"Yeah, you already said that. How much?"

"It's covered."

"Yeah? Where'd you get the money?"

Conner had run out of ways to not look at him, and put his phone away "From somebody who has money."

"That's good to know. What did you have to do to get it, huh? What's going on here that all of a sudden, you got money?" It made him furious that in all their time of barely getting by, or not getting by, it was only the dog that called up this kind of effort. "You better tell me what you been up to, sport."

"Just drop it, OK?"

They stared at each other. There had been those times, in Conner's growing-up years, when he seemed to take a leap into some new phase of growth, baby to toddler, toddler to little kid, and so on. Now he had a man's height and a man's hard arms, and there was something both wonderful and sorrowful in this, because now he would be left behind.

So he dropped it, because what other choice did he have. He'd started off all wrong and fumblefucked. It shook him up to see the dog so sick. And if the dog died, he couldn't think of one reason for Conner to stay here.

You could get another dog, the same way you could get more sheep, he guessed. But what was so great about getting all new children? What the hell was God thinking?

Sean lay on the sofa next to the dog's bed. They took the cone collar off to give him a break, and Sean scratched him under his chin the way he liked. Conner fed him a plate of the special food, and Sean said that he looked a little better, and Conner agreed, and that was at least a start at conversation.

Later Conner coaxed the dog to his feet, and took him out in the yard to hobble around and pee. Sean got up and went into the kitchen. The cans of dog food were on the counter, along with a sheet of post-surgical instructions, and a small plastic bag that Sean inspected. Inside was a bottle of tramadol. He shook it, then opened it and counted out the pills, twenty of them.

"What are you doing?"

Conner standing at the back door, incredulous. Sean let the pills rattle back into the bottle. "Just . . . nothing."

"Those are for Bojangles! I don't believe you."

He didn't have any good reason for opening the bottle. He had acted without intention. He said, "I wasn't going to take any of them." Although maybe he would have. He didn't know. "Here," he said, handing the bottle to Conner. "Take em. Put them some place and don't tell me."

In the bathroom Sean scooped up every pill bottle he could find: the Percocet, Vicodin, Dilaudid. The Oxys.

"You don't have to make a big production out of this," Conner said, when he came back into the kitchen and dumped them on the counter.

"Call it whatever you want."

"What am I supposed to do with these?"

"I don't care. Flush em. Sell them. No, don't do that."

"Yeah, you can always go get more."

"I can but I won't." He didn't know if he meant it. But he wanted to mean it.

"Come on, Dad," Conner said, sounding weary. Like this was just one more dumb stunt.

Sean raised his hand, enough. He was through with talking. With everything that went into or came out of his mouth.

He got ready for bed and laid himself down. He didn't figure on sleeping. God was a whirlwind, ready to blow him to bits. Was there still such a thing as love in the world, and could he latch on to some corner of it?

And just at that moment, someone somewhere tapped out letters on a keyboard, and the letters were converted into electrons, and the electron stream sped along a connection that spoke to a specified server, a specified account. The electrons were retranslated into a pattern of light and dark and blink, a line of type waiting to be called up out of the hum and glow: *Steve, is that really you?*

TEN

After the morning's class session, in what he meant to sound like a spur-of-the-moment idea, Art had asked one of the other instructors in the tutoring program if she wanted to grab some lunch. She had surprised him by saying yes, so that he didn't have to produce any of the regrets or backpedaling speeches he'd rehearsed. Half an hour later they were sitting on a creosoted log at Rodeo Beach, trying to keep their sandwich wrappers and paper napkins from blowing away in the walloping ocean breeze. The takeout sandwiches and the beach had been her idea, and Art was glad, since that meant he didn't have to apologize for the inconvenience of attempting to keep sand out of their food. Not that she was apologizing. She was delighted, she was chatty chatty chatting away, while Art made ignoble attempts to look down the front of her shirt.

The woman's name was Beata, and she was Polish, had been in this country since she was a teenager. Her English was very good, certainly good enough to coach the program's glum underachievers, with a faint, lilting accent that occasionally made the emphasis land in unexpected places, as in, "Good morning, *happy* people!"

She had a small head with straight black hair cut to chin length. Every so often the tops of her ears showed through, like a child's. Her eyes were wide and gray, her skin thin and blue-veined and bruisable-looking. Art guessed she was somewhere near thirty. He found her only fitfully attractive, but he had to start somewhere. Worse men than him—dumber, uglier, meaner—had girlfriends. Sex lives. You saw it all the time.

Beata wore clothes that made her seem older, or maybe just Old World: filmy scarves arranged over one shoulder, then belted at the waist. Blouses with crocheted sleeves. Quantities of twinkling glass jewelry. Today she wore a woolly blouse with folkloric embroidery and a dark full skirt that wadded up around her and made it difficult to see her figure, let alone imagine her naked, as Art's base instincts urged.

"Look, look!" Beata pointed out over the water. She had an enthusiastic disposition. "You can see so many miles! There is such a great big boat!"

"Yeah, probably a tanker." Art tried and failed to find anything remarkable about it, but chose to humor her. "Like, an oil tanker." He didn't know if there was any other kind.

"A beautiful day," Beata said, gazing around her with approval, and Art agreed with this also, although he was too full of edgy lust to get into the right carefree mood. It was windy but bright, and warm enough for families to lay down beach towels, and for rampaging kids and dogs to run through the shallowest waves, and for an old VW van in the parking lot to serve as headquarters for a group of surfers, their boards and gear and coolers and lawn chairs set out under an awning. The wind made it hard to carry on much conversation, the kind of mandatory getting-to-know-you conversation he'd imagined, but maybe that was all right. Maybe they could just nuzzle and smell each other, end up in some friendly place.

Because he didn't really know her, had only traded hellos and small talk in the hallways of the community college where the summer tutoring program had set up shop. They'd groaned and raised their eyebrows in mock despair, which was meant to disguise their real despair, at their students' lack of basic reading skills, motivation, civility. "If I can learn English," Beata said, "you would think the big babies who are born here can too."

Maybe she had a boyfriend. Girlfriend. You never knew. Once they spoke for a few minutes as they walked to their cars, their longest conversation. He mentioned that he had a teenage daughter. He figured it was something that women would like to hear, it gave him an air of responsible maturity. At least, as long as he didn't get into the particulars. He was fishing around, waiting to see if Beata volunteered any children or other domestic entanglements of her own. But she had only shaken her head and said that not for any money, or in any country, would she wish to be a girl again, that miserable state of wanting, wanting, wanting, with no chance of having.

But what did Linnea want? She wouldn't say. She slumped around the apartment, and the bathroom filled up with her makeup and tampons and shampoo bottles, and her music elbowed his out. These days, with the issue of her immediate future still unresolved, there was a bulky fake politeness between them that they kept bumping into. She was mad at him for everything that was his fault, but also for everything that wasn't.

Art watched Beata throw a piece of bread crust to a parading seagull. "Uh-oh. Now you've done it. These guys are professional beggars."

"Well, I am a professional feeder." She wrinkled her nose. "Not a word?"

"It's sort of a word." He tried to realign his ass on the log perch. The wind lifted Beata's cap of black hair into a crest. He didn't like to think what his own untidier scalp looked like. Not that she seemed to be paying him any particular attention, which was a little disappointing, even if this wasn't really a date, even if he'd gone out of his way to make it seem like it wasn't. He obviously needed to put himself out there. Grow a pair.

"So," he said, making an effort at flirtation. "I guess you're kind of a nature girl?"

She turned and gave him a brief smile. "We are all of us a part of nature."

"Yeah, I just meant—" Art tried to formulate exactly what he meant. Not that much. It was only lighthearted conversation, rapidly gaining ballast. "You really seem to enjoy it. Because some people, they spend all their time in front of a computer, or watching television. They wouldn't have thought about going to the beach." Of course, he had not thought of it himself.

Beata said, "I live in the city"—her speech giving it the rising tone of a question: I live in the city?—"and this is an easy beach to visit after work. I come here when I can. You are so lucky, you live so close. You are a nature boy?"

There was a hint of teasing in this, and Art rallied himself to meet it. "Oh, not really. Maybe you could teach me how. We could run away together, live in a tree."

She giggled. Art found this encouraging. "Like Tarzan and Jane," he added daringly, but just then Beata was distracted by a howling child, a little boy knocked over by an incoming wave and sitting on his bottom at the water's edge. Before Art could fathom what she was doing, Beata jumped up and went to him, her big dark skirt flapping around her like a witch costume. She bent over the screaming boy, who didn't appear to have anything wrong with him except the indignity of having fallen, making solicitous inquiries.

Then a fattish woman in shorts and a tank top approached, hoisting the boy up by one arm and marching him off. She gave Beata a narrow, unfriendly look.

Beata gazed after them, then returned to Art and sat down on the log, her face clouded over. "What is wrong with that lady? She acts like I will steal her child. And she not even watching him!"

"Just grouchy," Art said, though he guessed the mother, who in fact had not been paying much attention to the boy, was angry at having this publicly demonstrated, and that Beata, with her peculiar clothes and pale Polish skin, was the perfect target for righteous, misplaced indignation. "Maybe she was trying to teach him not to talk to strangers."

"Ridiculous. What is she doing instead, while her child cried? Or drowns? Eating disgusting food."

The woman was consoling the boy with a cellophane bag of potato chips, holding it so he could pull the chips out in fistfuls. "Oh well." Art felt moved to offer some defense of inadequate parents. "Sometimes, you know, just to calm them down . . ."

Beata didn't answer. She was still staring at the mother and child, preoccupied with her disapproval, so he pulled his phone out of his pocket. "Excuse me a minute."

He'd been trying to reach Linnea, without success. This morning Art had asked her if she'd thought any more about schools, if she'd come up with any new ideas about schools. Linnea said she was keeping her options open. He hadn't liked the sound of that, snotty and menacing, but he hadn't said anything. He'd missed one more opportunity, hadn't chosen to confront her. Had more or less let it slide. He guessed he'd been handing out his own kind of potato chips.

The phone clicked, sending him to Linnea's voice mail. Art hung up without leaving a message. He'd already left a couple. He was never at all sure where she was, how she spent her time. When asked, she said she was just hanging out, or had walked down to the market for something, or taken a bus to the mall. He assumed she was being untruthful, at least part of the time, on principle.

Whenever he spoke with her mother, Louise talked about Linnea as if she were something broken that could not be fixed. "She's three years away from eighteen," Louise said soberly.

"What's that supposed to mean?"

"When she's eighteen, she's a legal adult. Responsible for herself."

"You sound like you can't wait."

"No, Mr. Clever, please do not presume to tell me what I sound like. It means that once she's eighteen, whatever trouble she gets into is adult trouble."

"She hasn't gotten into any trouble out here," Art said. He didn't really count her filching his marijuana as trouble. It was more like bad manners. "She's just kind of difficult. In a kid way."

"Could I make a suggestion? Birth control."

"Come on, Louise. She isn't doing anything with boys. She doesn't know any boys." Although once he said it, doubts set in. Just because he hadn't seen boys didn't mean there weren't any. Like having mice, or termites.

Louise said that there was this narrow window of time when they would be able to function as parents. It was unclear whether she meant herself and Art, or herself and Jay, or perhaps all three of them. Parents could still make decisions for their minor children, therapeutic choices. She started in talking about the Montana school again, the desirable combination of discipline and support, the beautiful ranch setting, the not inconsiderable amount of money she and Jay were willing to pay out. Art let her talk on. He'd seen the brochures too. He was supposed to present them to Linnea, but he hadn't dared. It was too easy to imagine her scorn and fury at those bright pictures of happy, chastened young people sitting around campfires, or paddling canoes, or bonding with horses.

He came to realize, not while Louise was talking, but later, thinking about it, that she had mentioned how expensive the school was not just to prove how much money and effort she was willing to put forth for Linnea's sake (Art had not been asked to contribute), but because the cost of the place was a point in its favor, a measure of its worth. Serious money produced serious results.

He and Beata had finished their sandwiches, and Art gathered up the wrappers and napkins and paper bags, stood, then realized the trash can was all the way over in the parking lot and sat back down again. Beata had turned away from the distressing family group and was once more looking out over the rolling waves. Art tried to get absorbed in them, but really, they were just waves, doing the same thing over and over. "Well," he began, signaling that they should get going. He was giving up on the idea of her as a frisky date.

Beata said, "When I first came here, to the United States? I had no idea how big a country could be. Back home, countries are one next to the other. A train ride. First we lived in New York. On the other ocean. Then here I come to go to college, San Francisco State."

"Come here to go to college," Art corrected her, but she only looked perplexed. Her eyebrows, he noticed, had been drawn into thin antenna lines with hard pencil. "Never mind."

"And everything was different. Different weather. More cars, less people. Even this different ocean. And I was different too. Before, I was so very shy. Hard to imagine? What could I say in English? I was still learning. And who to speak to in Polish, but my mother and father? So once I came here, I decided, I would be a cheerful person. Talk to everybody, go everywhere, be brave, be someone not expected."

"That's very positive. Good for you. We should probably start back." He checked his phone again to see if Linnea had called, but she hadn't. He was wondering if he should text her instead of calling. There was probably something dumb and parental about voice mail.

Beata stood up and brushed the sand and crumbs from her skirt. Art watched his feet as he followed her, trying to keep his ankles from collapsing sideways in the sand. Beata kept turning back to look at the ocean, making little regretful sighs that struck him as affected. There was a reason he usually avoided the cheerful types.

Once they were in the car, Beata insisted they stop to see the seals at the rescue place up the hill, a new building that was half zoo, half hospital. "More nature stuff!" Art, heavily patient, trooped after her. At the rescue facility, workers in yellow rubber coveralls hosed down the concrete. The seals lay around like fat gray sausages. The seals made an *awk awk* racket. Some of them were wriggling up the ramps to flop into raised tanks, where they dove and bobbed to the surface. They looked out over the edge of the tank with big wet black eyes. The workers held up fish by their tails and dangled them. The seals rose up to take them, swallowing them down whole in an instant.

There was a fishy stink to the place, not that unpleasant until you thought about it. There were a number of educational exhibits, and Art dutifully read these displays as Beata exclaimed over them. The text was about the fragility of the oceans, the threat to marine life from pollution, floating trash, depletion of fishing grounds, climate change, and so on.

The place depressed him. Most places depressed him these days. He wasn't sure what he was meant to do about the never-ending supply of bad planetary news. He felt like some overlarge and overdeveloped mammal who had strayed out of its range.

Maybe he would have been more successful at being a different kind of creature, all instinct and no confusion of motives or choices. Everything would come naturally: eat, fight, migrate, breed. He guessed he might just as well turn out to be a failed animal. A woodpecker hammering away at a concrete post. A scrawny hyena pushed out of the pack.

Beata was off talking to one of the guides, and so he tried calling Linnea again. The phone clicked and a man answered. "Hello?"

"Linnea?"

"What?" The voice was annoyed, suspicious.

"Where's Linnea?"

"You have the wrong number," the man said, and hung up.

Stupidly, he stared at the phone in his hand. He dialed back, got Linnea's voice mail. He checked the phone's history. He hadn't misdialed. He tried again and the same man answered. "What?"

"Please put Linnea on. This is her father."

"How about, take a flying fuck at a rolling doughnut, dad." He hung up again.

Beata came back to him then, full of happy information. "Do you know that this place used to be where they kept missiles? Underground. A missile silo. What is the matter?"

"I keep trying to call my daughter, and some man answers instead."

"Huh. Wrong number?" Art shook his head. "Boyfriend?"

"I don't know. I hope not." The seals cackled and barked, the noise echoing off the glass enclosures. Below them, workers were herding the seals around the pens, using big pieces of plywood with handles. Maybe Linnea had loaned her phone to somebody. Maybe it had been lost or stolen. The man had sounded like somebody who might steal a phone. Or do worse things.

Or else it was nothing at all, some kind of mistake.

"Art?"

Beata had a hand on his arm, trying to angle herself into his field of vision. "Is something wrong?"

"I don't know." He took a step toward the glass and looked down at one of the seal pens. Some smaller seals that looked like stuffed animals were being lifted and rearranged. Dread and stupidity paralyzed him. He thought he would just watch the seals for a while.

"Let's walk." Again the hand on his arm, propelling him. A troop of schoolchildren marched down the hall toward them. Beata steered him around them and down a flight of stairs. A window looked out over the ocean, and below them, the beach where they had eaten lunch. "Tell me," Beata said.

"I don't know why she isn't answering her phone. I don't know where she is. I never know."

"Teenagers," Beata said wisely.

"No this is different. Worse." The ways in which it was worse seemed complicated beyond his power to explain. "I have to go home and see if she's there." He had no real hope that she would be. "I'm sorry. I can drop you off at school."

"I think I should come with you." Art started to protest. "The truth? You look like you need some help. You look like a rock. Rocky."

They reached the parking lot. The sun had flickered out behind a layer of fog and the wind was chill. Art had a headache, as if weather systems, lows and highs, were booming through his skull. "What about our classes?"

"We'll tell them, family emergency. I can call."

"It really will look like we've run off together," Art said, reaching for his earlier joke. "Look, you don't need to come along. I bet this is just her trying to aggravate me. Or maybe she's not even trying." He felt queasy about allowing her to witness the abject disorganization of his apartment, not to mention that of his life.

"I'm calling right now. The number is on my phone."

Art drove and listened to Beata manage the call to the program secre-

tary, with whom she seemed to be on first-rate and familiar terms. Without exactly saying so, she was able to paint a picture of a distraught young
girl, one of those teen heartaches, requiring both her daddy and some
specifically female sympathy and support. Then there was some further
cozy talk between the two of them, something solicitous and fond, and
then Beata said her good-byes.

"Thank you," Art said. He accelerated up the 101 ramp, as if being in a
hurry was going to help.

"You're welcome. She said she didn't know you had a daughter."

"It wasn't a general topic of conversation."

"You see, Art? Girls like it when you talk to them. Pay attention.
Do you even know her name, the secretary? Katherine. She has three
boys, one of them is Navy. When a language is new to you, you have to
listen."

"Yes." He had to keep himself from grabbing his phone and calling
Linnea again, shouting curses at whatever pissant scum answered.

"Do you listen to your daughter?"

She was looking at him with her thin antenna eyebrows raised. Art
said, "She doesn't like talking. She was in an accident. Not an accident,
a murder, a shooting. Some other girls were shot. She's very disturbed. Nobody knows what to do about her. So there's a lot to not talk about."

"Watch your road, please."

He was coming up too fast on a lumbering panel van. He braked and
changed lanes. "Her mother and I split up when she was a baby. I hardly
know her. I'm supposed to be keeping her out of trouble. This phone
thing—" He wanted to impress the seriousness of the situation on Beata.
"She's only fifteen, and this guy with her phone sounds—older," he finished lamely.

"We'll find her. She'll be all right."

"She's already not all right." His exit was coming up, and he dove
for it.

"You know," Beata said, crossing her legs somewhere beneath the vast
territory of her skirt, "it's not always a bad thing, to have trouble when

you are young. You can make yourself a stronger person from it. Our troubles make us who we are."

"Sure. Great." Art was scanning the sidewalks, hoping to see his daughter slouching along, her hair newly dyed a Mercurochrome red. "I feel so much better now. Thanks."

Beata was silent. Art made the turn into the cul-de-sac, reached the apartment complex and his parking space. He shut the engine off and they listened to its ticking as it cooled. "I apologize," Art said. "I'm just upset. I appreciate you trying to help. I appreciate your being here. You didn't have to come."

"I can wait here if you want."

"Please come with me. I'm sorry."

She opened her car door. "Sometime soon? You'll have to tell me all about you being married."

Just as they reached the stairs, Christie's door opened. "Oh, hi Art." He saw her looking Beata over, then attempting not to.

"Hey Christie. Have you seen Linnea, she up there?"

"I think she went out after you left for work. I think I heard her." Christie was wearing her nurse's clothes, a printed smock and white pants. Art had been guilty of any number of stray fantasies involving old-fashioned starched nurse's whites and those little caps.

"She didn't say when she was coming back?" As soon as he said it, he wondered if it sounded as if he was hoping for a little private time with Beata. Well, hadn't he been?

"I didn't get a chance to talk to her."

There was a moment when he could have introduced them to each other but it passed, and Art said, "OK, thanks, bye," and started up, embarrassed for no reason, Beata following him to what he was pretty sure was an empty apartment.

When he unlocked the door he called "Linnea?" for form's sake. No answer. "Well," he raised his arms and let them fall to his sides. "Come on inside, so I can figure out what to do next."

Art stood back to let her enter. Beata advanced to the midpoint of the main room, taking it in. He was glad she didn't offer any opinions or commentary. Maybe there just wasn't that much to say about the place. He opened the refrigerator, moved to make some hostlike gesture. "You want a Coke? Beer? Orange juice?"

"No thank you. May I use the bathroom?"

"Down the hall."

He waited, looking out the front window for any sign of Linnea. Right about now his afternoon class would be assembling, and, finding the cancellation notice on the door, disassembling. No one, himself included, would be disappointed.

When Beata returned, she had taken off her dark stockings and was barefoot and bare-legged. "Too hot," she said, as if he had said something, and he guessed his face had. Her legs and feet were very white and somehow foreign-looking, as if they had spent the summer in a pale northern country. "So. Are you going to call her again?"

"I don't know. That guy, I wasn't getting anywhere." He didn't think he wanted Beata listening. It wasn't likely to be a conversation that made him look, or sound, very good.

"How about I try." She nodded. "Yes." She moved a pile of magazines to sit on the couch, opened her handbag, and extracted her phone. "Number please."

"What are you going to say?"

"By ear. Oh don't worry, I can be very sneaky. The number."

She dialed, and Art heard the small leakage of the man's grouchy voice through the phone's earpiece. "Hi!" Beata said. "Who is this?" Her tone was frisky, giddy. It made you think of someone chewing bubble gum. She listened a moment, then giggled. "My name is Tara." More listening. More giggling. "Thank you."

Art was standing in front of her, mouthing questions. She shooed him away. "Listen, is my friend there? Can I talk to her? No, it's about the party. She said there was a party.

"Sure, I can come.

"Old enough to party. Ha-ha-ha.

"Oh, I don't know about that. It sounds kind of wild.

"Ha-ha. Well tell her to call me, OK? This number. I'll think about it. Byee."

Beata held the phone away from her and shut the call down. Her face lost its frivolous expression and her mouth tightened.

"What did he tell you? Was Linnea there?"

Beata shook her head. "I think so. He didn't want her listening in. We have to wait now."

Art sat down next to her on the couch. He was hollowed out with fear and nervous sickness. Beata's hand curled around the back of his neck, a cool pressure. He hoped she wouldn't say anything else and she didn't. There was only this space of silent sitting.

Finally he sat up and pushed some air in and out of his chest in an inelegant gulping laugh. "Some lunch date, huh?" He had forgotten that it wasn't supposed to be a date. He didn't know what to do about the hand on his neck, so he reached up and patted it with one of his own. Then, because that seemed presumptuous or unwise, he took his hand away.

"Does your daughter look like you?"

"A little. Except for the hair. She has teenage hair."

"Ah. It's always hair, isn't it?"

"You were really something on the phone." Art wasn't sure what he meant by this. Admiration, yes, but also some alarm at how easily she had switched tones. Technically, she had not been talking dirty, although that was the impression he was left with. This was not a good time to let himself get distracted.

"I am really something even off the phone."

Art considered this. "Yes, I believe you are."

She rubbed the back of his neck, then released him. "Tell me more about your girl. Her troubles."

"Not right now." Not with Linnea once more out in the dangerous world. There was a confusion in his head, he had to stop himself from rehearsing that earlier nightmare, what must have happened in that school bathroom with the boy, the gun, the screaming girls. He had to remind himself that this had already happened and was not happening to her now. Or was it? Or something worse? And along with the dread there was anger: why had somebody else's random horrible life landed on top of her, and now on top of him? That boy and his craziness, no one he would ever know, but once you started asking why terrible things happened, you had to ask why good things did too or why anything at all was the way it was in the whole world, and then you were completely screwed.

To drown out the awful sound of the phone not ringing, Art asked Beata what time it was. Two-thirty, she told him, and Art said good, good, as if two-thirty meant something that two twenty-five had not. Could he call the police? He didn't think so. That wasn't the kind of call you made at two-thirty in the afternoon, and anyway, no visible crime had been committed. He needed some other kind of public servant to drive up with sirens and whirling red and blue lights, take his statement, fix him a cup of tea, massage his scalp, and in general feel sorry for him, and it was this kind of need and maybe some other kinds that made him thrash around in the couch cushions, attempting to get some purchase, and clutch at Beata's shoulders and kiss and kiss and kiss again her small, soft face.

He drew away. "Sorry," he said automatically, although he wasn't sure if he was or not. His mouth was still wet and he tried to be discreet about swiping at it with the back of his hand. "Oh boy."

"Tarzan," Beata said. Art felt a dopey smile spreading over his face and tried to get his feet underneath him so as to manage the uncooperative cushions, and then Beata's phone rang, a frolicking, instantly annoying tune, and she pushed it at him saying, "Answer, answer."

It wasn't Linnea's number; she still had an Ohio area code. "Hello?" He heard music in the background, something jazzed up and scratchy.

"Jesus Christ," Linnea said. "You?"

"Honey? Where are you, are you all right? What happened to your phone?"

"Who was it that called about me?" Linnea asked, managing to sound as if the answer was entirely uninteresting to her. "That was just weird."

"Tell me where you are."

There was a jumble of noise, the phone dropped, or juggled, then re-trieved. "Sorry. I think there's some kind of filter, I can't hear stupid things."

"I want you to come home. Or I'll come get you. No questions asked."

"Such a good one," Linnea said, meaning, she didn't believe him, he'd say anything. And he guessed he would.

The music in the background had a voice in it. Billie Holiday? Art got himself free of the dratted couch, stood. "I don't suppose you'd care to share who was answering your phone?"

"Just this guy. You don't know him. I gave him my phone. It's com-plicated."

"Please, Linnea."

"It was like, a deal. I can't talk very long, OK? This is somebody else's whole different phone. Do you want to make a deal too? Say yes."

"Yes." When he turned and looked back at Beata, she had removed her blouse. Underneath it she wore a pink and white bra, high-cut and prim. He wouldn't have suspected that she had especially large breasts, but she did. Mother of God.

"So here's the deal," Linnea said. "I don't have to go to Camp Who Gives A Happy Fuck."

"That doesn't sound like such a great deal, where's the deal in that?"

"Wait wait, there's more. If you promise not to send me there, I won't, like, run away."

"What are you talking about, run away?" Unwisely, Art let his glance stray to Beata, who was busy unfastening the waistband of her skirt. "You can't do that, it's dumb."

"See, I can handle stuff. I really can. You would be surprised." She sounded pleased with herself. "Look, I gotta go now."

"Linnea, honey? Just come on back. You don't have to go anywhere." He was sure that kids threatened to run away all the time. But he was just as sure that some of them actually did it.

"What are you doing? You sound weird."

Beata stepped out of her skirt. Her underpants were pink cotton, and the dark fan of her pubic hair showed through. "Nothing," Art said.

"It's really OK if you don't want me to live with you. I would totally, totally understand. But I'm not going back to my mom's. I mean, hello! Not an option."

"I do want you here." And he did. Some instinct he didn't know he had, descending on him in a wave, or maybe he just didn't want to fail at one more thing. "We can figure everything out."

"Um, I need a new phone?"

"New phone. Done." Beata was walking down the hall in her underwear, stopping to look into the different rooms. "Linnea?" The phone was muffled while she spoke with someone she seemed annoyed with.

She came back on the line. "OK, but could we go to the sushi place for dinner? Please? I'll be home by then. I gotta go. Bye."

Beata was waiting for him in his bed. She'd gotten underneath the covers and pulled them up modestly to her neck. "She's all right," Art said. "She's coming home."

"But not right away?"

"No, not right away." He sat down on the edge of the bed, drew the covers down, and kissed the skin just below her throat. She smelled of some dark and complicated fragrance, like the scent of tea leaves. He said, "I think I need to just lie down for a minute, if that's OK. Come down from one hill before I climb the next one."

"I am, what, the Tour de France?" But she moved over in the bed and he lay back and fit himself next to her. "You were really, really worried. A good daddy."

"I don't know about that. I haven't been, like you said, paying enough attention to her."

"Right this minute? I think I am the one needing your attention."

He let his hands stray over Beata's body. The covers were in his way, but he still found things that he liked. "You're sort of, what? 'Not someone expected.'"

"Thank you. You too. Not such a sack of sadness as you look."

He wasn't? He considered this new possibility, this new, unsad self. A little while later, but not before talking became entirely impossible, Art stopped and raised himself up to look down on her. The ink lines of her eyebrows arched, regarding him. "Hey," he said. "You have to tell me, this isn't happening because—" He had meant to say "because you felt sorry for me," but that would have been entirely too pathetic.

"Because you wanted it to. Yes. Now, I can teach you some Polish, if you like. The words for this, and for this."

ELEVEN

If only their father was still alive, or if only he had gone about his dying differently. Every unhappy phone conversation between Leslie Hart and her sister, Deirdre, always came around to that wish, bumped up against it, and stalled out. Certainly their father had done everything he considered right and necessary. There was a will, there was money in trust for each sister. There were the formidable investments, in stocks, bonds, Treasuries, currencies, commodity futures, real estate, and other funds so complex and fine-tuned that they were in perpetual vigilant motion, turning fractions of pennies into larger fractions, and eventually into measurable wealth. And this largest portion of the estate was under their mother's direct control, which their father might have reconsidered in time, if he had been given more time, since she seemed determined to throw it all away with both hands.

Leslie hadn't seen any of it coming. No one had. Oh, she could scream. She wasn't a bad, greedy person. She wanted people to be happy, to have enough to eat, and good dental care, and their educational opportunities. But even if you gathered up all the money in the world and sprinkled it over everyone on earth, it wouldn't make any big difference. What was giving away her father's money meant to accomplish? It would be gobbled up like flakes of fish food.

Her mother certainly seemed to be enjoying herself. And while it was a relief that she'd pulled herself out of her period of decline, there was something alarming and unnatural about her new enthusiasm. Honestly? Leslie and Deirdre had grown used to their mother's fretful ill health, had accepted the prospect of a long (or short) period of semi-invalid life. It sounded cold, but you readied yourself, you made adjustments for all the sad, necessary, and messy parts of life's final act. And you knew how you were supposed to feel about all that: the ways in which you would grieve, the ways in which you had grieved.

But you didn't know how you were meant to regard your seventy-nine-year-old mother's setting herself up as some kind of public phi-lanthropist, even if the seventy-nine-year-old was perfectly happy about it, and that made you feel like a bad person when you really were not.

"Mom," Leslie had asked on her last visit, "why don't you just make some charitable contributions, like you always have? Why do you have to go to all this trouble?" By trouble, Leslie supposed she meant, trouble for everyone else involved.

Her mother had been distracted by one of the horrible cats, who had managed to climb halfway up the living room drapes and get stuck there like a burr. "That's Mr. Darcy. He keeps doing that. I'm going to have some play structures built for them. The kind where they can hide and climb and pretend they're in a jungle." Her mother rose from the couch and tugged at the drape, which slid off its rod and landed on the floor in a heap of fabric and snarling cat. "Oh don't worry, he'll get himself loose. I'm sorry, I forgot what you were asking."

Her mother was smiling a bright, unfocused smile that didn't fool Leslie for a minute. She was pleased with herself. The pile of drapery thrashed and convulsed and Mr. Darcy ran away down the hall, his orange tail standing up as stiff as a bottle brush.

"Mom, why do you need a foundation?" Foundation, Leslie didn't even like the word. It made you think of makeup, underwear. "Why does it have to cost so much money?"

"Oh, Tweety Bird, I know you're unhappy about all this. But the Foundation doesn't mean I love you one bit less."

Leslie's mouth tried to bite down on a word but couldn't find one. Her mother was always doing things like this, coming at her with strange assumptions or accusations. The kind of thing that made Leslie want to double-check her own driver's license, reassure herself she was still who she thought she was, a grown woman, not an anxious, piping child. What did money have to do with love, anyway?

"I just meant, it sounds like so much work." Although that was not at all what Leslie meant, and she was angry, first at herself and then at her mother for putting her in this false position. "What if you change your mind, get tired of it?" She meant, get too old and addled to sign her own checks. These things happened.

"I'll have plenty of help." Her mother smiled and nodded as if to an audience of solicitous attendants, although there was no one in the house but themselves and the wrathful cats. "That's been one of the benefits. I have met so many nice people. Don't you ever feel the need to get beyond your usual routines, open yourself up to other possibilities?"

No, Leslie could have said, but didn't. Could have said, her mother's new and helpful acquaintances might turn out to be professional grifters. But her mother still had the power to reduce her to silence while she continued on, blithe and oblivious.

Growing up, both Leslie and her sister had their shifting sympathies and alliances with each of their parents. Their father had been what people called "difficult": moody, often silent, preoccupied with serious man-business. Their mother had pecked away at him for all the years of their marriage, wanting his attention, coaxing and complaining and making tearful accusations. They'd felt sorry for her, they knew she was unhappy, but it was exhausting to live with. And when the beam of their mother's restless discontent had turned to focus on her daughters, there had been nowhere to hide. Why did they not keep their hair out of their eyes? Why did they put that gunk on their faces, waste time on trashy television and worse music? Lie around eating snack food that was making their waistlines so sloppy, not to mention their behinds? Why had they not developed some discernible talents or interests, either athletic or artistic or intellectual? Why were they turning out so ordinary, when so much care and resources had been invested in them?

Then, after a time, their mother would give up, lose interest in them, return to her grievances with their father. And their father would do something wounding and unforgivable, like fail to come home for the birthday dinner prepared for him. Then their mother would appear at their bedroom doors late at night, weeping and saying that she couldn't stand it, she'd leave tomorrow except where would she go, she would have nothing, he'd see to that, she'd end up all alone in some tiny little apartment. Of course they felt bad for her, and indignant, and were frosty toward their father until he noticed and made amends, and then it began all over again.

So that, while their father had been often enough at fault, and sometimes seemed confused to find himself equipped with two daughters who required so much in the way of upkeep and acknowledgment, he was at least consistent. He could be a restful, oblivious presence, and more than once when their mother's anxious tides ran high, one or the other sister might seek him out in his basement domain, where he crafted small rocket engines or produced ornamented and scrolled woodwork with the thrilling, dangerous saws they were forbidden to approach. "Don't even pretend to touch these," he'd thunder at them, making them wonder what was so awful about pretending, and they would promise never ever to do so.

They would spend a silent hour or two, watching him like a naturalist observing wildlife from a blind, until he forgot they were there, and went about his work, the muscles of his arms and back and neck moving with perfect economy and ease, in perfect contentment. In this way Leslie gained a piece of knowledge that would serve her well in her own marriage: Men were often happiest when left alone.

How could they blame their mother for taking her turn now, for whatever mixture of pleasure and spite came from having her way with his money? Hadn't she earned it, put up with enough? Cared for him during his difficult illness?

But Leslie had been expecting her own portion of the estate all this time. Not in a greedy, impatient, unseemly way where you actually hoped people would die—except of course they had to eventually. But the inheritance was something that was due to her, a deferred payment for whatever had been wounding or neglectful in her growing-up years. Her father's gift emerging from his long silence, his final pronouncement, and when you looked at it that way she guessed money really did have a lot to do with love.

Now she was back in town for the Foundation's first official board meeting. She'd been surprised and skeptical when her mother had recruited her, and her mother had been vague about her reasons, beyond saying that she thought Leslie would enjoy it. As if she was talking about a ski vacation! Someone had put her mother up to it. Most likely the mealymouthed nurse. What was supposed to be so great about her? Her mother didn't need a nurse anymore, she was fine.

Her sister, Deirdre, said it wouldn't be such a bad idea to do a background check. "I mean, who is she anyway? Mom's never careful enough, she's always taking in strays."

"Funny," Leslie said, but even though she'd told her sister about the cats, she didn't get it. "I think she's some holier-than-thou type. You know, never says two words about herself, just goes around ministering to lepers."

"Lepers? Isn't that contagious?"

"It's a joke. Never mind." Her sister had a cast-iron resistance to humor. Also, Deirdre was older than she was by five years, and Leslie suspected that her hearing wasn't what it used to be. "I guess you can do that kind of thing on the Internet. Look for criminal records. But I think she's just a goop, she likes making other people look bad."

"She sounds awful," Deirdre said, in her too-loud, deaf-lady voice. "Daddy would have made sure she knew the limits."

Leslie said he certainly would have, but there was no force left behind her indignation after so many repetitions. She couldn't help thinking that maybe the nurse was the kind of daughter her mother had wanted all along, someone to fret and fuss over her and listen to her complaints.

Everyone, meaning Leslie's husband, Roger, and Deirdre, and Deirdre's husband, agreed that Leslie should serve on the Foundation's board, for the same reasons she had been chosen to attend the initial meeting. She was family, she lived nearer than Deirdre, and she had, at least in everyone else's view, fewer obligations now that her youngest was on his way to college. As if she no longer had her job as a mother, and needed a new one. She was not to worry about the actual business of the board; they would all consult among themselves on what should be done as issues came along. What if their mother decided to liquidate everything, give it all away to some guru or con man? Con woman? Wouldn't it be best to keep an eye on things? Yes, it would be the best thing, she agreed, although you could get tired of other people deciding things for and about you.

Her flight from San Diego had been delayed, and then she'd had to wait a long time to get her rental car, and traffic on the bridge was backed up for no reason at all except to pile on the bad luck. This first meeting was to take place at her mother's house, and Leslie had planned on arriving at least an hour beforehand to freshen up and attempt to take her mother in hand, impress on her the importance of sound judgment and caution.

Instead the driveway was already filled with cars, and Leslie had to park at the bottom of the hill and walk with care up the steep slope in her pumps. When she stepped inside, there were people standing around with drinks and little plates of food, like a cocktail reception. Her mother stood up from her chair to be embraced. "Tweety Bird! Why didn't you call, I was getting so worried." Then, looking her over, "What's the matter with your hair?"

Leslie extracted herself from her mother's hugs and hand-patting and excused herself to use one of the upstairs bathrooms. A smell of cat rolled toward her from the far end of the hallway, but the bathroom itself was clean and cat-free. The upstairs cats must have all been confined to one or another bedroom for the occasion. Hopefully not the one she was meant to sleep in during her visit.

Her mother was right about her hair; it looked like a badly fitting hat. Her skin was as parched as a dried apricot. There was nothing about her that said Tweety Bird.

The board members, ten of them in all, were still where she'd left them, trying to balance their drinks and plates of shrimp and melon and stuffed endive. Her mother had decided to start things off as a sort of party, although no one seemed sure if they were supposed to be having fun or not. Leslie recognized some of them, the nurse, of course, in another of her long cotton dresses that looked like she'd made it in high school home ec class. The lawyer whose name she'd forgotten. Her mother was having an animated conversation with a man in a white turban, oh great. It would be just like her mother to think they needed a few turbans around the place.

The plane had made Leslie's feet swell, and her pumps felt as rigid as horseshoes. But she took care to keep her shoulders back and her chin up as she made her way across the room. This was her house, after all, and she wasn't going to slink in sideways. From one corner, Marietta Draper, whose parents had been such good friends of Leslie's parents, waved. Leslie was relieved to see her. Marietta was at least a normal person who knew that you dressed up for occasions like this. And here were the Keoghs (also waving), who were such reliable fixtures of any local civic endeavor. Leslie began to feel more hopeful.

Leslie's mother clapped her hands together. "Could I get everybody to move into the dining room? We're all set up for you there. Thank you so much."

The group began to migrate across the hall. Leslie made her way to the other side of the room to intercept her mother. She was giving instructions to a caterer, or so Leslie thought him to be, a teenager wearing the usual badly fitting white shirt, tie, and black pants. ". . . then if you could run down to the bank for me? Everything's all filled out. And have the garage check the tires and the oil and I don't know, whatever else they like to check."

The boy said something Leslie didn't catch, picked up his tray of plates, and carried it off to the kitchen. "Who's that?" Leslie asked her mother.

"One of my helpers." Her mother had gotten herself up in a yellow summer suit with pearls at her neck. She wasn't wearing her glasses and she kept turning her face this way and that with an all-purpose smile.

"Helper? You're giving him your car and your bank information? Where are your glasses?" Leslie tried to keep her voice down. Marietta Draper and the Keoghs were advancing toward them. "Who is he, did he show up with Cherry Ames, Student Nurse?"

"There's no need for you to be so unpleasant. Her name is Christie Schuyler, as you know very well. Now I know you think I can't be trusted to wipe my own behind, but please stop rolling your eyes that way. You were never a girl who could think one thing and have her face say another. Marietta!" Her mother advanced, arms extended. "Alicia dear, and Sim! I don't think I've seen you since the funeral!"

Since Alicia Keogh was staying behind to keep her mother company, there was nothing for Leslie to do except walk in with Marietta and Sim, talking pleasantly about the news of everyone's children and grandchildren, and wondering what her face had to say about it all.

Place cards had been set out for them, and Leslie found her seat midway down the long table. Marietta was seated on her right, and to her left was a man who introduced himself as a researcher at UC Berkeley, a sociologist, which Leslie supposed had something to do with poor people and their terrible problems. Seated directly across from her was the man with the turban. Either this was her mother's idea of being funny or else she had not given it any thought at all.

Christie Schuyler and the lawyer shared the space at the head of the table. They were thick as thieves, bending over a sheaf of pages and conferring seriously. The woman had the most annoying hair. It was that frizzy kind of blond that needs hair spray in the worst way, but instead she'd allowed it to grow out in all directions. Someone should tell her she was getting too old for the no-makeup thing. You saw women like her cruising the health food stores, buying organic beets and deodorant in the form of rocks.

Marietta nudged Leslie. "Is that her? The boss lady? She looks awfully—"

"Yes, doesn't she," Leslie whispered back.

Then Christie Schuyler stood up and started talking. Her voice was too soft for anyone to hear much. The room quieted, people leaning forward. ". . . wonderful opportunity," she was saying. "And I'm sure we're all very grateful."

If any of it had been worth listening to, Leslie might have been distressed that she couldn't hear. Maybe she was going deaf, like DeeDee. Someone, the lawyer probably, must have told the woman to speak louder, because her voice went up a notch, an earnest, straining treble: "So often we look around us and think, 'What is my responsibility to the world at large? How can any one person make themselves felt in the tide of events that so often seems chaotic, insurmountable, wrong?' Well, here is our chance. I intend to be worthy of Mrs. Foster's trust in us, and I know you do also. Now I'd like to call on Mr. Kirn."

Kirn, that was the lawyer. There was a bit of light applause when Christie Schuyler sat down, but most people were unsure whether or not applause was called for. Kirn didn't stand up to speak. It wasn't necessary for him to project himself, since he obviously loved hearing himself talk, and probably listened to tapes of himself while driving. He called their attention to the bylaws on which they would be voting, asking if there were questions or discussion. Leslie didn't trouble herself with these; Roger and the others had read them over already, looking for tricks or traps, and had pronounced them unobjectionable.

The man next to Leslie, the sociologist, had a question. It was the kind of what-if, overcomplicated question you expected from somebody who wanted to show how smart they were. She let her attention shut down.

She was so tired. She'd had to get up early to catch her flight. She'd spent the last three days packing, organizing, and making arrangements, since, in spite of what Roger and her son thought, a house did not run itself, and a refrigerator did not magically refill itself with groceries.

A little filtered sunlight fell across her face. She let her eyes close. Next week she and Roger would deliver their son to the University of Colorado, along with all the electronics and sporting equipment and wardrobe items that were necessary for his comfort, well-being, and enjoyment. There was also meant to be some provision for classes and study, but mostly you worried about your child getting beer-drunk and falling off a balcony onto his head, or getting arrested for drugs, or for molesting girls who would later change their mind about their willingness to be molested. Not that Josh was a wild kid, or a problem kid, given to bad behavior. But she'd been a mom for a long time now. She knew some things. Turn eighteen-year-olds loose for the first time in their lives and they were like, what was it, that movie where the boys were marooned on an island and became bloodthirsty little savages? Like the feral cats.

She'd wanted Josh to stay home for a year and go to community college. She and Roger had argued about it. Roger said she was attempting to baby him, she didn't want the last of the kids to go and leave her with an empty house. Oh didn't she? She couldn't wait. If it was possible, she'd send Roger off to college too. She wanted to wake up and go to sleep without a thought of anybody else in her head.

Anyway, Josh wasn't going to community college, he'd decided himself. Fine. Roger could be the one to go pick him up when he flunked out of school for not going to class, or not turning in papers, or decided he hated his teachers. Not that you wanted distressing things to happen to your child just to prove your husband wrong. But say they did. Poor Josh. With her two older kids, she hadn't been as vigilant, hadn't seen the pitfalls so clearly . . .

Marietta nudged her and Leslie straightened herself in her chair. Had she been asleep? Had anyone noticed? No one seemed to be paying her any attention; they were still going on and on about the bylaws. It was only two or three of the board members keeping the discussion alive, batting questions around among them.

Sooner or later she guessed they'd vote, and then there was to be a series of reports and proposals. The meeting could go on for hours if somebody didn't shut the yakkers up. Wasn't there some kind of rules of order? Could you call for a vote?

Leslie hadn't noticed him before, but the boy she'd thought was a caterer had come in and was standing against the back wall, where a coffee service had been set up on the buffet. Coffee, she was dying for some. Were you supposed to get up and serve yourself? She imagined that some of the others were wondering the same thing. And she was, after all, a kind of hostess. People might be waiting to see what she did.

She tried to catch his eye, not wanting to raise her hand and risk being called on by Kirn when all she wanted was coffee. The boy—how old was he? Josh's age?—wasn't being especially attentive. He seemed more interested in the bylaws discussion, which surely was not any of his concern.

Finally she managed to signal him over to her. "Could you bring me a coffee with cream, please? Marietta, did you want anything?"

"Yes ma'am," the boy said, and returned with a small tray of coffee cups, saucers, spoons, cream, and sugar, unloading them with a clumsy kind of carefulness. His hands were rough-looking, with scabs across the knuckles and the white marks of old scars. You could tell he'd tried to scrub his nails clean, but they were still rimmed with indelible grease. Lord have mercy, where did her mother find these people?

But then it was time to vote on whatever it was they had agreed to, and Sim Keogh, who was the executive secretary, called everyone's name and recorded their votes, and nobody said no. Well at least they were getting somewhere. People shifted in their seats. Across from Leslie the man in the white turban was trying to be discreet about cracking his knuckles.

Next they heard from Christie Schuyler about the new office—which they were all invited to visit!—in an undistinguished neighborhood in San Rafael. "We've been very budget-conscious, since foundations such as ours need to report the percentage of funds used for overhead.

We've made six hires so far, with a seventh pending. We've been fortunate to find qualified personnel from some of the same populations we hope to serve—that is, underrepresented groups, and those with demonstrated needs."

"We"? Who was "we"? The woman talked like she was Queen Victoria. And what did she mean, "those with demonstrated needs"? They found some homeless people who could type? She was getting into one of her moods. Now they were talking about projects, about assistance to food pantries and health centers and after-school programs. You didn't want to be against such things, did you?

But she really, really did not like Christie Schuyler, and she would never understand why her mother thought she was so perfect.

From somewhere within Leslie's purse, her phone buzzed. She pulled it out and read the screen. Roger. He wanted to check on her, make sure she was up to the job.

It pleased her to be able to ignore him. She knew he was worried about their own finances, and for that reason if nothing else, he didn't want to see her father's money pissed away. Not that they were anything like poor, or broke. Just undercapitalized.

Back in the palmy days when the real estate market could do no wrong, they had been considered wealthy. But it was a different world now. How many glittering office buildings and condo developments stood empty, with Roger's firm's green and white signs advertising vacancies? Leslie suspected that the company was in worse shape than Roger let on. He got irritated when she asked him questions about it, questions that she intended to be non-irritating, as opposed to the other kind.

The income from her trust fund had paid a lot of the kids' college bills, and in time the trust would pass to her children, and to their children, in smaller but still shiny nuggets. Roger had hinted around at changing this. She'd like to see him try.

In fact—her phone jingled, he'd left a message— who said she had to share any of her father's money with him? She allowed herself the pleasure of imagining Roger surprised that no fat check had been deposited in their joint account. Then anxious, then mad, and then . . . Well, it would be cutting off her nose to spite her face if they really needed money. But he was going to have to be a lot nicer to her.

Of course, this assumed there would be any money left after her mother and Christie Schuyler ransacked the estate.

Leslie hadn't been paying much attention to the talk going on around her, only wanting the meeting to be over so she could change out of her pantyhose and wash her face and sit her mother down for another attempt at a reasonable conversation. Tardily, she became aware that the lawyer, Kirn, was beaming at her, singling her out. ". . . and maybe Mrs. Hart should have the honor of starting us off." What?

"I'm sorry, would you mind repeating . . ." Marietta was trying to whisper something.

Kirn was smiling his fake jolly smile.

"Humanity," Kirn said. "What it means to each of us. In light of the Foundation's goals."

"I was never very good at pop quizzes," Leslie said, which was just funny enough for people to laugh, and to buy her a moment's time. Oh screw you, Kirn. What did he mean, honor? Was he making fun of her? He was one of those guys who liked reminding everybody they were in charge.

"Humanity," Leslie said, waiting to see what would come out of her mouth next. Why was Kirn's face so pink? It looked like a big boiled ham. "Humanity is people I don't know. Who are they? What do they want? It's something different for every different person you ask. Humanity is very confusing to me."

They were waiting for her to say more, but she didn't. "Thank you," Kirn said after a moment. "Now that we've got the ball rolling, I wonder what other perspectives are out there?"

Leslie sat back and traded glances with Marietta. Marietta pulled her mouth into a humorous, sympathetic shape, as in, What was all that about? Leslie shook her head slightly. Other people were making speeches

"Mr. Kirn does like his little stunts," Leslie said, although she had not intended to bring it up. But the more she thought about him putting her on the spot in that way, the more it steamed her. What humanity means to me? Maybe, aggravation.

"I'm sure he's a good lawyer. Otherwise your mother wouldn't be working with him," Christie said reasonably.

Leslie had her own ideas about her mother's judgment in hiring people, but she did not voice them. After some more awkward standing around, she said, "You know those ads about kids born with their upper lips all curled and twisted, what do you call that?"

"Cleft palate."

"Yes. Those really horrible pictures. We could send them some money." She was pleased with herself for the idea.

"If they have enough money to run national ad campaigns, they probably don't need our support. And they aren't the kind of local cause your mother wants to sponsor."

"Well, forget it then."

"But please do keep suggesting projects," Christie said encouragingly.

Leslie had already lost interest in making suggestions, since they didn't seem to be of the right sort. Did anybody in the world ever listen to her, take her seriously?

"It was just an idea. Never mind." Leslie waved it away. "Don't let me get in the way of all the important things you have in mind to do. Excuse me."

Leslie crossed the hall to the den, sat down on the couch, and pried her feet loose from her miserable shoes. Her father had died in this room. Leslie tried to feel some trace of him there, some grumpy ghost, and failed. Maybe money was the only thing he'd left behind.

She was in the worst mood. She hated everyone, not only Christie Schuyler and Kirn, but all the wretched people in the world, including the cleft palate children whose distressing photos ambushed you from magazine pages. There was no one in her family who had not disappointed her: her father by dying, her children by growing up. Her mother with her

now. Humanity was this or that. A recognition of their shared blah blah blah. The challenges they all faced in blah blah blah.

She guessed they all thought they could come up with something better than she had.

They hadn't used this room for normal meals when she and Deirdre were growing up. Most of the time the dining room table was piled with stacks of mail, school projects, craft projects, folded laundry, whatever migrated from other parts of the house. For holidays or company, her mother had bundled the mess away and set the table with all the grand dishes and serving pieces. Certain foods appeared that they did not eat except on such occasions: roast turkey, a Brussels sprouts dish involving chestnuts, a fancy custard. It was like eating in a church or a museum, some place where more was expected of you besides simple eating. So that in one sense, it was not as jarring as it might have been to sit in this room in the company of so many strangers, since it had never been a place of familiar comforts.

But where was there such a place? Her old room had long since been turned into a combination guest room and storage room, its bed piled with boxes. The kitchen had been redone, with upgraded appliances and black granite countertops and artful skylights. She couldn't steal away to her father's basement domain; the wildest of the wild cats lived there now, defecating in corners and clawing through the ceiling tile to hide in the insulation.

It was sad, really. Everything changed. Kids grew up. Old people got older, and if you took your eye off them for the space of a second, they were gone. She wished that when Kirn had called on her, she'd said something about her father. Told them this was his house, he'd built it, and that was his seat at the head of the table. Marietta and Sim had known him. She could have at least made them remember him. But the moment had passed, one more thing gone.

The meeting seemed to be over. People were scraping their chairs back from the table, standing, stretching. Marietta said, "I'm going to have to run right out the door, I have to pick up Jordan. How long are you in town? Call me, maybe we can have lunch. I think this is off to a really good start. Whoever humanity is, they should be pretty happy they're getting all this attention!"

Leslie said good-bye to the sociologist, and to Sim Keogh. The boy who had served the coffee was cleaning up. The sleeves of his shirt were rolled to just below his elbows, and Leslie noticed how brown his arms were, a deep, burned brown, his face and throat also. One of those blond boys who spent so much time in the sun, they looked like a photographic negative. He must have felt her staring at him. He raised his eyes to hers and Leslie glanced away, pretending to be preoccupied with something else.

Her mother appeared at the dining room door, looking anxious. "Did everything go all right?" she asked. "I didn't want to eavesdrop."

"It was fine, Mom." How were such things supposed to go? She had no idea. She stood next to her mother and shook hands with everyone who was leaving, exchanging introductions, since she'd arrived too late for that. The man in the turban was the semi-famous author of a travel book series called Spiritual Destinations. There was a woman who sat on the board of a charity for children with cancer. A man who ran a drug addiction program, who of course looked like he'd taken every drug in the world himself.

The boy clearing away the coffee cups waited politely, since there was no space for him to get through with his tray. Leslie's mother beckoned him, moving people out of his way. "Just leave everything in the kitchen, thank you."

"Who is that?" Leslie muttered, once he'd made an excruciatingly awkward job out of getting through the door. She really hoped he wasn't in charge of washing dishes.

"That is someone whose family has not had all the advantages that yours has." Her mother propelled Leslie toward Christie Schuyler and Kirn, the lawyer, who were approaching the door, the last to exit. "Now I

would really like to see you being pleasant to Christie, it won't cost you a thing. Do you think she'd stay for dinner? Is it too hot for moussaka?"

"I don't like moussaka," Leslie said, as Mr. Kirn advanced, smiling like a species of big, happy fish. Christie Schuyler trailed behind.

"Joyce, you really should have sat in with us." Kirn pretended to scold. He was in an excellent mood. "Tell your mother what a terrific meeting she missed."

"It was super."

"You know you didn't need a nosy old woman taking up space," Leslie's mother said, pleased. "I'm glad it went so well. Christie, you see how silly you were to worry about anything?"

Christie murmured something by way of acknowledgment. She hadn't looked all that worried, either then or now; she didn't have the kind of face that said much. But this was Leslie's mother's method, to pronounce people one thing or another. Leslie's phone buzzed again. She guessed if she'd wanted her husband's attention all this time, she should have gone into finance.

Kirn was speaking to her mother in vibrant, thrilling legal tones, dropping his voice so that Leslie couldn't catch what he said. "Girls," her mother said, meaning Leslie and Christie, "I'll be right back. You two can catch up on your chitchat."

Neither of them looked inclined to start chitchatting. Christie was taller than she was, and Leslie found it irritating to be at eye level with her freckled, unpowdered jaw. She could find some excuse to leave, but she didn't like to abandon the field just yet, while the two of them, Kirn and Christie, were up to who knows what. "What was that about?" she asked. "What did he want with my mother?"

"I don't know. Probably some documents she needs to sign."

"He was certainly very hush-hush about it."

"I expect it was something confidential. Lawyer business." Christie shrugged and one sleeve sagged off her shoulder. She reached up and pulled it straight. The woman dressed like a milkmaid.

new, exciting project that shut her out at every turn. Her husband, for being exactly who he was for all the years of their marriage. Even DeeDee, remote in her deafness and her faraway city and no help to her at all.

She knew she was being unfair, unreasonable, sulky, childish. She didn't care. She could have driven a nail through her own hand, just for spite.

In a little while she'd have to pick herself up, go in search of her mother, listen to Roger's message, argue, sigh, take up the sword again. But for just these few minutes, she wanted to rest. Be someone other than herself. You were supposed to be able to do that if you meditated, but maybe you had to be Indian too.

Something beneath the couch made a soft, bumping noise. Leslie jumped out of her seat and pulled the couch away from the wall by its armrest. An orange cat, either Mr. Darcy or one looking just like him, cowered in the corner. His tail lashed back and forth in agitation.

"Shoo," Leslie said, but there wasn't anywhere for him to shoo. Mr. Darcy's face was the usual frozen cat mask that seemed to doubt your existence. The creature opened its jaw and gave a low, guttural war cry.

"Nasty thing," Leslie told him. "I hope they at least neutered you." She took a half-step toward him and he scrabbled across the floor, clawed at a curtain, and hoisted himself to the closed window. He rubbed against the glass, making more of his strangled noise.

"Shoo," Leslie said again, flapping at him with a magazine. Mr. Darcy hopped down from the windowsill and watched her from the corner. Leslie went to the window and looked out. The backyard was leafy and tranquil, the late-summer ferns bronze, the fountain catching the sunlight and sending it skyward in a glittering loop. Mr. Darcy raised his tail and backed up against the wall to spray it with urine.

"Oh for Christ's sake." Leslie struggled with the window lock and slid the glass up. Quickly, because she heard voices in the hall outside, she unlatched the screen and raised it until it caught.

She backed away from the window. Mr. Darcy hunkered down on his front paws and stared at her. "What are you waiting for?" she asked him.

She picked up another magazine to throw at him. He reached the windowsill with one leap, hauled himself over with his front paws, gave Leslie a last view of his pink anus, and was gone.

Leslie looked for him in the yard, but he had already vanished. She lowered the screen and closed the window and latched it. She wasn't sure if what she had done was a good or a bad deed. Her human heart had been filled with black and spiteful things. But she was pretty sure that Mr. Darcy hadn't cared.

TWELVE

Hi,

Yes it's me, except you got my name wrong, its not Steve. But let me guess yours isn't exactly Laurie, is it.

—

Ha ha ha. I guess when you put it that way . . .

—

Where are you?

—

Right behind you, boo!

—

So your not going to tell me?

—

You going to buy me another drink?

—

Depends. You need one?

—

ROTFL. Always!

—

So where are you?

—

I don't think I should say, Steve. You sound like you might have some kind of bug up your ass.

–

Hi again, sorry, I use this computer at the library and the library
was closing. But that's OK because I had to think some about
what to say. Which is funny because I have thought a lot about
you and things to say to you. Oh well. Laurie or whoever you are
wherever you are. Maybe you can tell me how the car wrecked
and how I was the one they had to cut out of it in about five different
pieces. I don't think I was that drunk. It's a brain thing from the
accident.

My luck wasn't that great before, but thanks to you its pretty much gone
now. I won't sing you the rest of that sad song, but the other thing I
would really really like to know is: why me? Why pick me out of the pile
to play your crazy sick games with?

I guess it makes sense for you and me to have a conversation with a
couple of computers in between us since that's how we started out.
Anyway, whatever.

–

Dear Steve, I hope I can keep on calling you Steve because why not. I
gave up what you might say is my real name a while back. I had my
reasons, but now I think it's a good idea in general for people to change
themselves over every so often when they find themselves in different
circumstances. The one thing you can count on in life is different
circumstances.

I'm sorry you've had bad luck and if it's in some ways my fault, I am
sorry for that too. I will try to explain some things, but here is one
answer for you: I picked you out of the pile because you said you had a
boy who was the same age as my boy.

–

Steve? Are you still out there?

THIRTEEN

Now that things between him and his dad weren't so great, Conner spent more and more time at Mrs. Foster's. There was a room over the garage with its own bathroom and he moved some of his clothes into it. Every so often he drove Mrs. Foster around town to visit her friends, or to do the kinds of errands for which she dressed up. The car was a big Lincoln and his nickname for it was the HMS *Titanic*, but he kept this to himself. Mrs. Foster liked the small ceremonies involved in being driven around, such as having him open and close doors for her, and cautioning him to speed up or slow down. Conner guessed it was one of those things she'd always wanted and was finally getting around to doing. The steering wheel had a loose and floating feel, and he had to take care not to scrape the tires against curbs. Iceberg, dead ahead! It was the kind of car that automatically turned you into a little old lady.

When he was doing other work for her, landscaping or repairs, he had the keys to a small Nissan pickup that he didn't like any better. It shouldn't have bothered him, since it was free and after all it wasn't even his, but it did bother him. It was the kind of truck he liked to make fun of. He was aware that his situation had its embarrassing aspects.

He left the big Ford truck with his dad, not that his dad did much driving now, but it wouldn't have been right to strand him without it. And leaving the truck was another part of their quarrel, meant to demonstrate that Conner had his own life these days and could provide for himself. He was eighteen now—his mother sent a birthday card with a twenty-dollar bill in it—and no one else had to worry about him.

His dad had just worn him out, was the way Conner came to think of it. His dad hadn't meant to do anybody harm, and most of the harm he'd done was to his own self. But he'd been careless in the way he lived and people got tired of it, first Conner's mother and now Conner too. His dad said he was through being a pillhead, he'd cleaned up his act, and maybe that was true. It just didn't matter as much anymore. Conner still went back there to give his dad money, and to make sure Bojangles had what he needed. He wished he could have brought Bojangles to Mrs. Foster's, but with all the wild cats on the place it would turn into an ugly situation, and right now it was important to keep everything there humming along.

His dad gave him all kinds of a hard time. "What are you supposed to be, the pool boy?"

"There isn't any pool."

"You know what I mean."

"Just drop it," Conner told him. He never used to answer back but there were things you got tired of hearing too.

His dad made one of his obnoxious faces, like he knew things nobody else did, and no one could get anything past him. Which was why he spent his days wearing a hole in the couch inside a half-empty house that didn't belong to them anymore, with no visible plan to do anything else for the rest of his life. Conner thought he understood how pride could back up in somebody, get turned around and come out as meanness. But that didn't make it any easier to put up with.

Tonight Conner had brought dinner from the barbecue place his dad liked, hoping it would put him in a better mood. So far it only had the effect of keeping his dad's mouth full of cornbread and slaw and rib tips so that there was a halt to anything unpleasant he had a mind to say. Conner couldn't tell for certain if his dad was through with the pills—he'd quit worrying about it the same way you'd quit a job—but at least his appetite seemed better lately, if not his disposition.

The dog was stretched out on the floor, and every so often he sniffed around to see if any bits of food had fallen, and every so often Conner's dad picked out a bone with some meat on it and tossed it to him. The dog hadn't been the same since his operation, even though the vet said that everything was all right now, the cancer gone. But he didn't have his old happy energy. It was like his sickness had made him afraid somewhere deep down in himself. And so his busted-up dad and the busted-up dog spent their days and nights together doing nothing, and every time Conner walked into the house, the sadness of it made him want to walk right back out again.

He'd planned on spending the night there, but once they were through eating and Conner had collected all the paper plates and napkins and wrappings, he stood up and said he'd better be getting back to Mill Valley.

His dad tilted his head so as to see him better. "Get back, what for?"

Conner couldn't think of either a good reason or a good lie, and so he said, "She gets nervous nights when there's nobody else there."

Which was true enough, although Conner came and went as he pleased, and the most Mrs. Foster ever did was to call him, saying, I thought I saw a light, I thought I heard a car, I just wanted to make sure it was you.

His dad turned back to the television, even though it was only commercials. "Huh."

"I can stay here if you want."

His dad kept his eyes on the television, its hectic color and noise, and raised one hand in a wave, meaning, do whatever you want.

"I'll walk Bo first."

His dad said Fine, sure, and Conner coaxed the dog up from his spot and out the back door. The ground was dried and summer-hard and the dog walked like it hurt his feet. He sniffed around in the bleached-out grass and foxtails, not finding anything of interest.

It was almost Labor Day, and already there was less daylight, minute by minute. By the time he reached Mrs. Foster's, darkness would have come down like a lid. Back when he was in school, this was the time of year when you looked forward to a certain energy, different routines starting up. He hadn't liked everything about school: a lot of it had bored or aggravated him. But at least he'd had his place there, and a sense that there was meant to be progress, one year piled on top of another as you went along. Now the thought of fall, and of the winter beyond it, felt only cold and final.

Conner knew that his dad would have liked him to stay over tonight, just as he would have liked things to be easy between the two of them again. But his dad didn't have it in him to come out and ask, or apologize, and that was something else Conner had grown tired of, arranging it so his dad could act like he didn't care if the things he wanted came his way.

When he brought the dog back inside, Conner said, "Don't you have a doctor's appointment tomorrow?" He said this as a reminder. He hadn't entirely cured himself of the habit of worry on his dad's behalf, afraid he would forget, hurt himself, screw up one more time.

"What about it?"

Conner couldn't tell if this meant his dad had only just now remembered, or say that he did, if he intended to go. This was a new doctor who was supposed to treat pain through hypnosis and electrical stimulation and other methods that you wanted to believe would work, although they probably didn't. "I hope it goes OK."

"Ah, doctors. They just gnaw parts of you down so you fit better in your coffin."

There were a lot of cheerful observations like that these days. Conner drove away wondering if that was really what it came down to for his dad, getting ready to die, and if Conner should be getting ready for him to die too.

It was more than an hour's drive back to Mill Valley, and that was if he was lucky with the traffic. He was beginning to hate the 101, the backups, the miles of stinking exhaust in your face. The highway brought out the worst in people. He'd seen it happen, felt it in himself, cursing whoever was ahead of him the same way people behind him probably cursed him. Road rage, they called it. Like it was really the road's fault.

He guessed he didn't think as highly of humanity as Mrs. Foster did, with her happy little charity. Yeah, but he didn't think all that highly of himself these days.

He'd stolen from a dead man the first time he'd been inside her house, and he had gone there intending to steal again.

He'd needed money for Bojangles, twelve hundred dollars for the surgery, and another five hundred for what he already owed. The vet clinic suggested he take out a loan. They were not unsympathetic. They saw this kind of thing all the time now. People gave up the pets they could no longer afford to feed. Animals turned up in shelters half starved, and with heartworm, unhealed fractures, mange. They wished they could treat them all, save them all, but, etc.

"Christ," his dad had said. "I need another operation myself, you see anybody lining up to pitch in?"

His mom had said, "Oh honey, I can send you a little, and a little more next month, but they just cut back my hours, do you want me to talk to them? Oh honey, this is all just so unfair."

And so he'd gone back to some of the places where he'd had luck with stealing before. His method was to park the truck on the street and knock on a front door, and if anybody answered he'd ask if they needed yard work done and either they did or they didn't.

If there was no answer, he unloaded his rake and clippers and worked industriously in the yard for a time, since no one ever noticed the people doing such things. If the homeowner happened to come back, he would say it was a mistake, his boss had sent him out, he must have gotten the address wrong.

And if nobody came back, you'd be surprised at how many people were careless about locking their doors, or installed substandard locks, or didn't think about the ground-floor windows, at least not in the middle of the day. Once an alarm system had screeched at him and he'd had to get away fast, but he hadn't been caught and he thought that the owners of the house had gotten their money's worth, good for them.

If he did get inside a place he was quick, in and out in a couple of minutes. He knew by now where he might find the extra keys, the fireproof safety box, the credit cards nobody bothered to carry with them, the phones and cameras he shoved into his pockets, the computers small enough to hide beneath his sweatshirt. There were always flea markets, and certain people who hung around the flea markets, and little punk kids with too much money who'd buy whatever new and shiny stuff he had. But all that took time and effort when what he needed was cash, and right away.

He hadn't meant to ever go back to the Fosters' house, where it had all begun. It had been too creepy and shaming, and besides, he could have been recognized. But the house wouldn't quit him, and stayed in his head for every bad reason. He had found items of immediate and portable value there, and no consequences had come his way. And say he got caught, there or anywhere else. He was almost ready for the worst to happen, his life going into some blazing flameout tailspin, just so he wouldn't have to keep worrying about it happening.

And so he had parked in the driveway and rung the front doorbell. It had a deep, underground sound, as if the house itself meant to warn people away.

No one answered, and Conner walked away back down the drive, thinking things through, telling himself he hadn't done anything yet, only knocked on a door, nothing he couldn't explain or take back. There was always that too-late moment—a door forced, your hand in a drawer—but he hadn't reached it yet and didn't have to. He could follow his instinct, which was to leave it be, go somewhere else, and so he would have done except just then an old lady in a quilted bathrobe ran around the corner of the house, waving her arms as if trying to signal a boat.

"Are you from the gas company?"

He froze. But she didn't remember him; why should she? "No ma'am. Is there a problem?"

"The house is full of gas, you can smell it everywhere!" With her snarled hair and pinched, gray face she looked like an escaped hospital patient. She took a step, wobbled.

"OK, easy there." Conner moved closer, ready to prop her up or catch her if he had to. "You want me to call somebody?"

"I called already but nobody—" Her fingers plucked at her bathrobe, then her hair. "Would you just look at me, running around like a goony bird!"

"What happened?"

"I didn't even have time to get dressed!" She appealed to him with the unfairness of it. Her mouth gaped and she labored to breathe. He couldn't tell if she was woozy from a gas leak or if it was just distressed vanity.

Conner said, "Maybe you should sit down." There was nowhere to sit. "Did you want me to go in and check, see if I can find anything?"

"Be careful! Don't turn on any lights, it can spark an explosion!"

He went in through the kitchen. He smelled cat piss, not gas. The smell rose up and ballooned inside his head. She must be so used to it, she could detect some other, different stink on top of it. Conner looked around him, not finding anything in the way of a gas leak or anything of value he could lay hands on. He took a few quick steps into the den, feeling thick-headed from the smell. There was a way in which the room did not match up with the room in his memory, and a way in which it did. He turned, blundered into a wall, and walked back through the kitchen and outside.

An orange PG&E truck was just pulling up in the driveway, and a worker in a vest and helmet got out. Mrs. Foster—he had forgotten the name, but it would come back to him soon enough—was telling the worker the details and urgencies of the situation. Conner waited. He had an unreasoning fear that she would drop dead, and it would be his fault.

The PG&E guy walked around the house to investigate. "It'll be all right," Conner told her, although he didn't know that.

Mrs. Foster stuck her hands in the pockets of her bathrobe, pulled out a pair of eyeglasses, and settled them over her nose. "What if the house blows up?" she asked plaintively.

"It won't."

"Well you sound very sure of yourself." She contemplated him. "Do I know you?"

"No ma'am. But I'm glad I was in the neighborhood and could help."

She looked him over again, either trying to remember him or trying to fit him into a recognizable category, but she didn't say anything more. They waited for the PG&E guy to finish. Conner wondered about the cats. He hadn't remembered cats.

The PG&E guy came back out and said there was a pilot light out on the water heater, that was the only thing he could find, there was a lot of pet hair blocking the oxygen feed and he'd cleaned it away. He said this without seeming to criticize or draw conclusions. It was probably the sort of job where you saw all kinds of things.

They watched him back his truck down the drive. "Well if that isn't mortifying," Mrs. Foster said. "All that fuss over a water heater."

"You didn't know what it was."

"My husband always took care of the house things."

Conner said nothing. She turned to look at him again, her eyes magnified and swimming behind the lenses of her glasses. "And what exactly were you doing in my yard?"

"Actually," Conner said, and it was another too-late moment, a step through another sort of doorway, "actually, I was looking for work."

The next day he went to a health club that was advertising free trial memberships, filled out a guest pass with a name not his own, and stole two wallets and an iPhone from some unlocked lockers.

And so he had gone to work for Mrs. Foster, and the vet allowed him to set up a payment plan for the rest of what he owed, and things were all right now but not really. He told Mrs. Foster enough about his father and his father's situation and his own situation to enlist her sympathy, while also managing to suggest that he was holding back because of the exquisitely painful nature of it all. Mrs. Foster's capacity for sympathy was a bubbling spring, a geyser barely capped, and it was not difficult to siphon enough of it off to work to his benefit.

He admired her generosity; he also felt a contempt for how easily she could be manipulated. He was ashamed of his talent for ingratiating himself, even as he had every intention of continuing to do so. He felt protective of Mrs. Foster, of her bouts of frailty and distress, she was useful to him, she annoyed him. His dealings with her were in large part motivated by self-interest and in some smaller part by dread, guilt, obligation, and wanting to do the right thing, and all the people she brought around who kept trying to figure out the definition of humanity? That was it right there.

Mrs. Foster delighted in coming up with large and small chores for him. He planted shrubs and replaced the worn stair tread. He cleaned up cat mess and built gates and pens to contain them in the basement. He liked cats, in general, but he did not like these cats. He could be entrusted with lists of supplies to purchase, and more involved transactions that required negotiations with tradespeople. He helped her do battle with the new computer her daughters had insisted on buying for her. "It's too complicated, it won't let me do anything."

"It just looks different from what you're used to." What she had been used to was a ten-year-old PC.

"I told everybody at the Foundation, if there's something I'm supposed to know, type it up and put it in an envelope."

"Now that's just being a quitter," Conner said, in a pretend-scolding tone. He knew by now what he could and couldn't get away with around her.

"Young man," Mrs. Foster said, pretending to be severe, enjoying every minute, "when I make up my mind to quit, I don't expect to be talked out of it."

She liked having some company in the house, she said, someone to help her with all those things she tended to fuss about. She said she didn't know what to pay him, he was going to have to help her with that too, and Conner said he didn't know, he guessed whatever she had in mind would be all right. Instinct told him it would be best to be vague here. She made special trips to her bank in order to have clean twenties and fifties to hand over to him, always with a hesitation as she did so, always adding one more bill and asking him, is that all right, is that enough?

There were times he felt he was taking advantage of her, and times it felt the other way around.

He didn't steal from her, unless being overpaid was stealing. He told her that he was saving money for college, which was not a lie unless he never went. He still did the occasional odd job for other people. It seemed like a good idea for him to have somewhere else to be once in a while. Between paying off the vet and giving money to his dad, there wasn't any huge amount left to him. He held on to what he could. He didn't steal, but honesty was a luxury he wasn't yet sure he could afford.

He used to believe that he would grow up in pretty much the same way everyone else did, the same way all his friends went about it. At the end of high school you were propelled into the next phase, like an exit on the highway that shot you in a certain direction, and then it was a matter of choosing lanes (work, school, what work, what school), and your choice carried you forward without much further effort. Now he saw that you couldn't count on moving forward. He could end up like his dad, just going along and going along and never much thinking about things until all of a sudden life did something unforgiving to you, and made you realize you were old.

"Why don't you have a girlfriend?" Mrs. Foster asked him straight out, when she was in one of her playful moods. "A good-looking young man like you."

"I don't have time for one."

"Nonsense. There's always time for that."

"It's OK, really." He liked her better when she didn't try so hard to be pals.

"Are you shy? Girls always warm up to the shy ones."

No, he wasn't shy. He watched the girls who drove around town wearing their sunglasses and trailing bright bits of music, he watched the joggers in ponytails and shorts and bra tops, he beat off in the shower as he fucked them again and again, their legs pushed apart and dangling, their pink faces wincing. He wasn't shy but he didn't know how to get from watching to fucking. He would have scared them if he'd tried. There was meant to be conversation and flirting and some effort made, and he didn't care to make the effort, or he'd forgotten how. He couldn't bring himself to talk about all the small and meaningless things girls required to prove you were paying them attention.

He hadn't even noticed the girl behind him in line at the Mexican place where he sometimes bought lunch. He was waiting for them to call his number when she walked over and said, "So I guess you liked the burritos."

"What?"

"He doesn't remember," she remarked, as if to a watching audience, although there was no one with her and no one paying attention.

"Oh, hi." She had red hair now. "Yeah, good burritos."

She took a step toward him and regarded him as if he was something hung on a wall, a picture, or maybe a bus schedule. "What did you do to your hair?"

They called his number then and he picked up his food. When he turned around the girl managed to be in his way without looking like she was trying to. "Wait for me, OK?"

He didn't have to but he did. When she had picked up her own food, Conner said, "Looks like you did a number on your hair too."

She raised a hand to flick the hair away from her eyes. The red color was a little faded, some of the dye rinsed out. "This is my natural color. Didn't you have some weird name?"

"Conner. Yours was weirder." He remembered hers all right, Eowyn. But he didn't want to admit to it if she had forgotten his.

She shook her head. "I'm kind of between names right now. You want to sit down?"

He'd been intending to eat in the truck, but instead found an empty table. They sat across from each other and started in on their food. He was able to look her over, make up his mind about her. The hair was sort of freaky, but she was wearing ordinary clothes, jeans and a T-shirt. The skin of her face was pale for the end of summer, and she'd drawn smudged black crayon around her eyes. She saw him looking. "What?"

"Why do you put that black stuff on your eyes?"

"You don't like it?"

"No. It makes you look like a raccoon."

"Well thanks so much. Raccoon is exactly what I was aiming for."

Conner couldn't tell if she was pissed off or not. He'd finished his food but she was still working on hers, cutting it with a plastic knife and fork. He said, "How old are you anyway?"

"Older than I look."

"Come on, just tell me."

"I'll be sixteen in February. See, I knew you wouldn't believe me."

"Did I say anything?"

She shook her head and went back to poking at her food. Conner guessed she looked about fifteen, sure. He didn't think she was hitting on him. She was just weird. "So, why aren't you in school?" he asked, just to be saying something.

Her face closed down, went flat and sullen. "What are you, the truant officer?"

"Aren't you supposed to be there?"

"This week is just some meetings and stuff."

"Oh, so you're a little badass. Skipping out."

Her black-smudged eyes contemplated him. "I don't know anybody there yet. Which is both a good and a bad thing. I think I need to go to a beach or something."

"What, and work on your tan?"

"No, just, be someplace where there aren't any people." She finished eating and gave the straw in her drink a final noisy pull.

More customers were crowding in at the door for the lunch rush. They cleared away their trays and walked out into the hazy hot day. The restaurant was on a frontage road parallel to 101. The traffic was like water from a running tap, pouring over the highway. "You see what I mean?" the girl said. "Is there anything here that wasn't made by, what do they call it, the hand of man? Except I guess the sky?"

He hadn't really thought about it. "Well, nice to see you," Conner said. He had to raise his voice over the traffic noise.

"Yeah, you too." She was occupied with looking through her bag.

Before he drove off, he tried to call his dad. He got the message saying that the number was temporarily unavailable. This meant the bill hadn't been paid, which was aggravating because he'd given his dad the money for it. One more way-to-go-Dad moment.

When he started down the frontage road, he saw the girl trudging along the edge of the parking lot, past the vaguely Spanish-style building complex that housed other restaurants, stores selling baby goods, luggage, stained glass. She'd put on an oversized pair of white sunglasses that took up half her face. Conner lowered the window. "Do you need a ride?"

She opened the passenger door and got in. "Thanks. It just sucks not to be able to drive around here."

"Where did you need to go?"

She turned the sunglasses in his direction. "I don't actually need to go anywhere."

"School," he reminded her.

"I haven't entirely decided about school. I'd have to repeat some courses, that's another sucky thing." She looked around her. "What kind of a truck is this? It's very lame-o."

"Yeah, well, so are those sunglasses."

She turned her face toward him and peered over the tops of the glasses. "I like them. They're like, a spy who's trying to look Hollywood."

"The last time I saw you," Conner said, "you were trying to sell me pot."

"That didn't work out very well. Not just with you, I mean in general." She shifted around on the seat until she had one leg tucked underneath her. "You were so majorly offended. Don't tell me you never in your life smoked."

"I wouldn't say that." He'd done his share. But he'd pretty much quit when his dad started having his problems. He didn't want both of them staggering around the house stoned. "If you want to go someplace, you need to tell me where."

"The beach? Come on. Pretty please? I can't get there by myself. Where were you going instead?"

"Back home." Although saying this, he didn't know if he'd meant Mrs. Foster's or his dad's. If he went to Mrs. Foster's, she'd want him to do some made-up chore so she'd have an excuse to pay him again. Sometimes he felt like an African orphan, like a poster child for her charity empire. If he went to his dad's, he'd have to listen to a lot of snot about being a pool boy. Not yet ready to decide anything, he said, "I need to get gas, OK?"

He filled up at a Stop N Go and tried to call his dad again. Again he got the same recorded message. Was there ever going to be a time when he didn't worry about his dad? The answer came to him right away: when his dad was dead.

Conner got back into the truck. "Which beach did you want to go to?"

She said, Oh, excellent, she said she didn't know, she hadn't been to any of them, she was still kind of new here. Conner asked her where she was from and she said a galaxy far, far away. "Fine," Conner said. "Have it your way. The mystery girl from Planet Weird."

She was quiet then. "Hey," Conner said. "I'm just messing with you."

"An asteroid crashed into my home planet and we had to activate our escape pods."

Conner drove back through Mill Valley, then onto the Shoreline Highway. It was a weekday and there wasn't any beach traffic to speak of. "It could be cloudy at the beach," he said. "Colder."

"I don't care. This is just excellent. I wish we could go all the way to the Arctic Circle."

He thought they could head to Muir Beach, that was the closest. The road wound along the cliff edge with the ocean far below. The girl hugged the door, shrinking away from the drop-off, even as she craned her neck to see it better. "You haven't been up here before, have you?"

"Don't talk, just drive, OK?"

The road led them down again, past a cluster of mailboxes, a pasture of grazing horses, then a short tree-lined lane to the beach itself. He steered into the parking lot, found a spot, and killed the engine. "Here you go. Beach."

They got out and made their way along paths through an expanse of clumpy ice plant, then sand, then down to the smooth wetness at the water's edge. A dozen or more other people sat or strolled, all of them giving the impression of trying to ignore everyone else. Muir was small, a pocket beach, with cliffs on either side and houses on one slope of the peak above it. To the north you could walk around a cliff shoulder to a narrower rim of sand. Farther still there was supposed to be a nude beach, or so his pals always said, but Conner guessed that was wishful thinking.

It must have been close to low tide. The waves were small and orderly, rinsing in and out, leaving a deposit of kelp and sticks. Seagulls marched back and forth, only bothering to fly off when people came right up on them. The sky was thin gray with a mild, eddying breeze off the water.

The girl bent down and untied the laces of her sneakers. She took one shoe off and hopped around, trying to kick the other shoe loose. "Here," Conner said, holding an arm out.

She leaned on him to steady herself and managed to get the shoe off. "Thanks."

He hadn't meant anything by it. But it took on some kind of meaning, touching her, if only because he couldn't remember the last time he'd touched anyone. The girl was looking out at the ocean, scowling. He couldn't tell what she was thinking.

He watched her roll up her pants legs. "That water's cold," he said.

"Sissy."

"Fine. Knock yourself out."

She took a few steps until she was ankle-deep in the surf, then set off walking the length of the beach. Conner kept pace with her from above the tide line. He pulled out his phone. You couldn't get service out here, but maybe his dad had left a message. He checked but there weren't any calls. They hadn't talked for a couple of days. His dad was still doing his pissy act, where everything was Conner's fault. He was welcome to keep it up and see where that got him. But the phone being turned off was something new.

At the end of the beach the girl came out of the surf and sat down in the sand to put her shoes back on. After a minute Conner sat down too, on a ridge of sand just above her. "Was that fun?"

"Oh yeah. Big fun." She was brushing sand off her bare feet.

"Why don't you want to go to school?"

"I got my reasons."

"What are they? Come on. Did you flunk math or something?"

She was still wearing the white sunglasses, but they were a little too big for her and kept falling down. She pushed them up to the top of her head. "I thought I wanted to go. I really did. Because it would be all new, a new place. I don't know." She was still picking grains of sand from her toes.

"Don't know what?"

"If I can . . ."

"What?" Conner said, because she was mumbling.

"Can be around other people."

"You're around other people right now," he pointed out.

"Not really."

They watched the ocean for a while. He thought he saw something dark rise above the white collar of a distant wave. A seal? But he didn't see it again, and he wasn't certain enough to mention it, and anyway it was one of those times when talking embarrassed him, made him feel he was going right off the edge of a cliff.

After a while she turned around to look at him. "So, Conner"—it was a mild shock to hear her use his name—"I need to ask you one of those theoretical, hypothetical questions, like, if somebody had a small amount of marijuana right here and right now, would you smoke it with them, or would that freak you out?"

"You little druggie." He was relieved that she was back to her more or less normal, smart-ass self.

"It's just the one jay." She dug into the lining of her purse and held it up.

"Why don't you either smoke it now or get rid of it so it's not in the truck." He didn't think Mrs. Foster would appreciate any police actions involving vehicles registered to her.

They climbed up on some rocks at the far end of the beach, away from the others, not that you figured any of them really cared. Conner let her smoke most of it herself, and only palmed it for a quick couple of hits. It gave his head a pleasant, spacious feel.

They got back in the truck and the girl tucked her legs underneath her and said, "You know all the drugs in the world, the ones people invent, there's not a one of them that does as much good as the all-natural kind."

"Penicillin."

"That grows from a mold. Where are we going?"

It hadn't occurred to Conner to go anywhere else, but now he considered. "I don't know. You want to just drive around for a while?"

"Yes yes." She pulled out a set of earbuds and fiddled with them. "Do you have any extra? These are shot."

He was trying to concentrate on his driving, he was just high enough that it was making him stupid. "What? No."

"That's the problem with people now. They aren't natural enough. They've lost their natural, ah, natures. You shouldn't need some machine to listen to music. You should sing, or play an instrument."

"What are you talking about? This is your brain on drugs, I'm thinking."

"Are you some evil character I shouldn't be riding around with? Huh? I guess you probably wouldn't tell me anyway. Never mind. Sorry. Don't mind me. I'm just practicing my people skills."

"You need to calm down some." He had an intimation of the many bad things that might come from his original bad idea of letting her into the truck.

"Sure, OK. Sorry." She shook her head, then looked out her window. "This is pretty here, wherever it is."

They were back on the Shoreline Highway, headed north. The ocean was now at a little distance from them, a flat silver in the hazy afternoon sun. There was more traffic now, people heading out to Stinson Beach. "If you want to see more of a beach beach, you know, people lying out on towels in swimsuits, there's one coming up."

"Not really."

They were both quiet then. Conner let the road decide for them, carry them along past the Stinson turnoffs, along the lagoon and the unmarked road to Bolinas, into the trees then out again on the other side. It had been a long time since he'd driven out here and he waited for landmarks he recognized, a crossroads, a sign for horseback riding. "If you keep going," he said, "you reach Point Reyes, which is like a big ocean park, with beaches and hiking trails and a lighthouse. It's a peninsula, and it's on a fault line. They figure the next really strong earthquake, it'll probably just break off."

"Then let's go there and hope we get an earthquake."

At Olema, Conner made the turn onto Sir Francis Drake Highway. Cows grazed in pastures edged with blackberry bushes and white and yellow wildflowers. The girl pointed to a house set back along the road, with a front porch made out of timbers. "That's where I want to live."

"Yeah? What would you do there?"

"I could be an ecoterrorist."

"A what?"

"You heard me. Burn things down or blow them up if they hurt the environment. Like, housing developments and ski lodges."

He thought that was pretty funny, but just in case she was serious, he kept his mouth shut.

They stopped at the grocery at the last little town before you entered the Point, to get bottled water and a couple of bags of snacks, since there seemed to be some munchies in play. Conner stood outside next to the car, waiting for her to get done with the restroom. The narrow bay behind him was at low tide, ribbons of water laid out along stretches of mud and kelp. His head still had blank spaces in it, so that he had to make an effort to link one thought to the next. He knew the sequence of events that had brought him here, and he knew what was before his eyes, but he couldn't fathom any particular reason for his presence.

But where should he be instead? Nowhere else made much sense these days. He was an amateur thief, an odd-jobs man, a hustler, and maybe he was something even worse and hadn't yet found it out.

The girl came around the front corner of the store. He couldn't tell what was different until she came closer. She'd washed all the heavy black makeup away. Her eyes were pink and scrubbed. "Hey, no more raccoon," Conner said.

"I can put it back on, you know."

"No, don't. You look better without that crap."

She opened the truck's door. "Wow, you'll probably be buying me a corsage next."

The sky had been blue above them, but as they headed toward the ocean once more, the air turned to a kind of gray glare, a layer of clouds that seemed to barely hold back the sun. The hills and woods gave way to long sandy flats, a branching lagoon, and in the distance, the ocean. The road straggled on ahead as far as they could see. A single car approached them; they saw it coming from a long way off, then closer, then it passed them and was gone. The road was now the only thing visible that had been built by the hand of man, and it seemed like a place where anything could happen, something from a movie, or a fairy tale, or a dream.

They'd been quiet for a while. When Conner looked over at the girl, she was watching the horizon where the ocean came into brief view beyond the hills. Conner said, "You know, when you go to school, they'll have to call you some kind of name. So why don't you tell it to me. It's sort of freaky that you won't."

"I will, OK? Unless you keep bugging me. Don't make such a big deal out of it."

"Fine, mystery passenger."

She rolled her eyes but didn't answer. A little while later she said, "I want to live out here. Right here."

"Sure. You could dig a hole in the sand and eat seagulls."

"Do you think people are naturally bad? You know, evil?"

"Why are you asking me?" Did she never stop saying bizarre things?

"Because you're the only one here," she said, reasonably. "Because I wonder about it. If people start out that way, or if things happen that aren't their fault."

"It's always their fault," he said, angry at her for never shutting up.

"What's the matter with you all of a sudden?"

"I have a headache from answering dumb questions."

He felt her looking at him, then she said, "Can we get closer to the ocean? Can we see it from up close?"

He sighed. He couldn't win with her. He'd been thinking of heading all the way to the lighthouse at the end of the Point, but instead he took the turnoff to South Beach, the road curving around small, sandy hills until they reached the parking lot. There was one other car parked at the far end, and it had a broken-down aspect, as if it had been there a long time.

They got out of the truck and stood on the overlook above the beach, a straight expanse of shoreline in both directions as far as they could see. The wind was strong enough to make them squeeze their eyes shut against it. The ocean beyond was enormous and wild. Huge gray-green waves broke and re-formed again and again and again. It was cold in the wind, and the girl jumped up and down and hugged herself. "Whoo-oo!"

Conner went back to the truck and found one of his old sweatshirts. "Here," he said, handing it to her. She looked at it as if she didn't know what it was. "Put it on."

She pulled it over her head and poked her hands out of the too-long sleeves. "Thank you." She studied the signs posted along the overlook, warnings about sneaker waves and sharks and cliff erosion. "Do they really have sharks? Let's get down by the water."

The path wound through the ice plant and beach grass. There were steep places where they skidded in sand. At the bottom the wind was less. Up against the cliff face, driftwood logs had been dragged into a space for sitting around a fire pit. "Come on," the girl said, trudging toward the waterline.

"Look, they aren't kidding about sneaker waves and rip currents. Don't go in the water."

She started running. "Hey," Conner shouted. "What did I just tell you?"

Once she'd put some distance between them, she turned around, walking backward, and shouted something he couldn't hear. "What?"

"Never mind. Another dumb question."

"Don't be that way," he said uselessly.

She cupped her hands around her mouth. ". . . something really, really bad."

He started toward her, walking slow and deliberate so as not to seem he was chasing her, in case she was out to do something stoned and stupid. "I can't hear you."

"I said, do you think if you do something really, really bad, that means you're always going to be bad, from then on?"

"Now that's an interesting question. Come on back and sit down so we can talk about it."

"I'm looking for more of an . . ."

"What?"

". . . off-the-top-of-your-head answer."

She was skipping along the frill of water where the waves ran in. He counted ten of his heartbeats. Maybe she was one of those mental health cases who tried to kill themselves five times a week. Maybe she was just screwing around. Conner looked one way and then the other along the beach, saw no one. The waves rose up behind her. For a few moments the ocean's force balanced their immense weight far above her head, then they broke and came booming down. Again he had the sense that anything could happen, as if the huge sky and the huge ocean were a kind of theater they had wandered into without knowing.

He raised his voice over the noise of the wind and surf. "Hey, I'll tell you what I think if you'll tell me your name."

"You first."

"I think"—he didn't know what he thought but he kept on talking— "you don't have to go on being like that. Like whatever shit you did. It's just what happened. Hey! You know when's the only time you can't fix shit? Make up for it? When you're dead."

The girl was a good twenty yards away. She began moving toward Conner, not in a straight line, but angling and dawdling, as if to hide any intention of reaching him. But when she did, she looked him full in the face, and her eyes were roughened from the wind and stinging sand. "My name's Linnea."

"Linnea." He'd never heard it before as a name. "Well that's nice."

She was curling herself inside the sweatshirt, trying to get more warmth from it, and there was a blue tint to her lips that didn't look good. He stooped down and used his arms to warm her and they kissed, just once, confusing them both, and then they started back up the slope to the truck without saying more.

Once they reached the parking lot another car was there, with an older couple just getting out, and another car pulling in, and Conner thought that whatever had just happened between them, it would not have come about if anyone else had been there to see.

When they had driven back as far as the turnoff to Route 1, Conner said, "Do you have time for a detour? I wanted to swing up north a ways, stop at my dad's."

Linnea—he had to keep the name in front of him—lifted her head. "I've got time. I think I'm still supposed to be in school. So, do you live with him? Your dad?"

Conner said yes, because that was the simplest answer, and she said, "Me too. I mean, I live with my dad, not yours."

He was relieved that she sounded just as casual and offhand as he did. He guessed he should ask her about her mom, and she could ask him about his.

But they could save that for later, once they decided what else to ask and to tell, and he would have liked to think some more about the kissing, but for right now it was best to act as if none of it had really happened.

It was a long slow road going this back way into Sebastopol, and Linnea slept for most of it. Conner called his dad again and got the same message. He tried to keep his mind empty and open and not think about anything more than getting where he was going, and then dealing with the next problem, namely his dad, who wasn't going to stop being a problem anytime soon.

Linnea woke up just as they were entering town. "Is this it? Where we were going?"

"Yeah, and now it's where we are."

"It's so hard to get a straight answer around here. I have to go to the bathroom."

"Noted."

She sighed in pretend exasperation. "Sometime, just for fun, let's act like normal people having a normal conversation. We could find a conversation in a book and read it out loud, take different parts."

Conner stopped the truck on the street across from the house. Linnea started to say something, then closed her mouth. The driveway was filled with things that looked like the wreckage from a flood: mashed cardboard boxes, clothes spilling out the top, a sofa leaning up against a fence, a pile of black plastic trash bags, stacks of books that had been kicked over or otherwise scattered, splintered kitchen cabinets pulled out of the walls and disgorging some cookware, a trail of papers in wads and in single sheets, more, all of it ruined, soiled, abandoned.

"Stay here," Conner said to Linnea, and he saw in her face what his own must look like. He got down from the truck and checked the front door, blank and locked as always, then ran around to the back, stumbling, made stupid with dread, already knowing what he would find: the house emptied out of their squatters' possessions, his father, and the dog too, long gone.

Did we still believe in heaven? Some of us were raised up righteous and kept the faith. But for those of us who had fallen away from theology, there was no clear notion of what awaited us after the final lights-out, or even what we might wish for. Most of us would rather just go on living, although in more easeful circumstances. Heaven for us might be one big television commercial, a place of beatified food items, miracle cures, and brand-new cars that transported us to places we had never been but longed to go to, like the seaside, or the wilderness.

In this our heaven, instead of angels we would have celebrities, those luminous two-dimensional beings who came to us by way of screens or magazine pages. As it was, they were hardly real, and if ever one of them appeared in person, it constituted a visitation.

In this our heaven, instead of hunger, there would be simple appetite. Instead of loneliness, there would be the fellowship of major brands.

Anyway, we didn't much like thinking about things like death, or the failures of the body, or the disapproving God who had been totting up demerits all our lives. We had to get through our day, and stack it on top of the day before, and then pile the next day on top of those. We had to keep the wobbling stack in some kind of balance, and only every so often did we attempt to discern the shape of it, or draw a line around it with a story, something like "A long time ago, I was a bride," or "Nobody ever paid that much attention," or "I went away to war and when I came back, everything was different."

When you died, it was the end of the story.

Oh but we wanted to keep starting over, rewinding our stories back to the beginning and making them better, and maybe that's what our heaven would be, one more chance and then another and another, an infinity of chances to get it right.

Because whether you called it sin or mistakes or something else, there was so much that had turned out wrong.

We didn't want to wait for heaven. We only had our one lifetime, not long enough for history or evolution to wash over us and make us into something different. But surely even within our brief and mortal selves there were possibilities. Amazing transformations. Changes of luck or circumstances. And while some of these had to do with money, which might always be beyond our reach, there was also love, which was not.

FOURTEEN

Seek out your own salvation with diligence.
Be a lantern unto yourself.

A skinny adolescent cat, white with a black question mark across its face, was sunning itself on the window ledge in Mrs. Foster's breakfast nook. Mrs. Foster made small coaxing noises to try and get its attention. Christie warmed her hands on her teacup and waited to see if Mrs. Foster wished to hear any more from her. She'd already covered the basics of the Foundation's progress and now she was down to things like grant deadlines and tax filings. Mrs. Foster said, "There's something about a sleeping cat, isn't there? You just can't leave them alone."

Christie was pretty sure that she herself could, but she made a noise of mild agreement. It was Mrs. Foster's prerogative to tease cats, to ask questions and ignore the answers, or any other behavior she had a mind to engage in. Now that she was Mrs. Foster's employee, rather than her nurse, she was obliged to put up with such things.

Mrs. Foster gave up on the cat and turned back to Christie. "It's nice we're giving money to the food pantry. And the affordable housing program too. You have to start with the basics. Food and shelter."

"You can make a real difference," Christie said, hoping she didn't sound entirely fatuous. She was here at Mrs. Foster's request, since Mrs. Foster said she preferred such updates to all those tiresome written reports, which Christie suspected she did not read. Christie had brought her medical bag along and checked Mrs. Foster's vital signs and asked the routine questions about her well-being. Although there seemed no need. Mrs. Foster was enjoying a spell of elderly good health, as if giving away money had been just the tonic for her. These days her makeup was always gallantly applied, her fingernails lacquered either rosy pink or a dark plum shade that she told Christie was called "Man Eater."

As for Christie, she was discovering unexpected and not always attractive talents in herself. She could do the things necessary to running a business, if you thought of the Foundation as a species of business. She was learning to read financial statements and grant applications; they no longer made her feel thunderstruck by her own ignorance. She issued press releases and made phone calls to strangers, with more ease than she might have imagined. She tackled spreadsheets. She held people to account, she was unmoved by the excuses and sullenness of bad employees. She told sass-mouth Janelle to either get off her cell phone or go home for good, and when Janelle left, she didn't stop her. When Kenny didn't take his meds and started following everyone around, standing too close and asking them intense personal questions, Christie put him on medical leave and changed the building's locks.

It had been Mrs. Foster's wish that the Foundation employ the otherwise unemployable: the drug-addled, the belligerently untrained, the mildly nuts. Christie had gone along with this, not because she'd thought it was a good idea, but because it seemed her job to follow instructions. Now she was retooling the office staff one by one, trying to make it into something other than a sheltered workshop. She didn't discuss this with Mrs. Foster, since one of her new, unappealing talents seemed to be strategic sneakiness. Besides, she wanted the Foundation to succeed, she wanted to do a good job.

They were beginning with a series of small-scale initiatives, making contributions to already-established organizations. A mental health out-reach program. Groups that provided youth mentoring, or community-based medical screenings. Christie was familiar with some of these from her work at the clinic. She had her own opinions about which of them got results and which of them were badly managed, and she made decisions accordingly. Those applying for the grants made efforts at flattery and courtship, and these efforts annoyed or amused her. At the same time, she was beginning to enjoy the small amounts of power her position gave her. She believed this was another unwholesome development, one more of her recently discovered and distressing moral failings.

"But I can't help feeling," Mrs. Foster said, still distracted by the sleeping cat, "that all these very practical efforts—and this is in no way meant as a criticism of you, my dear, because I think you are entirely wonderful—that these basic, practical things don't really address the kinds of broader issues I had in mind."

Christie didn't entirely disagree with this, but she needed to be cautious. "What broader issues are those?"

"Oh, I don't know. Something"—a wave of Mrs. Foster's manicured hand, the knuckles now larger than the fingers themselves, which were so wrinkled as to appear corrugated—"significant. Now, this is going to sound insulting, and I don't mean it that way, I don't mean for you to take it at all personally."

Christie braced herself for the insult that she was not meant to take personally. ". . . but you can be a nurse, and take care of everybody's small, immediate needs, or you can be the researcher who cures cancer." Mrs. Foster sat back, pleased with her rhetorical flourish.

"I'm not sure that's a good example. Or a fair choice."

"It's a figure of speech. Oh heavens, don't sulk. Would it make you feel better if we gave money to a nursing school? I'm just saying, we haven't yet hit our stride. Found our true calling."

Christie said that she assumed that living up to the mission statement would be a gradual, evolving process. Glibness came out of her effort-lessly these days.

Outside, a power saw started up. Christie could see a portion of the backyard and the drive, where the boy who served as Mrs. Foster's handyman and houseman was making a racket. He always seemed to have some noisy carpentry project going on these days. He'd set up a workbench and Christie watched him lifting one board and then another, bending down to position them, then using a circle saw to slice them through. She didn't know his name, but he was always around, and Christie believed, from something Mrs. Foster had said, that he lived on the premises now. Another of Mrs. Foster's projects. Christie wondered what was wrong with him, since there was most often something wrong with the people Mrs. Foster bestowed her favor on. But she didn't like this line of thought, since then she had to wonder what was wrong with her too.

She'd crossed paths with him a few times as she came and went, but they'd never spoken, and it would have been awkward to start doing so now. He was unnervingly good-looking, young and tall and trimly muscled, with dark blond hair and dusky, sunburned skin. She was almost embarrassed to look at him, yes, it embarrassed her, she'd thought she was beyond any such stray thoughts or urges.

Or say she wasn't. She didn't have to do anything about it.

Mrs. Foster was still on the trail of her argument. "Well, suppose you managed to give everybody what they needed, food and shelter and medical care and whatnot. Got rid of the real inequalities and wants, made everyone share."

"I think that's called communism."

Luckily, the cat raised its head just then and stared at them with its question-mark face before it leapt from the windowsill, and Mrs. Foster had not seemed to hear her unwise wisecrack. "Say you did all that," she went on. "Wouldn't people still act badly? I mean, be greedy and violent and unpleasant?"

"Probably. I guess." More like, of course.

"Because people are naturally self-centered and awful," Mrs. Foster stated, more cheerfully than you might imagine.

"I don't know. I don't think you can generalize. It's more like, people are inconsistently virtuous."

"Exactly. That's exactly the way I started thinking. How imperfect human nature is. That's when I came up with my idea."

"And what is that?" Christie asked, as she was meant to, a small, spinning cloud of apprehension moving toward her over a near horizon.

"We could pay people to be good."

By the time Christie left Mrs. Foster's house, the cloud had taken the form of attacking winged monkeys. Mrs. Foster's new idea sounded, well, kooky. Would you hand out dollar bills for good deeds? Would you have to set it up like drug testing? Would you try to turn bad people into better ones? What about people who were already good? Mrs. Foster had not gone into great detail. It was likely that she had not yet considered the details. What was wrong with giving away food and housing vouchers? Why couldn't she just endow a library?

Mrs. Foster had told Christie to "give some thought" to this new mission and call her in a couple of days. It might be possible to stall, to say she was working on it, and hope that Mrs. Foster would forget about the whole thing. But that was wishful thinking. It was more likely that Mrs. Foster would set off full-speed in all directions, perhaps start talking it up with the board members, and Christie would be the one who'd have to put out the fires.

When she got home she called Mr. Kirn, and was unexpectedly put right through to him. Mr. Kirn was most often busy doing more important things. "Let me make certain I understand you," Mr. Kirn said. "'Pay people money to be good.' I don't suppose she said how much money?"

"No, and she didn't define 'good' either."

"Maybe she was just thinking out loud."

"Maybe," Christie said, and waited for the idea to work itself through his lawyer's brain. For want of any better alternatives, he was the only board member she turned to for advice. Not that she had much in common with him. Or perhaps this new job was making her more Kirn-like—a thought that depressed her.

"How, exactly, do you think she wants this 'project' to work?" Mr. Kirn asked. "Like a psychology experiment, with questionnaires and interviews?"

"I don't think so." Christie tried to sort Mrs. Foster's vague directives into something resembling a course of action. "More like a tent revival. Advertising for people who want to 'improve their moral nature.' Preaching to them about virtue and personal responsibility."

Mr. Kirn sighed. "And then?"

"Something about them signing a contract, and getting a check. I know. Think of all the con artists. How fast the money would go."

"Huh. I suppose you could think of it as incentivizing behavior. In the same way the law does. Although then you get into negative incentives. Penalties for bad behavior."

"I don't know how set on this she is. But I wanted to give you a heads-up, in case she talks to you." Meaning, of course, that she hoped he would see it for the bad idea that it was, and join forces with her.

"Huh," Mr. Kirn said again. Christie guessed they might both be thinking of the hazards involved if Mrs. Foster insisted on moving forward, how foolish the Foundation might be made to look. You couldn't imagine that Mr. Kirn would enjoy looking foolish, even by association.

Of course, neither would she. And she felt guilty, disloyal to Mrs. Foster for maneuvering behind her back like this. As if she had become too attached to the idea of a job and a salary (although out of principle, the salary was not large), rather than acting out of any feeble altruism.

"I'm glad you called," Mr. Kirn said. "Let me give it some thought and get back to you."

They hung up. Mr. Kirn called her again a half-hour later. "Tell her you want to hold a conference. A conference to examine the relationship between economics and behavior."

"Is there a relationship?"

"We don't know yet. We haven't examined it. That's what the conference is for. You'll have to think up some catchy title. And get speakers lined up. I'll talk to some of the other board members. You can rent space in a college or somewhere. And you'll have to hurry, because it takes time to organize these things."

"Hold on a minute. Why would we want to have a conference?"

"I'm sorry, I can't stay on the phone, I'm due in court. You have a conference because then you don't have to do anything else. Think about it. I have to run."

Christie hung up. She couldn't help feeling she'd just made a deal with the devil. Not that Mr. Kirn was the devil. But how neatly and easily he'd come up with a perfectly cynical idea.

She took her shoes off and did some spine stretches, rounding then flattening her back. Her back had been acting up ever since she took on the Foundation job, which she thought meant something organic and sinister and subtly wrong was announcing itself. She sat down at her little shrine, which she'd been rather neglecting lately. Every time she tried to clear her mind, all her small and large responsibilities pestered her. *The name of God is Truth. The name of God is call Mr. Sebastian about the next session of the Zoning Commission and see if it was too late to get an item on the agenda about the need for low-cost multifamily housing.*

She had wanted to engage with the world. And now the world was engaging right back.

She didn't succeed in meditating, because she didn't really try. But by the time she stood up, she had decided that if there was to be a conference, and especially if there was going to be all the work and effort of a conference, then it would have to be undertaken with an open mind and an open heart, and it would be meant to accomplish something.

We do not so much look at things as overlook them.

Mrs. Foster liked the idea of a conference. She liked the idea of people meeting in assembly rooms with microphones and coffee cups, having impassioned discussions. She wished there to be distinguished guests and hobnobbing. Christie laid it out for her, assisted by some judicious follow-

up from Mr. Kirn. She had come up with a few possible study-session topics. How could you best explore the issues and questions that linked
economics and behavior? Did poverty in itself lead to moral failings, such
as crime? Was "goodness" something that could be objectified and measured? Did society benefit directly from individual virtue, and therefore
have incentive to promote it? Did our concepts of goodness have their
foundations in religious and spiritual practice? What about the notion
that money was the root of all evil, and those monks and nuns who felt it
necessary to deny themselves material wealth? If people were paid to be
good, would you be setting up a kind of capitalism of virtue, with everyone competing among themselves to be the most worthy and rewardable?

"Congratulations," Mr. Kirn told her in one of their flurry of phone
calls. "Those are exactly the kind of windy, unanswerable questions that
you organize a conference around."

"I'm not intending to simply waste everyone's time," Christie said
stiffly.

"Of course you aren't," Mr. Kirn reassured her. It was that easy for him
to switch tones. He probably argued both sides of his legal cases, just for
practice.

"We're planning on two months from now, right before Thanksgiving.
It won't be very large. It can't be for a first-time conference. But it's something you could build on in the future. There could be different topics
each time. Workshops. There's no reason you couldn't have some practical
applications. Why are you laughing?"

"I'm not."

"It's more like sniggering."

"I apologize. I'm not laughing at you. I'm envious. I wish I had your
energy. Your positive attitude. Your belief in possibility."

"By which you mean, naive."

"Promise me, if you are ever on a witness stand, do not volunteer
characterizations of yourself. No. I meant it's admirable. I'm sure you've
seen your share of ugly situations. Human beings who make you want to
resign from the species. As have I. And yet you persevere."

"As do you," said Christie, wondering if Mr. Kirn was being sincere and if there was any possible way of telling.

"Not at all the same thing. So much about a law practice is competitive. Who wins what. So much ego involved. I have to say, it's what keeps me going. But you operate out of a"—he paused, either to find the right words, or for effect—"disinterested interest. You really are a remarkable young woman."

"Thank you." Christie's interpersonal radar chimed a warning. A vision of the sort considered "unbidden" rose up of Mr. Kirn's pink and gleaming face. And surely there was a Mrs. Kirn? "I'd say that Mrs. Foster is pretty remarkable also."

"Absolutely," said Mr. Kirn, but with decelerating enthusiasm. "Let's talk again soon, shall we?"

She didn't have time to worry about Mr. Kirn, or even time to worry about whether she should be worried. There was too much to do in the way of the Foundation's ordinary operations, and now the conference on top of it. Fortunately, one of the original hard-luck hires was turning out to be an excellent worker. Her name was Imelda and she had felony convictions for check fraud and identity theft. In most places this would not be considered a desirable résumé. But Imelda was one of the prison ministries program's success stories, with a new husband and a new baby girl, and if you didn't believe that people could turn their lives around, why bother with the enterprise of humanity in the first place? Besides, the skills she had used in her previous criminal life—confidence, cajolery, cunning—served her well in dealing with vendors and booking agents and the media.

Christie was able to get one genuine celebrity for the conference, a best-selling author of inspirational books who would be in San Francisco as part of a national tour. The rest of the panelists would be local notables with expertise in fields such as sociology, in philosophy, in economics, and religious studies. Mrs. Foster was persuaded to add to the existing budget for their honoraria. A nearby seminary had conference facilities available. The machinery of publicity was set in motion. The Foundation's new website bloomed with information about the conference, which was called "Investing in Our Better Selves"—not catchy, but Christie hoped it conveyed something aspirational, not just another investment seminar.

People began to send in their registration fees, a rush of them at first, then they dribbled in until they reached thirty, or half of what they'd hoped for. Time began to grow short. Christie and Imelda sat together in front of a computer, refreshing the web page every so often to see if other registrations had come in. They wanted enough of a crowd so that it wouldn't look forlorn, and they wanted to cover some of the expenses. Imelda said, "I don't suppose we could hire some people to go. You know, like placeholders."

"That sounds a little bit like, I hate to say it, fraud."

Imelda shrugged. "Not according to statute."

"We're supposed to be aiming for a higher standard," Christie told her. "Although it's not a bad idea." She admired Imelda's enterprising spirit and hoped it would find some appropriate and ethical outlet. It wasn't hard to imagine how she might have bluffed and charmed her way through her different profitable scams. She was tall and black-haired and glamorous and she still wore the excellent suits and shoes she had acquired pre-prison. She kept her hair in a sleek updo and her taste in jewelry ran to discreet gold. Anyone walking into the office would take Imelda for the boss and herself for the secretary. "Hit refresh again," Christie said.

Nothing. "Maybe tomorrow," Imelda said. "Don't slump. You look terrible when you slump. Up with the chin, back with the shoulders. Like me, see? Even in the prison, I worked on my good posture. Why does the old lady want to give all her money away?"

"Don't call her that, please. She's not giving it away. She's investing in human nature."

"Human nature," Imelda said, "is not the best investment the market has to offer."

"It's her money and she can do whatever she wants with it." Christie hoped that Mrs. Foster would back off her original plan before she, Christie, had to hand out checks to a bunch of reprobates and pirates. And did she even believe that wealth allowed people to spend their money in whatever mean or foolish way they wished? Did wealth convey such entitlement? She was too tired to start thinking in this way. "Let's pack up," she told Imelda.

Imelda shut down the computer and helped Christie empty the waste-baskets and turn off lights and lock up. It had been raining for the last two days and Imelda took her own immaculate raincoat from the closet. "Is this yours?" she demanded of Christie, holding up a baggy olive green slicker. "Sweetie, you have to let me take you shopping sometime. You dress like a refugee and you will never get yourself a man."

"What would I do with one of those?" Christie was used to Imelda's bullying by now.

"Have a baby," Imelda said promptly. "My little Gracie angel, she's the best thing I ever did. If you don't want a man, at least get yourself a baby. You can do that, you just go to a clinic. Tomorrow I am bringing you a trench coat I never got around to wearing. Very sharp, metallic gray. A Burberry. The tags are still on it. You try it and see."

They said good night and Christie walked to her car through the puddling, lake-like parking lot. It was the end of October and the clocks hadn't yet been turned back, but the drilling rain made for an early, lower-ing darkness. Traffic on the freeway moved at a stately pace. The wet pave-ment mirrored the red, smeared taillights. Her defroster wasn't keeping up with the moisture and she had to keep clearing the windshield with her hand. Once you allowed people familiar access to you, as she seemed to have done with Imelda, they felt free to make their suggestions. What would she do with a man—or a baby, for that matter? She'd spent a long time not thinking about these things. She wasn't even sure about the trench coat.

When she reached her apartment, Art and his girlfriend, the one with the name like the water filter, Brita or Berta or something, were camped out under the overhang of the parking structure, grilling their dinner on a hibachi. Art waved her over. "Hey Chris, we're having a rain party. Want some wine?" He wagged a bottle at her.

Christie started to say no out of reflex, then told them she had to go in and drop some things off first. She changed into sweatpants and a heavy sweater and socks, and wrapped herself in a blanket against the chill.

Lawn chairs had been set in a circle around the hibachi. Christie eased her sore back into one of these and accepted a paper cup of white wine. Maybe Imelda was right, it was all a matter of posture. Or the bad ergonomics of her office chair. "Thanks." The rain had eased up into a steady light fall, and there was a pleasant sense of shelter in looking out at it.

"We're making fish tacos. Want some?" Art prodded at the foil bundles on the grill.

"Do you eat fish? I forget. I can make you one without fish."

Christie told him not to bother, the wine was all she wanted. Now that Art had himself a woman, it was easier to spend time with him. Although he sometimes annoyed her with his solicitude, as if Christie was an ex-girlfriend and Art was trying to console her for things not working out.

Beata. That was her name. Beata said, "I wish I had your pretty hair! What is it you do to it?"

"Wash it, mostly." A little too much effort on Beata's part as well, as if Art had cast her as an object of pity. Beata's dark hair was cut all one length, like a paintbrush.

Talk about dressing like a refugee. When Christie had first seen her, Beata resembled some kind of Eastern European nun. There had been a remarkable transformation, to a look that the fashion people called "flirty." Tonight she wore unseasonable white jeans, a tight white T-shirt encrusted with sparkles and dangling ribbons, and a pair of bare pink sandals. Christie noted, unkindly, that this was a difficult look for someone with as much in the way of boobs and butt as Beata had, though Art didn't seem to mind. There were more sparkles and ornamentation and dangling stuff around her neck and wrists. Art had not undergone any big makeovers, but Christie did notice that his shirt had been ironed. Why was she so concerned about appearances these days? Maybe because everybody else around her was.

"We have chips," Beata said, offering a bag to Christie. "Or fruit? Arthur, shall I go upstairs and find the grapefruit salad?"

"Please don't on my account." Something about her made people keep thinking she needed things. She drank some of the wine. It had a friendly taste and she drank a good bit more. "How's Linnea doing?" she asked, attempting to deflect their attention from herself.

"Pretty good. Not bad. OK."

"Not so OK," Beata said. Then, to Christie, "Boyfriend."

"He's not her boyfriend. He's too old for her."

"Oh, well then." Beata raised her pencil-thin eyebrows and made a droll face.

"She says he isn't."

"She is lovesick for him."

"She's fifteen years old," Art said doggedly. It had the air of an argument they'd had before.

Again Beata turned to Christie. "As if fifteen is too young to be in crazy hopeless love. It is exactly the right age."

Christie wished she hadn't asked anything about Linnea. Now she found herself appealed to, as if she were some arbiter of crazy lovesick behavior. "Teenagers, who knows."

"He's such a nice-looking boy," Beata said.

"He's entirely too full of sperm."

"It's just nature. Relax, Dad." Another conspiratorial glance in Christie's direction. Did she look like somebody who knew about these things?

"I guess I should be glad she's interested in normal teenage experiences," Art said, looking glum. "Even risky, promiscuous, normal experiences."

"They are not having intercourse," Beata said. "Of that I'm sure. You watch them together, you'll see."

"She should have been home by now. I need to call her, excuse me."

"Poor Art," Beata said, once he had gone upstairs. She bent over the hibachi and used a spatula to turn the fish over. Her white underpants rose up above the line of her jeans. "He could not protect her from the one terrible thing, so now he tries to protect her from everything else."

It had sounded terrible. The boy with the gun, the dead girls. There were parts of it Christie could not fully imagine—blood, terror, pain— and at least one part she could. The fear that some pointless and evil act could single you out at any moment. You didn't let yourself dwell on such things. Unless they had already happened to you. "I'm glad she's doing better."

"Better, who knows. At least different." They were quiet, watching the rain blow and mist around the streetlights. Where it hit the metal edge of the roof, it ran together and dripped to the ground in threads. Beata said, "We have other food too. A rice casserole. Cheese? Bread and jam?"

"No thank you. I'm going to go in and eat my own dinner in a minute." She was getting hungry, she ought to leave before she had to watch Art and Beata feeding each other and licking each other's fingers. But she was tired, and not in a hurry to be in a hurry about anything. She finished the wine and Beata refilled her glass.

"I'll get drunk," Christie said, and laughed foolishly. She already felt a little blurry, a little drunk around the edges. She wasn't that used to drinking. In order to try and cover up, she said the first thing that came into her head: "You look different these days."

"Good or bad?"

"Just different. I mean, good."

"More modern American girl."

"Yes," Christie agreed. Although "modern American girl" had many gradations, and Beata had staked out a certain territory for herself.

"Do you have an opinion about tattoos?"

"I suppose I have different opinions for different tattoos. Depending on where and who and what. Some of them are OK. Most of them are a waste of perfectly good skin." Christie realized she was doing what drunks do, talking to show how undrunk she was, and digging herself a deeper hole. *Do not speak unless it improves a silence.* There were times she thought she was forgetting everything she ever knew. "Do you have any tattoos?" she asked, as she should have to begin with.

"Art wants me to get one. Somewhere personal. I have yet to decide."

It was possible that Beata was a little drunk herself. Before Christie had to ask, or not ask, about the prospective tattoo, Art came bounding down the stairs. At the same time, Linnea stepped out of the rain and into the circle of lawn chairs. With her was the boy who lived at Mrs. Foster's.

It took Christie a moment to sort it out, to try and to fail at understanding what he was doing here. With Linnea? She didn't get it. But here he was. Full of sperm. Oh thank you, Art, for that thought. What was she, a child molester? He wore his usual jeans and hooded sweatshirt and his neck and throat even in this light were sun-colored.

Art was saying, I just called you, why didn't you answer, and Linnea said Because I knew it was you and I was almost here. Art threw up his hands, meaning, Teenagers, while the boy stood there with the polite, sulky face kids wore when they were around parents.

Nobody was paying any attention to Christie yet. She would have liked to get up and leave, or not be there in the first place. She wrapped the blanket closer around herself. Maybe she'd be taken for a homeless person trying to stay out of the rain. Linnea always ignored her anyway, and for once Christie was glad.

Linnea had gone back to brown hair again, with a carrot-colored stripe in the front. She flopped down into one of the chairs. "Is it food yet? I'm hungry."

"Almost," Art said. "What do you want to drink?"

"A margarita."

"Ha-ha. Coke, 7Up, or milk. How about you, Conner?"

Conner, that was his name, said he'd have a Coke. He sat down next to Linnea. He hadn't looked in Christie's direction and maybe he'd join with Linnea in ignoring her. She was pointlessly embarrassed by his presence. The grown-up thing to do would be to introduce herself and say, surely I've seen you at Mrs. Foster's. There was a moment when she could have done this, but she let it get past her. Art and Beata went up and down the stairs, fetching drinks, plates, silverware, taco fixings, salad. Christie drank more wine.

"Here, try a taco," Art said, offering her a plate. "Or I guess this is two."

"No thanks," Christie said. The hunger had gone right out of her. The boy gave her a quick sideways glance, then looked away. She felt sure he knew who she was.

The others sat down to eat, balancing the plates on their laps. It was all good, they agreed, yes, very good. The rain had picked up again. It landed hard on the pavement and rebounded so that the ground was alive with water. Christie had the sensation of her foot falling asleep, except it was her whole body, gone numb and tingling. She knew she was halfway to being drunk and stupid, and the best thing was to sit there quietly and not call attention to herself. She watched the boy and Linnea. What an odd pair they made. She thought Beata was right, they weren't sleeping together. She couldn't have said how she knew that. The alcohol was making her notice such things, as if she was a sexual Geiger counter. Here were Art and Beata, finding excuses to brush up against each other, two people remembering the last time they made love and looking forward to the next. Here were her own furtive feelings, which were like a rash that should not be scratched in public. She didn't have any designs on the boy, or any fantasy imaginings. At least, she didn't think so. He only triggered other disreputable designs and fantasies.

Of course Linnea was lovesick. How could she not be? The boy was too perfectly beautiful. But Linnea was keeping her face blank and indifferent, that useful all-purpose teenage pose. Every so often Art looked over at her, and Linnea made a point of not looking back. Beata had draped a dish towel around her neck to protect her white clothes. She ate her tacos with a knife and fork, in tiny bites. Everything the others did seemed to amuse her.

And the boy himself? Christie couldn't read him. He drew the others in and gave nothing back, like a dark-burning star. Beata finished with her plate and brushed at her clothes with the dish towel. "Linnea, are you dressing up for Halloween?"

"I don't know. They're having a zombie apocalypse at school the Friday before. Maybe I'll do something for that."

"Zombie apocalypse," said Art. "You'll have to explain this to me."

"See, some people are zombies, and they've attacked the school and eaten people's brains and stuff. Some people play victims and lie around being dead. Other people are the survivors and they try to keep the zombies from killing anybody else. Meanwhile, society breaks down because everybody who's supposed to be picking up trash and growing food and taking care of the power plants is either a zombie or else they're hiding from the zombies. I don't think that part goes on at school. They just have bulletins over the loudspeaker."

Nobody said anything. "I want to be one of the zombies," Linnea said. "The makeup is really cool."

Art said, pleasantly, "Whose idea was it, spending a school day on this stuff?"

"Dad, it's only the last couple of periods. We had an assembly and we voted. Lighten up."

"Honey, I just don't think it's very healthy."

"Fine. I'll dress up as a big plate of broccoli."

"Please take the zombie makeup off before you come home. I hope you will please do that much for me."

After a moment Beata said, "How about you, Conner? What is your costume going to be?"

"Just what I always wear."

He didn't seem to mean it as a joke. There was another silence. Beata stood and began clearing up the plates and food. Art helped her. Conner said he had to go, and Linnea got up also. Christie did a good job of not watching him. "Back in a minute," Linnea said.

Art waited until they were gone. "I'm going to call the goddamn school."

"No," Beata said. "Leave it be. It's just pretend."

"She can pretend to be something else."

Christie said, "At least she seems to be looking forward to it." The other two gave her a weary look.

Art said, "I'm going to talk to a counselor. I guess they haven't had themselves a school shooting in these parts lately. Lucky them."

Linnea came back then and stood with her hands in the pockets of her denim jacket. "Did you get enough to eat, honey?" Art asked. "Come on upstairs and we'll fix you another plate."

"No, I'm going to hang out here by the campfire a while longer."

Christie got up to go and Linnea said, "Wait a minute, I want to ask you something."

Christie sat back down. Art gave her a different look: what the hell. "Thanks for the wine," Christie told Art and Beata as they started upstairs. She thought she'd come out on the other side of drunkenness and furtive desire. She was only tired now, curious about what Linnea had to say, but wishing it was already over.

Linnea took out a pack of cigarettes and lit one. "Are you going to narc me out?" She meant the smoking.

"Not unless I'm asked a direct question about it."

Linnea considered this, exhaling the smoke to one side. "I don't want to go back up there until they finish getting their freak on. You know?"

Christie thought she knew. She was pretty sure she heard such things from downstairs. She didn't know what to make of this sudden chattiness. Linnea said, "I bet that was Beata's Halloween costume she had on tonight."

"If you're going to talk about somebody, you should do it to their face."

"Like people always do around me, right?"

One reason not to have a baby was so that you would not eventually have a teenager. "What was it you wanted to ask me?"

Linnea hitched her chair closer. The orange stripe of hair was distracting. It looked like a caterpillar clinging to her head. "Con says you do work with homeless people."

"Yes, that's part of it." He knew that much about her.

"Where do people go when they're homeless? Are there places they end up? Like, camps or something?"

"There are shelters. And a few places you might find people under a tarp, or living in a vehicle. It's nothing organized. They go wherever they can. They leave town. They turn up in emergency rooms, or jail, or the morgue. Why?"

"So there's nothing like, police records, anything like that."

The girl seemed serious, or at least, more serious than she'd been about the zombie apocalypse. "If you get arrested, there's a record. There are social services that try to do a homeless census once a year, but it's a difficult population to reach." Christie waited. "Maybe if you told me what this is about?"

"Con needs help finding his father."

FIFTEEN

In an effort at building a more honest and authentic relationship, from time to time Art smoked marijuana with his teenage daughter. He hadn't begun out of any such hopeful motives; Linnea had simply come home and caught him lighting up in the kitchen. "Busted!" she said happily.

"Oh well, ha." Art was already a little messed over. His brain had that Swiss cheese feel. "I was just, ha." He opened the refrigerator and closed it again.

"You gonna share?"

What else could he do but hand the pipe to her? He watched Linnea fire up the lighter and play it over the pipe bowl. "Careful. This is pretty strong stuff."

She spoke with difficulty through the smoke she was holding in. "S'not bad."

Art sat down at the kitchen table. He shook his head and its insides joggled. "This is just . . . Honey, I don't know about this."

"Your eyes are all red. You are wrecked."

He tried sounding stern. "What do you think your mother would say?"

"She'd say she was right about both of us."

It was funny enough to make them snicker and snort. Art took the pipe back from her. "Seriously, this isn't a good idea for you. You can get kind of dependent on it. You can spend too much time just sitting around getting high and neglecting, ah, stuff you need to do." His daughter's expression was one of huge merriment. "You're young, you're still developing," Art said. "It can screw up your . . . development."

"Yeah, can't have that."

"And you really, really shouldn't do other drugs. Or drink. If I catch you doing anything like that, I will pack your young ass off to Montana."

"No prob."

Of course she'd say anything. How would he know what kinds of shit she did? What were you supposed to do, lock them up? "Linnea! Don't push me on this!"

"All right, all right." She waved a hand in dismissal. "I'll just be a little pothead."

"Don't even be that."

"Use, not abuse," she suggested.

"And quit filching my stash." He'd meant it seriously, meant it to come out seriously, but little laugh bubbles kept rising up in him, like carbonation. He really was hopeless. He should have read one of those books, *How to Talk to Your Kids About Drugs*. There was probably a chapter in there somewhere, "Special Situations." He didn't think he was the only parent who had to hold up their lame end of similar conversations.

He wished he had the courage of his stoned convictions. Marijuana was a natural substance, a mild and harmless euphoric. Linnea already smoked it and did God knows what else. But now it was his job to worry about it.

Although she seemed to be doing better lately, settling into school, coming home when she was meant to, well, more or less. Gradually, Art had been able to imagine a longer timeline than getting through the next few days or weeks. He didn't envision and dwell on every calamity that might befall her every time she left the apartment, or at least he did so less often. Louise still called him every other week or so to fret and complain, but he was more used to her by now, and she only bored him.

"What is she up to at school?" Louise demanded.

"Geometry, Spanish One, Intro to American Civilization—"

"You know what I mean."

"She's fine, things at school are fine. She sees a counselor, it's all good." He decided not to tell her about the plans for the zombie apocalypse. "She does her homework, she goes to class. I don't know if she's made a lot of friends yet, but she's new, give it time."

In fact Linnea's only friend, as far as Art could tell, continued to be Conner, whom Art disapproved of on the general grounds of his being male, and older, and fully capable of sexual misdeeds. He wasn't going to tell Louise about him, either. "Everything's going well, why do you keep worrying?"

"Because worrying is what you do with children. You missed out on a dozen years of training. You're still playing catch-up."

"Yeah yeah yeah."

"Art? If you think she's doing just great, you aren't paying attention."

"Maybe you could give her some credit. People do change."

"I'll believe that when you get a real job." No matter what he said to Louise, she was always able to serve it back up to him as new and tasty fare. "You think I don't know about change? Didn't I watch her change from a normal child into a nightmare? You think it didn't break my heart? It did. You think I didn't try to help her, to get her help? She didn't want to be helped. She took pleasure in pushing me away."

"All right." It was time to get off the phone, before Louise got too carried away with the vision of her own suffering. "I'll tell Linnea you called."

"I had to give up on my own child. Not entirely give up, I mean, you always hold out hope. You say she's doing better, that's great. It's probably easier for both of you since you're so much more objective about her."

"What's that supposed to mean?" he asked unwisely. "'Objective,' like, I don't care about her?"

"I'm sure you at least think you do," Louise said, and hung up.

The next time Art smoked marijuana with his daughter, they were sitting in front of the television watching a reality show that Linnea enjoyed because it was "so sick." The show was about girls Linnea's age who got pregnant and had babies and then found out it was a big drag. Linnea and Art passed a joint back and forth and Linnea hooted at the television. She made fun of the teen moms for being dumb and for having dumb boyfriends.

Art was encouraged by this. It seemed like a good opportunity for some sort of teachable moment. At the next commercial, he said, "You have to wonder, did they have any idea what they were getting into?"

Linnea pinched the end of the joint open so it would draw better. "You mean, do I realize that being a teen mom would put a crimp in my exciting, fast-paced social life? Yeah, I do."

"Well that's good. I mean, good that you know . . ." He had to stop attempting heavy-duty parental conversations when he was drug-addled. Maybe he wasn't the best person to be giving lectures about the serious, long-term responsibilities of family life.

"Besides, don't worry, if I ever got pregnant, I would definitely have an abortion."

"That's not the point. Let's back up a minute."

"The social life thing?" She gave him a cracked smile. "It's OK. It's not like I have these great expectations."

"How about, 'Don't get pregnant,' and the best way to do that is not to have teen sex."

"No kidding. This is like, kaput." She dropped the stubby remnant of the joint into the ashtray. On television, one of the teen moms' moms was hollering about the teen mom letting her baby drink soda pop from a baby bottle. Why did these people agree to be filmed? Did they think they'd end up looking good?

They both watched a while longer. Somehow, television made behavior that you would go out of your way to avoid in real life into something fascinating. Linnea yawned. "These guys, they're so stupid, they all should have been sterilized. So if Beata got pregnant, what would you do?"

"Huh." It was an unwelcome thought—that is, he hadn't bothered thinking it.

"I'm sorry, that's not the right answer."

It had been embarrassing enough to talk about his daughter's sex life; he surely didn't want to discuss his own. "That would be up to Beata," Art said, meaning to put an end to the discussion.

"So if she said, 'I want to be your baby mamma, let's do this,' you'd go along?"

"I don't know, I haven't thought about it. It's not going to happen, anyway." Beata took birth control pills. Or so she said. Was it something he ought to worry about? A pregnancy trap?

"You could have a little boy. Name him Jerzy or something else Polish. Then I'd have two half brothers. Just from different halves."

She didn't say anything more, and Art was afraid of saying anything more, so they sat in silence, watching the teen moms and their hapless, adorable babies.

Things were going just fine with Beata. Weren't they? He thought so. This fall they were both teaching the usual patchwork of courses that made up a part-timer's life, the usual composition and remedial composition, at night classes and refugee centers and adult education programs and online courses. They were both busy with their comings and goings and with the mounds of grading. Sometimes they were able to manage a quick meal and a tryst at Beata's apartment in the Sunset. On weekends Beata usually came up to Marin and stayed overnight, and she cooked big dinners and they watched television, and there wasn't pressure for something more.

At least there didn't seem to be. Beata didn't complain or hint around that she wanted him to take her on expensive wine country tours, or they should move in together, or any other change in their routine of modest entertainment and good old reliable sex. When she wasn't around, he didn't have to worry about her. Was that so wrong?

But he wasn't always the best judge of women, what they wanted and what he was supposed to do about it. Usually they blindsided him with accusations, the things he had failed to notice, the offenses he so willfully committed against their needs, their natures, their exquisite sensibilities. Louise had turned this sort of denunciation into a minor art form, but Art had to admit, he had heard similar speeches elsewhere.

The problem with women was that they were always planning some future that involved you and that you were not aware of, as if you'd signed up for a credit card without knowing it. Once, the two of them sitting at opposite ends of his couch, each of them hunched over their laptops making frantic grade entries, Beata had asked him what he wanted to be doing in ten years. "Fishing up at my cabin in the Sierras," Art had said.

"No, I mean doing with your life."

"I don't know. Retire." He hadn't thought about it. He seemed unlikely to be doing anything that much different. "Win the lottery."

"I want to be entirely new," Beata announced. "New work, new house. Everything new and amazing."

"Go for it," Art had said, humping to get his grades turned in before the online session closed. He hadn't thought much about it at the time, and Beata had not said anything more. At least he didn't think she had. Among the other things Beata had not said were that she wanted to have a baby, or get married, or any combination of these. Surely he would have remembered something like that. But of course such things were seldom spoken outright. They were implied, assumed, conveyed through an indirect language that everyone expected him to speak fluently.

Linnea wasn't in the habit of offering observations about Beata, and Art didn't know why she'd done so now, aside from teenage brattiness, and wanting to unnerve him, and if so, good job. He'd almost forgotten the half brother back in Ohio. And the stepfather, and the dead girl, the stepsister, well, he hadn't forgotten them, but it was too distressing to think about them. What a lopsided stumpy mess people made of a family tree these days. The last thing any of them needed was some new little sprig grafted on.

Then it was only a few days before Halloween, and Beata surprised him in a different way, which he guessed was the nature of surprises. She called and said she wanted them to go to a costume party together. A friend of hers in the city was hosting it. "You're kidding," Art said, though he was pretty sure she wasn't. "You mean, dress up?"

"Yes, that's usually what people mean by costume."

"Who is this friend?" Art asked, stalling for time. He wasn't a big Halloween fan. In San Francisco, you were talking serious drag queens.

"She is a friend from college, she lives in the Mission. I think you should meet some of my friends. I would say, I should meet yours, but you don't have any."

There was a certain crispness in her tone. So here it was: the voicing of discontent, the required changing of his ways. He guessed it had to happen. "Can I go but not dress up?"

"Not allowed."

"Why didn't you tell me sooner? How am I supposed to get a costume together?"

"It wouldn't make any difference if I gave you a month. You would still do it at the last minute."

The whole idea was dismaying him. "Honestly, I usually don't do Halloween."

"Make an exception."

"Do you already have a costume?"

"Yes, and it is a surprise."

"Don't you think you should tell me? I mean, shouldn't we match or something?"

"I will look amazing, and you should too. Saturday night, come pick me up at eight. Oh stop groaning. Be fun."

Art hung up the phone. He was not feeling fun. This was a test of some kind. He would have to be a good sport, enter into the festive spirit of the occasion. He wondered what Beata might have told her friends about him already. He didn't like the idea of them looking him over, comparing notes, deciding if he measured up. He wasn't a great party person at the best of times. Usually he hung on to a drink and communed with the host's bookshelves.

"What do you think I should be?" he asked his daughter. "A vampire, maybe?"

"Everybody goes as a vampire."

"Right. Skip it." Anyway, the vampires in television and movies these days were all young and handsome, more like your average brooding fashion models than the undead. "I'm supposed to look amazing."

Linnea hooted at that. "Just be something completely different than normal. That's the whole idea." She was fixing herself breakfast, a bagel with peanut butter and banana slices. She was good about feeding herself, which was a lucky thing, since he had never really gotten it together when it came to cooking. Beata made a point out of cooking for him. He should have been more wary about that.

As if he had just thought of it, he said, "Hey, isn't it the zombie apocalypse today?"

"Yeah. I decided not to be a zombie. They already have too many of those."

"Oh." Cautious now. "Were you going to be anything else?"

"Maybe I'll be a zombie slaughter victim. That's easy, you just lie there. Con and I are going to hang out on Halloween," she added, overcasually.

Art was still trying not to visualize her as a victim of slaughter. "Hang out, what? What's that supposed to mean?"

"Nothing. Just hang." She rolled her eyes. Dumb Daddy.

"Honey, I don't want him over here when I'm not home, and I'll be at the party."

"Did I say we'd be here?" Linnea applied another scallop of peanut butter, as if it was icing, and gave the bagel a critical, appraising look. "You know, I didn't even have to tell you. But I don't want you to worry if I don't get home until real late."

"All right, but . . ." He tried to climb down from the ledge, decided instead to jump to the next one. "Does Conner smoke pot? Or do anything else?"

"Not really."

"I didn't hear a yes or a no in there."

"He used to. He doesn't anymore, but it's not like he took some vow not to. We need more peanut butter." She threw the empty jar into the trash under the sink. "I have to go, I'll be late for Zombie Home Room."

After she'd left, Art poured another cup of coffee and sat on the couch, attempting to sort through his worries. He didn't know what he could do about the Conner situation except make vague, fatherlike noises of concern. He had to admit, he pretty much allowed Linnea to do as she pleased, as long as she didn't run entirely off the rails, get herself hurt or arrested. He hadn't lied to Louise; things were better, if being a typical pain-in-the-ass kid was better. But how could she be all right, really? How could you tell? Her counselor said she was not "forthcoming." She evaded questions, the counselor said. She gave flip answers. Yes, she did. Art recognized this as self-protection, but of a worrisome kind, as if the girl carried herself through the world like a full glass of water.

And what was he supposed to do about Beata? It had been so pleasant not to have to do anything. Now she wanted him to up his game and be more (or less) of one thing or another. Whatever that was. He wished he knew. The Halloween costume was going to be a tough call. Obviously, some effort was required. It wouldn't be enough to put on a football jersey, or a funny hat.

He had to teach most of the day, but he managed to get to one of those temporary costume shops that opened in malls. He looked through racks of limp and picked-over outfits: pirates, Frankensteins, Klingon warriors, various ghouls. He could be an alien, a biker, a cowboy, or, somewhat confusingly, a cactus. There were furry suits in fluorescent colors that he guessed were meant to represent Muppets or cartoon figures; they looked unclean and possibly contagious.

Finally he found something he thought would do: a caveman costume, a leopard-print tunic and britches. It came with a foam club, a wild black wig, and a sinister rubber mask. It was newer-looking and there was a reasonable chance he would not contract scabies from it.

The tunic left one shoulder bare, but he thought he could wear some kind of shirt underneath if he wanted to. Or maybe just throw the bathroom rug over his exposed arm and pretend it was a fur. The mask was Neanderthal in inspiration, with a huge, jutting forehead and flattened nose. Art thought the idea had possibilities. It showed him to be a man with a sense of humor. And it sent a certain signal—namely, he wasn't one of those guys who would let himself get pushed too far by girly discontents.

Linnea wasn't back from school yet when he arrived home with the costume packaged in slippery plastic. The zombie apocalypse might be carrying over into after-school hours, a whole troupe of zombied-up kids fooling around downtown. He hoped that for Christ's sake she hadn't gotten too tangled up in what was meant to be a joke, good, clean walking-dead fun, and had freaked out. Somebody would have called, wouldn't they?

Art hadn't wanted to change clothes in the store's makeshift dressing room. He struggled into the short pants, which were just a shade too small, and felt rather like a leopard-print diaper. The tunic was a better fit. He wished his arm was meatier, but he could swing the club around for menacing effect. He settled the black wig on his head and pulled the mask over his face. The eyeholes took some getting used to, but his reflection in the bathroom mirror was rather thrilling, he thought. He practiced walking caveman style, knees bent and shoulders pulled forward. "Guh," he said, experimentally. "Guh-ugh."

A knock on the door startled him. "Hello?" It was Christie, peering in through the front window.

He couldn't pretend he wasn't there; she would have heard him moving around.

"Just a sec," he called. He took the mask off and opened the door just enough to poke his head around it. "Hey Christie."

She stared at him in wonder. Art realized the wig was still on his head. "Oh, ha."

He pulled it off. "Halloween," he explained.

"Let me guess. Eighties rock star."

He scoffed at this. "Naw. Give me a break." Not wanting to open the door further, he said, "It's supposed to be a surprise. So, what do you . . ."

"Is Linnea here?"

"She's not home from school yet." He waited. "Did she do something?"

"No, she'd asked me a question, that's all."

It was an oddity for Linnea to have talked to Christie about anything, but he wasn't really in a position to be inquisitive at the moment, hiding his caveman self behind a door. "OK, I'll tell her you were asking for her." He felt compelled to add a little small talk. "How's the job going?"

"I'm planning this giant conference from scratch. It's really a lot of work."

Art thought she looked tired, though he had learned that women did not welcome hearing this kind of thing. She looked dragged down. Still pretty, sure. Now that Beata was signaling her intention of putting the hammer down on him, he looked at Christie with some of his old interest. Not that she'd ever given him the time of day. He'd better try to mend things with Beata, who was, among many good qualities, a terrific piece of ass.

He said, "Keeps you running, huh? I'm sure you're doing some great work." He was getting cold, holding the door open in his flimsy getup. He was going to have to rethink things like coats. "You want me to have Linnea come see you or something?"

"Sure. Happy Halloween, Art."

Once back inside, he tried to call Linnea and got voice mail. Sometimes she'd text him back, but the phone stayed silent. He changed out of the costume and got dressed and turned on some lights as the sun began to ebb. It wasn't unheard of for her to be this late getting home, but he felt uneasy, as if he was the one waiting for zombies to attack.

The high school wasn't that far away—Linnea sometimes walked, taking a winding shortcut—and Art decided to drive over there to see if he could find her. A dreary dank wind was sending stray bits of paper trash skittering over the roads. Lowering clouds covered most of the sky, with the sun leaking through at the western edge. Art watched two buses pull up at the stop across the street, their lighted insides giving them the look of rooms in motion. A few people got off, none of them Linnea.

He followed the road where she might have walked, then doubled back along it. He tried the shopping center where the kids sometimes hung out. He idled in the parking lot for a time, but didn't spot her going in or out of the Safeway or the drugstore or the smoothie shop. The school was just across the road. Cars were still pulling up and waiting there, an hour after the last classes. He crossed over and joined the end of the line, tried calling her again, no luck.

Kids were standing around talking, or leaning into car windows, or getting into cars and being driven away. Some of them were in full zombie regalia: chalk white faces, torn clothes, blotches he guessed were meant to represent decaying flesh. A couple of them were staggering around, stiff-armed and stiff-legged, while their audience hooted in approval. It looked like the apocalypse had gone well, even if the school was still standing.

Art was about to give up and go home to wait for Linnea when he saw her coming down the school's front steps, alone. She stopped to hoist her backpack higher. The weight of it made her bend forward, as if she was walking into the wind. He thought she had earbuds attached to her ears. He could have honked, or called to her, but he watched her for another minute. She jammed her hands into her jacket pockets and walked out to the sidewalk, through the crowd of zombies and other kids horsing around under the light from the streetlamps. She didn't speak to any of them and none of them spoke to her. She reached the bus stop and stood there waiting. Two or three buses were coming up behind him, their lights flaring in his rearview.

He could have reached her before the parade of buses, and he would have done so if she had not seemed so entirely alone, if he would not have embarrassed her by witnessing it.

. . .

The next day was Halloween and the party. He called Beata around noon to see if she was still determined to go. She was. "You have a costume?" she asked, sounding mistrustful.

"I have a costume."

"Will I recognize you?" A note of teasing. He was glad to hear it.

"No, I'll just be the guy who shows up at eight o'clock and ravishes you."

Some confusion; Beata thought he'd said "radish." She said she was glad they'd gotten that straightened out. "There will be no radishing beforehand. It will spoil my looks."

"Afterwards, then," Art said. "Radish, radish."

"Such a silly man. I have to go, I have things to do to get ready."

She hung up. "Ugh," Art said. He thumped his chest, practicing. "Gromph." He wondered if he was going to have to stay in character all night, talk nothing but caveman talk.

Before she left to do whatever it was with Conner she wouldn't tell Art about, Linnea stayed in her room, playing her music. She seemed entirely uninterested in what Art had procured for a costume, and for once he was glad to be ignored. He made her promise she would at least answer texts, and she said Yeah, sure. He made a show of worrying, enough so that Linnea sighed dramatically, but even though he cautioned and harrumphed, Art had come around to appreciating that Conner was a little older. At least he wasn't a kid with a learner's permit and the keys to a Lexus.

After she was gone, Art got his caveman ensemble from the closet and climbed into it. He had tried to loosen the elastic waistband of the pants, ripping out a seam and restitching it. Now he had more room, but the elastic had lost some function, and just to be prudent, he pinned the pants to his undershorts. He put the tunic on and struck a muscular pose in the bathroom mirror. He wished he had thought to get body makeup, some kind of bronzer. He looked sort of pasty for an outdoor type.

He was nervous setting out, but it was a fine night. Crossing the great bridge in darkness, its views of ocean and city lights spread out beneath him, he always felt his destination invested with a certain grandeur. The metal plating made his tires thrum, the vast cables soared overhead. He found an old Tom Petty CD and played it loud, a soundtrack to the night's adventure, singing along gustily, since there was no one there to hear: "And I'm free-ee, free falling."

He couldn't drive with the mask on and he pushed it up on his forehead, so that it resembled the head of a vestigial twin. He was cheered when the car in the next lane honked at him, and he looked over to see two people in gorilla masks in the front seat, waving in a companionable fashion. Or maybe they really were two gorillas. What did he know?

At Beata's he had to park more than a block away. He had a coat but that would spoil the effect. He had decided that his only option was to go for it. What the hell. It was Halloween. He got out of the car and balanced his foam club on his shoulder, and swung his head from side to side as he walked, caveman style. He didn't see anyone else in costume, well, it wasn't exactly a party neighborhood. Elderly people with shopping bags veered around him on the sidewalk. His pants took a hitch downward and he had to stop and readjust them.

Beata's apartment was a third-floor walk-up. He rang the buzzer and the door clicked open.

On the last landing, he paused to get his breath, then bounded up the last stairs and beat on the door with his fist. It opened, and the two of them beheld each other.

Beata gave a little shriek.

She had gotten herself up as a Roaring Twenties vamp. She wore a short red dress with fringe, and a string of pearls. Her hair had been lacquered into tight flat curls and there was a jeweled band across her forehead. Red red lipstick and black-rimmed eyes.

Art spoke first, forgetting to be a caveman. "Wow. That is some fancy getup."

The mask made his voice come out muffled.

"And you. You are very . . ."

"Very what?" He pushed the mask off his face. It was hot and he could tell there was going to be a sweat issue.

"I don't suppose you brought a pair of pants. Real pants."

Art looked down at his bare legs. He couldn't remember her complaining about his legs before. Beata said, "In case of, what is it, wardrobe malfunction."

"Pants? Cavemen don't wear pants." He waved the club over his head.

"Please be careful with that."

"Hey, you wouldn't tell me what you wanted me to wear." He was sensing a quality of reserve in her attitude that did not augur well.

"We should go, the party is already started."

"I haven't had a chance to look at you yet." Art dropped his club, which bounced. He caught her around the shoulders. "You are one red-hot mamma."

"Thank you." She ducked underneath his hands. "Do not mess up the hair. The hair is very nervous-making."

Things got a little better on the drive to the party. Once they reached Market Street, almost everyone was dressed up. There were nun costumes, long black capes, many tutus. At Guerrero Street, three men dressed as condoms were chasing three girls dressed as Playboy Bunnies. Beata's mood seemed to lift as she pointed out all the different revelers. Art wished he knew what she didn't like about his costume, or maybe about him, but decided it was better to leave well enough alone. "So, is this supposed to be a big party?" he asked, just as a way of making conversation.

"It's a pretty big apartment."

Art waited, but she didn't say more. "What's your friend's name?"

"Susan. Maybe some other old friends will be there too."

"Old boyfriends," he said, reduced to ponderous teasing.

"Maybe so."

Was that what this was about? Or was she saying it just to make him jealous? Was he going to have to hit people with his club? "M'booga," he said. "Gumbo gumbo."

Beata gave him directions. He parked and she led the way down a side street to a warehouse, or so it seemed, its street level given over to a car repair business. Overhead, lighted windows, signs of habitation. "What does Susan do?" Art asked belatedly, realizing he should have taken an interest.

"She works with taxis."

"Oh, that's nice." She wasn't going to unbend, make any effort. They were climbing the stairs and he paused. "Hey." Beata stopped and looked back at him. "What's the matter with you?"

"Nothing is the matter with me." Emphasis on "me."

Art sighed, aiming for a tone of heavy patience, but his heart clenched up, *Aw shit.* Had he forgotten her birthday? He didn't think so. Nor was it Valentine's Day. Had she unilaterally declared some anniversary, and not told him? Whatever it was, he'd been weighed in the balance and found wanting. "What did I do? Mind giving me a hint?"

"Nothing, Art. You have done nothing. Let's try to have a pleasant evening." She scrutinized him. "Your pants are falling down."

He'd shoved his wallet, keys, and phone into a small front pocket and the weight of them was dragging. It wasn't like a caveman could carry a purse. He took the keys out and managed to tie them around his neck with a stringy piece of the tunic. "You don't like my costume," he suggested.

"It's perfect for you. Primitive Man."

"Primitive," Art echoed. He recognized this as the opening shot in a longer battle. "How, exactly, am I primitive?"

"There is more to life than just sex, Art."

"Huh." He was too shocked to make any other answer, perhaps because there was no good answer. You couldn't really argue back that no, sex is the only thing in life, or maybe in biological terms you could, but that was not what she had meant. What did she mean, and what was he being accused of? They had great sex together, didn't they? He'd always thought so, right from the start, and if Beata did not, you could have fooled him. More to life? What did she want him to do, not have sex with her? He was bewildered, and then angry. Women never fought fair. It was always the knife in the ribs when you least expected it.

Beata had already turned and was knocking at the apartment door. Art pulled the mask over his face. The hell with everything. He might as well go for being Primitive Man.

The door opened. He couldn't see clearly through the mask's eyeholes, but there was a swell of noise and jazzy music. Beata was greeting people and being greeted back, voices rising in delight.

"Oh my God!"

"And you! You are the gorilla of my dreams!"

"Where did you get the . . ."

"I'm thinking of wearing it to work."

Art pulled at the mask so there wasn't so much of it bunched up and misaligned. Beata was having an animated conversation with a blond woman who was also dressed as a flapper, except that her shimmy dress was yellow. There was also a gorilla—on the short side, for a great ape—and a pink flamingo—that is, a man in a flamingo-head hat and a feathery pink body held up by suspenders. Beata waved a hand in Art's direction. "And this is—"

Art leapt forward and hit the gorilla over the head with his foam club. "Ow," the gorilla said, a girl's voice. He reached out and pawed at the blond woman's hair, making guttural noises of appreciation. "This is Art," Beata said. "What a kidder. Art, that's your hostess, Susan." Art leaned in to sniff her neck. The woman made a faint strangled sound and pushed him away. What else did cavemen do? He was running out of ideas.

The pink-flamingo man said, "Does he eat birds? Do I have cause for concern?"

"Beer," Art announced. "Give beer!" He whomped on the floor with his club for emphasis.

Susan and Beata had taken a few steps back and were watching him in a way that did not seem friendly. "Sorry," Art said. "Got a little carried away."

"The bar's over there." Susan pointed. "Please, help yourself." Art was startled to realize that she was older than Beata, older than he himself. The blond hair he'd been fondling was a shiny wig.

"Thanks," he said, and headed bar-ward, doing a little bit of the old caveman swagger. Screw em if they couldn't take a joke. He heard the gorilla girl behind him, asking, "Is he the one with the master's degree?"

"Yes," Beata said. "That is he." Not, "Yes, that's my boyfriend, he has a master's degree." Although technically, he was ABD.

The pink-flamingo man said, "Grad school. Not everybody gets through it unscathed."

Screw him. Screw them all. He needed a drink and he needed it now. The apartment was one big open room with a baby grand piano at one end, a number of angular sofas and modern chairs, and at the far end, a kitchen. This was where the bar was set up. The party wasn't crowded yet, and he felt self-conscious about his bare arms and legs, the way he might not have if the place had been packed with more and drunker people. The floors were glossy varnished wood and his sandals squeaked on it. He nodded to a couple dressed up as robots, he guessed. Their costumes required a great deal of aluminum foil, and they might also have been a pair of oven-ready baked potatoes.

There were wine bottles and liquor bottles on a kitchen counter, and a cooler with bottles of water, also beer of the expensive sort bought by people who did not drink beer themselves: Harp, Anchor Steam, Beck's Dark. Art settled for a Beck's and took it back to one of the sofas to drink. Beata was still by the door, ignoring him. New guests had arrived. A man in a white nurse's uniform complete with starched cap and white stockings. Another who was either on his way to a leather bar or was just trying on the look for tonight. Whatever else people thought about his costume, at least he didn't think it said gay.

Art pushed his mask up and out of the way so he could drink his beer. He took his phone out to check it, nothing. He sent Linnea a text: *How's it going kiddo?*

After a couple of minutes his phone chimed back: *R U the life of the party?*

Yeah, I M killing em.

She didn't send anything back, but it cheered him to hear from her. He drank the beer down as fast as he could manage, which made him burp. What the hell. Caveman. He got up, went to the bar, and brought back two bottles. More people were coming in now, and he toasted them from the sofa. "Beer," he said. "Beer good."

He'd lost sight of Beata. Someone was playing the piano. He had to find the bathroom. The couch held him in its soft grip and he struggled to stand. His pants were drooping badly and he had to use his free, non-beer hand to hold them up. The bathroom was beyond the kitchen, off a hallway with closed doors—bedrooms, he figured. After he peed, he nosed around for a minute, entertaining the notion of invading his hostess's closet, dressing up in her clothes, and making his escape out the front door, unrecognized.

Back in the main room, he grabbed another beer and looked around for Beata. He still couldn't fathom the fight she'd picked with him, and now, with his head inflated by alcohol, it seemed like a simple matter to set it right. He would get her to explain herself. They would agree to have, in the future, whatever variety of sex she wished, and a great deal of it.

He found her standing next to the piano. A group had gathered there to listen to a man who was playing some sweeping, classical piece. "Hey," Art said, sidling up to her. "I missed you."

"I have been right here." She was drinking a glass of wine, red, like her dress. Her makeup, the black eyes and red mouth, had smudged a bit. He found this alluring, in a slutty sort of way. Beata looked him over. "Did you lose your club?"

He hadn't realized it was gone. "Yeah, I'm, ah, trying to invent the bow and arrow."

He laughed foolishly and drank down half the beer. OK, not funny. He wanted to tell Beata how good she looked, like a red fruit. He wanted to eat great mouthfuls of her, feel the juice dribble down his chin. But you couldn't say something like that, and besides, there he was making every-thing about sex again, well EXCUSE ME, but sometimes it really was all about sex, that was why it felt so good, why you'd crawl over broken glass to get it, how you'd do anything for it except pretend it didn't matter.

On impulse, he grasped her around her fringed hips and lifted her to sit on the piano. "Art! Stop!" A dribble of wine spilled onto her lap. He thought of slurping it up with his tongue, then thought better of it. He laughed again, beer-buzzed but not quite as drunk as he would have liked to be, and struck a caveman pose with both hands on his hips, which had the advantage of keeping his pants from falling any farther.

"Honestly! Art!" Someone handed her a napkin and she used it to blot at the wine.

"You look good up there," he told her. She was sitting primly, as if making a point of how uncomfortable and unwilling and disapproving she was. What he'd had in mind was a more seductive, reclining pose. "Relax," he said, ineffectually.

The man playing the piano had stopped playing. "That's really not the best thing for the instrument."

"For crying out loud, it's a piano," Art said.

The man shook his head. He was one of those droopy blond types that women always got excited about for reasons Art never understood. His hair fell over his eyes and he had a long, narrow face to go with his long, narrow, piano-tickling hands. "Hey!" Art said. "You aren't wearing a costume!"

"I came dressed as a piano player." The blond man let his hands drift over a chord, and smiled up at Beata. Art wondered if he was one of the old boyfriends. It wasn't fair. He could have avoided all sorts of trouble if he hadn't had to dress up.

"This is ridiculous," Beata said. "I'm getting down."

"Nonono, just stay there a minute, please?" He wanted her to go along with it, smile, flirt back at him. "It's OK," he said. "You're like, what do they call it, a hood ornament. Except on a piano."

"Ridiculous," Beata said again. She drank more of her wine.

The rest of the crowd had retreated. Art hoped they were afraid of what he was going to do next. What was he going to do next? He finished his beer and looked around for someplace to put the empty bottle. He couldn't find a coaster. He'd get in some kind of new trouble if he didn't use a coaster. He hung on to the bottle.

The blond man started playing again. He played as if he was a little bored, as if he was somebody who performed in front of audiences every night of the week, no big deal.

"What's that called, what you're playing?" Art asked. "It's kind of a nice tune."

"I don't think I've ever heard anybody . . . call Claude Debussy's *La Mer* a 'nice tune,' " the piano player said, in between banging away on the keyboard.

"Clyde Debussy? The same Clyde Debussy who ran the vacuum cleaner repair shop back in my hometown? What a coincidence."

"Art," Beata said, "are you aware that you are speaking very loudly?"

"Well, sorry." He had only been trying to make himself heard over the music. The caveman mask had been pushed up to his forehead, but now he pulled it over his face and swung his head from side to side. "I apologize," he told the piano player. "In my culture, we express our appreciation of music with enthusiastic mouth breathing." To Beata he said, "You want to dance? Come on, I'll get you down."

"I'm fine here," Beata said. "Hi, Susan. Come sit with me."

Susan had come up behind Art. "Wow," he said, catching sight of her. "You sure are yellow." She was blinding, especially the wig.

"Thank you. Everything all right here?"

"Everything is very all right," Art told her. "This is a beautiful apartment. So, you drive a taxi?"

Beata said, "Taxes, Art. She is a tax attorney. You weren't listening."

"Like anyone could hear with all this racket."

"You need to not drink any more."

"What?" He cupped a hand to his ear. He had forgotten he still held the empty beer bottle, and smacked himself just above the eyebrow. "I meant to do that," he informed them.

"Art?" Beata wiggled off the piano and put a hand on his arm. "Time-out. Let's get some air."

"Bye," he said, to whoever else was there. The mask cut off his peripheral vision. Someone handed him the foam club. He followed Beata down the stairs, and although he knew that things were not turning out well, and in fact might have already turned, for the moment he was happy to be alone with Beata again, just the two of them. When they reached the sidewalk she said, "What in the world is the matter with you?"

"You know that guy? Clyde? The piano player? He somebody you used to date?"

"Don't change the subject. You humiliated me. Not to mention yourself."

It was cold out on the street after the overheated party. He felt his sweat turn into a chill, heavy layer. Instant pneumonia. "Sorry."

"Don't mumble. A minute ago you were shouting."

The caveman mask smelled of every synthetic substance in the world, a dead, chemical smell. Art pushed it off his face and tried to clear his lungs. The beer sloshed in his stomach. Heavy seas. He started walking to the car, careful about putting one foot in front of the other.

"Where are you going?" Beata came after him, her shoes clippety-clipping on the sidewalk. "We need to talk! A serious talk, there is never such a thing with you. Art! I am unhappy!"

He kept walking, giant-stepping his way along the street, Beata still going on about the things that made her unhappy, which were mostly him. Later, tomorrow or the next day, he would feel bad about the accumulating consequences of his behavior. There would be regret, and guilt, and carnal deprivation, but there would also be relief, because if he was purely honest, he had arranged his entire life so as to avoid, as much as possible, any serious talks.

SIXTEEN

Maybe his dad was already dead. Conner made himself think it, dead, again and again, until the word was hollowed out and meant nothing. But it didn't keep on meaning nothing. It came back to him on the edge of sleep, when he couldn't guard against it, it made him angry, it made him scared, and he got tangled up in all the different things that might have happened or might still be happening. If his dad wasn't dead, why hadn't he called? Was he in a hospital again? Or maybe he was mad for some stupid reason. Why was it always Conner who had to worry about him, or decide not to worry and then feel bad about it?

Linnea said she'd help him look. Conner didn't want her to. She'd already gone and talked to that weird hippie woman, the one who worked for Mrs. Foster, and now somebody else was all into his business. "Why did you do that?" Conner asked her, and Linnea said because she knows stuff, she knows what hospitals do when people come in without money and she knows where the homeless shelters are and what happens when the police get called and what's the matter with you? Do you want to find your dad or not?

"Fine," Conner said. "OK." But it wasn't her dad. She didn't have to keep doing things for him.

The hippie woman had suggested places they look—places around here, that is. Maybe his dad had driven off north, south, east, or west. There was no telling. Conner had already gone to Floyd and to anybody else he could think of and come up with nothing. Floyd said, "Could be your dad doesn't want to be found, he's embarrassed, you know? He doesn't want you to think he's some kind of bum."

Then he shouldn't be a bum, Conner thought but did not say. Don't look like one and live like one. That was what Conner figured had probably happened. His dad had run off so he could be a bum. Conner had gone to the humane societies a couple of times, the one in Marin and the one in Sonoma, to look for Bojangles. He wasn't there but the places were full of miserable dogs, cowering and barking. He couldn't forgive his dad for taking Bojangles with him when he couldn't take care of himself.

Linnea said she wanted to go with him to the shelters the hippie woman told her about. She said she wasn't afraid of the places they'd have to go, places where drunks or worse hung out, he wouldn't have to worry about her or anything. Except that of course he would. She said she didn't have anything else to do on Halloween, she was such a loser.

"You're not a loser," Conner told her, because she was always saying things like that, and now if he didn't let her come with him, he'd be one more person who didn't want her around.

So on Halloween night, when all the little dressed-up kids were being led door to door by their parents, and the big kids were out looking for trouble, he told Mrs. Foster that if she didn't need him, he was going to spend the evening with some old friends, and Mrs. Foster, distracted by arranging trick-or-treat candy in a bowl, waved him away, fine, fine. He didn't need to ask her permission, but sometimes she decided she needed something from the drugstore, or some other excuse to talk to somebody besides a cat.

He knew he'd gotten lucky with Mrs. Foster; he didn't make the mistake of giving himself any credit for it.

Conner gassed up the truck and drove to Linnea's apartment. She was already waiting for him in the parking lot. "There's the St. Vincent de Paul in San Rafael," she told him, even before she said hello. "You want to start there?"

"Sure." He didn't want to admit that he didn't know what that was, St. Vincent de Paul.

Linnea perched up on the truck seat the way she always did, looking around her like there was something to see, not just the same old stretch of 101 and the same old landmarks that made you impatient to get past them. "What's the matter with you?" she said after a minute.

"Nothing."

"Yeah, I can tell."

"I think my dad might be dead."

"No way."

"How would you know if he is or not?" It was a relief to at least say it.

"Because you would of heard. There's nothing on TV about anybody dead. Take the Central exit," she added. She looked out over the lights reflecting and pooling on the surface of the water as the highway passed over the bay. "Is that San Quentin?"

"Yeah. You know anybody in there?"

She whipped her head around. "What?"

"Nothing."

"Why'd you say that?"

"It was a joke. Jesus." He never knew sometimes what was going to get her going.

Linnea's phone beeped, a text. She pulled it out of her pocket to read it. "It's Art," she announced, tapping back a reply. "He's at a party with his girlfriend. You met her, remember? The Polish Bombshell?"

"That's messed up, that you call him Art."

"Well it's not like he was around during my formative years." They pulled up to a downtown stoplight and they both scanned the sidewalks, looking for anybody who might be just hanging out. "There's all kinds of fathers, you know."

"Yeah, at least you know where yours is."

St. Vincent de Paul was a charity, a place that handed out meals and clothes. It was closed for the night, but a half dozen people were killing time at the end of the block, on the steps of an antiques store. "Dining room opens at six for breakfast," one man told them. He looked young, no more than thirty, but the top of his head was bald. The rest of his hair was long and fine and tangled.

"We were looking for somebody," Linnea said. "His dad."

Conner said, "He has a bad hip that makes him walk crooked. He might have a dog with him." Nobody spoke. It wasn't a hostile silence, just a reluctance to give anything up, even words. "His name is Sean McDonald," Conner added.

"They don't allow dogs in there," an old man said. "They have rules for things." His face was so lined and shriveled, it looked like a special effects from a movie.

"So where would you go, if you had a dog?"

The bald man said, "I trained dogs in the army. The Special Forces. German shepherds, mostly. And Dobermans. Train them so all you have to do is nod your head and they'd tear somebody's throat out. They'd do whatever I'd tell them. Wouldn't let anybody mess with me. A guy tried to jump me once. Dog ate three of his fingers."

Linnea looked at Conner and shrugged. "Well, you guys have a nice evening."

"Hey, trick or treat," somebody yelled after them as they walked away. "Hey!"

Once they were sitting in the truck, Linnea said, "I didn't know places like that weren't open at night. I guess we should come back in the day-time. Talk to somebody who works there."

"Yeah." Except his dad wouldn't go anywhere like that. He wouldn't want to be around those people. He'd keep to himself. "Where else did she say?"

"There's different churches that have shelters, but that's mostly in winter. There's another place in San Rafael . . ." She had things written down on a piece of notebook paper that she fished out of her bag. "It's where you can get a cot for a night, and take a shower."

"Jesus." He hadn't thought about things like showers, his dad not being able to take a shower.

They drove past it. Through the front windows they could see some kind of kids' Halloween party going on in a front room. Little kids were running around with plastic orange treat bags. Some of them had their faces painted to look like cats or clowns. Some of them had masks made out of construction paper. "It doesn't look like a dad kind of place," Conner said.

They circled the downtown blocks. No businesses were open, and the half-lit storefronts had the look of empty fish tanks. The deserted streets reminded him. "Hey, how was the zombie apocalypse?"

"It sucked. They wouldn't let me be a zombie. It was only for the cool kids."

They drove in wider and wider circles, beneath the freeway and back again. Linnea said, "Ah, this is going to sound strange, so don't get upset, but did you think about putting an ad up about your dog? People notice dogs, you know, if they're hungry or lost. More than they do people."

That was true. "Talk about suck," Conner said. He hadn't let himself think a lot about Bojangles. He kept a bareness all around his heart.

"So Christie"—that was her name—"said, if he has a vehicle, he could be sleeping in it. People find parking lots where maybe they won't get hassled, like, twenty-four-hour restaurants. And there's people who camp."

"Camp, where?"

"Anywhere. Open space."

There was open space all around them. Even downtown, all you had to do was raise your eyes to the hillsides. There were a few houses on the lower slopes, their lights showing through the trees. Beyond them, solid black. And beyond those hills were other hills and canyons, the whole of Mt. Tam, and beyond the mountain were more wild and secret places, and beyond them was the rest of the world.

"This is stupid," Conner said. He meant, stupid to even try and find anyone.

"Let's just drive around for a while," Linnea said.

Conner got back on the freeway and headed north, hitting the accelerator hard. Sometimes he forgot it wasn't really his truck. It wasn't like Mrs. Foster ever checked the mileage, and even if she ever did, it wasn't like she cared, and even if she cared, she could afford all the gas on the planet. What did it matter that she was trying to give her money away? She was still keeping plenty for herself. And giving money to him by the handful. Money he couldn't afford not to take. It made him angry, like it was his fault for his dad being broke and beat down, like he was just one more part of the howling unfairness of it all.

Linnea said, "Maybe your dad got a ticket. You know, for sleeping in public or something. I'll ask Christie if she can find out."

"Fucking incredible."

"What is?"

"They make it illegal to be homeless."

He was glad she didn't say anything to that. He didn't want to have to explain himself or have some big heavyweight conversation. But in his restless bad mood he was ready to find fault with her silence also, her willingness to put up with him. Why did he hang around with her so much anyway? She was the only person he ever talked to, and she was just this freaky little girl.

After twenty minutes or so, she said, "You headed anywhere in particular?"

"You got somewhere you need to be?" he asked, and she gave him one of her looks.

Out of some need to be spiteful, or hurtful, either to her or to himself, he got off in Santa Rosa and steered his way to his old girlfriend's house. Linnea sat up and took in the streets of ordinary houses and lawns. Some of them were decorated with carved pumpkins or fake cobwebs or paper cutouts of black cats, witches, ghosts. "Nice neighborhood," Linnea said. "You think your dad's around here?"

"I got tired of the freeway." His girlfriend's house was dark and quiet.

She was probably out somewhere sucking dick, either the rancid beach boy's, or somebody else's. She was drunk at a party and guys were taking turns with her. He wanted to imagine all the worst and ugliest things.

"Hey, watch it," Linnea said, because he had veered too close to a curb and had almost taken out somebody's mailbox.

He jerked the wheel back in the other direction. "You want to drive?"

"What crawled up your ass and died?"

"You really need to cool it with the potty mouth, you know? Guys don't really like it."

"You mean, you don't."

"It doesn't matter what I like. I'm just telling you."

Conner hit the accelerator hard enough to jolt her back in her seat, and she gave him an evil look, though she didn't say anything. There were times when they got mad at each other for no reason, or not much reason, because they could never figure out what they were supposed to be. She wasn't his girlfriend and wasn't ever going to be. He thought maybe that was what she wanted, with all her hanging around, but it wasn't going to happen. She was too young and too weird and not really pretty. Anyway, he didn't want a girlfriend, unless he could find one that didn't speak English and liked being naked a lot.

He had his computer set up in Mrs. Foster's basement, and sometimes, if he was pretty sure she wasn't going to come downstairs, he watched porn on it. But that never really worked because he had to keep one eye and ear on the stairs, and besides, he always wondered about the girls, if it hurt them, and why they let somebody do these things to them, and what happened to them once the camera was shut off.

Conner turned and headed back toward the freeway. They were sitting at a stoplight. The truck had a rough idle. He thought it was probably going to have to have some work done before the next emissions inspection. He thought about calling his old girlfriend and saying whatever she wanted to hear, doing whatever it was she'd want, walking through fire, anything to get himself laid.

Linnea said, "I do know somebody in jail. Just not in San Quentin."

"Huh." Conner waited. She was either going to say more or she wasn't.

"He was sort of my boyfriend."

"Sort of, what does that mean?"

"Just, it didn't go on very long."

Again he waited, but she only said, "The light's green," and he drove through the intersection and onto the southbound freeway ramp.

"So where is this jailbird boyfriend, if he's not in San Quentin?" He resigned himself to asking questions.

"Back in Ohio."

"You write to him?"

"I'm not allowed to."

"Yeah, and I guess he's not on Facebook." Traffic was moving fast, careening along like nobody was ever going to stop again. He had to change lanes a couple of times. "You going to tell me what he did?" he asked, making sure he sounded only bored and patient.

"He shot some people."

"Come on."

"You don't have to believe me. It was all in the news and you can look it up."

"Thanks, I'll do that."

"Fuck you. I mean, sincerely." She switched on the radio and ran the tuner up and down the dial, coming up with squawks and banshee music. Conner switched it back off.

"OK," he said. "So how did you end up with this desperado character? What was the big attraction?" He hadn't been paying enough attention to her, he guessed, and now he was going to suffer for it.

"Forget it."

"All of a sudden he's this sensitive subject?"

"Pull over. I want to get out."

"Come on, Linnea."

"You're just a big turd, you know?"

"Thanks. Constructive criticism, always good."

"Everybody thinks I'm some big joke."

"I do not think you're a big joke."

"Say you're sorry."

"I'm sorry, Christ. Don't keep messing with the radio. It's annoying."

"Yeah, you're the only one allowed to be annoying."

"I said I was sorry."

"I know you're upset about your dad, but you don't have to be a total asshole."

"There's that potty mouth," he reminded her.

"I beg your pardon. I mean, a total douche."

"Tell me more about Mr. Wonderful."

"Only if you really want to hear it."

"Sure," he said. "Why not. What's his name?"

She gave him a sideways look and Conner had to figure that at least some of what she had to say was lies, but it was hard to tell how much or what part. "His name's not important."

"It's usually considered kind of important."

"It's not important for you to know it."

"OK, fine. Did he shoot a lot of people?" He hoped he wasn't going to have to keep playing Twenty Questions. "Was he in a gang or something?"

"No," Linnea said, like this was a dumb thing to ask.

"So tell me about his life of crime."

"He killed these people, three of them. One of them was my step-sister."

"All right," Conner said after a moment. He didn't think he believed it but his heart was sending the blood up into his ears, pounding away. "Stepsister, how is it you had a stepsister?"

"My mom married this guy, a long time after her and Art split up, and he already had this daughter. So she was a stepsister. Like Cinderella."

"Why did he, what, he was at your house or something?"

"No." Again, using her pitying, aren't-you-ignorant voice. "She didn't even live with us. She was one grade ahead of me. She was kind of a bitch. I know how that sounds, because she's dead and all, but it's true."

They drove in silence. Except for the dash lights and the moving lights around them, everything was black. Conner kept waiting for her to say more. He wasn't sure he wanted to hear any more. But waiting made him feel like something was creeping up the back of his neck. He said, "How about the other two?"

"I didn't know them. I don't know why he shot them, he was kind of crazy."

"Yeah, I guess," he muttered.

"He shot my stepsister because he knew I didn't like her."

The truck jittered on the curves. Conner had to clamp down on the wheel so they wouldn't go sailing off into the blackness. Linnea said, "I didn't ask him to. It wasn't anything I made happen. But I got blamed for it anyway."

Conner coughed and tried to get his throat working right. It was rasped dry. "You didn't shoot anybody." He was pretty sure she hadn't, whatever else she said.

"No, but I kind of wanted to."

Then she said, "That was why I got shipped out here, you know. Because my mom decided I was this evil creature."

"Evil, come on."

"Well, I did some sort of evil stuff afterwards."

After a while Conner asked, "How long is this guy in jail for?" He still wasn't sure how much of it he believed.

"He's in the crazy jail, they can keep him as long as he's crazy."

"I guess you don't miss him."

"I do and I don't." She'd been slouched down in the seat on her tailbone and now she wriggled her way upright. "I sure do think about him."

They were coming up on San Rafael and the traffic slowed. Linnea said, "When somebody you know is dead, they're like a ghost in your head. They keep on bugging you. It pretty much sucks."

"I don't believe in ghosts," Conner said.

"That's because you don't have any."

Maybe his dad was a ghost by now. It was lonesome to think it. His dad would be one of those sad ghosts who kept coming around wanting something, and trying to get you to laugh at some dumb joke so you'd be more inclined to give it to them.

He said, "Remind me not to spend next Halloween with you."

"You are so, so hilarious. Maybe I should just go home. Unless you have some other big fun plans."

He guessed he'd given up on finding his dad tonight. He couldn't think what else to do or where to go. He'd talked himself into the notion that anything he did really mattered.

Linnea said, "Like, we could find a party and knock on the door and say, 'Is this the Halloween party I was invited to?'"

"Don't tell me you ever really did that."

"No," she admitted. "But I heard some people talking about doing it."

There wasn't anywhere left for them to go. They could drive up and down the freeway all night, going nowhere. It was like they were the ghosts. What if he was the one who suddenly disappeared? Would anybody notice? His mom, sure. And Mrs. Foster, until she found somebody else to take out the trash and clean up after the cats.

And if Linnea was gone, her dad would miss her, and the mother she was always so mad at. But she was like him. She didn't belong to much of anything except herself.

They were almost to her exit when Conner asked her if she wanted to go get something to eat. She gave him a quick, startled-rabbit look. "Sure."

"Is pizza OK?"

She said it was. Conner took the exit to the shopping center to one side of the freeway.

He parked in front of the pizza place, got out, and waited for her to catch up with him. "Are we getting takeout?" she asked.

"No, we can go in and sit down."

He saw her thinking this through. They'd never done such a thing as sit together in a restaurant before, like a couple. It was no big deal. Ordering a pizza together wasn't like getting engaged.

They found a table and opened the plastic-coated menus. Conner watched her read her menu. She'd done some new thing to her hair in the last couple of days, put some all-over bright brown color on it and got it cut so it stayed out of her face. He hadn't noticed it until now because it actually looked good. She saw him watching her. "Something bugging you?"

"Nothing. You know what you want?"

"Green peppers, mushrooms, and black olives. And whatever you want on it. Except pepperoni. Pepperoni gives you pepperoni breath."

"Can't have that." It confused him; was she saying she didn't want him to have bad breath, it was something she cared about?

"Ever since I mostly quit smoking, I have a more sensitive, uh, palate."

"I guess you would, yeah."

The waitress took their order and brought them Cokes in tall glasses. They looked out over the room without saying anything. It was like talking was something they could only do while driving. Conner was thinking about all the weird things that had to happen for the two of them to end up here, sitting at the same table. First he guessed they both had to get born, and their parents had to get born too, and all the generations before them. Linnea had to get herself mixed up with some wild bad trouble that either was or wasn't her fault, and either had or hadn't really happened in the first place, anyway, whatever she'd done to get herself shipped out here to live with her dad.

And if Conner's dad hadn't gotten himself smashed up and useless, Conner would probably be in school by now, the community college in Santa Rosa, taking computer courses.

He'd have a normal life. It was all just stupid random shit that happened for no reason and nothing you could do about it.

The pizza came. Linnea ate just as much as he did, slice for slice. She said that when you stopped smoking, you got this huge appetite, and Conner said if she didn't watch it, she was going to get fat. "Show me where I'm fat," she said, pulling her jacket open, and Conner got a view of her unbuttoned shirt front and the undershirt beneath it and some little black straps beneath that.

"Nice," he said. "Flashing the whole restaurant."

She yanked her jacket shut. "You are vile."

"Ha-ha." But he'd seen what he'd seen. Her nipples stood out like twin targets.

They finished eating and Conner paid the bill. Linnea dug in her bag looking for her wallet and he waved her off. "I got it."

He saw her trying to figure it. "Well, thanks. I have to go to the restroom."

Conner watched her get up and walk away from him. She wore one of those shortie skirts over a pair of jeans, like he'd seen other girls wearing. It was disappointing when you couldn't see the girl's ass. Well it was, he couldn't help thinking it.

He waited at the front door for her, then pushed it open so that she walked beneath his arm. They got into the truck and he started the engine. Linnea said, "Got any ideas?"

"What?"

"Is there anywhere else you wanted to go? Or maybe I should just boogie on home."

"Yeah, I'll run you home." It wasn't that late, only around eleven. She lived just on the other side of the freeway and it didn't take more than a couple of minutes to make the turn onto the frontage road. Her apartment building was almost at the end. He was tired from all the driving but restless too. He had nothing to show for himself, tonight or any night.

Conner pulled into a far corner of the parking lot and kept the engine running. Linnea said, "I'm sorry we didn't find your dad."

"Well, we tried." He didn't want to think about his dad. He didn't want to be reminded of everything that was lost, failed, lonesome.

"Crap." She had dumped her purse on the floor of the truck and she bent over to pick it up. Her hair fell to one side and the back of her neck was bare. Conner reached over and held the palm of his hand just above it, close enough to feel the warmth from her.

Headlights swept over them. He pulled his hand away and Linnea straightened up. "Hey. It's Art."

They watched the car pull into its space across the lot. Linnea said, "I don't see Bombshell. I guess it's no sugar tonight for the Artster."

"Heh-heh, yeah." Conner tried clearing his throat. It made a thick, bestial sound, like a warthog in rut.

The taillights shut off, and a moment later Art got out. He wore a huge shaggy black wig with a dent in it, as if he'd slept wrongways on a pillow, and drooping leopard-print shorts. There was some kind of leopard top also, slung around one shoulder. He started up the stairs, then turned back, unlocked the car, and rummaged around in it. He emerged with a club shaped like an oversized drumstick. This he balanced on his bare shoulder as he trudged up the stairs, opened the front door to the apartment, and shut it behind him.

Conner and Linnea looked at each other. Linnea said, "Seriously. WTF."

"No words," Conner agreed.

Linnea opened the passenger door. "I'm going to count to one hundred real slow, then go up. Call me, OK?"

He waited until she was inside, then drove off. There was the totally random shit of the universe and then there was a whole other, stranger universe you didn't even know you lived in until it showed its face.

Conner posted a picture of Bojangles on Craigslist and offered a cash reward. He found out there were a lot of black dogs running loose in the North Bay, or maybe a lot of people willing to trade a dog for money. For the next ten days people wrote in about dogs that were female, or spotted, or Chihuahuas, or other depressing bad ideas. A woman in Fairfax wrote to say she was feeding a stray that might have come down from the hills, and Conner drove out to see it. He found a dog that was so lean and grizzled and weary that, even after it padded toward him and buried its head in his lap and thumped its tail, he had to check its collar and find the extra star-shaped hole he'd punched himself to convince himself that it really was Bojangles. His heart cracked open and flooded all the space around it.

SEVENTEEN

Sometimes he thought he'd discovered something amazing: the peeling-away process of all his worries and hassles, his shoulds and oughts, which left him feather-light, unencumbered, free. Like being a monk, maybe. An economic monk. He'd taken a vow of poverty, or more like, somebody else had drawn up the paperwork and handed him a pen to sign with. Anyway, once they kicked your legs out from under you, and stomped on your knees, and spat in your face, what else could they do to you?

Now he was free to look at the sky and think sky-thoughts. He smoked weed and let the clouds in his head drift and lumber into one another. He was fine, he was getting by, and he felt sorry for all those poor rat bastards who were sweating it night and day, hating their jobs and all the things that went along with the jobs. His life had been whittled or polished down, and was now so beautifully, beautifully simple.

Then there were other times, when the mechanics of living, matters of food and hygiene, exasperated and defeated him, when there was nothing to do and all day in which to do it. And then the next day and the one after that, each with its privations and inadequacies. He had his clothes and tools and a few other things he'd saved from the wreckage of his house under a tarp in the truck bed, packed into plastic bags and five-gallon buckets like a goddamn hobo, which he guessed he was now. When it rained, he stayed in the truck. When someone made him, he moved the truck from one place to another. Sean slept in the front seat, the dog in the small backseat. He figured that he and the animal smelled pretty much the same by now.

His clothes were still good enough to go into Home Depots or bookstores and use the bathrooms. He tried to walk briskly on his crippled hip. No matter who you were or what your circumstances, people looked at you cross-eyed if you had something wrong with you that showed, as if they were afraid your bad luck was catching. One of the colleges, the trusting kind that didn't always ask for IDs, had a locker room with blissful hot-water showers. At McDonald's and other fast food restaurants he ordered the dollar specials. He lingered over his coffee and a newspaper, taking note of everyone else doing likewise, the people he kept seeing in such places, none of them ever acknowledging the others.

Nothing stayed the same. Not the place he went to sleep or the place he woke. Not hope or the lack of hope. The difference between a good and a bad day as small as the presence, or the absence, of clean socks. Sometimes he was pleased with his own resourcefulness. He had it knocked, and if he wasn't good enough for some people, namely his ungrateful son, screw them. Then a bleak black mood would slam him sideways. Who was he kidding, trying to shine up the piece of shit that was his life?

For the last three nights he'd stayed in Bolinas, with a woman he'd met here. Sometimes a thing like that just came your way. He'd been sitting on the beach, with the dog hunkered down next to him, watching the kids on their boogie boards. The kids wore wetsuits because of the cold ocean, and it was pretty cold on the beach too, so he'd brought a piece of cardboard to sit on. You couldn't camp on the beach, just sit. But the sun was out and he had a paper cup of hot coffee to warm his hands and the waves were the perfect entertainment for somebody who had nothing else to do but to watch them. Did anybody ever ask a wave if it had plans, or prospects, or any business taking up space? Not likely.

He could have slept right there. Curled himself up next to the dog. But he kept an eye on the kids, who had come out of the water now and were hanging out at one end of the beach, milling around and jeering at one another. A couple of years ago, in this same little peace-and-love hippie town, on this same beach, a bunch of kids, not these same kids but some just like them, had beaten a homeless guy half to death with skateboards and bottles.

A woman walked past him on the sand and stopped. "Hi."

Sean squinted up at her. She had silver hair, trailing down past her shoulders. She wore a long skirt and silver bracelets around one ankle. "Hi," he said back to her.

"What's your dog's name?" She said it like it was some kind of test question.

"Bojangles. After the famous dancer."

"Does your dog dance?"

"Not while I've been watching him."

"How about you, do you dance?" She did a little dipping, twirling step in the sand. Her feet were bare except for flat sandals. She looked like somebody's crazy grandmother.

"Nope. My dancing days are over."

"Well that's a shame."

"Uh-huh." He wasn't so sure. Dancing wasn't one of those things he spent time feeling bad about.

The woman gathered her skirts up in a flounce and sat down next to him—that is, next to Bojangles, who was next to Sean. Bojangles wiggled his nose into her side to get himself petted. "Pretty pretty boy. I like dogs. Is he OK with cats?"

"He and cats usually work things out."

"Because I've got two cats."

"That's nice," Sean said. It was easiest to keep on being agreeable. She wasn't as old as he'd thought at first, at least not as old as her hair. Maybe she wasn't much older than he was. He was waiting to make up his mind about her. He figured she was one of the town's herd of hippies, people who went around talking about energy and astrology and who grew psychedelic mushrooms in their closets. "I like your necklace," he said. It was made up of yellow stones that were the size of gravel. Admiring the necklace gave him an excuse to look down her shirt.

"It's amber. That's fossilized tree resin." She picked up one of the stones and held it for him to see. "This one has a little bit of something inside it, maybe part of an insect."

"Oh, yeah. Pretty cool." He leaned in closer to look. He didn't think she was wearing a bra. Her skin and clothes gave off a smell that was part ashtray, part incense, part cat. An unfresh smell, soft around the edges, like the crumbs you found in the bottom of a coat pocket.

"Or a dinosaur. Because they had dinosaurs back then. My name is Dawn."

"Sean. Nice to meet you." He put his coffee down and held out his hand and they shook. Unlike most women, who didn't put any effort into a handshake, she pumped his hand up and down, cowgirl-style.

They sat and watched the waves pile up. Sean drank his coffee. He hadn't spent a lot of time talking lately and he was out of practice.

Dawn said, "Which one's the biggest ocean, do you know?"

He tried to remember the other oceans. Atlantic, Arctic, Indian. Were there others? "I guess I don't know. It might be this one."

"Well it doesn't seem all that big from right here. You probably have to look down on it from outer space."

"Uh-huh." Maybe she was stoned. It was the kind of thing stoned people got really intense about.

"Which do you think is more important, air or water?"

Stoned. Or something. There was an annoying little-kid quality to her questions. He said, "I guess it depends if you're a fish."

"Ahh." She nodded. "That's funny."

It wasn't all that funny. "Ha-ha," he said obligingly. Maybe she was some kind of village idiot, or a burned-out druggie casualty. He decided she wasn't bad-looking. Just a little crispy around the edges, like she'd spent too much time in the sun. "So, Dawn, you from around here?"

"These days I am. Uh-huh."

Some old dread rose in his throat, *you from around here?* But he was just spooking himself. He said, "You mean, you moved here from some-place else?" She didn't answer, only occupied herself with pushing her tongue around the inside of her mouth in a systematic fashion, as if she'd lost something in there. "Never mind," Sean said.

The dog rolled over on his back and Dawn rubbed his stomach. "Why did you name him that really? Bojangles?"

"I dunno. It was just one of those names that wasn't nailed down. No-body else was using it." He didn't want to tell her that it had something to do with drinking a lot of beer and watching an old movie and making the clever observation that the dog, like Bojangles, was black.

"You can change a dog's name, can't you?" She asked it like she really didn't know.

"Well yeah, it's not illegal or anything. But then the dog wouldn't know when you were calling him. Why would I want to change his name anyway?"

"I don't know. He doesn't look happy. Sometimes the wrong name can do that."

"He's fine," Sean said. He didn't want some nutty woman telling him he couldn't take care of his own dog.

"See, if you change a name, the universe will call you by the new name."

"All right. Fair enough. I'll put it on the to-do list." It was just mystic hippie talk, like crystal healing. He guessed if he was going to hang around here, he ought to learn the lingo.

"Sean. Hey! It rhymes! Sean and Dawn."

"Yeah. Who knew."

"What kind of a name is that, Sean?"

"Celtic. You know, Irish. Some places in Ireland, it's pronounced 'Shayne.' It's a form of John, and, ah, the French 'Jean.' "

"So you really have a whole lot of names." She made it sound as if he'd said he had a whole lot of money.

"If you look at it in a certain way, yeah." His name was Shit For Brains, and Broke Ass, and Gimp.

Dawn got up and brushed the sand from her skirt. "You want any vegetarian chili? I made some last night."

"As it happens," Sean said, "I'm a huge fan of vegetarian chili."

And that's how he'd come to be sitting on Dawn's front porch three days later, with his truck parked in the driveway and his dog in the yard and his boots under her bed. He'd felt sort of bad at first, like he was taking advantage. There was probably some law meant to protect the borderline mentally deficient or the seriously high—he still didn't know which she was, or maybe she was both—from, well, from people like himself. But she was allowed to run around loose and walk the streets on her own. Though in this particular town, home to the spiritually inclined and the drug-inclined and people who called themselves poets or artists because nobody told them they weren't, that didn't signify much. Anybody could, and did, have full citizenship rights here.

After the first night he stayed there, he woke up with the fattest of the two cats perched on the end of the bed, staring him down. It was an orange cat with flat green eyes, and Sean's heart seized up like somebody had injected solder into it, but really, the cat was no stranger than anything else he'd woken up to, namely this bed with a woman in it, and so he calmed himself and wiggled his toes for the pleasure of feeling the sheets around them.

Dawn said she used to live in Utah, in the desert. She said she used to have a husband and three children. In Utah! Then one day she had been struck by lightning, lightning in her head. After that everyone "kept trying to make me stay inside." So she ran away and came to the ocean, because all along she had really been a water person. She had changed her name too, although she wouldn't tell him her old name because then her old life might hear it and track her down.

Sean said Well, that sort of thing could happen. The old lightning-in-the-brain problem.

It wasn't exactly an explanation, but it sort of explained things. She surely didn't seem to like staying inside, and often enough Sean was left alone with the cats to make himself at home. On one such occasion, he nosed around and found some Social Security check stubs made out to Cheryl Krupalija.

He tried to find out just how much money Dawn had, both because he was curious and for more suspect motives that he didn't care to admit to himself. She had a small coin purse, like a child's, and she kept her paper money in it, folded up like origami. There didn't seem to be that much of it, but he hadn't seen her buy much either. The Social Security checks weren't very large, not enough to pay a lot in the way of rent. Her shingled cottage had only two rooms, a bedroom and everything else, but here in the Land of Ridiculous Real Estate, it was probably worth a few hundred thousand dollars. How did any of the longhairs and people who made driftwood sculptures get by around here? Did they all sell drugs?

He'd noticed that just up the hill from Dawn's place, at the far end of the same driveway, was another, grander house, shingled in the same style as hers. You saw a lot of such add-ons, or studios, or guest cottages tacked on to larger properties. "Who lives up there?" Sean asked her.

"Roberto," Dawn said. She was sitting at the kitchen table, pushing marijuana stems through a screen. The resins collected on a small mirror below.

"And who's he when he's at home?"

"He isn't home right now."

"It's just a way of speaking. Forget it." He should have known better than to attempt any kind of clever conversation with her. "Is he a friend of yours?"

"Yes. But he's allergic to the cats."

"Uh-huh." Sean watched her to see if she might be interested in coming back to bed, but she was hell-bent on processing the bag of stems. She tended to get involved in a project once she started it. Sean went out to the front porch. It was one of those mornings of high overcast and fog you got so often along the coast, the gray air blotting out all the colors of the world. It made you feel like you were inside of something and couldn't get out. He wondered what Conner was doing right now. Following that rich woman around and cleaning up after her.

He was going to call Conner, once he got his feet underneath him and had something to show for himself and didn't have to put up with a lot of pissy attitude. After all, who was it that had raised the kid pretty much single-handed after Conner's mother bailed on them? Who'd paid for his food and clothes and all his computer toys? If you turned it into math, calculated his effort times days and weeks and months and years, wasn't that enough to earn him some credit in the lean times? Buy him a little forgiveness if he'd done a few things wrong?

He was down right now but he could still get himself back up. Already Sean was sketching out a life for himself here. He still had his tools, and there was work he could do if it didn't involve climbing or too much lifting. He could fix a few things up for Dawn. Make some contributions to the household.

He didn't like the idea that if his son was living off a rich woman, he might be living off a poor one.

Dawn wasn't the best cook in the world—meals involved lots of carrots and beets and other gnarly things that grew in the ground—but at least it was cooking. Most of what he'd been eating were things that didn't require preparation, bread, mostly. She seemed OK with Sean being here— that is, she didn't tell him he had to leave. It was a funny feeling, being in the same room with somebody who from time to time seemed to forget you were there. As much as you could get tired of women who talked and talked, the ones who wanted to know what you were thinking, which meant, were you thinking of them, with Dawn there were silences like blank spots, like a record skipping. It made for a lonesome time.

"Tell me about your kids, your kids back in Utah," he said, and she said she didn't think they were in Utah anymore. She was petting the skinny cat. The skinny cat was long and narrow, and it bent around corners like it was a sheet of paper.

"All right, where are they? Where do they live now?"

"I don't know."

Sean waited, but she wasn't saying more. "Were they boys or girls?" he asked.

She shook her head, fast, as if trying to get what was left of her children out of it. She said, "Can animals be vegetarians? I mean, cats and dogs."

"That cat's already too skinny," Sean said. "Don't start feeding it a lot of vegetable slop."

"It could eat fish. I guess that still counts as vegetarian."

What kind of woman didn't know or care about her kids? It wasn't human. It wouldn't even do credit to a cat.

This morning, the third in a row he'd woken up in a bed, he heard a car pass by on the driveway. He and Dawn were enjoying some private time together, and Sean was disinclined to interrupt it. Later, he looked out the window to see a sporty red car, a BMW, parked up at the larger house uphill.

"Is that your pal Roberto's car up there?" he asked her, in case Roberto was anybody he ought to be prepared to say howdy to.

Dawn was in the bathtub, squeezing water over herself with a big sea sponge, the kind that looked like it might start crawling around on its own. "He has a lot of cars," she said.

"Well, somebody's up there," Sean said, trying to sound serious and important but getting distracted by the view. Naked, Dawn was saggy in some places and worn down in others, but he didn't mind, not one bit. In one way at least, he was a lucky man.

He was so grateful that she put up with the complications of his own beat-to-shit body, the ways in which he had to labor and arrange himself, all the worry and relief. He'd been afraid that after so much time of doing without, and so many insults to his system, his poor old dick was going to hide between his legs and refuse to come out, and that no woman would look on him without pity. Maybe she was brain-damaged, simple-minded, but thank God for her.

"Hey, look." Dawn raised herself up in the tub until her nipples broke the surface of the bathwater. "I'm a mermaid!"

"You sure are. That's a great trick. Do you have any more tricks? I want you to practice them. I'm going out for a while, OK?"

He whistled to Bojangles and they set off down the road to the beach. Already he'd established something of a routine: park himself in front of the waves for a time. Next head into town and equip himself with some small purchase—mints, a nail clipper, a can of dog food, anything to give himself the pleasant sense of spending money—then end up in the saloon where he drank one beer, making it last a long time. Then, in the late afternoon, feeling like he'd accomplished, if not a day's work, then at least something close to a day's occupation, he'd collect his dog again from the sidewalk outside and head back up the hill to Dawn's. He could get used to living like this. He was already used to it.

But this time as he approached he could see a man standing in Dawn's yard. He was a big man with heavy shoulders, dressed in a leather jacket and jeans. He was studying Sean's truck, taking it in, moving to one side of it, then another. Sean quickened his step as best he could. "Hi there," he said, once he was within hailing distance. Keeping it cautious, ready for things to go either way.

"This your truck?"

"That it is."

"Mind if I ask what it's doing here?"

"Mind if I ask why you want to know?"

They looked each other over. Big tub of tripes. His belly riding the front of his T-shirt. The T-shirt was red and featured a picture of a cowboy on a bucking bronco. He had a lot of wiry black hair going gray, and a gray mustache and beard trimmed so as to make a hole for his mouth. He said, "Because I take a particular interest in who parks in my driveway."

"I bet you're Roberto. Hi. Sean. Sean McDonald. I'm a friend of Dawn's."

Sean offered his hand. Roberto took a step forward and shook. "Friend of Dawn's. You must be a new friend."

"That I am."

"Well, well," Roberto said. "She does get around, our Dawn."

Sean didn't say anything. It didn't seem like a conversation that was going to end up in a good place.

But then Roberto laughed and pointed to Bojangles, who was lifting his leg on the garbage bins. "That your hound?"

"Yeah, he's mine."

"That's gotta be the most pitiful-looking dog I've ever seen."

"Ha-ha," said Sean politely. Though he didn't appreciate having his dog insulted.

It seemed to put Roberto in a fine mood. "How about you come up to the house, I'll cook us a little dinner. You object to steak?"

"No, steak's good." He didn't want to say yes or no. "I should talk to Dawn first."

"She's already up there. She's doing her laundry. You have anything you want to throw in the machines?"

He sure did, but he wasn't going to get that chummy yet. "Thanks, but I guess not."

"Or maybe what you really need is a car wash." Roberto leaned in to run a finger over the truck's tailgate. "Honestly? You should try to keep your vehicle in a little better shape."

"Yeah, I keep meaning to take it in somewhere." Roberto had already turned his back and started up the drive. Sean stumped after him.

At the front door, Roberto waited for him. "You are one slow motherfucker. You must not be that hungry."

"I'll be hungry enough by the time I get there." He was getting pretty tired of all the grief he was getting. But if he was going to keep hanging out at Dawn's, he figured he had to go along with it, Roberto being the landlord, he guessed. "Hey, nice place," he said, hoping that didn't sound too bootlicking.

Because it was a sharp house, with walls of windows and one of those giant fireplaces that was designed to look like a rockslide. Sean went over to it and ran a hand over the large and small boulders. "What you got here, river rock?"

"It's Chief Cliff stone. Dry stacked. With a reinforced wall behind it, earthquake-proof to 8.5. Get you a drink?"

"Yeah, sure. Thanks. Beer, if you have it." Roberto had started off down a hallway, but Sean lingered, taking in the view from the oversized windows. It was one of those houses designed around a view. Here was Bolinas Bay far below them, the line of breaking waves, and the sun lowering itself into the water, flooding the sky with gold. He wondered how much it cost to buy yourself a piece of ocean like this one.

Where was Dawn? He nosed around a couple of the rooms, which struck him as expensive and uninteresting. They all had things that you were meant to admire, like the black leather lounges or the oil painting slashed with colors. All of them huge, enormous, the same as the fireplace. It was like walking into the giant's house in the fairy tales, though he couldn't remember which one. The Fee-fi-fo-fum one.

Sean found the kitchen because of all the racket Roberto was making, banging around with pots and pans. He had two steaks the size of city phone books out on a butcher-block island and he was rubbing them with different dusty-looking spices. The kitchen was all stainless steel and black tile. There were pools of light on the black countertops from the discreet undercabinet fixtures. The kitchen sink was a tub of stone with a Japanese-looking faucet that would probably take him ten minutes to figure out how to turn on and off. "You must be quite the cook," Sean said.

"There's your beer." He'd set a Sierra Nevada Ale next to him on the butcher block. "And, if you don't mind, use the coaster."

"No prob." He took a long pull of it. Cold. Good. "So, where's Dawn?"

"She must have finished up and headed home. I expect she'll come around later. How about I put a couple of big-ass potatoes in the oven? Bake em up, then mash them with garlic and cheese."

"Sounds excellent."

"You want tofu or soy or bean sprouts, you go get your own. I expect you got your share of healthy eating at Dawn's place."

"She does like her vegetables, yeah."

"Here." Roberto was using a long thin knife to trim up the steaks. He heaped a pile of fatty ends onto a paper towel. "Why don't you give these to your scrawny dog? No, the back door." He used the knife to point.

"Thanks." Sean thought the guy could lay off about the dog, but he wasn't really in a position to complain. He carried the meat scraps out through the kitchen, onto a big outdoor deck set up with a gas grill, wet bar, fire pit. Everything new-looking, like the tags had just come off. There was an ocean view from here too, the water more distant across a shoulder of land. Ornamental bamboo grew in huge glazed pots. He whistled for Bojangles, who came skulking around a corner. Sean threw him the scraps one by one and the dog gobbled them.

Roberto came outside and stood behind him. "This is the life, huh? The beauty of nature. The comforts of home."

"Yeah, it's real nice." The breeze had picked up as the sun was going down, and even though Sean had his jacket, he wouldn't have minded an extra layer. "Scram," he said to Bojangles, but out of the corner of his mouth.

Roberto went to the bar, filled two highball glasses with ice cubes, and poured from a bottle. "I'll get those potatoes working in a minute. Soon as I have me a little cocktail time. Here, try a bourbon chaser with that beer." He set both glasses on a low table, then sat on one of the upholstered lounges. "Come on, take a load off."

Sean sat too. He'd lost track of his coaster, and even though Roberto hadn't used any coasters himself, he put his beer on the ground next to him. He waited for Roberto to pick up his drink before he did so himself. They both drank. "Whoa," Sean said, putting it down again. The bourbon whomped him upside the head. "This is some firewater."

"You like? It's Booker's. Small batch, aged six to eight years." Roberto took another sip and set the glass down. He had a face like a statue, with a jutting nose, craggy eyebrows, and a red, fleshy mouth. "Bet you don't usually drink hooch this good."

"I'd have to say you're right about that." Sean took another careful sip. He was getting hungry, and he didn't want the alcohol to start eating through his stomach lining. Roberto didn't seem to be in any hurry to start cooking. "So," he said gamely, trying to keep the small talk going, "what line of work are you in?"

"Entrepreneurship. I'm self-employed. Self-made. I'm involved in a number of ventures."

Sean waited for him to say what kind of ventures, but Roberto didn't elaborate. "I'm self-employed too," Sean offered. "I'm a contractor. Home repairs, remodeling, that kind of thing. New construction."

"A jack-of-all-trades," Roberto suggested. His belly rippled and the cowboy on his shirt disappeared into a fold of fat.

"Yeah, I guess so."

"From time to time I need a few things patched up around here. General maintenance. Taking care of the leaks and squeaks. You available for that sort of thing?"

"I sure could be."

"It's not too small-scale for you? You being used to, I'm sure, running bigger projects?"

Roberto's nostrils, Sean noticed, were furry with black hair. Somebody ought to tell him to trim that shit. It was really kind of disturbing. "Well, it's a recession," Sean said, "and that's made for a slowdown in the building trades. You have to roll with the punches." His bladder was cresting urgently. Ever since his accident, he had trouble holding it. "You mind if I use your restroom?"

"You can use the one off the kitchen."

"Thanks." Sean shifted his weight, leaning on his good hip and pushing off with his hands. He didn't like looking all crippled up in front of somebody he didn't know, especially if there was the possibility of getting some work thrown his way. "Hey, while I'm up, you want me to bring those steaks out, anything?"

"You can take the potatoes that are sitting out and put them on the rack in the top oven. You think you can handle that kind of executive, command-and-control mission?"

"Right." Sean headed inside, found the bathroom, relieved himself, and washed his hands. The guy was kind of a prick. But it wasn't like he hadn't worked for pricks before. In the kitchen, the oven was already turned on. He found the potatoes and put them in the center of the rack. He looked around in case there was any food lying around, a box of crackers, maybe, found nothing. He guessed it wouldn't be a good idea to go cruising the fridge. The steaks had blood pooling on their surfaces.

He went back out on the deck. "Done," he said. "Maybe I should run down to Dawn's, make sure she knows I'm up here."

"I wouldn't worry too much about that. With Dawn it's out of sight, out of mind."

"Yeah." That was exactly what he was afraid of. He needed to get his ass down there.

"We ought to talk about Dawn, you and me. I try to look out for her welfare. Because she has a piece or two missing upstairs, you know what I mean? Sit down, OK? I don't want to have to keep turning around to talk to you."

Sean sat. The sun had dropped into the ocean by now and the shadows on the deck were cold. He said, "Well sure, you can't help noticing a thing like that. When something's wrong with a person."

Roberto finished his drink and got up to pour another one. "You want that freshened? You sure? I don't regard Dawn as having anything 'wrong' with her. In some ways, she's lucky. She doesn't worry about the crap everybody else does. Global fucking warming? Collapse of the international banking system? What does she care? As long as she can dance on the beach and find somebody to spread her legs for when she's in the mood."

Sean kept quiet. Roberto got up and went inside, came back with the steaks on a platter.

He set the platter down and turned on the grill. There was a whoosh of gas as the flames caught. Sean wished he was sitting a little closer so he could get some of the heat.

Roberto said, "She's almost a kind of talking animal. Eat, shit, scratch, fuck, sleep. Life reduced down to the basics." He slid the steaks onto the grill. They hissed and crackled. The smell of the cooking meat made Sean's mouth ache. "It doesn't sound so bad, does it? Be a happy little, furry little creature. Sleeping in the sunshine. Singing in the rain." He poked at the steaks with a long, two-pronged fork, occupying himself with the cooking. They sent up a fragrant, meaty smoke. Sean had thought the conversation was at an end, but Roberto wheeled around to him. "Does it?"

"Yeah. I mean no." He'd forgotten what they'd been talking about. He wondered how long it was going to take the steaks to cook through on one side.

"The only problem with being an animal, sometimes you get eaten by bigger, smarter animals. What do you think you'd taste like, fella? If somebody made you into a burger?"

"Ha-ha," Sean said, as if this was funny, then, seeing as how Roberto was expecting an answer, he said, "I don't know. Salty, I guess."

"This cow was probably pretty happy when it was running around on its four hooves. Probably just as well."

"It's kind of a complicated way to think about dinner," Sean offered.

"The top of the food chain. That's what we are."

"Lucky for us, huh?"

Roberto swung around to stare at him. "What's that?"

"Nothing. Say, you aiming for rare, medium-rare? You might want to turn those dudes over."

Roberto gave him another glowering look, but he flipped the steaks. They hit the grill and the flames licked up around them. Sean drank some more of the head-slamming bourbon, just enough to be sociable. He was already tasting the cooked meat. He knew how the first bite of it would feel in his mouth, how it would give way and release its juices.

Roberto said, "You know how you tell the difference between a food animal and a predator? I mean, with humans."

Sean shook his head. What was with the weird questions?

"It's all about the bones piled up at the mouth of the cave. Look around you, sport. You want a house like this, cars like mine, all the toys that go along with them, you have to have the smarts and the hustle to go for it. Not to mention the killer instinct to take what you want."

"It's a nice place," Sean said, wanting to steer the conversation into more normal channels. "Really nice. What's this deck, redwood?"

"What if, just imagining, just as a kind of theoretical thing, somebody gave you a hundred thousand dollars. What would you do with it?"

"A hundred thousand dollars," Sean repeated, to give himself more time to think. It had to be some kind of a trick question. The guy was turning into one of those screwy drunks. "Well, for starters, I'd go out and have a hell of a party."

"Party." Roberto nodded. One of his eyelids had developed a bad twitch that pulled his face in different directions. "I could have told you that's what you'd say. Because it wouldn't occur to you to think of it strategically. How to leverage that money to make you more money. How to use money as a weapon. No, it's all about the pleasure principle to people like you."

"Hey, buddy? No offense, but some of your remarks, they can get a little personal."

"The ones who think they deserve a living. The lazy. The feeble-minded. The crippled."

"How about," Sean said, "you pull those steaks off the fire, and I'll go check on the potatoes, and we can eat instead of talk. Change the mood here."

"Because now I'm supposed to feed you? It's not enough that I come home and find you getting all the pussy in the place? All moved in and making your ragged gimp ass comfortable?"

Sean started to say, This is a simple misunderstanding, but Roberto took a step toward him and then he took a leap, his hands clutching and his red tongue working between his teeth.

Sean got himself out of his chair faster than he would have thought possible, dodged, and shoved a foot in Roberto's path. He tripped over it and went down hard, face first.

Jesus shit fucking Christ.

He backed away from Roberto, who was motionless on the ground and making mewing, kittenlike noises. He grabbed the grill fork in case Roberto got up but when he didn't, he speared one of the steaks instead. The steak dripped hot grease and he held it away from him. Quick as he could, he went back in through the kitchen and the echoing hallways to the front door. Once he was outside the dog trotted up to him in the near dark. He did a happy dance, smelling meat.

"Christ. Here." Sean bit off a piece for himself, for the dog, then another for himself, for the dog. It was too hot to taste it right, and his head hurt and his body shook from adrenaline, *fucking loony!* Why did he keep finding these people? The house behind him was dark and silent. There was a light on at Dawn's place. He ran downhill, his *goddamn hip* like running on knives, trying not to fall down or get tangled up in his excited dog.

He couldn't find his keys. The sweat rolled over him. Here they were, on the truck's seat, *dumbfuck.* "Get in," he told the dog, who didn't want to leave his true love, the steak, behind. "In there, Christ!" The curtain in Dawn's window was yellow from the light behind it. He'd left some things inside that he would have liked to get back, but maybe some other time, since vacating the premises ASAP was the best idea he'd had in a long while.

He held on to the rest of the steak with his teeth as he climbed into the truck and started the engine. It always took some effort to turn around in this steep, narrow space. You had to throw the truck into reverse and back up the hill, then forward, then back again, all the while trying to keep the gearshift from popping out like it wanted to and this without having the heebie-jeebies like he did now and a hunk of meat in his mouth and the dog trying to get to it, and the last thing he needed was to run a wheel over the edge of the pavement and get hung up there, or go sailing off into the trees below, rolling end over end like he was in some *goddamn movie.*

"Off," he told the dog, "get off." But the dog wouldn't shut up, yapping and throwing himself at Sean's window, and just as he got the truck pointed downhill and in motion, there was a noise, CRACKWHUMP, and a singing zinging rush of air and glass breaking behind him and he couldn't believe this asshole was FUCKING SHOOTING AT HIM!

Sean hit the gas. The truck bumped down to the edge of the driveway and he took off through town at high speed and it would be really, really all right if some officer of the law saw him and decided to intervene, but no such luck.

Once he reached the road that led back to Route 1 he eased up a little and checked himself and the dog for blood, found only a sparkle of glass across the back of the seat. A new layer of sweat crept over his scalp. Did he have some sign on him that said, "Please make use of me for any and all crackpot purposes"? Did he send out secret homing signals on the crazy radio? Somewhere in all the panic he'd dropped the remains of the steak and the dog was finishing off the last of it, fine. Just fine. "Don't say I never did anything for you."

Headlights were coming up behind him on the road. It could have been anyone, but they were traveling fast and gaining on him, and his mouth went dry and his hands turned slick on the wheel. Sean sped up. The lights kept pace. It was dark now, and the road was dark ahead and behind, and here was the highway, two-lane, empty, miles from nowhere in either direction. He turned right, south, then, wanting to get off the main route, jogged to the left on a road that opened up before him, powering the truck through the flats and uphill, hoping the trees would hide him.

Sean slowed, waiting, telling himself he was probably just being paranoid. Yeah, except for the actual bullet hole through his back window. No lights behind him. "Get out of there," he told the dog, who was noodling around Sean's legs, licking grease from his jeans.

Where the hell was he? The road was climbing up the mountain grade, narrow, twisting, practically doubling back on itself, maybe a fire road? He nudged along, looking for somewhere to turn around. The trees closed in and his headlights swung back and forth around the curves like he was on some funhouse ride. There were supposed to be mountain lions up here. People took pictures of them with trail cameras. Big tawny cats padding around with killer jaws and a hungry attitude.

Now why was he thinking about that? Couldn't he stay positive for five minutes at a time? He wrenched his mind away, back to Dawn, sweet Dawn, fare thee well! Once he got past the actual death threats, this night might make a good story. He could even tell it to Conner, turning it into something comical, as if all this time he'd been gone he was only off having wild and crazy adventures. He'd leave out Dawn being mentally whatever she was. He'd feel funny about that part.

Behind him on the road, the noise of a car accelerating effortlessly through its gears as it climbed the grade, an expensive sound, and here he was already so wasted, so truly tired, but OK, let's do it. He downshifted and heard the transmission drop and put his foot on the gas to take a curve. The next instant he skidded sideways with trees snapping and filling the windshield and the metal bones of the truck breaking and *shit not again.*

EIGHTEEN

Dear Sean,

See, I actually do know your name. I knew it all along.

I hope your OK. That sounds pretty funny coming from me. Maybe you
don't write back because you are way too disgusted with me and who
could blame you? Anyway, for what it's worth I really did like you. I
thought you were kind of cute and funny. I was just so screwed up.
I am doing better now. I don't expect you to congratulate me or anything
but I am.

You said you do not remember the accident. Do you remember what I
told you about my son who is in jail now? I had two kids, a boy and a girl.
Well I still have them. My girl is from my first marriage, she is twenty-
three now. Her dad and I split up and that was sad but it happens and
there wasn't anything too ugly about it. Then I married this other
character and I guess we are still married because I can't find him to
divorce him. He wasn't the best idea I ever had. He is the dad to my son.

So when you said you had a boy who was the same age as mine that
made me I guess mad at you before I even met you. That somebody

else had a boy who wasn't in trouble. I don't claim this was a good way to feel. But I did.

I also did not plan anything out in advance. I did not know I was going to do anything until I did it.

My son wasn't any problem growing up by which I mean only the normal things for a boy. I think you will know what I mean. Because of your own boy. They like to get into things! He always did OK in school. He liked riding his bike and playing games on the computer. The same as other kids. I made sure the games weren't bad ones. It's not like he was raised in a house where there was no attention paid. And there was never such a thing as a gun on the premises. Never. I had no use for them.

I don't know whether his father is to blame for never being much of a father or if it was a bad mental character being passed on and nothing anybody could have done. But his father at least did not end up in all the newspapers and television for killing two little girls and one man which is what my boy did. I still can not get used to saying that.

He was my own child and I loved him the same as any mother although it was easier when he was just small.

How is your boy? I hope he is doing well. The way you talked about him I could tell you were so proud of him and happy.

Our problems started up when he was a teenager but nothing big at first with answering back and disrespect. What can you do about that but hope they get it out of their system. He was not easy to live with but in no way a matter for law enforcement. When he was not being snotty to us he was very quiet which was not like him and there was no way of telling what was in his head. I still don't know, how could you? People sure seem to think I should have. Or that I raised him to be vicious and we all sat around pulling knives on each other. Anyway it was all my fault one way or another for doing or not doing what I should have.

I could not stay living where I was. My daughter left too because all of a sudden we were the evil ones. She is a good girl now living in Kentucky and sometimes we talk but that is still hard for us.

I send my son cards for his birthday and Christmas but truth is I do not want to do even that much.

When I told you about my son and his troubles you said something like you were trying to be funny and that flipped the switch in me. I think you did not actually mean it, you just didn't know what to say like most people don't know. And I had been drinking a lot which sounds like a big fat excuse but it's the truth. Plus I'd been riding that crazy train for a long time.

I was so heartsick. And lonesome. But who would want to be with me if they knew who I really was?

My son was seventeen at the time of his crime but he was considered an adult due to the serious nature of his crimes. The court determined he was not mentally competent and so he is incarcerated where he can get treatment. This is the best outcome for him. But I had not thought he was crazy! When did that happen? They worked backwards from what he did and decided that anyone who killed people he never even knew would have to be crazy. If I acted crazy myself it was out of trying to understand him. He was angry and unhappy and frightened. I could have told them that much. So I became angry and unhappy and frightened.

He had gotten so he did not like going to school. He would not say why. It was supposed to be his senior year. I wanted him to at least finish up and graduate because if not you spend your whole life working jobs where other people tell you what to do, it is hard enough to earn a living these days anyway. I myself have worked many different jobs as head of a household, sometimes two or three at once.

He stopped having friends. They didn't come around any more. I saw this happening but what could I do? He didn't want to talk to me about it or about much of anything.

I think he is one of those people who feel there is not enough of him and too much of everybody else. That he was not important. Or that everybody else was a different sort of creature than him and it wasn't like actual killing.

There is one thing I know I should have done different. Tell him I loved him more often. Back when I still did.

Anyway when I told you about my son and you tried to say something funny, I don't even remember what it was, I said the hell with you and everybody else. I did not think it through at the time. I was surely trying to hurt myself and you were just along for the ride. Maybe I wanted to do the same as my son did and make an evil act against someone I did not know and for no real reason.

I opened my car door and you said Hey watch it and the air was black and loud and seemed like a solid thing you could jump onto. You started hollering and then the noise of it was cut off because I stepped out into the air. I don't know how I did it I just did. I was driving in the left lane and I went right on past the road shoulder and into the dirt beyond. It knocked me on the head but no worse. I did not see the car go off the road or hear it wreck.

It was like I had jumped out of my whole life. I wasn't thinking in any normal way because of my head. I think I thought I was already dead and it took me a while to decide I was not. I picked myself up and walked back the way we had come and after a while I came to where I could look around me and decide what way of living I wanted to start new with.

That is what happened and some of the why. I apologize for bringing you distress which you did not deserve any more than the rest of us deserve our bad fortune. I will sign with my real name and you can look it up. But you will understand that I do not tell you the name I live with now or where I am making my new life.

Sincerely yours,

Shelly Ann Rosa

NINETEEN

During the last week of conference registration the Foundation had a peculiar kind of luck. Their only real celebrity, the author of those aggressively marketed and widely consumed inspirational books, was involved in an irresistible scandal. An old mistress was cast aside for a new mistress, and there followed vengeful acts and public statements by the discarded lady. There was a showy, unserious suicide attempt, and the release of some equivocal e-mails, and interviews with sympathetic media: "Serenity and compassion? He pees serenity and shits compassion. He's just in it for the money and the sex."

"Oh dear," Christie said, reading Imelda's computer screen over her shoulder, inhaling her heady, expensive perfume. "I hope she doesn't show up at the conference."

"Are you kidding? I hope she does. This is gold. I should get ahold of all the press contacts and remind them he's speaking."

"I have to introduce him. What am I going to say?"

"How about, 'Here's a man who needs no introduction.' You know how many Twitter mentions he has?"

The author released a statement referring to the old mistress as "a longtime friend of my wife and myself, currently undergoing some personal challenges," and the new mistress as "a young person who has attended my seminars, along with so many others, in the hope of building an authentic spiritual self." The author's wife stayed silent, in public at least. Her husband's books, with their gauzy celestial covers, were always dedicated to her.

Christie found it all depressing. These guys never disappointed in their ability to disappoint. The same grubby behavior, the same rooting and burrowing and penis-driven folly. She told herself that there were many decent men in the world who lacked fame and the ego that went along with it, who lived tranquil, honorable lives. You didn't hear about them because virtue wasn't a good story, didn't offer up any momentum or trajectory or thrilling sense of what awful thing might happen next. Virtue only kept on being itself, unchanging, like water trapped in a stopped drain.

Maybe that was why she'd given up, without knowing she was giving up, her own insignificant attempts at being virtuous. It bored her.

The conference was taking up not only most of her waking hours, but also most of the available space in her head. It was either a good idea gone wrong, or maybe it had always been a bad idea, or maybe they'd pull it off in spite of themselves, and redirect Mrs. Foster's project into some better channel. She'd hoped it would produce some clear-minded wisdom, or kindle some blaze of good feeling, and perhaps it would, but not for her. She was too mired in the details of chair setup and parking passes. Not to mention her own machinations—who would need flattering, who would need chiding—which she observed in herself with distaste. Humans just didn't do a very good job of rising above human nature. And here she'd thought it a good idea to arrange for some number of her fellow creatures to congregate in one space and ask each other searching questions.

Certainly all of Christie's skills were needed when the scandal broke. Mrs. Foster had seen the famous author's news coverage also, and she called Christie in distress. "We can't have him on the program! Call him and tell him he can't come."

Christie, unprepared, only managed, "Um, why's that?" She'd come around to Imelda's point of view. They'd been clobbered with new registrations.

"I hardly think he sets a good example," Mrs. Foster said sternly. "The conference is called 'Investing in Our Better Selves,' not 'How I Get Away with This Sort of Thing.'"

"I doubt if that's going to be—"

"Did you hear what that woman said about him? The kinds of filthy activities he enjoyed?"

Christie murmured that she had heard about something of the sort. Along with most of the English-speaking world. She rather wished she had not. "You know, we did sign a contract with his booking agent."

"Well get Allen on that part." Allen being Mr. Kirn. "He'll know what to do." The matter settled, Mrs. Foster was ready to get off the phone.

"I believe this represents an opportunity for us," said devious Christie. "I believe it makes the conference even more important, because people will be thinking about moral failures and confusing impulses and good old hypocrisy, all the really truly human things. If there wasn't any scandal, he'd just show up and talk about finding God by putting your ear to a seashell." Christie had perused the great man's books and had come away with a rather unfavorable impression.

"Well . . ."

"I expect he'll speak from the heart. He'll have to." Of course it was just as likely he'd use the occasion to find new groupies.

Mrs. Foster wavered, and the conference went on as planned.

Imelda took Christie shopping, as she had long threatened to do, and picked out her conference wardrobe: garments in charcoal and teal and peach, in linen and fine wool and silk. Shoes to go along with the clothes, and, over Christie's protests, makeup. "If you don't wear makeup, people think you don't care what you look like," and when Christie objected that she didn't care, really, Imelda looked at her severely.

"You can keep it at the office. I'll put it on for you, what are you so afraid of? Somebody might pay attention to you? Here, let's practice."

And so Christie sat at her desk while Imelda patted and fluffed and dabbed with her deft, well-tended fingers. The conference was three days away and she still had a long list of chores to attend to. It wouldn't matter how good she looked if the caterer didn't show up or the programs weren't delivered. "Make a kissing mouth," Imelda instructed, and Christie pushed her lips forward. "Big kiss," Imelda urged her, then sighed and muttered at the clearly inadequate effort.

Finally she was finished and held up a hand mirror. "Meet the new you!"

Christie looked into the mirror at her new and bedizened self. Her eyes were outlined in green and gray and her eyebrows were darkly feathered. Her skin's surface was a layer of rosy sheen, her mouth glossy and pink as candy. Imelda's face appeared behind hers in the mirror. For two entirely different people, blond and raven-haired, they now looked remarkably alike. "Too much?" asked Imelda. "Here, blot your mouth." She held out a tissue.

"Thank you," Christie said. Her face felt sticky. "It's amazing."

"Now don't go washing it right off. Leave it on all day, get used to it. Would it kill you to smile?"

Christie made an honest attempt to leave her face alone that day. She mostly forgot about the makeup, except when she caught people giving her puzzled or intense glances. It was the new her, whoever that was, imperfectly attached to her old, tired self. Other people must be better at the makeover, transformation thing. Like Imelda, with her former and profitable career in identity theft.

She was kept busy with the hundred and one chores, large and small, that needed her attention. Almost none of them could be crossed off a list with finality. Almost all of them required more follow-up, more phone calls, more checking back. Not until she got home, late at the end of a long day, did she take another long look in a mirror.

The lipstick had pretty much worn off, but the eye color had smeared and smudged into startling green puddles beneath both eyes. Only the eyebrows had survived unchanged, dark and angry, giving her something of a Kabuki aspect. She was still scrubbing and rinsing and toweling off when Art knocked on her door.

"Hey, Chris? You in there?" Of course she was. It wasn't like she had anywhere to hide.

She opened the door to find Art, his hands engulfed in oven mitts, holding a large cooking pot, heavy, by the look of it. "Chicken vegetable soup," he said. "I made this big old batch and there's not even room for it in the fridge."

"Since when did you turn into a cook?"

Art attempted to shrug, but the soup pot was too full. "It's just soup. Like, boiling stuff. Want some?"

Christie said that would be nice. Art took careful steps into the kitchen and set the pot on the stove. "It turned out all right. Pretty good, actually."

"Thanks, Art." She'd been eating a lot of sandwiches from the 7-Eleven lately. "I just got home, so this is good timing."

Art said he'd eaten, but he'd keep her company. Of course he would. She couldn't very well tell him no. She set out bowls and spoons, bread and butter. The soup was hot and tasty. Every so often a piece peel, of carrot or potato, surfaced in her bowl, or a limp, flowerlike piece of celery green, but she navigated around them.

They finished eating, and when he made no move to get up and go, Christie put the teakettle on. "How's Linnea?" she asked, since Art wasn't providing any conversation himself.

"Good, she's good." He wasn't the right fit for her small kitchen chair; he kept recrossing his legs and hitching himself up. His long hair floated into his long face and he swatted it out of the way.

"Did her friend have any luck tracking down his father? I hadn't heard." Art looked uncomprehending. "It was something she mentioned a while back."

"I don't know anything about it," Art said, but he wasn't inclined to be curious. He seemed to have settled himself at her kitchen table for some other, unknown purpose. The kettle boiled and Christie got up to make the tea.

"Work keeping you busy?" She guessed it was up to her to drag whatever it was out of him.

"Yeah, the usual. I've been thinking of looking for some other kind of job."

"Really?" This was something new. Art had never seemed to put much energy into vocational matters. "What kind?"

"I dunno, maybe something in high tech. Information systems. Web design. Software applications. There's a lot of places where they need worker bees, where they train you."

"What brought this on?"

"I need more of a steady paycheck. For Linnea, you know, she's a smart kid, she'll want to go to college. Plus I might want to retire someday. So I better get to work."

"Good thinking. I hope you find something you really like." She wanted to be encouraging about this newly birthed Art, peeking out from behind a cabbage in the cabbage patch.

"As long as it really pays, it'll be just fine."

They drank their tea. Once the tea was gone, she could shoo him out, get ready for bed, and pick up where she'd left off worrying about the conference. Art put his cup down. "Beata and I broke up."

"Oh, I'm sorry, Art. I mean, if you're sorry."

"Ah, shit happens."

More gloomy silence. Christie got up and cleared the table, set the dishes in the sink, and started washing up. She wished she knew what it was he wanted her to say so she could say it and be done with it, and him. But that wasn't a charitable thought, when the guy was so clearly miserable. She said, "Maybe you could make it up with her. If you want to."

"I don't think she'd be very interested in that."

So it was as she'd guessed: Beata was the one who'd ended things. "Care to say what went wrong?"

"I guess I'm just crude and insensitive." Art laughed unhappily.

"Ha-ha," Christie echoed, but she didn't rush to say, Oh no you're not, as she was meant to, because she was tired, and Art probably had behaved in some way as to merit complaint, and then, because the hair on the back of her neck was prickling, she whirled around from the sink to find Art nuzzling up against her, his mouth grazing her ear, his hands patting her up and down in a tentative, hopeful fashion.

"Art!" She pushed him away. She grabbed a spatula and flapped it in his face. "What the hell?"

"Take it easy with that thing."

"What is the matter with you, have you lost your mind? Are you drunk?" She raised the spatula again and he retreated.

"I'm sorry, I guess I'm just . . . Shit."

"I'll say." Christie folded her arms. So much for the new Art.

"I really miss Beata." He was mumbling now, his head drooping.

"Well what does that have to do with me? With groping me?"

"Not groping," he protested.

"Your girlfriend breaks up with you, so you grab the next available woman?"

"I didn't grab you either," Art said, sounding cross. "I was being affectionate."

"Any old port in a storm, huh?"

"Now that's not fair. You know I always liked you."

She knew. "I wouldn't use that as an excuse." She had to give up being angry with him. He was too pitiful. "Honestly? It's kind of insulting. Who wants to be the rebound assault victim?"

"I miss her perfume. You know how she always wore that stuff that smelled like peaches?"

"Well go tell her that! Call her up! Ask her how her day went, and how she's feeling, and what's new, and then listen to what she says!"

"You think that would work?"

"What do you mean, 'work'? Act like you're interested in her as an actual person. Or act that way with the next woman you take up with. Thank you for the soup, I'll put the pot outside your door."

"So what would I say? If I called her? How would I start?" Christie gave him an incredulous look. "All right, sorry, I'll see you around, we're cool, OK?"

"And check up on your daughter!"

The door closed behind him. Christie heard his feet on the outside stairs, then on the floorboards over her head, Art walking back and forth for a time, and then nothing.

The conference was scheduled to begin Friday afternoon and go through Sunday morning. On Friday, Christie dressed up in her new finery, and the least amount of makeup Imelda would let her get away with, and drove out to the seminary where the Foundation had rented space for the event. The seminary was a complex of basilicas and stone chapels, set up in the San Anselmo hills. Its white spires rose from the trees and wisps of morning fog like a fairy-tale castle. The weather was chilly, but not miserable, the view from the broad terrace was green and tranquil, and Christie took heart. She'd prepared, and then overprepared, and everything was in place, and in forty-eight hours or so it would all be over and she could worry about something besides name tags and honorarium checks and whether or not anyone would actually show up.

The famous author was not due to speak until Saturday night, the main event. Imelda was going to attend his bookstore reading in the city tonight and keep an eye out for any vindictive ladies or problem behaviors. And at some point tomorrow, Mrs. Foster would arrive and be installed in the reception suite that had been set aside for her use, where she would welcome selected notables and accept tributes. The board members had been invited, of course, and Mrs. Foster was expecting her unpleasant daughter, Leslie. But there was really no point in being nervous about her or anyone else, Christie decided. No one was likely to pay Christie the slightest attention, a minor functionary stumbling around with a clipboard.

She set about unloading the boxes of programs and posters. The posters had turned out nicely. They were full-color, printed on glossy stock, and showed a cluster of tiny buildings, like a Monopoly town, beneath a perfect, vaulting blue sky. The sky was meant to suggest, in a tactful, secular fashion, the Infinite. One of the tiny buildings was a bank, with Greek columns, and tiny figures walking in and out, carrying fat little bags with dollar signs on them. Printed across the sky:

INVESTING IN OUR BETTER SELVES

a gathering and an inquiry

exploring the relationship between economics

and personal virtue

The best-selling author was billed as giving one of his standard talks, "Aspirations to the Divine." Which more or less suited the conference theme, at least closely enough, since most of the audience would be there to gawk and get a whiff of those lower aspirations. There were more speakers and discussion groups, among them: "Learning from the Rural Poor of India." "How Nonprofits Can Profit." "What We Talk About When We Talk About Wealth." And "Hard Times and Social Pathology."

The first conference attendees began arriving after lunchtime. They had the look of people who would enjoy spending a free weekend in serious-minded discussions. Some of them might have been earnest graduate students, given to eccentricities of jewelry and footwear. Some of them were a good deal older and more prosperous-looking, friends of Mrs. Foster, perhaps. (A discreet fund-raising effort was going on all weekend.) Christie and one of the office interns greeted people and found their names on the list and passed out name tags and programs. The keynote speaker, an eminent biologist who had written a book on human evolution, would take the floor at three o'clock. After he spoke, there would be a question-and-answer session, followed by a reception. The guests would mingle over plastic cups of wine, platters of cheese, olives, roasted baby artichokes, purple grapes, hummus, pot stickers, and cookies.

Then, both energized and sated, people would go home and return the next day for more speakers, workshops, "lunch on your own," a buffet dinner, and the marquee event of the conference, the talk by the adulterous, spiritual-heavyweight author. Sunday morning there would be a meditation session in the seminary's beautiful chapel, followed by coffee and pastries, and some wrap-up discussion sessions organized around the topic "Blessed Are the Poor in Spirit: Toward a Better Marketing Plan."

Things got off to a good start. Some attendees weren't going to show up until Saturday, but some fifty of them, enough to make a crowd, arrived for the first speaker, and chatted among themselves in a good-humored way in the lobby. The eminent biologist arrived on schedule and Christie took his coat and handed over the white envelope containing his honorarium check, made certain there was water at the podium and that the microphone worked, herded the audience inside to sit down, welcomed everyone "to the first installment of what we hope will be a thoughtful, invigorating time of learning, discussion, and fellowship," introduced the biologist, listed his many honors and accomplishments, led the applause, resumed her seat in the second row, and fell asleep.

She hadn't meant to. But she was tired, and the chair was comfortable, and the biologist had a soothing way of speaking. Christie woke in a panic, hoping she hadn't snored. No one was sitting near her, and fortunately her head had fallen forward rather than tilting back. She straightened and discreetly checked her mouth for drool. Some of what the biologist had said while she slept clung to her ears without her taking in its meaning: the biological basis for social behavior, and highly social species needing bigger brains, and the altruism of vampire bats, of all things, and was there an altruism gene? "The same authority," the biologist was saying now, "equates altruistic, that is, cooperative, groups with virtue, and selfish, that is, competitive, individuals within groups, with sin. Although he is careful to say he regards this as an oversimplification."

Christie wished she'd been able to stay awake and follow the argument, but she had no chance now, since the intern came in to summon her outside so she could deal with somebody who was insisting they had already sent in their registration fee, and after settling that, she had just enough time to go back in and start the question-and-answer session, then out again to oversee the caterer, then back in as the questions were starting to straggle so she could thank them all so much and please join us for refreshments. The intern was in charge of the wine, and making sure that no one was overserved.

The biologist was a pro at these things. He held his glass of wine without actually drinking from it, and chatted with anyone who had a mind to chat. As Christie approached the little group around him, a woman was saying, "I appreciate that you left enough room in your thesis for the possibility of a Supreme Being."

"One must always leave room for possibilities," the biologist said diplomatically. "Although I think you'd find that for many biologists, genetics are their version of God." He saw Christie and smiled at her, twinkling. She had the horrible intuition that he'd probably seen her sleeping.

"Is accumulating money an example of individual selection?" an intense young man asked. "That is, a selfish and even sinful trait?"

The biologist considered this. "It could be looked on as a survival skill."

"So it's survival of the richest, then."

"Evolution is more complicated than that. And of course, it can take millions of years, we can't see it from close up. As Darwin said, 'Individuals do not evolve, but populations do.'"

"But we want to," Christie said. "I mean I'd want to. Evolve into something better." Immediately, she felt stupid for opening her mouth.

The biologist smiled and put his wineglass down. "A faster ocean swimmer. A louder singer of mating songs. A keener hunter. Who wouldn't aspire to that? Now I hope you'll excuse me, I have an early appointment tomorrow."

Saturday was the big day, with more attendees, more speakers, more of everything. None of Christie's feeble confidence after Friday's session had survived the night. Today would be the day she'd be exposed as incompetent, ineffective, insufficiently ardent about the transformative powers of big-time money. She met Imelda for an early breakfast at a coffee shop in San Anselmo. Imelda looked her up and down. "Not bad," she pronounced. "You know what that jacket is screaming for? A statement necklace." She herself was wearing one of her snazzy suits, eggplant-colored, with a vermilion blouse. Christie asked her how the famous author's bookstore appearance had gone.

"I don't suppose I could talk you into getting a manicure. Would that be pushing my luck? It was fine, he's done this kind of thing a million times. He has this very theatrical delivery, very hammy, you know, grabbing the podium and casting his eyes to heaven. People ate it up. His little girlfriend was there. She has the strangest hair, it looks like she put it in a waffle iron."

"He'll be here for the dinner, then he gives his talk. Were there press people?"

"Oh yeah. Video cameras, feminist bloggers, indie reporters. He got a few pesky questions. But really, the guy is slick. He managed to say he was praying for guidance and he hadn't done anything wrong, both."

Christie finished her coffee, gathered her bags, and told Imelda to call the caterer and see if they couldn't get a couple of trays of sandwiches to supplement the dinner, in case there were reporters expecting to be fed. "What's the matter with you?" Imelda demanded. "Quit trying to button that, it's supposed to stay open. You look like a million bucks. Why you so sad-faced?"

"I don't know, it's this whole thing." She wasn't even sure what she meant, *thing*. The conference? The Foundation? The foggy muddle of her life? "Here we start off trying to do something positive and worthwhile and *good*, and we get thrown off track by all the petty, sordid stuff. Like this ridiculous man and his girlfriends. Why should anyone care? People are disgusting."

"People are people, you worry too much. Like my husband says, 'On the sixth day of creation, God must have had a hangover.'" Not for the first time, Christie found herself wondering about Imelda's home life. "Come here a minute." Imelda leaned over the table and smudged something beneath Christie's eyes. "Concealer."

By the time Mrs. Foster arrived in the late morning, the conference was rolling. Who would have thought so many people would sign up and pay out money in order to hear about the economics of virtue? But they did, they had, or it was likely that some of them just wanted to gawk at the famous author, now famous disillusionment. There were a number of inquiries about whether he had yet arrived, and disappointment when Christie told them not until this evening.

Still, the mannerly crowds filled the lecture rooms and workshops. From the main entrance, where she waited for Mrs. Foster, Christie heard applause and laughter coming from behind the closed doors. Then, just as Mrs. Foster's huge, champagne-colored Lincoln eased up to the curb, the sessions ended and the conferees emerged, looking pleased, chatty, ready for the next scheduled event. She couldn't have arranged a happier backdrop.

The first person out of the car was Leslie Hart, who looked around her as if she was a Secret Service agent on alert for snipers. "Good morning," Christie said. "How nice to see you again."

Leslie stared at her. "Oh, it's you. Could you get my mother a Coke or something? She was feeling a little carsick."

"Certainly." Christie stepped around the front of the car to greet Mrs. Foster. She wondered if Leslie had been confused by the makeup and clothes, or was just being rude. Then the boy, Conner, stepped out from behind the driver's seat to open Mrs. Foster's door, and Christie had her own moment of slack-brained staring. It had not occurred to her that he'd be here, although it should have, and she had not anticipated that he too might have been made to dress up, or how good he would look in an ordinary jacket and tie, all sulkiness and dark gold skin, like a statue come to life. Down, girl. He looked at Christie and then away, and Christie thought that there might be more they could say to each other but not now, as he helped Mrs. Foster out to the pavement and stood aside. Both of them were servants, in their different fashions, supporting the grand enterprise of Mrs. Foster's wealth.

Mrs. Foster was wearing oversized tortoiseshell sunglasses. She turned her head slowly this way and that, taking in the crisp sunshine and the purposeful crowds. "My goodness. What a lot going on. Did we do all this? How extraordinary."

Christie escorted her to the reserved room, with Leslie Hart trailing behind, sent the intern for Cokes and a coffeepot, then back again for the tomato juice that Leslie wanted instead. She got both of them settled in comfortable chairs. "What is this place?" Leslie said. "A monastery?" She took off her hat, black and strangely shaped, like a small lampshade, and Christie saw that she was doing a new thing with her hair. She'd changed the color from gold to platinum and cut bangs. It looked unconvincing, like a wig.

"It's a theological seminary," Christie said. "Presbyterian. Ecumenical. They've all been very nice."

Leslie picked up a program. "What are these? 'Who Put the Nature in Human Nature.' 'The History of the Sin Tax.' 'I Am a Fugitive from a Hedge Fund.'"

"Those are some of the scheduled speakers. Would you be interested in attending any of the talks?"

Leslie tossed the program aside. "No thank you. How are you feeling, Mom? How's your tummy? Do you need more ice in that?"

"I wish you'd stop fussing, Leslie dear." Mrs. Foster sat with her feet on the floor and her handbag in her lap, like the Queen of England on a reviewing stand. "Where's Conner? He wasn't going to stay with the car, was he? We should call his phone. Maybe he got lost trying to park."

"Oh please don't worry about him. Are you hungry yet?" To Christie she said, "She doesn't eat enough. Her clothes just hang on her."

"Tiresome child," said Mrs. Foster. "I'm fine. Everybody wants to fatten me up like a beef cow."

Christie didn't know why they were snapping at each other, unless it was that Leslie Hart felt it necessary to reclaim her mother from everybody else circling around her. Luckily, two of Mrs. Foster's friends showed up and settled in to talk, and Christie was able to make her escape.

After this next session they would break for lunch, and most of the attendees would head into town to eat. Christie went back to the registration table and tried to tidy up and clear the decks. She took some of the speakers in to meet Mrs. Foster, as well as the seminary's marketing director, and a few others who needed to be thanked or solicited. A journalism instructor at one of the community colleges had sent his class to write articles about the conference and a dozen of them were wandering the seminary grounds with homemade press passes around their necks, helping themselves to the free snacks and mostly interviewing one another. A lady with hearing aids in both ears complained about the acoustics. As Christie was enunciating, loudly, her sympathy and concern, Conner came in at the front entrance and looked around. Christie pointed around the corner to the suite.

He came out again after the hearing aid lady had departed. "Hey." Christie flagged him down.

He detoured toward her, reluctantly, Christie thought. "I have to go pick up lunch."

"I wanted to ask if you'd heard anything about your father." He was so young, a kid. She realized she couldn't even imagine having sex with him. Maybe she could help him with his homework instead.

"Not really. But thanks for telling us some places to look."

"What does that mean, 'not really'?"

"Somebody found my dog, my dog that was with my dad. Not real far from here, in Fairfax. But not my dad."

"Oh." She considered this. She guessed it didn't mean much of anything helpful. "Well, I'm glad your dog is all right."

"Yeah. Sorry, I really have to go." He crossed the hall and stepped out into the sunshine, just as the bell tower from the chapel next door chimed its twelve singing notes. What if she were to allow herself to feel everything she really felt? Lust after the boy? Dislike Leslie Hart? Stop making excuses or telling herself she ought to feel something different or more worthy? Would anyone like her? Did they even like her now?

The bells chimed, the questions seemed to drop through the top of her head one at a time, like something heavy and silver. Did she need to build an authentic spiritual self? Did anyone else care? Did she? Why fight against her every instinct and impulse, bend herself into some impossible and hobbled shape, hold herself back with every step?

The bells stopped chiming. She put the questions aside, *all right*, because there was work to do, and anyway, it seemed a little silly that she'd taken so long to even ask them.

Meanwhile, there were calls from one of the local television stations, and from the bookseller who was handling the sale of the famous author's books at the lecture. A freelance investment broker had set up his own table and was handing out flyers and had to be shooed away. Mrs. Foster went home for an afternoon nap before the dinner. Conner opened the car door for her, and Leslie Hart, wearing her peculiar hat over her peculiar hair once more, hovered nearby. Maybe it really was a wig, maybe Leslie had cancer and Christie should feel sorry for her. But she didn't, she wouldn't. It felt exhilarating not to.

In the lull between the last sessions ending and the evening events, Christie and Imelda supervised the setting out of tables and chairs, inspected the kitchen, double-checked with the caterer, with the media escort who would deliver the famous author, then sat with their shoes off and their feet up in the ladies' lounge, drinking sodas.

Imelda called home, cooed to her baby, instructed and reinstructed her husband. "He sucks at child care," she announced, hanging up. "He wants a kid who can go to the refrigerator and get him a beer. Can I ask you a dumb question? What does it mean, 'The Humanity Project'?"

"It's an initiative to help, ah, people. Determine their material, social, and moral needs and how best to meet them." She'd helped write this stuff, and now it hurt her ears. "To help us be more comprehensively human."

"What would people act like instead, angels? By the way, His Famousness is big on angels. Expect to hear a lot about the spirits that walk among us."

"You say that like it's a bad thing."

"Listen to you, all snarky! Girl!"

"Snark," Christie said. "Snark walks among us."

Maybe she was just tired. Or maybe she had been tired for a long time. Well, she was going to be tired for a while longer. The conference attendees were drifting back, thirty hopeful minutes early for the cocktail reception, milling around outside the doors. Racks of glassware bumped into walls, ice cubes rattled, something heavy landed on the floor. But then the doors opened, and the guests found their way among the tables to the drinks and the serving platters of bruschetta and mini-quiches and vegetarian spring rolls. At the far end of the room, other servers were busy setting out pans of food for the buffet, surely too early if they had to sit for another forty minutes. Christie added food poisoning to her list of things to worry about.

"Hello there!"

She turned to see Mr. Kirn, wineglass in hand, smiling fondly at her. He was dressed in his usual lawyer's full-dress uniform, and a faint scent of barbering rose from his pink, well-tended face. "How's it going? It looks like everyone's enjoying themselves."

"I hope they are. So far, so good." She was relieved to see him. He was going to sit at the head table with Mrs. Foster and the famous author and keep the conversation from straying into unpleasant areas. "As long as our main speaker shows up on schedule."

"He'll be here. He's not one to miss out on television coverage." Mr. Kirn pointed to the camera crew setting up in one corner.

"I should go check the sound system." She was having trouble standing still for more than two minutes without fretting.

"Could you spare me a moment? I'd really appreciate it." Mr. Kirn took hold of her arm with his free hand and steered her toward one of the windows looking out on the terrace. She had to admire the way he always got his way, even as it irritated her. Once they reached a corner out of the traffic pattern he said, "I'm sorry, I didn't offer to get you a drink."

"Thank you, I'm fine for now." His oily manners. She could get her own drink.

"This is really amazing. Everything you've done here." He nodded at the room, the sociable crowd. He seemed to want to commend her as well for the beautiful parquet flooring, the massive hearth, the general excellence of the setting.

"Thank you. I had a lot of help." Waiting. What did he want? She had things to do.

Mr. Kirn smiled. Christie found herself fascinated by his white, fortunate teeth. What care, and how many resources, had gone into that smile. How many dental professionals had labored over it while Mr. Kirn lay back in the dentist's chair, mouth agape. His flossing habits were excellent, his X-rays without flaw. Never once had he worried about cavities, impactions, gingivitis, halitosis. His teeth were a perfect instrument of mastication, the front line of digestion. There was nothing he could not engulf and devour. After the examination he shook hands with the dentist, thanked the hygienist in a way that made her blush, then went about his business, on good terms with all he surveyed. Christie became aware that he was speaking, and that she had not been paying attention: ". . . entirely too modest. It's just like you, not to take all the credit you deserve."

"It is?" she said stupidly. It confused her that he was speaking about her as if she were someone he knew particularly well.

"I don't think you realize your own power. The effect you have on other people."

She was attempting to connect the notion of "power" with anything about her, she was thinking, *Aw crap*, first Art, now this, but Mr. Kirn's voice had turned husky and urgent, startling her in a different way. "When I first met you, I'm afraid I didn't take you that seriously. You were in so far over your head."

Was she supposed to agree? Demur? She didn't like that phrase "in over your head." It made you sound as if you'd ignored a No Swimming sign.

"But by God if you didn't just keep going, working hard and letting your faith in the basic decency of people carry you through."

"I'm not sure I really have that, you know? Faith in people's basic whatchamacallit. Decency."

"I have to tell you, all my smart, cynical, self-serving attitudes began to seem so . . . unclean."

She wanted to say that "unclean" was the last thing that came to mind when one thought of him. But Mr. Kirn was hurrying his speech now, fumbling his way through, words and whole ideas dropping off the edge of his agitation. "Because of your example . . . your, may I say, purity? Yes, purity of motive. Your, what this whole conference is about. Personal virtue. I feel like, who is it in *Hamlet*? 'Thou turnst mine eyes into my very soul, and there I see such black and grained spots . . .'"

"Mr. Kirn, I can't imagine you've ever done anything that terrible." At least, she didn't want to imagine it, and if he had, she didn't want to know.

Mr. Kirn shook his head. "There have been occasions . . . I have not always been worthy of the trust placed in me."

Oh please, she begged silently. No more. But he staggered on. "My own arrogance. My own stupid greed . . ."

What was he mumbling about, had he stolen money? Had he stolen from the Foundation? Why was he telling her this? Was she supposed to call somebody? Make a citizen's arrest?

He seemed to catch himself then, recovering his professional caution. "But never mind any of that. It's nothing that can't be set to rights. Because you would want me to make it right. You are my, I know how it sounds, so trite, my polestar." Mr. Kirn squared his shoulders and held out his free hand. "So no matter what happens from this point on, I want you to know and believe that you've been a profound influence in my life, and a force for good." Christie extended her own hand, and they shook. "Thank you."

"You're welcome."

He hurried away and Christie lost sight of him in the crowd.

She was not a repository of personal virtue. She was not pure of motive. She didn't even especially *like* Mr. Kirn, either the old, crass version or this new, ranting one.

She went to the bar table and picked up two glasses of wine, one for each hand, and drank them in quick sequence. Across the room, Imelda was waving at her, semaphore-style, as if she were trying to signal a ship at sea. Christie put the empty glasses down and went to join her. The alcohol made her feel ever so slightly brain-damaged, slow and blurry.

"He's here," Imelda told her, once she'd come into hailing distance. "Mr. Higher Wisdom."

At the entrance to the room was a small crowd of excited people, and video cameras held aloft. The crowd parted enough for Christie to view the figure at its center. "Wow, he's short!"

It was true. She recognized the massive shoulders, the craggy face, the white hair and stern black eyebrows, from the book jackets. But this edifice was balanced on top of a runty bottom half.

"It's because of those feet of clay," Imelda said. "So how about I introduce you before I leave." Imelda was going home to tend to her baby. She peered more closely at Christie. "You OK? You look a little, I don't know, cross-eyed."

"I'm fine. My strength is the strength of ten because my heart is pure."

She waited in line and was duly presented. The great man clasped her hand in both of his and gave her his trademark searching, bullshit look. The pale and dolly-like mistress drifted in his wake. She did have peculiar hair, crinkled and nearly colorless. What did they see in each other? What did anyone ever see in anyone? It was a mystery. She was happy to keep it that way.

Christie put one of the office staff in charge of fetching them drinks and leading them to their table. Mrs. Foster and Leslie Hart were just now coming in from outside, and she went to meet them. "Is that him over there?" Mrs. Foster asked. "Is that why everybody's milling around and rubbernecking?"

"Mom, chill," Leslie Hart said. "Try not to say anything too awful to him." She rolled her eyes at Christie, to indicate that awful things had already been said, or at least rehearsed.

"And that's the—what do they call such people these days? The girl-friend?" Mrs. Foster sniffed. "Surely she's up past her bedtime."

"You don't have to talk to her, Mom. In fact it's better you don't."

Christie smiled. She didn't much care who fought with whom. She had already checked out, in some sense, and was done with worrying, and with worrying about worrying. The wine had turned her good-humored. If people decided to make faces, or hit each other with their shoes, well, that would be interesting. She steered Mrs. Foster and Leslie to the head table. Mr. Kirn was already there, once more his smoothio self, smiling as he stood to greet them. Had she hallucinated everything he'd said earlier? Had he always had his secret yearnings, so well concealed? The famous author and the pallid girlfriend were advancing from another direction, trailing a crowd of admirers. Christie dispatched a waiter to their table and left everyone to sort it out for themselves. Then she stopped by the bar table for another glass of wine.

Some of the attendees decided that dinner must be ready, and lined up to get their plates.

Christie saw Conner come in at the door and look around for Mrs. Foster. Then, once he'd located her, he strolled around to the back side of the food tables, procured a plate, and, managing to avoid the entire line thing, filled it from the different foods and retreated to a corner to eat, standing up. He moved with such slouching grace, even as he was trying to evade attention. Most of it was youth, of course. Bye-bye, she said to Youth, waving from across the abyss.

It was hard to tell how things might be going at the head table. The two men, the author and Mr. Kirn, appeared to be engaged in some agreeable conversation, while Mrs. Foster, Leslie Hart, and the girlfriend each looked off in different directions. Then waiters arrived with their wine, salads, entrées, and those who were in a bad humor already were able to feel bad-humored about the food. Mr. Kirn spotted Christie across the room, nodded and raised his glass to her.

Polestar? Who wanted to be a polestar?

She decided it would be nice to be an engineer, somebody who worked with blueprints, steel, equations, building bridges or roads. It was possible to build a better bridge. But how did you go about building a better human?

Most of the guests were seated by now. Christie was thinking she might have to eat something herself, as well as locate the introduction she had prepared for the famous author, several painstakingly typed sheets that she could not remember having seen lately. But then a new commotion announced itself at the room's entrance.

A dozen or so people stood in the doorway, and Christie, craning her neck to see, was at first unable to make them out, or determine who they might be. Three of them—a man, a woman, and a little boy—were Mexican or Guatemalan, short, dark, watchful. The rest were ordinary-looking men dressed in army surplus jackets, knit caps, different flapping layers. They seemed stuck in the doorway, neither advancing nor retreating. Then a young man with a furry chin and an untidy head of dark hair stepped forward, his voice loud and shaky with self-importance.

"May I have your attention, kind ladies and gentlemen! I hope you're enjoying yourselves this evening, this lovely evening, in this lovely spot, and that you've had some really great discussions, you know, theoretical-type discussions about pressing social issues and all, and I sure hope you got your money's worth. But meanwhile, I'm here to ask if you're willing to share your actual food with actual hungry people."

The young man raised an arm to indicate the group in the doorway, who seemed to have shrunk together, timidly staring.

The camera crew and the other journalists, who had been lounging around in the back of the room eating sandwiches, came to attention.

Silence, and then the occasional voice, rising in whispers and questions, and everybody looking around the room to see what was going to happen next, and then Christie, unhurried, walked up to him. "Hi, Scottie."

"Oh. Hey there, how you doing?" He looked a little wild-eyed, and he was breathing strenuously.

"Tell your guys to come on over."

"Yeah?" He considered this. Christie thought he would have been just as happy to create a big stink and get thrown out.

"Sure. More the merrier." She beckoned to them; they hung back, unsure. "Go on, tell them."

Scottie went to confer with his followers, and pointed to the food. The Latino family led the way, then the men, hesitant at first, shuffling along the line of pans holding the dilled salmon, the vegetarian lasagna, spinach with feta, couscous with dried cranberries, pasta primavera, and the rest. "What is this shit?" Christie heard one of the men mutter.

"So, you guys hungry?" she asked cheerily, and another man said something about how he could always eat.

"Go ahead, help yourselves, and grab a seat wherever you can."

She watched them heap their plates, then wander the room until they found empty chairs at the various tables. The conference-goers, puzzled at first, seemed to decide that this was included in their registration fees: personal interaction with genuine poor people. They scooted their chairs over to make room, they seemed delighted to have these shy and furtive visitors in their midst.

Scottie was still planted at the front of the room, eating a piece of stuffed endive. Christie said, "This really was a stupid stunt. What were you going to tell these people if we turned them away?"

"I was going to take them to the pancake house," he admitted.

"It was crummy to use them as props."

"Not props," he argued. "Protesters. Why waste all this money so people can sit around on their asses eating snazzy food? What's it supposed to accomplish?"

There was a whole list of things: Dialogue. Engagement. Information sharing. Consensus building. La la la la la. "You know, here's your chance to argue your case in person. Ask for a piece of the action." She nodded at Mrs. Foster's table.

"You think I should?"

"Sure. Nothing ventured, nothing gained. Let a thousand flowers bloom."

"You're right. I mean, you work for a useless, wasteful boutique charity, but you're right."

He raised his arm and, belatedly, Christie managed to bump fists with him. She watched him go, then turned back to the buffet food, or its remnants. By now it looked as if it had been trampled underfoot. She picked up a dinner roll and contemplated eating it.

Leslie Hart came up to Christie, her heels clattering on the parquet floor. "What on earth is going on? Who are these people?"

"Um, you'd have to ask him." Christie indicated Scottie, who had made his way to the head table by now and was glad-handing the famous author, Mrs. Foster, and a couple of the waiters. "Don't worry, there was plenty of food. It's sort of like, the miracle of the loaves and the fishes."

Leslie exhaled and her fringe of bangs puffed up. "You're all nuts. Everybody in your whole nuthouse foundation, including my mother. The lawyer's just the last straw."

"Mr. Kirn? What's he done?"

"Oh don't tell me you don't know."

She didn't, but for a moment she was transfixed by Leslie's glaring staring eye, intent and hostile, the iris yellow-green, the pupil shrunken to a point. It looked like the eye of an angry chicken. *Pawk pawk pawk.* "What about Mr. Kirn?"

"He says he's leaving the board. He's giving up his law practice and he wants to go on a Buddhist pilgrimage!"

Yes, and Christie herself was going to attend clown college and join the circus. "Oh, really?" She tried and failed to come up with some sufficiently distressed response to this news. She was distracted by a small commotion. One of the homeless men had grown comfortable enough to begin an animated conversation with the others at his table. He was entertaining them with some story told at full volume: "Dude! Where's my dawg? Du-ude! Where's my dawg!"

"Would you excuse me?" Christie turned away from Leslie and her indignation, walked over to the man, and put a hand on his shoulder. They spoke together for a while.

The waiters brought out coffee and desserts. The booksellers had set up a table along one wall and people were browsing through the offerings. It was almost time for the famous author to speak. He was making his way to the podium. Christie walked over and met him there.

The famous author began speaking to her in his deep, authoritative, media-tested voice, telling her how pleased he was, how honored, how grateful for the excellent hospitality, and so on. At some point Christie became aware that his hand was climbing over her forearm on its way up toward her shoulder. She looked down at it and eventually he stopped talking and the two of them stared at the hand as if it were some alien entity. Then he took the hand away and sat in the chair next to the microphone.

Christie picked up one of the books from the booksellers' table. She figured she could at least read his list of publications and accomplishments from the jacket flap. The book was called *The Journey to the Mountaintop: A Seeker's Guide.* Its cover art showed a snow-covered peak, vaguely Himalayan in aspect, tinted with rainbow shimmer. People bought this stuff, they couldn't get enough. They wanted stories of affirmation and purpose, and hardships overcome. They wanted to believe in happy endings in the face of all evidence to the contrary. She guessed she wasn't any different. Maybe just more easily disappointed.

She stepped up to the microphone and tapped a finger against it to make certain it was on. The room began to quiet down and settle itself for listening. "Good evening," Christie began. "If I could have your attention, please." She felt a little dizzy, all those faces watching her. She had no idea what she was going to say. "Thank you so much for being here tonight and lending your voices and your presence. Thank you to those who have supported The Humanity Project with their resources and hard work. And to our honored guest, tonight's speaker, who, as we all know, has many demands lately on his time and energies."

A perceptible shift and murmur in the crowd. Was she referring to . . . they were uncertain if . . . A few sniggers, of the nervous sort.

Christie referred to the book jacket. "He has written . . . 'nine best-selling volumes that explore, in eloquent yet straightforward language, our quest for meaning and purpose in a world that so often seems to lack them. His words have brought comfort and inspiration to millions.'"

She stopped reading. The faces of the audience were turned toward her like flowers. The anxious earnest conference-goers, the homeless men waiting for the next good or bad thing to happen to them. The Latino family, who did not appear to understand English, let the amplified noise wash over and around them. If she turned her head enough, she would be able to see Mr. Kirn, Mrs. Foster, Leslie Hart, and the others. "I don't have much to add to what others have said about him, those who know him far better than I, and those who have studied his eminent works with care. He is, in many ways, so much more . . ."

She paused, vacantly. The room was silent. A tide of dread gathered in it and rippled toward her. What if she flaked out? Stopped talking? Someone would have to do something!

". . . so much more celebrated than the rest of us. But every bit as human. Because to be human is to be broken. To be of the world is to be soiled by the world. To be alive is to be, in spite of everything, hopeful."

She looked out onto them. They looked back, stricken. Except for the Latino family, who had no expectation that she'd make sense to begin with. "Please join me in welcoming our distinguished guest."

The audience applauded, as much from relief that she'd gotten through it as from anything else. Christie walked away from the microphone and over to the corner where Conner stood. She said, "I think I might know where your father is."

Conner didn't want to wait until morning, so Christie said they could take her car. He offered to drive. Christie said that would probably be a good idea. She was on the downslope of drunk, and she was tired and hollowed-out. "You don't really have to go," he said. "I mean, I could drive Mrs. Foster and all back home when they're done here and get the truck, and you could write everything down for me."

But he was so clearly anxious to leave that very minute that she waved this off and said she didn't mind. Mr. Kirn was given the keys to Mrs. Foster's car. One of his last official duties before hitting the Buddhist trail. Oh surely he wasn't serious about that; there were things she simply could not fathom about people. Conner spoke with Mr. Kirn about the new arrangements and Christie hid in the ladies' room until Mr. Kirn was out of sight.

"I might have gotten your hopes up for nothing," she told Conner once they were under way. "It's not like it's a sure thing."

"We'll find out pretty soon." He'd retrieved a hooded sweatshirt from Mrs. Foster's car and taken off his coat and tie. He looked like an ordinary kid again.

They weren't going that far, in terms of distance, but they would have to travel down one set of hills, then west on the flats, and up more hills, a half-hour's drive to this place where the homeless were said to camp. They might have moved on by now. Or the man at dinner could have been mistaken, or lying. Or it was just as likely that Conner's father might not want to be found. But it wasn't her job to point any of this out.

Meanwhile, here was this peculiar interval, peculiar to be sitting in her own car as someone else drove, hurtling through darkness and this boy beside her, whom she could once more allow herself to admire as if from a distance, and without distress. She said, just for the sake of saying something, "Have you seen Linnea lately?"

He looked over at her, then away. "Not really. I think she's going out with some guy from her school now."

She probably shouldn't have asked. She tried to remember anything Linnea had said about Conner's father. He hadn't been able to work and he'd lost his house and when did that turn into something you got so used to hearing about so many people, and so used to saying? She would have liked to ask Conner more about him, but he didn't seem like a boy who was in the habit of talking about things, and she thought she understood that right now the mechanics of driving were what he needed to do in place of talking, and furthermore that in all her besotted staring she had overlooked everything that was fragile about him.

She sat back and closed her eyes. She was going to have to tell Mrs. Foster she was leaving the Foundation, going back to nursing. Imelda could step up and run things in her place. Imelda would be a whiz, all enterprise and energy. She wouldn't spend time worrying about whether money was either a good or a bad thing. She wouldn't take herself too seriously.

Maybe she dozed. When she opened her eyes again they were driving through Fairfax, the downtown left behind them, the houses rising street by street into the hills. "Go up to Deer Park Villa," Christie directed him. "You know where that is?"

"Yeah, I do." After a few more blocks he said, "They found my dog right around here."

"I don't suppose," Christie said, "that you're keeping your dog at Mrs. Foster's?"

"I've got him up in my room. I only take him out when she's not around. I guess I should probably tell her."

"I wouldn't bother thinking about it right this minute."

They reached the gates of the Villa, closed now. "Take that turn," Christie directed him. Then, later, "Turn right." Conner slowed as the road narrowed. The trees were closing in around and above them and the car's headlights didn't penetrate the green walls. They both leaned forward, trying to see. "Look for a white sign."

"What is this place anyway?"

"There's some man who lets these guys camp on his property."

The road was barely more than one lane and didn't seem to be going anywhere. Christie began to doubt the directions and hope they could get themselves downhill again. Then Conner said, "Is that it? The sign?"

A rusted white No Trespassing sign was attached to a chain, but the chain had been taken down and the sign lay on the ground. Conner downshifted and they bumped along a grass-grown drive, still slick from the last rain. It didn't look like anywhere that humans had been for a long time.

The drive came to an end in a half-cleared field. Conner brought the car to a stop and kept the engine running. The headlights showed an empty, weedy space, a ring of cinder blocks around what might have been a burn pile, a heap of rebar and rusted barrels. Christie said, "I don't think—"

"I saw something."

"Where?" She didn't see anything but the end-of-the-world landscape. "Let's just go."

"After I get out, lock the doors," Conner told her. "Do you have a phone?"

Christie fished it from her purse. "No service. Please don't go out there."

"All right, look, can you turn this car around if you have to? Can you get out to the road and into town again? If I don't come back in ten minutes, that's what I want you to do. Sound the horn before you start back, and keep hitting it as you go. Don't stop anywhere until you're in Fairfax."

"We can get the police and come back here."

"These aren't people who hang around waiting for the police." He opened his door. "Ten minutes."

Conner got out and she watched him moving along the beam of the headlights, the gray sweatshirt ghost-pale, then take a step into darkness, hesitate on the edge of her sight, and vanish.

She didn't want to keep track of time because it would run out and she'd still be sitting here alone, as she had been, in one way or another, all her life, and there was nothing out there in the dark worse than that.

Conner came walking back along the trail of light, and someone else was with him, a limping figure so encrusted with leaves as to look like a walking tree. Every so often the figure stopped and brushed at himself and shed some leaf clumps. Christie opened her door and got out to meet them.

"I wrecked the truck, sport," the man said. "I'm real sorry."

"That's all right," Conner told him. "Don't worry about it."

"I lost Bojangles."

"Somebody found him. I have him, he's fine. Christie, this is my dad."

"You got Bo? No way. No . . ." The man shook his head. The front of his shirt was matted with dried blood, one of his eyes was black and swollen, and there was a long scabbed-over place on his scalp. He smelled like something that had been buried and then dug up again.

"How's he doing?" Christie asked. "Can you get him in the backseat? We'll take him to Marin General."

"Aw, I've hurt myself worse having a good time."

"Dad, quit trying to talk. Just get in back here and chill out."

As if all he had needed was someone to tell him what to do, the man limped a few more steps and leaned against the door Conner was holding open. "I'm going to get this nice car all goobered up."

"It's my car," Christie said. "Don't worry about that either."

He cocked his head so as to look at Christie with his good eye. "I know you from somewhere."

"I'm pretty sure you don't."

"Come on, Dad. Get in."

Conner's father balanced on the car door and reached out to brush Christie's face with the tips of his leafy fingers. "Nursie."

She remembered him then. She did. Her skin felt burnished. How strange to be so remembered and so touched, in so much forlorn darkness. It was another mystery.

EPILOGUE

It's been five years now, and five years is a long time when you're talking about the difference between ages fifteen and twenty, between the sad girl I was back then and the trying-to-get-it-together one I am now. But of course, she is me and always will be. I know her terrors, her anger, and her shame.

I didn't see Conner anymore, not after his dad came back. Whatever it was, desperate friendship or peculiar courtship, it was over. The two of us were always some kind of accidental, lost-in-space collision anyway, a pair of separately damaged goods. I think I knew that all along, even when I was all moony over him.

The old lady loaned Conner money to go to school, Sonoma State, and he and his dad moved back north somewhere. You know who told us that? Christie! She went with them! Up and left! She turned out to be this secretly nuts person, just waiting for a chance to bust out and show it!

Ordinary life accumulates a day at a time, and only after a long stretch of it can you look back and see how far you've come. I went to school, I did my homework, I moped around. I nudged my way into a couple of friendships. I acquired a boyfriend, a sweet, dopey guy who played jazz piano and aspired to hipsterdom. We hung around together in coffee shops and other people's basements and had a lot of enthusiastic sex. My dad didn't much like him and kept saying rude things about piano players.

We were going to take on the world as a couple of wised-up cultural renegades. Of course that didn't happen, we broke up, but no hard feelings, I'm grateful. He was my claim to an expanding patch of normal—that is, normal, age-appropriate teen heartbreak and pissed-offedness.

I graduated from Tam High without any visible evidence of aspirations, talents, or inclinations. I enrolled at College of Marin and took a class in mass media that got me into film. Not making films, and not "cinema," please! But camera work, lighting, and sound. All the backstage stuff. Something just clicked. I liked the idea of being the one behind the scenes who made it all happen, who could break it down into the basics.

I worked a bunch of jobs when I wasn't in class, saving up money. I got into the film program at Cal State Northridge this year and right now I've got an internship with a production company, working in the digital film lab. We call ourselves lab rats, and of course the interns have to do the most boring, suckiest things. But dudes, we are right behind you, we are paying attention, and we are coming for your jobs!

I live in the dorms with a roommate but I'm almost never there because of work and classes. The hours are long, but like they say, at least the pay is shit. Everything in the movie business is need-it-right-this-minute drama, and huge temper tantrums from people who get paid way too much, and are way too important for their own good. But I'm going to be one of the ones they don't even notice. Like a mouse in the walls, going about my own business, darting out when nobody's watching.

My mom and Jay and Max came out here for my high school graduation. That was quite the occasion. I hadn't seen any of them for three years. My mom had gotten kind of fat, like a big bowl of blond pudding. She kept grabbing me and hugging me and smashing me into her boobs. I guess it was OK to see her, aside from the hugging thing, but I wished she could have just owned up to basically throwing me away. She chose a husband over a child. I can understand it, but don't expect me to give her a total pass on it.

Jay looked older too. Him and me didn't say much, but we didn't have to. We'd both had the same piece cut out of us.

Max was now this long-legged snaggletoothed boy who of course didn't remember me. I got him to play Call of Duty with me and by the time they left, we were on mellow terms.

It was so strange to see my mom and dad together, doing the Dance of Awkwardness. You could tell they were embarrassed that they'd ever set eyes on each other. If you want a good reason not to get married to whoever you're in love with when you're in your early twenties, look no further. Don't think I haven't taken that to heart.

But here they were, at least going through the motions of doing the right thing by the product of their unfortunate union, me. They acted, if not exactly proud of me, at least relieved. They didn't buy me a car or anything, they weren't that kind of people, but they did all chip in for an iPhone, which was kind of sweet. My dad, being a giant dork, also bought me the Concise Oxford English Dictionary. My mom rolled her eyes. She is famous for her eye-rolling. She got that it was a lame gift, and at least we could bond over that.

They are my past, the movie already made, one I can't go back and edit so I came from somewhere different.

There are parts of that movie I shouldn't let myself go back and watch. But sometimes, in spite of myself, I do. After every lie I told, the movie is the truth.

There's a window letting in bright sunlight. That's one of the things that throws you off, how mild and pleasant the light is, how it is reflected off the mirrors and chrome fixtures. There is nothing that is even worth paying attention to in this ordinary, utilitarian room. Two sinks, three toilet stalls, a paper-towel dispenser on the wall, and a wastebasket to receive them.

Since we're all just harum-scarum kids, the school bathrooms are important to us as places to congregate, places the teachers mostly leave us alone, clubhouses, repositories of bodily distress and bodily secrets, our faces presented to the mirrors as we tried to puzzle out what we looked like to everybody else.

I've just had my rumble with Megan and her friend, and my heart is still crashing around in my chest from it. I can't even remember that much of the fight, so it's not in the movie. But I know that I hate Megan. The fact of her existence devalues and negates my own. I pace back and forth, exhilarated with hating her but scared too, because the pushing and shoving and threatening is something new and I don't know what's going to come of it.

Now there is background noise, a popping, and someone at a great distance shouting something you can't make out, and sounds of running and slamming. You can tell this is unusual, unexpected, by the way I stop my pacing and try to listen.

After a while I creep up to the door and wait. There aren't any locks on these school bathroom doors so that the teachers or the cops can bust in whenever they want, and the one window, over a radiator, has a metal grate over it to keep us off the roof, and anyway, I have not yet fathomed and won't until it's too late that I ought to be thinking about running or hiding. If anything, I'm still afraid of Megan, and getting beat up.

So when the door opens and Megan comes in, I take a step back, ready to take a punch or throw one, and her friend Eyeliner is right behind her (I did not know her name then, but I was to learn that and much more about her), and right behind them was this boy. A boy in the girls' bathroom! This is more remarkable than the gun he is holding, which I don't even see or maybe don't comprehend because I've never been around an actual gun before. And maybe the trespassing is what Megan has in mind when she says, in what seems like her normal, hateful voice, "You are going to be in so much trouble."

The boy doesn't say anything. He's nobody I know, he's tall and weedy and wearing an army jacket. He's got this pale pale skin, and his hair's combed back so his face stands out, big and white, like a sign. The gun is flopping around in his hand in a nervous way and he says, "I am the Angel of Death."

"That's just stupid," Megan says, and she starts to cry. Her face gets red again. Anything pretty about her just falls away when she cries.

There's a moment when you're not yet able to think anything through, but you know there's some bad, wrong, mortal danger staring you down, and if only you can accomplish this one simple task, get on the other side of the door, you're safe. And so you take a step toward the door but the boy is in the way and your robot brain doesn't understand, because it has already managed the task and is rejoicing in its relief and freedom, because things cannot be otherwise.

But they are otherwise. Another kind of understanding comes over you.

The Eyeliner girl is crying too now. Her eyes are all black and runny. She says, "Please just let us go. We won't say anything, we'll forget we ever saw you."

The movie slows down here because the boy with the gun slows down, he is not in any kind of a hurry. His big white face looks sleepy. From a certain angle it almost looks kind, although it is not.

Megan says, "Look, you don't have to shoot anybody. We'll do whatever you want. Won't we?" She looks around at me and at Eyeliner. "We wouldn't care, I mean, we would want to."

Poor dumb Megan, thinking it is possible to have a conversation here. Thinking that what this boy must want is the treasures of her body, a body that she only has about five minutes more to inhabit.

The boy says, "In my one hand is vengeance, in the other mercy." He says it like he is ordering a sandwich when he's not very hungry.

The Eyeliner girl tries to get her phone out of her purse without anybody noticing but he sees her and uses his gun hand to hit her in the mouth. We all scream then, and the scream is something black pulled out of my throat by its roots. Eyeliner girl is on the floor but he makes her get up. I keep thinking that someone will come help us, save us. Nobody does.

The boy shoves Eyeliner girl into one of the toilet stalls and Megan into another one and me into the last. I sit down on the toilet because my legs aren't holding me up. Megan is next to me and I can hear her working the latch, locking the stall door. The boy hears it too and kicks the door so the latch breaks and Megan yelps a little. The boy goes in there with her and I think, maybe he'll do things to her, maybe that's all he wants.

But no, he goes right back out again, and when I look out through the place where the door doesn't shut, the boy is at the sink, washing his hands, with the gun resting on the shelf below the mirror where we always spread out our combs and makeup.

I look down and I see Megan's feet in their suede boots with the tassels and I nudge my own foot up against hers and she presses back and later I'm really glad I've done that, done something to her that wasn't horrible.

The boy is talking to himself, at least his lips are moving. His eyes are heavy, almost closed. Then he opens them and in the mirror he sees me looking at him.

"Come out here," he says.

It's like I'm already dead. I can't get my legs to work right, they're flopping around all loose. I'm not anybody brave. I open the stall door and prop myself up against a wall and I just want to get the part that will hurt over with.

He says, "Do you have a boyfriend?"

I don't think I've heard him right. He's picked up the gun again. Maybe he said, "I'm going to shoot you now." I don't know anything about guns, real ones. He's crazy and this is some intersection of crazy and real. Do I have a boyfriend? Is there a right answer or a wrong one? I'm too stupid scared to know which is which, so I just say, "No."

He says, "Well I'm your boyfriend now."

I'm so out of it, I've peed my pants, and my ears aren't working right, there's a scratchy, magnified echo to everything, Eyeliner girl and Megan scrabbling around in the stalls, the boy's voice landing in my head too loud.

He says, "You aren't like them, are you? They are unclean beasts. They were going to hurt you, but I stopped them." He holds up the gun. "This is the sword of righteousness."

Oh let me speak up for the wretched girls, or for myself, anything except snivel and pee myself, faint and fall. But that's what I do. That is all I do.

The boy says, "We should kiss."

So he shuffles over to where I'm propped up against the wall and he puts his big white sleepy face up to mine and this is meant to be a big moment, this first time I kiss a boy and there's nothing to say about it. It's like putting my mouth up to a blackboard.

He says, "You should go now."

I'm so used to the idea that I will never get out of this room that I don't understand him at first, and he gives me a little shove. He says, "When this is all over we can be together. You have my blood promise."

I'm out in the hallway then and I'm running and it's like running downhill even though the floor is level. I'm trying to get as far away as I can from what's coming, the sound of the shots, but I'm not fast enough not to hear them and they echo forever.

When I have the bad, black dreams, or daylight spells of shaming fear, I tell myself one more time that nothing was my fault. That boy did not really know me or my kid's grievances, and I didn't summon him forth to act them out. I don't want him thinking about me. I hope that where he is, they give him the kinds of pills that make you forget your crazy self.

But sometimes I have a different kind of dream, and in it we're both different people, in the way that only makes sense in dreams. We are shy about being together. And we love each other as we have promised to do, hand in hand, our hearts made clean. When I wake up I'm still in love, and I go out into my day as if no other day matters.